DELL SHUDDERED AS SHE LOOKED AT THE HUGE
SILVER WOLF. . . .

"He's mine," said the wolf in a menacing growl.

"He's not yours," Dell argued. "He's just a little boy and
he belongs to me and his father."

"His father! Merely human," the wolf said. "His father
cannot stop me."

"Tell me what you want with my son."

"I want to make sure he doesn't detroy those like you
and me."

"You're vampire?" The thought startled Dell.

The silver wolf transformed, becoming a tall, slim male
dressed in a fine charcoal suit.

The transformation caused Dell to step back. She had
never seen a Predator like the one who stood before her.
He possessed a terrible, spellbinding beauty. He towered
above her, opening his mouth to let her see his fangs—
fantastically sharp and pointed as the teeth of a shark.

The Predator spoke in a very deep voice. "Your son will
one day hope to dispatch me and all like me to the devil.
He'll find us abominable and track us down, one by one.
He'll raise a secret army to aid him in his quest. He is the
single most destructive *dhampir* ever to draw breath. We
have been warned he would come one day. . . ."

The Vampire Nations Novels:

RED MOON RISING (Book One)

MALACHI'S MOON (Book Two)

MALACHI'S MOON

Billie Sue Mosiman

DAW BOOKS, INC.
DONALD A. WOLLHEIM, FOUNDER
375 Hudson Street, New York, NY 10014

ELIZABETH R. WOLLHEIM
SHEILA E. GILBERT
PUBLISHERS
www.dawbooks.com

First Printing, January, 2002
1 2 3 4 5 6 7 8 9

DAW TRADEMARK REGISTERED
U.S. PAT. OFF. AND FOREIGN COUNTRIES
—MARCA REGISTRADA
HECHO EN U.S.A.

PRINTED IN THE U.S.A.

This book is dedicated to my son
Brandon Lee Mosiman,
lost but not forgotten.

"Stranger by whom these lines be read,
Weep for the living, not for the dead."

—Tombstone Inscription

BOOK ONE

THE RAISING
OF THE CHILD

1

"Who are you?" Malachi asked.

In the dream he was no longer a little boy of three, but a grown man. His mind was adult and full of experience. In sleep, he had somehow stepped into the future.

Looking around, he saw he was standing in a dark wood with a rising red moon. Beside him, looking out over the blasted landscape of a forest of bare trees and putrid ground glowing with scarlet light, stood a giant creature in black clothing, an ankle-length cape shrouding his shoulders, a hood covering his head.

"I'm the Master," the creature said.

"Why am I here?"

"To be instructed in the ways to bring about my victory on Earth."

"Victory? Over what? Will I lead a war?"

"Yes, a war between my creatures and the Others who are weak. We are made of three kinds. I am Predator. I am as ancient as the world and have been here from the beginning. Until now we have shared the world with those Others, the Naturals and Cravens. Your coming is a sign my battle to reign alone is at hand. You'll lead this battle, a captain in my campaign."

Malachi began to tremble from the inside out, his muscles dancing beyond his control in fear. Somewhere deep in his mind he touched the child he was, lying in his bed, sleeping. Even as he stood here, in a world so real he could feel the debris beneath his shoes and the intimate brush of the fetid wind against his manly face, he knew it was all wrong. He shouldn't be in this dream or having this conversation. The giant creature that called itself a Predator wasn't human, but he wasn't the Christian God or an alien either.

He was as he had described his enemies—Other. His power was tangible, projected as it was from the statuesque figure so that it engulfed Malachi, who, even as a grown man, was dwarfed by the being.

"I must go, I can't stay here." Malachi turned away from the horrid red moon filling the sky and the Predator that dictated his future as if it were predestined. He stumbled along the path, shaking as if a gale blew at his back.

Hands latched onto his shoulders and spun him around. The giant Predator was inches away. It was the first time Malachi saw his face. It was a ravaged nightmare, with haughty Roman nose, full lips, and eyes that blazed with amber depths and black reflective pupils. The lips pulled back in a smile that revealed fangs lowering from red gums.

Malachi screamed, unable to help himself. He turned his head away, believing himself in the clutches of the devil and his soul in peril.

"Go, then, but remember me," the creature said, holding firmly to Malachi. "One day you will do my bidding. With your help, the world will be ours."

Malachi wrenched away, stumbled back, and, with a scream lodged in his throat, he turned to run.

It was as if he ran instantly from the dream world into reality. It was no more than a hasty step from nightmare to night shrouding his child's room. He woke in his bed, trembling and sweaty, crying out in terror. His mother and father rushed to his room, turning back the covers and soothing him, thinking to dispel his nightmare.

He hadn't the words to tell them what he'd seen or the prediction that had been laid upon him. He simply cried against his mother's breast, too scared to speak, too lacking in language to explain, too afraid to close his eyes for fear the dream would return.

By morning he had forgotten the nightmare and bounded from bed to find his parents where they sat in the dining room. He climbed into his father's lap, adoring the strong hands that lifted him. He reached for a piece of toast from his father's plate, plucking it from the contagion of the runny yellow yoke of fried eggs.

He would not remember the awful night and the conversation with the Predator again until years had passed and, as an adult, his mind opened to reveal the cryptic message told him when he was just a boy of three.

Was it true?

Was it nightmare fantasy?

Only Malachi could answer the questions in the fullness of time. When he did, his whole life would change forever.

* * *

Twilight crept into the cell through a small barred window high on the west wall. Night in Thailand brought a chill that caused the stone blocks to weep with condensation. The damp cell smelled of rusting iron from the rivets in the wall and the chains that bound Charles Upton.

Outside, Charles could hear temple bells and believed the vampire monks used them to indicate a call to prayer. *Prayer* and *vampire* did not seem to be a reasonable combination, but after three years of imprisonment Charles had nominally accepted the idea. His captors were some manner of creature so unlike him they might as well be aliens from another world. *He,* by glory, was a true, legendary vampire. Though he was newly made, compared to the ancient monks who watched over him, he felt no urge to call on God to save him.

Becoming an immortal had rescued him from an ignoble death. He had been dying of porphyria, a disease that had plagued him for the latter years of his mortal existence. It was a scourge running through his life like a firestorm, stealing away joy and hope. To become vampire was all the miracle he could have wished for. He'd been granted life eternal. He'd never fear the darkness again. His pain was lifted, the sores scarring his body disappeared, and he was stronger than any man on Earth. If there was anyone to thank, it was Ross, the Predator living a life of ease back in Texas. Meaning to kill him, at the last moment Ross listened to Charles' plea for mercy and his promise to share his vast wealth and power.

But then Ross betrayed him. Along with Mentor, the strongest and oldest vampire in the entire western portion of the United States, Ross decided to simply *take* what he wished rather than share it.

Charles seethed at the old memories. They set him afire just as the disease had done his mortal body. He would get his revenge. Oh, yes, he would, for he had eternity to carry out the threat, didn't he? He had never been thwarted in his life as a businessman and would not allow this to stand—this disgusting imprisonment . . . this unending silence . . . this life in death forced upon him. No creature as majestic as he should be treated this way. The difference between him and his old mortal self was as great as that between a June bug and a man. If the vampire had evolved, which he didn't, but if he had, it would have taken millions of years to bring man up to this incarnation. That some of them imprisoned their brothers seemed an insane act of treachery.

He thought the monks of the monastery deluded and superstitious anyway, them and their precious, unfeeling god who so far had turned a deaf ear to any plea for redemption. His disdain for the monks rivaled the hatred he felt each morning at six and again at noon when the bells sounded in the courtyard. *There they go again,* he thought twice daily, hearing the bells. *Praying for control over their evil hunger.*

Charles thought they ought to be out preying on victims, not praying for their dark souls. They should be taking new blood rather than going down onto their knees in the chapel and bowing their heads to a nonentity. *Insane,* he thought. *They are absolutely mad.*

Hearing the bells during the day reminded Charles where he was and why. But it was the tolling of the twilight bells that always produced an eerie shiver. One more day lost, they said. Another day shut away from the world. If he were to live forever in this prison, it would not be like living at all. He had come to abhor the end of day—and the third ringing of the bells. He had taken to covering his ears with his hands in order to shut out the resonating sounds.

However, one twilight in the thirty-eighth month of his incarceration, he was too busy concentrating on the cards spread before him on the cold stone floor to bother with the peal of bells. In the dwindling light the ancient figures on the cards seemed to shimmer and move about, changing posture and intent.

Earlier in the day he had created a ruckus sure to bring one of the monk guards running. Often they ignored his rages, knowing eventually he would spend himself and lie down in exhaustion to sleep. Charles had to devise new ways to attract their attention when he wanted something. He discovered if he drew the rage up from the center of his chest and let it explode in his brain, he could close his eyes and shout in a voice of thunder that even angels could hear.

There were many things he could do now that he was vampire, and though he had been without instruction, he was slowly acquiring knowledge of those powers. He could throw his voice, making it seem he was on the other side of the cell, talking to himself. He could speak with insects and rodents when they invaded his space, frightening them away. He deeply despised the roaches, silverfish, spiders, lizards, scorpions, and mice that came with wriggling antennas and whiskers to quiz him in his sleep, creeping as they did onto his eyelids or snuffing curiously at the white hair in his ears.

Using his voice to its fullest extent and backed with his rage, he could force the monks to attend his needs, as he had done this day. Joseph, one of the regular monks who brought his daily ration of blood, appeared at the cell door, unlatching the small iron grate covering the window.

"What is it you want now, Charles?" he asked in exasperation.

All the monks disrespectfully addressed him by his first name, which Charles found annoying, but less annoying than their neglect.

"I am bored," Charles said. "Could you bring me some cards to play with? It would keep my mind entertained." Charles had asked for other small items during his time in the cell, and usually his wishes had been granted. Once, in the dim past of his youth, he remembered playing solitaire aboard a merchant ship, and how the cards helped pass the time at sea.

Joseph brought a deck of cards covered with worn velvet cloth and thrust them through the window bars. Dust motes flew from his hand and the package, creating a small swirl in the air before Charles' face. Joseph said, "This is all I could find. Brother Hadeem said they've been on the library shelves forever, perhaps since we took over the monastery, and no one has found any use for them. They're yours if you want them."

Once Joseph had left, bolting the iron grate over the bars,

and Charles had removed the soft, dusty cloth from the cards, he could see they were not normal playing cards. He couldn't play solitaire with them. He couldn't do anything with them. They were some sort of tarot divination cards. They were so old the parchment and cardboard edges flaked off in his hands and the prominent colors of gray, violet, and ruby were muted and aged with an overall yellow cast.

Charles nearly raised his voice again in rage, demanding a regular *American* pack of playing cards. The monks could surely send for a deck at some nearby village, if they wanted. They might be in the wilds of Thailand, the monastery hidden in the jungle at the base of mountains, but they could reach into the modern world for their needs any time they liked. What was he supposed to do with tarot cards so ancient they might crumble to dust if he shuffled them?

Then, just as he was about to return to the door and yell, the cards grew warm in his hands. He looked down and, fanning the cards out, saw the figures on the cards begin to shift slightly, taking on more vibrant colors. He blinked and rubbed at his eyes, thinking he was imagining things or maybe the dim light in the cell was playing tricks on his vision. Still the figures moved, some of them presenting their backs to him, some bending to fetch an item from the ground or a table, others backing up from their position on the card face so they appeared to be farther distant, as if walking off into another dimension.

Charles sat down on the stone bench that served as his bed. What did he have here? What sort of magic had the monk innocently placed into his hands . . . and how might he use it to release himself from the monastery prison?

He had gotten down onto the floor and spread out his long, skinny legs. Between them on the rough stone he began to place the cards, turning them over one by one and lining them up in columns of eight. The figures had ceased their movement as he did this, but as soon as they were all laid out in a grid, the shimmering began again, the figures moving about as if alive.

"Who are you?" he whispered, leaning over to watch the figure. "Where are you?"

He knew the question he should be asking. *What can you do for me?* But he would come to that if he could ever find a way to communicate with the cards.

Even as twilight descended and night rushed on, long after

the bells had been silenced and into the late darkness, Charles leaned over the magical cards, running his fingers over them. His brow furrowed as he quested for understanding. What were they trying to tell him? What gave them life and what dimension were they locked in?

He forgot the usual hunger that sometimes drove him to claw at the stone walls and beg for relief. He forgot the betrayal that brought him to this horrid place where he was chained; watched over, and sentenced for life. Time did not exist, the hours speeding past unnoticed. Charles didn't sleep until he passed out, falling right where he sat, legs spread-eagled, the cards between them, his head lying on the stones.

*   *   *

At the ringing of the morning bells, Charles woke and remembered the cards. His tossing and turning in his sleep had scattered them about. Reaching to gather them, he sensed something happening in the corner of his cell. He saw a mist seeping through the stones there, rising in a gray cloud that elongated within seconds to touch the floor. From the mist twirled tiny electrical storms of twinkling lights that came together even as he watched, mouth agape. The mist formed into a human form and finally into a female.

Before him stood a tall slim woman with wild long hair covering her shoulders. She wore an ankle-length brown dress with tattered wisps of beige lace at the high throat and wrists. She appeared to be a woman transplanted from Victorian times.

"Where did you get the cards?" she asked.

"Who are you?"

"Madeline. I occupy the cell next to you."

He had heard the monks call her name over the months, admonishing her for a volatile temper. He had never seen or spoken to her, however, and did not know she could migrate through walls.

"How did you do that?" He rose to his feet, a few of the cards still held in his hands while the others lay about him on the floor.

"Never mind. Answer my question first. Where did you get the cards? I only have paper and pen. No one has ever offered me cards."

Her voice was quiet and controlled, very unlike how it sounded when she was in a rage and the monks stood in the hall threatening to bind and gag her if she didn't shut up.

"I asked for them so I could play solitaire. Joseph brought them yesterday."

"Yes, I heard him," she said. "May I see the cards?" She floated to him and bent to retrieve a card from the floor. Suddenly Charles knew he must stop her. He couldn't risk her seeing how the figures came to life. He snatched the card from her hand before she was able to do more than glance at it.

"No, you may not," he said. "They're mine."

"Unfriendly cuss, aren't you?" A hint of a smile turned up her lips. "I've thought of visiting you before, but now I see it was a mistake. I should have stayed away."

Her form shimmered and retreated. Charles, feeling an urgent sense of abandonment, stepped forward with his hand outstretched to stop her, and said, "No, wait! Don't go."

The shimmering ceased and she was solid again. "Why did Mentor bring you here?"

Charles lowered his head so she could not see the hatred he felt. He knew it disfigured his face. "He was scared of me." He lifted his gaze. "Why did he bring you here?"

"I lost my mind."

Charles found her honesty startling. "Are you still mad?" he asked.

"Not as much as I was a hundred years ago."

"You've been here a hundred years?" The very thought of spending a hundred years in this dreary place made his heart constrict, as if a knife had been plunged through it.

"A hundred and eight years, actually," she said. "But that's old news and boring besides. Do you never answer questions put to you?"

He'd forgotten what she'd asked. The thought of a century imprisoned behind these walls had completely filled his mind with despair.

"Why did Mentor bring you?" She repeated the question for him as if she knew his confusion.

"I told you, he was scared of me and how much power I might one day have over him."

"That's ridiculous." Madeline leaned now against the wall

and stared at the small barred window where morning light filtered into the cell. "Mentor is not afraid of anyone."

"You know of Ross?" Charles asked.

"The Predator who controls the blood in the southwestern area of the United States?"

"The very same. He wanted my companies and my tremendous wealth. He and Mentor decided I'd be better off out of the way."

"Poppycock."

"What?"

"You lie." She turned from the window and began to shimmer out of existence. "Everything you say is a lie. I don't even care about your cards. I shouldn't have visited."

"Wait, stop going away like that."

"Why should I? I hate few things more than a liar."

"All right, then! Mentor knew I was planning to take over operations. I was going to get Ross to help me. Or I thought I was. . . ."

She solidified again, turning her face to him. He could see her intelligent eyes questioning the veracity of his words. He would tell her the truth, by glory. He had been alone so long without seeing anyone but the damned wordless monks. He hadn't held a real conversation with another being in over three years. Her appearance was thrilling to him.

"Go on," she said. "You have my attention."

"I don't know exactly how Mentor did it, but he knew what I had thought secret. I was working with Ross, letting him use my resources to expand the blood bank and start more of them—one in Oklahoma, another in Arizona. When he controlled the blood, he controlled the Predators who worked under him, and they controlled the Naturals and Cravens with their deliveries. Once I had Ross on my side, I was going to convince him he needed to kill Mentor. Incinerate him. He doesn't like him much anyway. They're always fighting."

"While I've been here, Mentor and Ross have re-created their uneasy alliance in America. I know how they are," she said. "Before the Colonial days in that country, they were aligned in the French countryside, bringing together the clans who wandered in separate sects, living in hovels, mainly, preying on travelers along the roads. It's fair to say the two of them argued and fought for a couple of centuries before they ever laid eyes on you."

He didn't care how long they'd worked together. Wasn't she listening to him? Then he understood what she was getting at. He'd been fighting a long-standing, if ill-tempered, alliance. "Then my plan to push the wedge between them even deeper might never have worked, but I didn't know that." Charles sat down on the stone bed, the knowledge he'd been rash and ignorant causing him to feel tired. He continued slowly, looking up at Madeline. "I had money. Lots of money. A disgraceful amount of money and companies and holdings, some would say. Once I had Mentor out of the way, I was going to get rid of Ross and take over everything."

"And why would you do that, if you'd managed it—besides being a greedy little new vampire?" she asked.

He felt scolded, but realized he deserved her contempt. He might have been sixty-eight when he'd become vampire, but in terms of age he was a babe compared to his enemies. "Because I think the way things are run is stupid."

"You mean how the Predators allow the Cravens to live?" She seemed genuinely perplexed, as if he were a Chinese puzzle she could not decipher.

"Yes."

"And how the Naturals walk among men?"

"Yes." He knew he would not insult her, for it was obvious to him she was Predator, the same as he. He could sense her warrior spirit. She had never taken blood except from living beings before imprisonment.

"So you would make changes." She seemed intrigued with his plan.

"I would definitely make changes," he said, encouraged. "I would destroy the Cravens wherever I found the mangy things. They're useless, a drain on our blood supplies. I'd have the Predators rise up and rule the world, as they should. I'd stop the supplies of blood to the Naturals. They could prey, the way their nature dictates, or they could starve for all I care. We've *been* human., It's not that great."

"Isn't it?"

It was the first time since he'd begun his confession to

Madeline that he sensed she'd been leading him on. She was mocking him now.

"You miss being human?" He was sincerely curious.

"I miss the human who loved me," she said, fading from the cell. "They say it's why I'm mad."

"Why are you leaving?" He felt desperate to keep her. "I told the truth. That's what you want, isn't it? The truth?"

"Your truth is cold as the grave and just as sordid. It makes sense only to you. It is an ugly truth you want to make reality. You may keep that truth to yourself."

"But I don't understand . . ."

"No, I guess you wouldn't."

Then she was gone, disappearing right before him. He knew vampires could change themselves into animals, though he had no idea how, but he did not know they could become mist and invade the minute spaces between ancient stacked stone. He had wanted her to tell him how to do it. He could escape if she'd only told him.

"Madeline?" he called, rushing to the cell door and pressing his face against the little barred window there. "Madeline!"

Joseph came down the dark, sooty corridor lit with kerosene wall lanterns even during the day as no light pierced the space between the cells. Joseph frowned and said to him, "Stop that yelling. Madeline does not speak to inmates."

Unlike many of the other monks, who went about with their shaven heads uncovered, Joseph wore a cowl of orange cloth that matched his robe. He peered now from beneath it, his eyes like flat red coals.

Charles almost told him he was a fool. Madeline had left her cell and come into his. She knew things he must learn. She did not like his truth, but she did indeed speak to him.

Once Joseph was confident he had stopped calling into the corridor, he went away again, his robe swishing along the cobblestone floor. Charles moved from the door to the cards on the floor. He picked them up, caressing their strange warmth. Smiling to himself, he sat again on the stone bench. What did he need with mad Madeline's secrets when he had a better one of his own?

He simply had to make out what the cards were telling him, that was all. It might be magic much stronger than Madeline possessed. It might be something that would set him free.

2

Della Cambian Major had been a vampire nearly four years and her son, Malachi, born from a union with a human, was not quite three. Having moved from the suburban neighborhood in Dallas where she'd lived all her life with her family, she had begun a new existence with her husband, Ryan. They now lived in a small Texas country town best known for potluck community dinners and old cowboys and ranchers spending their waning years sipping black coffee at the one little convenience store. Here Dell's secret was easily concealed, as people kept to themselves and were especially cautious with newcomers to the vicinity. Dell loved the privacy afforded her so easily, so naturally, but she often felt isolated and lonely. Were it not for Malachi's company during the day while Ryan worked on a nearby ranch, Dell was not sure she could have remained on the two-hundred-acre ranch they called home.

She had her studies, which were coming to an end, via Internet classes offered by a highly-regarded Texas university. She would soon have a degree in library science and might one day run a great library where she could research the world's knowledge and come to terms with her vampiric condition. She had already been reading whatever literature and nonfiction she could find that might give her a clue about her clan—its reason for being, its destiny. And in another year Malachi would begin preschool, which would allow her even more freedom to study, but until then her days were predictable and quiet, much too quiet. Some days she thought she lived in a world muffled by cotton.

In the mornings she worked at the local library as a clerk and at noon she picked Malachi up from day care and spent the afternoons in his company. At night she turned to her studies, preparing homework and reading assignments.

Today she was teaching her son something she'd learned in a book about hunters. She'd stumbled across the little volume at the library and found herself immersed for a couple of hours in the age-old rituals of hunting.

"Mommy, can I have a marshmallow yet?"

Malachi spoke better than his peers at day care. Most three-year-olds were able to speak in a few completed sentences, yet often they communicated in fragments. Malachi had been speaking well since he was two. Dell expected that was because he was *dhampir*. He'd inherited half-vampire and half-human genes. He was more advanced than other children and would grow into a superior specimen of a human who inherited some of the vampire's exceptional abilities. But he was not immortal, and when she thought of the day when she would lose him to death, she grew so cloudy and blue that she often took to bed and turned her face to the wall.

"Mommy?"

Dell realized she'd not answered him yet. He was relentless until his questions were answered. She knew this was typical of a toddler. In most ways he exhibited all the usual absurdities she loved best about small children.

"Uh . . . no, don't eat the marshmallows yet. Just hold onto the bag. We're going to roast the marshmallows."

Malachi pulled himself into a lawn chair and hugged the marshmallow bag to his chest. His legs swung loose over the edge of the chair. He was being as patient as he could. He had never tasted a roasted marshmallow, but she knew he trusted her. If she said they would do something as incredible as take a white fluffy treat and actually roast it over a fire, he would wait.

"Now watch what I'm doing. This is an experiment." She placed a new roll of toilet paper into a large empty coffee can.

"An experiment?"

"Yes. I read about it in a book at the library today. Hunters make a fire like this to warm their hands when out in the woods hunting for deer. They can't make a normal fire because deer would smell the smoke. This fire makes no smoke or smell. Or at least that's what the book said. Let's try it.''

"Okay, Mommy." Malachi's legs grew still and he leaned over his lap, squishing the bag of marshmallows.

"Now we pour a bottle of rubbing alcohol over the roll of toilet paper." Dell saturated the roll, then brought out a small box of matches. "We light it carefully. Once it's going, we'll put our marshmallows on sticks and hold them over the fire."

"We're gonna *cook* marshmallows? Over toilet paper?" He giggled. Covering his mouth.

"Oh, yes," she said. "You'll like them, wait and see."

The roll of toilet paper flared up bright and clean, burning without smoke or scent. Just as the book had said. It amazed Dell. There were so many things she didn't yet know—so much knowledge she hoped to learn. From the simple making of a hunter's fire to the intricate workings of the universe. It would take a millennium to find out even a tenth of what she longed to know.

Dell stood back, watching the fire burn for a minute. Fire always set off an alarm in her vampire brain. It could kill her. Fire was one of but two things that could.

"Wow," she said, shuffling aside the sudden little fear she always felt. "It works. I can smell it, but I bet a deer couldn't." As vampire, she had a heightened sense of smell that was better than any animal's, but that wasn't something she needed to explain to Malachi.

She broke two green branches from a flowering pear tree that grew close to the house. She stripped the leaves. She took the marshmallow bag from Malachi and speared a marshmallow on each stick, handing one to her son. "Okay, now hold it out over the fire until it gets all brown. After you eat that one, you can have this one to roast."

She showed him how. When the marshmallow browned, its skin rumpled and blistered, she blew on it to cool it before she plucked it from the stick and held it out to Malachi. He hesitated. "Go ahead, it's good."

"You've eaten it before, Mommy?" He wasn't convinced. "It looks like a caterpillar."

She laughed. "Sure, I ate them when I was a kid." Memory of consuming food was growing dim in her mind, but

the taste of a hot roasted marshmallow remained. The
burned skin crumpling sweetly in her mouth, the inner
white soft cloud of marshmallow running between her teeth
and coating her tongue.

Of course, since becoming vampire at seventeen, almost
eighteen, Dell had never eaten food again, and did not miss
it, but she always tried to remember her son was human
and that there were treats in the world he should not miss.

Malachi took the proffered sticky mess from her fingers
and bit into it. Dell watched his face, his eyes, and saw the
delight there. "You like it?"

After swallowing Malachi said, "Umm, good!"

"See? I told you."

Having seen how his mother speared the marshmallow
and held it over the fire, Malachi now roasted the second
one she'd speared and did the same with a third, and then
a fourth. While he roasted marshmallows over the coffee
can fire in their backyard, Dell relaxed, basking in his en-
joyment. Her little child was dark-headed with intelligent
cocoa-brown eyes and a build like that of his father in
miniature. Wide shoulders, long legs. He wore black cow-
boy boots, jeans, and a red pullover knit shirt with a
little alligator on the pocket. To any observer he was
completely normal.

But Dell knew he wasn't. Not only was his vocabulary
beyond that of other three-year-olds, his ability to learn was
enhanced. Show him something once—like how to roast a
marshmallow—and he remembered and could do it forever.
Read him a story and he never forgot a detail, repeating it
verbatim back to you. He could hear better than normal,
often surprising his father with how he knew a car was
approaching the ranch house from the distant road before
the engine's sound could be detected. His eye and hand
coordination was superior, so that he was already playing
skill games on their computer, racking up high scores before getting bored and moving on to another game.

He was also healthier, his immune system stronger and
more resistant to invasion than any other child his age. He
never came down with the usual childhood maladies, never
had colds or the flu, never ran fevers or lost his appetite.
Because it was state law for children to be inoculated before starting school, he'd been given baby shots and vacci-

nations, but hadn't really needed them. He'd been a perfect baby, giving his mother little trouble, and now he was a perfect toddler scarfing down roasted marshmallows like there was no tomorrow.

"Mommy, why don't you eat one? Why do I always eat everything alone? I thought you liked marshmallows."

Ah, there was the rub. She could not tell her son she didn't need food. Her sustenance came from the plastic bags of blood she bought from Ross and his blood bank in Dallas. She drank one a day—or night as it happened, for she didn't want Malachi to see her feed. Soon she would have to tell him the truth. She was not human any longer, though for many years she had been. She was less human than he was and not at all like his father, Ryan. Her body was, in fact . . . dead. The organs were renewed and sustained from the fresh blood, but she did not have to breathe, except when around humans, and the heart in her chest cavity was as still as a rusting bit of machinery in a closed factory.

She began to wave off his query. "I don't want anything right now, I . . ."

"Your mommy's sweet enough as it is," Ryan said, walking around the corner of the house. "Aren't you, Mommy?"

He bent down to kiss her, and she smiled against his lips. She sent him a mental comment. *Thanks. It's getting harder to fool him.*

Ryan straightened, walked near his son, and tousled his hair. "Can I have one, Champ? We might as well both ruin our supper together."

"Sure, Daddy. Here's another stick."

While Ryan pushed a marshmallow onto the end of the stick, Dell looked him over. It was her habit to search for any clue her husband might not be happy and content. Ever since they'd married, she'd feared he would leave her. He only thought he loved her, she was sure. How could a warm-blooded man love a cold, dead thing like her?

He was dusty from a day's ranch work. He hauled cattle to auction, rounded up herds and branded the calves, and helped the heifers during calving season. He gave the stock shots, watched for scours—a disease that could bring a cow down fast—inspected hooves, fed the herds, and generally made sure his employer's investment lived healthy and multiplied. It would be another two years or more before he earned his degree and could practice veterinary medicine. Until then he worked hard for a living, though he never complained.

Dell was afraid he'd tire of all the responsibility, that he would age beyond his years and resent her for it. She studied him now with Malachi. How he laughed and joked with their son. She inspected him to see if it was genuine. She could read his mind if she liked, but didn't do that unless he slept and was unaware of her intrusion. It was an invasion and he wasn't fond of it, but she told herself she had to do it to be sure. To be sure he loved her and Malachi. To have some certainty he wouldn't leave them.

"You made a hunter's fire," he said, jogging her from the reverie of her close inspection.

She smiled. "Yes, I read about it in the library today."

"My dad made fires like this when he took me hunting and the morning was cold."

"The deer really can't smell it?"

"I suppose not. Dad took a couple of deer every season."

Dell didn't like hunting, so Ryan didn't do it, turning down his father's invitation each fall. She hoped he didn't miss it. The thought of shooting a helpless deer turned her stomach. She knew it was a Texas tradition. The meat fed some of the poorer families who lived in the country. But to kill for sport, whether the man ate the meat or not, if that man could afford to buy his meat at the grocery store it seemed to her he was just indulging a primitive killer instinct.

Like a Predator. Predator vampires killed wantonly, killed humans. Naturals like herself, and the Craven, a type of vampire who was always sick and weak and hidden from the world, declined to commit murder. They had all been human once. Nearly every vampire in existence had once been a man or woman first. It was against unspoken rule to infect a human and leave him alive to become vampire.

Each of them might have changed as a child or as an adult, but they had all been born mortal. The mutated human disease, porphyria, caused them to change, to die and to rise again as vampire.

How the Predators were then able to forget their humanity and murder when the hunger drove them was beyond evil. Dell thought if she had to kill in order to live, then she would welcome the orange-and-blue flames of the hunter's fire and let them burn her to cinders and the final death.

"You're awfully quiet this afternoon." Ryan moved from his son's side and came to her. "Did anything happen?"

She looked up at him, and love flooded through her. All the sad thoughts about her kind fled, all worries over how her half-breed son would fare in the world vanished, and all fear of being abandoned by the one man she loved disappeared. She smiled at him. "No, nothing happened. I was just thinking."

"About him?" he asked softly, indicating their son.

"Some," she admitted. They had talked about Malachi since before he was born, wondering what it might be like to raise a child who would be so different. They had to prepare him soon. They couldn't wait forever. He was *dhampir*. He was not completely human. He might even contract the disease, as it resided in his genes from his mother, and he could one day be like her. Porphyria's mutated gene was like a twisted, hookworm latched onto the DNA chain. Some of the Naturals worked on research, secretly trying to discover just where the gene resided, hoping to manipulate it out of existence. One day maybe they'd be able to do that in living humans with a family history of the mutant gene. Until that time . . .

Mentor, the counselor to the vampire nations, and the wisest reformed Predator anyone knew, had told them chances were Malachi would never be infected. The odds were against it.

But still—just dealing with his enhanced abilities was going to be difficult. He'd live in the world and die like his father, but until then he would be more than human, enjoying supernatural talents, and how he used them would determine the state of his very soul.

"Don't worry so." Ryan pulled her by the hand from the lawn chair. "Let's make the champ some dinner."

Together they put out the coffee can fire and led Malachi into the house to wash his sticky face and hands. The farmhouse was old but comfortable, and Dell loved it. All the rooms, except for the old-fashioned kitchen, were large, with high ceilings. There was a fireplace, hardwood floors, and a wraparound porch on the front where Dell sat at night and watched the stars. When she and Ryan married right after high school graduation, his grandfather deeded the old house and the two hundred acres to them as a gift. They were eternally grateful. They both worked so hard to pay Ross for her blood supply and for the Internet tuition for college classes. If they'd had to pay for rent, too, they wouldn't have had two nickels to rub together left over. She didn't know how people managed to live. It surprised her that more of them weren't on the street or living under freeway overpasses.

Ryan turned on lights, as Dell often forgot, never needing illumination in order to see. In the small kitchen they worked together to make a pizza from scratch, rolling the dough, chopping up pepperoni and vegetables, grating cheese. In the living room Malachi, all washed up, and with his boots removed, sat in the middle of the floor playing with Legos. He built fantastic buildings, tall, futuristic, some of them standing beneath domes, as if he could see a Martian landscape in his imagination. He could be trusted to sit quietly and build things for hours and never clamor to watch television like other small children might. They let him watch cartoons on Saturday mornings and some educational shows, but she and Ryan were so busy in their lives with work and study, the television was rarely turned on.

"So what's up?" Ryan asked, pressing pizza dough into a pan.

"You know what it is." She didn't really wish to get into it. She was so tired lately. Despite the fact she never fell ill or complained, the psychic energy it took to maintain a believable humanity when out in the world doing her lowly job at the library seemed to sap her life force. It took the night—and the blood—to keep her moving.

"You'll have your degree soon," he said, knowing her concerns as well as she did. "Maybe you can work at Sam Houston University in Huntsville."

"I don't know. It's pretty hard to get in there."

"Well, there'll be something. . . ."

She wondered what. And where. There was the nearby state penitentiary, but the gloom of the place scared her badly. Already she had troubles dealing with humans who lived without any real sense of their frailty and finite life

span. How could they waste any single moment when they
had so few given them? But dealing with truly doomed
individuals, the prisoners, and working in a library donated
by kind individuals who gave the prison their cast-off books
and magazines might truly push her into a lasting depression.

"Malachi's going to be fine," Ryan said now, dumping
tomato sauce onto the pizza dough. "He really is."

"I know. Or at least I think I know."

"You have to stop making the salad," he said, hurrying
over to her where she had lettuce and tomatoes cut into a
bowl on the counter.

"What? Why?"

He grabbed her around the waist and pulled her to his
chest, kissing her hard and quick. When he let her go, she
said, "What are you doing?"

"I'm making sure you let go of the blues," he said, grinning. "You can't make salad when you're blue. It'll turn
the tomatoes sour and wilt the lettuce."

She laughed and hugged him. "Oh, Ryan, if it weren't
for you, my life would be so awful."

"I know. Or I think I know."

She swatted him on the forearm and pushed him toward
the pizza. "Finish up," she said. "I have studying to do. I
can't spend all night in here lollygagging around with you."

They finished dinner preparations and joined their son
in the living room while the pizza baked.

Malachi explained his newest creation. "It's a ramp," he
said. "For the air cars."

"I see," said his father seriously, with no hint of the grin
Dell knew he hid inside.

"And what is this?" Dell asked, pointing to a block of
interlocked Legos with a tall pitched roof, like a medieval
cathedral.

"It's the barracks for the army," Malachi said.

"Ah. Of course it is." Dell had no idea where Malachi
learned the word "barracks" or its meaning. Nor did she
understand how he'd come up with the idea of "air cars."
She rather missed the baby he'd been, lying quietly in her
arms, staring up adoringly into her face. He was getting so
smart. And so . . . strange.

"Where is this place" Ryan asked. "Is it the moon? A Mars base?"

"Uh-uh. It's the United Sates of America."

"But we don't have air cars and army barracks that look like big churches."

"We will," Malachi said with complete conviction. "One day when I'm a big boy."

Will we? Dell wondered. What did Malachi know they didn't? Was he a prophet? But she was worrying again; she was turning the worry wheel and all for naught. Whatever the future held, she'd find a way to protect her son and her husband from it, if need be.

After all, barring a catastrophic accident that set her on fire where she couldn't put herself out or if some malicious Predator lopped off her head, she would live forever. There probably were air cars and cathedral barracks up ahead or even things more fantastic that none of them could envision yet.

She would see it all.

3

Mentor picked his way through the litter in the yard, grimacing at the uncut grass, and opened the door into a house of squalor and darkness. None of this surprised him, but it always left him feeling discouraged to come to a house of Cravens. He had lived for centuries and he'd had to deal with every clan, as it was the job he'd carved out for himself. But no matter how many years he'd seen lairs like this, it always brought him low.

To his way of thinking, he had certain duties he could not ignore. He watched Ross, to keep him under tight control. He could never trust him, not even after more than three hundred years. He helped new vampires enter their moments of death, face the red moon, and decide with the willfulness of their spirits to be either a Predator, Craven, or Natural. He guided new vampires in the ways to progress in their new lives. He prevented rogues and renegades from spilling the long held secrets to the world. Most of all, as his name proclaimed, he mentored. When that meant visiting a house he would otherwise pass by, then it was ordained so.

*   *   *

"I can do this," Dolan said, showing his resentment at Mentor's interference. They sat in Dolan's shabby room in the desolate house full of Cravens moaning and sighing from other rooms.

"It won't work," Mentor said again. "Cravens haven't the strength to do what you propose."

"Why don't you let me try and find that out on my own?"

"Because it will only lead to more despair."

Dolan hung his head where he sat on the edge of his unmade bed. "I have to do something, Mentor. I can't spend my time, all the days of this long life, sitting in this house listening to them. Listening to *me*."

Mentor tuned into the sounds Dolan meant for him to share and mentally crab-walked back from the cacophony, shutting the other Cravens out.

"You have the freedom to leave here," he said.

"And go where? On my own, into loneliness? Or into the wilds where I'll live with the animals, like an animal?"

"It isn't as bad as all that."

"How would you know?" Dolan's voice rose.

Mentor had once counseled Dolan when he'd been suicidal and homicidal, hoping to burn down the Craven house and all in it. Now he had a plan, but Mentor knew it was a fantasy that must go unfulfilled.

"I know enough," Mentor said. "Do yourself a favor and leave them alone."

"Them?" Dolan pointed to the closed door. "When they could get up and try to change how things are?"

"You know there's no changing things. You chose this life, Dolan, did you forget? So did the others."

"Yes, I chose in death to live as a Craven, because I died a sick and depressed man, a human who had suffered too much. It really was no choice at all."

"You could have been . . ."

"A Predator like you?"

"Reformed."

Dolan laughed sarcastically. "Reformed my hind foot. If you wanted to kill humans, you could do it in a millisecond. I never wanted to kill."

"And neither do I."

"Now, you don't. Not now, maybe."

Mentor said, "You could have chosen the Natural life."

Dolan's laugh was even harsher. "Oh, of course, I could have come back into the same life I left. You know I was a suicide, don't you? Why would I want to be like that again?"

Mentor had not been there to guide this particular vampire through death. It had been at least two hundred years ago when Dolan had died of the mutated disease that made

him into vampire. Mentor had been in another part of the
world, only just becoming the man who mentored, the
strong and resilient vampire he was now.

"No, I'm sorry, I didn't know you had killed yourself.
Though I should have guessed it from our last visit with
one another." Then Dolan wanted to die, too, and take the
house of vampires with him—which was against vampire
rule. Neither Dolan nor anyone else had the right to judge
and execute another vampire unless that vampire was rogue
and beyond reach.

"Now listen," Dolan said, growing animated. "Just listen
to my plan, will you? I want to work with the other Cravens
like me. I want to help them get up and learn to fight, learn
to deal with the light of day. They need to find a useful
mission to carry out. I don't believe we're doomed to hand-
outs and begging and welfare. I don't believe we have to
stay hidden behind drawn drapes and weep and gnash our
teeth and feel powerless and so sick all the time. I don't
feel sick! Why should they? We could join together, we
could . . . maybe we could find work, pass as human the
way the Naturals do. Maybe we could be our old selves
again."

"Stop." Mentor raised the palm of his hand. "They don't
have the energy you do, Dolan, haven't you noticed? They
can't do these things you want."

"Why not? How can they be different from me?"

"Because you border, Dolan. You're Craven, yes, you
know that, it's what you chose for eternity, but you border
on being Predator and it gives you strength, it gives you
urges, it makes you think other Cravens can think the way
you do, can do what you want to do, can change their lives.
But they can't. They're lost to themselves and to the outside world. It's what they want."

"But . . . but . . ."

"You're not the only Craven to be borderline, Dolan.
It's happened before. I've listened and gone along with
other plans, only to see them fail. I really hate to take away
your dreams, Dolan, but it'll only mean more pain and
disillusionment for you. I want to save you from that."

Dolan seemed to think it over. Mentor reached out and
touched his arm to reassure him.

"I'll tell you the solution we might try," Mentor said.

"You come with me. I'll train you for . . . something. You are perhaps more like me than them." Mentor gestured toward the door.

"But I wanted to help them."

"You cannot help them. Be firm in your mind about that. There is no change for them. But for you. Perhaps . . ."

"I've never heard of a Craven living with a Predator. What could you train me to do?" Though he was doubtful, there was hope in his voice.

"We'll talk about that later. The point now is to get you out of this house where you're making everyone else miserable with your ranting and raving. Will you go with me?"

"You're not going to . . . kill me, are you, Mentor?"

It was the first time Mentor had seen the other vampire show fear.

"No, I'm not going to kill you. I'm going to make you more like me."

As the two vampires moved stealthily across the neighborhood toward Mentor's house, Dolan asking impossible questions all the way, Mentor received an alarming mental call from Dell, the young female vampire he had helped change four years before. It was about her son, the *dhampir*. The first *dhampir* to have been born in the clans on the North American continent in a hundred years. Dell's marriage to a mortal had been counseled against numerous times, but there was no changing the heart. Mentor knew this well enough since he'd married a mortal himself once. Long ago and lifetimes away.

He knew there would be offspring between Dell and her husband, Ryan. Mentor himself had never desired to chance making children with a mortal, but these were modern times and much had changed for young couples. Despite his wishes, vampires often did things he thought would bring not only themselves harm, but the whole vampire nation. Birthing a *dhampir* fell directly into that category.

Therefore, he was not surprised when he heard Dell's mental plea for help. He knew it would come soon, as the boy was already three and precocious.

"Dolan. Dolan! Hush and be still. I have to leave you. You know where my house is. Go there and wait for me." Mentor had him by the shoulders.

"Where are you going?" There was a little panic in Dolan's voice. He, too, needed Mentor to stay close by.

"Never mind. That's your first lesson. Don't be curious about anyone else's life or get into anyone's business. I have to attend someone; it's an urgent call. That's all you need to know. Now do as I say and wait for me at my house." With that Mentor raised his arms heavenward and swept from the sidewalk where they had been, spiraling into the black ink of the night sky. He knew Dolan stood there, staring after him long after he was out of sight in the clouds high overhead. He also knew that Dolan would do as he was told and go along his way.

*   *   *

Mentor stepped into a bedroom where the parents were frantic. Dell rushed over and grabbed him by the shoulders, crying blood tears. "He might be dying, Mentor! He's fevered and he's never even been sick before. He isn't dying, is he? Is he, Mentor? He won't go into the dark wood and face the red moon, will he?"

"Calm yourself. Let me see him." Gently moving Dell aside, he drifted to the bed and stared down at the little boy. He was handsome, his skin pink with the flush of fever, his hair and eyebrows and lashes dark as midnight. Mentor reached out and placed a hand on his forehead. It felt like a furnace.

"When did this start?"

Ryan said, "During his bath. We had eaten dinner, and I was bathing him before bed. He felt hot, then he began to complain his head hurt."

"Is he dying?" Dell wrung her hands, the blood from her weeping making red tracks down her cheeks to stain her blouse.

Mentor turned back to the boy and entered his mind. For some seconds he searched there, and when he was sure, he retreated. He turned to Dell. "He's not dying. He's becoming what he is destined to be. A *dhampir*."

"I thought he always was." She wiped the blood off her face with the wet washcloth she'd been using on her son.

"He was and he wasn't. He'll undergo the change in the unconscious state, the same as you did, but the difference is he will not die. Once the change is complete, he'll wake and be fine."

"Will he be different?" Ryan asked.

"Stronger than ever," Mentor said. "Everything you know about him will be increased. He'll be even smarter. His memory will be incredible, his stamina unimaginable for any normal man. He'll be able to move . . . fast. He'll be able to see better, hear better, and instinctively sense danger—all more than he ever has before. By the time he is grown, he will be as gifted as any of us who are full vampire. He'll only lack a few of our abilities, but the ones he's left with will be as strong or stronger than our own. A *dhampir's* instinct is to survive. This is a human instinct, as well, but in Malachi it will be extremely refined. In all situations he will struggle, using every gift he possesses, to survive."

"He's not suffering now?" Dell remembered her own death and the terrible trauma of it.

"No, he's not suffering."

"Oh, thank God." Dell collapsed by the bedside and took her child's hands. "I was so worried. I thought . . ."

"You thought it was the mutated porphyria," Mentor said. "Well, rest easy. It's a passage, but the only one he'll ever have. When he does die, it won't be like your death, Dell. He won't suffer then, either."

Ryan walked Mentor from the bedroom and to the front door. Mentor often liked to use conventional methods of entry and exit from houses and buildings, conventional transportation when he wasn't needed somewhere urgently, and tried as much as he could to move about in the world like the man he used to be so long in the past. "Dell seems troubled," he said. "Beyond this present crisis, I mean."

"She worries a lot," Ryan said. "About Malachi, me, her job, the future. I tell her not to, but . . ."

"She's stubborn," Mentor finished for him. "I certainly know that. And what about you? Are you okay with your life? With your family?"

"I love them," Ryan said. "No matter what they are."

"Or what they become?"

"Yes. No matter what they become."

Mentor patted the young man on the shoulder and let himself be shown out the farmhouse door. Mentor's own

wife had said almost the same thing to him when she'd
been alive and happy with him in their home in Scotland
in 1789. She would love him, she said, no matter what he
was—and he'd always been vampire when she'd known
him—and she would love him, she said, no matter what he
might become—murderous fiend, or a compassionate man
willing to forgo the quick, neat thrill of taking life. Until
her death in 1822, their love had been the abiding force of
his existence.

After her death he retreated into solitude in a cold deserted castle in Sweden to mourn. For thirty despairing
years.

He hoped Dell would not be so unfortunate when one
day she, too, lost her human family.

"Go to her," Mentor said, waving good-bye to Ryan.
"The boy's waking. Remember—though he will be
changed, he is still your son. He is more human than vampire. Remember."

Mentor took to the sky and headed for Dallas and home
where his protégé awaited him. It had come to him when
speaking with Dolan in the house of the Cravens. He could
use a partner, someone to help him with the burgeoning
population of vampires in the southwest region of the country. Dolan might prove helpful.

*   *   *

Ryan had long since gone to bed and now slept soundly.
He had to be up early for work. Dell, unable to sleep and
never needing as many hours of rest as her husband, sat in
the living room darkness, rocking her son in her arms.

Malachi had come from a fevered state of unconscious-
ness earlier that evening to surprise his parents with a small
joyful laugh. "I had a dream, Mommy," he said.

Immediately Dell had remembered her own nightmare
when she'd died and met the Giant Predator in the dreamworld. He had wished to devour her and make her his
own. But Mentor had assured her the same thing wasn't
happening to Malachi.

"What kind of dream?" she had asked her son, sitting at
his side on the bed. The sheets were damp from his perspi-
ration. His dark hair was wet as she brushed it back from

his forehead. But he felt cool to her touch now. The fever had broken.

"I dreamed I could fly!"

Ryan had looked at Dell. She had sent him a glance to let him know she'd handle this.

"You know you can't really fly, don't you, Malachi?" Though vampires, if they wished, and if they practiced diligently, could perform a kind of flying feat, rising above the ground and moving through the atmosphere across the globe, her son would never be able to do these things.

"I know, but in the dream I could fly," he had said. "And I went to a place where I saw a wolf. A very big wolf with silver fur."

Something inside Dell began to vibrate with apprehension. "A wolf?"

"Yeah, he was *big* and everything was silver. The wolf, the moon, the whole world was silver except me."

Now that Malachi had fallen asleep as she rocked him, Dell probed his mind for remnants of the dream he'd had when he'd fallen ill. Mentor said he would be changed, he would exhibit more of his innate supernatural powers. She'd seen no evidence of that yet, but trusted she would once Malachi had rested and the long night was over. She would have to discuss everything with him, tell him the truth of who and what she was and what he was becoming. She hated the thought he must handle such important information when he was not much more than three years old. How would he control himself and not let his secret out? He was just a baby.

As she carefully tiptoed through Malachi's memories, she found the one involving his recent fever dream. Entering the remembered dream, she flew across a dark sky and came down gently, floating onto an open, featureless, arid plain. Just as Malachi had said, it was as silver as an English sterling tray, bathed in light from a large silver moon. From out of nowhere the wolf appeared. He loped easily across the plain toward her, his snout down, his eyes silver disks. His coat was thick and heavy, black with striations of silver. She waited breathlessly on his approach.

When he was but a few feet away, he halted and lifted his head. He spoke to her saying, "Who are you? I always speak with the boy."

"I am his mother. What do you want with him?" She was not afraid of the phantom wolf, but understood well how a dream being could affect the living creature that met with it. She must take care.

"He's mine," said the wolf in a menacing growl meant to warn her not to interfere with the destiny he was there to deliver.

"He is not yours," she argued. "He's just a little boy and he belongs to me and his father."

"His father! Merely human," the wolf said. "His father cannot stop me."

"Tell me what you want with my son."

Clouds sailed across the face of the moon causing the silver river of light to dim. The wolf's eyes glowed fiery amber in the new darkness.

"I want to make sure he doesn't destroy those like you and me."

"You're vampire?" The thought startled her. She had assumed the wolf disguised something else, something sinister, certainly, but not a vampire.

The silver wolf transformed, rising from four feet onto two, his snout shrinking into the bones of the face until it was a human nose. The almond-shaped eyes rounded, the ears grew small and closer to the head. The wolf was no longer animal, but a tall, straight, slim male dressed in a fine charcoal suit.

The transformation caused Dell to step back. She had been in the presence of Mentor, one of the oldest and most powerful Predators on Earth. She had met Ross, the leader of the Predators in the whole region. And in her death throes as a human she had faced the raging visage of the great Predator-Maker, who might have made her like him if he'd caught her. But she had never seen a Predator like the one who now stood majestically before her. He possessed a terrible beauty, spellbinding in his brilliance. Silver light emanated from his very pores and from the fiercely determined eyes. He towered above her, at least seven feet tall, with broad shoulders, massive hands, and powerful jaws that seemed to strain beneath the silvery skin stretched over the bones there. He opened his mouth and let her see the fangs—fantastically sharp and pointed as the teeth of a shark.

She reminded herself this was the dream world and the wolf-turned-vampire could appear to her in whatever form he wished. Nevertheless, he struck fear into her heart.

"My God," Dell whispered. "Did Malachi see you?"

"No." The Predator spoke in a very deep voice that filled the plain and caused the cloud cover to scuttle from the moon. "He thinks me a wolf, which I am. I am also this." He waved one hand down the length of his body. "Your son will one day hope to dispatch me and all like me to the devil. He'll find us abominable and track us down, one by one. He'll raise a secret army to aid him in his quest. He is the single most destructive *dhampir* ever to draw breath. We have been warned he would come one day."

"I don't believe you," she said, scurrying away now across the empty plain, trying to will herself away from the dream and out of her small son's mind.

She was caught from behind and spun around. The huge vampire had her by the shoulders, shaking her. He then held her still, his face inches from her own, his incisors gleaming. "You stay out of my way," he said. "I can bring you down in the wink of an eye. You are nothing like me. You are like a fly crawling beneath the hand of a giant."

Dell trembled. Down the silver corridor of the vampire's eyes she saw reflected the moment of her death.

"Do you understand?" He moved in closer to lick the side of her cheek. It left a burning trail along her skin and his rank breath now lay across her face like a heavy woolen scarf. She had felt more than the flick of his fiery tongue. His incisors slowly pressed her flesh just below her chin, seeking the artery. She pulled back with a force that made him straighten and then smile horribly.

He said, "You're the one who made this child. It was prophesied he would come, but no one knew which of us would make him. He'll grow up to hunt us. We'll hide and he'll find us. First our legions and then our leaders. He knows."

Dell's voice was weak when she asked, "Knows what?"

"That we are unholy."

"We may be mistakes of nature, but we aren't unholy." Her soul raged against the idea her son might one day turn against her kind. He carried her genes. He was like her, too.

"Peer deeper," the vampire said. "Look ahead to the boy's future."

"I'll make a bargain with you." She had to do something. She realized the threat was real, dream or no dream.

The vampire seemed intrigued. He turned his head to the side, examining her sincerity. "What kind of bargain?"

"You know I'm vampire, like you. I'll raise the boy and insure he won't lead anyone against you."

"How could you insure it?"

"I'm his mother. He's a baby. I'll raise him to be peace loving and to live as a human. He'll have no animosity against vampires."

"And you promise this? With your life?"

"I do." Dell spoke without hesitation.

He let her loose, turned and went to four feet, changing to wolf again. He loped off back the way they had come when she'd sped away. "See what you can do, Mother of Malachi. I will leave him alone for a while, but I expect neither your firm teaching of the boy, nor your love for him, will turn him from his task. If that happens, there will be nothing you can do. If you get in our way then, you'll go to hell with him, your pretty head in your hands."

With a shudder and a jerk, Dell found herself free of her son's memories and his mind. She sat still in the rocking chair, Malachi sleeping peacefully in her arms. She felt dampness on her cheeks and wiped away the blood tears. The dream was terrible, but it felt too true to be merely an amalgam of fantasies either she or Malachi had manufactured.

She must see Mentor again. Now. She had to tell him what she'd learned from the wolf.

Mentor, she called mentally. *Come back, Mentor, I have to talk to you.*

It took him just long enough to appear for Dell to put Malachi down on the sofa, wrapped in a blanket. He slept on.

When she turned from him, Mentor stood in the center of her living room. "He's all right, just as I said, isn't he?"

Dell spoke softly as not to awake her son. "He said he'd had a dream during the fever. There was a silver wolf. I tried to find out about the dream and the wolf came to me."

"Balthazar." Mentor whispered the name.

"Balthazar? Who is that?"

"He's a lone Predator who favors taking the form of a silver wolf. It could be him. Tell me more. What did he say?"

"He said Malachi's destiny is to hunt down Predators and kill them. He said vampires would come to stop him and if I got in the way, they'd kill me, too. He said Malachi would be a hunter, a destroyer. But before that, he would be the one hunted. I made a pact with him. If he'd leave Malachi alone, I'd make sure he wouldn't grow up to be a threat. He reluctantly agreed to let me try." She paused, staring into the silence of the darkened room. "It was just a dream, wasn't it, Mentor? It wasn't this . . . Balthazar, was it?"

Mentor didn't reply for a few moments. When he did, his voice was strained, something Dell had never heard. "It sounds like Balthazar. He's been trying to create his own group for many years. He used to be an exile, having self-imposed the exile on himself rather than be hunted as a renegade and put to death. But for some time now he's become active in the Canary Islands, pulling several of the more disgruntled Predators under his tutelage, prophesying a coming war between the clans. He's never been . . . stable."

"He wants to lead a bunch of Predators?"

"Please, don't let this worry you. Most of us ignore him. He's more than a little paranoid. It would be just like him to hunt around to find *dhampirs* and threaten them. Not only would he like to see a war start, but I've heard news he's been talking about a *dhampir* who would come to do away with Predators. I shrugged it off as more unbridled paranoia, but if he's taken to coming as the wolf . . ."

"He's real, then." Dell sat down in the rocker, holding to the chair arms. "He's been inside Malachi's head. He's dream-walking." She looked at Mentor. "Can't you do something about him? Even with my promise, if he thinks my little boy is going to be a threat to him, he might still be dangerous. He might . . ."

"Take it easy, Dell. He still has only a handful of malcontents under him. He's neither a mystic nor a magician. He's just a little tin god in a lonely outpost, indulging in paranoid fantasies. It probably pleases him to enter a child's dreams to frighten him. It's the mark of a coward. It gives him something to do with his free time. Many idle vampires resort to such petty games. And Malachi's young. He's not afraid of him yet, not really. The wolf's just making threats."

"What about the threats? He scared me silly. He seemed extremely powerful."

"Did he?" Mentor touched her mind, exploring, finding the image of the silver wolf and the man being he showed Dell in the dream world.

Dell knew he was studying what she'd seen and had stored in memory. She said, "Well? Is it him?"

Mentor withdrew from the contact he'd made with her memory and now he frowned. "It's him. He's . . . grown."

"Grown?"

"He's . . . stronger."

"What am I going to do if he comes back? If he decides he shouldn't wait?"

Malachi put his hands on her shoulders. "I told you. He can't be afraid of a three-year-old. And if he accepted your promise, that means he'll leave him alone for a while. I don't think you have anything to fear right now. Balthazar is also known for a twisted kind of honor. If he gives his word, he means it."

"And the future?"

"I don't want to lie to you, Dell, but I don't want to alarm you either. Let the years pass. Watch for him, question your child if he seems unhappy or scared."

"And wait," she said. "That's what you're saying, isn't it? We have to wait."

"It's all we can do unless Balthazar moves against you or the boy. But he won't come or send anyone for a long time—if he ever does. Rest easy now. It's been a difficult night, and you're spending all your energy."

She did feel suddenly burned out. She said good-bye to Mentor and went to pick up Malachi from the sofa. She held his bundled figure close to her chest and gazed on his innocent face. Her boy must grow to understand the vampire nations and accept them. He should have no reason to want to hurt Balthazar or the Predators. But no matter how it all turned out, she would never let anyone do Malachi harm, no matter what. He was her child, flesh of her flesh, her only son.

Through the darkness, shadows draping over her as she moved, she carried Malachi quietly to the child-sized bed in the shape of a racing car they'd put into his room. She settled him into it; smoothed his hair, and tucked the cover around his body.

Then she returned to the chair in the darkened living room and sat rocking throughout many hours, worrying over the prophecy. It was fine for Mentor to reassure her, but he had never been a parent. He didn't know you couldn't put aside a real threat just because it wasn't standing on your doorstep yet. What if she failed to raise Malachi in a way Balthazar approved of? He'd be back. He was obsessed with Malachi. With no real reason at all! There were other *dhampirs*, why not threaten them? He must be really insane.

Thoughts of the dreamscape and the silver wolf who walked in it were enough to keep her up till dawn. By the time the sun rose, she had made a decision. She'd tell her family. She'd ask them all to help provide a protective circle around Malachi to watch over him. Her mother, her father, her brother Eddie, even her grandparents. They were all vampire and, together, they'd find a way to insure her son's safety.

4

Dolan sat in the dark on Mentor's sofa near the dead fireplace. Mentor didn't bother to open the door. He merely went through it and transformed in the center of the floor. Dolan glanced up at him, unsurprised. "That didn't take long," he said. "I thought I saw you here a little while ago and then you vanished."

Mentor sat in an easy chair and reached over to turn on a table lamp. Electric light was something Mentor liked very much. He had lived through the days before its invention and still recalled the thick greasy pungency of kerosene and, before that, of whale oil and stinking animal fat. "It wasn't as much of a crisis as I first thought. But I had to go back and see about something else. I'd just gotten here and was recalled."

"Ah." Dolan fell into contemplation. Mentor sat in the silence, resting from the day, thinking his own thoughts.

Finally Dolan said, "Why did you want me to come here? I'm not suicidal this time. You don't have to keep me in your basement, chained to the wall."

"No, but you have ambition, Dolan, and that won't do around the Cravens."

"I'm Craven."

"But you border on being Predator, as I told you before. That places you between worlds, between the clans. You don't quite . . . fit."

"Oh, great, just what I need. Lost in limbo." A sad chuckle escaped him.

"That's why I asked you here. I need some help."

"You? The Great Mentor, the Master Psychiatrist to the vampire nations?"

"There's no call for sarcasm. I'm trying to help you."

Dolan looked down at his hands. He pressed the knuckles of his right hand with his left thumb, massaging the bones. "I'm sorry. I'm just disappointed my plan to bring together the Cravens was shot down so fast. If only we could join our forces, we could elevate them."

"That's just it," Mentor said. "Cravens don't want your help. They can't see having the same ambition and energy you possess. In that, you're more like me."

"Like a Predator, you mean."

"Just so."

"All right, I'm convinced. What kind of help do you need? I'd rather work for you than sit around that dark house one more day."

"It wouldn't be working *for* me," Mentor said. "You'll be working *with* me. Our numbers are growing. Either I'll have to partition off part of my southwest territory and find someone to watch over it, or I have to have help doing it all myself."

"Wait a minute, you're saying you want me to do what you do? Are you nuts?"

"Sort of what I do. I think you'd be good at it."

Dolan laughed. "I'm a Craven. Who would listen to me? I'll be laughed at."

"Maybe at first," Mentor admitted. "But once you've been around a while, trust in you will build. They'll know I sent you."

"Well . . . what about the fact I don't know how to do what you do, Mentor? I can't guide new vampires through their mortal deaths. I can't counsel them once they're vampire. I can't hunt renegades and save suicides and deal with . . . with Ross."

"I'll always have to handle Ross. You're right, he's quite a handful. But I can train you to do some of the other work. Like tonight, when I was called away, when the alarm came and I was needed. You could learn how to handle minor disturbances such as that."

"I don't know . . ." Dolan had stopped rubbing at the knuckles of his hand and was now scrubbing at his cheeks in nervous worry.

"Relax," Mentor said. "You won't be sent out on your own for some time. You'll accompany me for a while, learn on the job, as it were." Mentor stood, crossed to the other man, and touched his shoulder. Dolan instantly lowered his hands from his face and was calm.

"How'd you do that?" he asked. "I was suddenly at peace, just from your touch."

Mentor smiled. "I'll teach you all the tricks. Just trust in me."

Once Dolan was settled into the spare bedroom, the heavy covers over his head to block out any morning light that might leak through the window shades, Mentor left the house again, soaring into Dallas' night sky. He came down again in a poor minority neighborhood, lighting on a concrete bench in a small backyard Japanese garden. Moonlight gleamed from the two large white stones placed in a sea of white, carefully raked gravel. Small conifers and holly bushes ringed the yard and a small stand of bamboo grew in a corner, errant breezes ruffling their long spiky leaves. Behind Mentor, a large old weeping willow drooped its lacy branches over his hunched shoulders. It amazed Mentor that the largest portion of Texas consisted of desert, but from Dallas or San Antonio all the way east to the Louisiana border a great variety of plants grew in the temperate climate and rich earth. Except for Thailand, which he loved very much, he felt the eastern parts of Texas were his favorite places in the world.

She lived here and had created the beauty he now beheld. Bette Kinyo, the Japanese-American hematologist he had saved from Ross' hands. She was married now, a woman of thirty-two finally wedded to Dr. Alan Star, the man Charles Upton had hired a few years in the past to find him real vampires. Star had been Upton's specialist in Houston, where Upton had the headquarters of his international oil and shipping company.

Mentor had formed a pact with the couple—with Bette, really—who convinced Alan to go along with their wishes. Bette and Alan would stop investigating the shipments of blood leaving the Strand-Catel blood bank run by Ross. Though they knew there were vampires, they would never speak of them or reveal the secret. It was either that or be at Ross' mercy. And Ross had no mercy. Given half a chance, he would have split both Bette and Alan asunder and drained them dry of their blood.

During the days when Mentor had dealt with the couple,

he'd unintentionally fallen in love with Bette. He'd entered her mind three times to wipe it of memories to keep the vampire nations secret. While immersed in her mind he had found her as good and decent and without malice as any human he'd ever encountered. But it was not just her inner spirit he began to love. He loved her small stature, the delicacy of her hands, and the porcelain skin of her heart-shaped face. He had lost himself in the depths of her fine dark liquid eyes.

She reminded him in some ways of his small Scottish wife, Beatrice, whom he'd loved so much that he hadn't been tempted by a woman in more than a century and a half. Beatrice, too, had been a superior woman, her heart as pure as a saint's. She had never raised her voice to another living soul. She had never harbored envy or longed to have more earthly possessions than her neighbor. To him, she was the embodiment of love, and from her, he had learned what it was like to put another person first in his life.

Bette might suspect he loved her, but they didn't speak of it. He tried not to see her, knowing it would be unforgivable if he were to interfere in her human life and the love she had for Alan.

Still, when he was overly tired from the work he did with other vampires, or when he was particularly burdened with all the memories he carried with him from centuries of living on Earth, he came to the little manicured garden and sat beneath the willow.

Staring at the gravel sea he was able to imagine white-capped waves breaking against the island rocks that rose from the "waters." All vestiges of his complicated life fled as his soul emptied, giving him respite. His consciousness floated on the white moonlit sea, free of encumbrance.

He had found other sacred places of peace during his sojourn on Earth, some of them just as necessary to him as Bette's garden. When he had first sickened and changed into vampire, he had gone nearly mad. No . . . he had actually gone mad. There was no point in lying to himself.

He lived then in a superstitious age that did not admit there were beasts such as vampires, but readily accepted the idea of demons from hell walking the land.

All the people around him who carried the same mutated genes as he only knew a terrible disease had afflicted them at first, carrying them inexorably toward death. They had no name for this disease then, and most often thought it was demonic possession. As the disease progressed, they weakened, their faces grew stony, they festered with sores, and sunlight gave them pain. Then some of them died, dying as naturally as all mortals, their breath ceasing, their pulses going silent. But they came back. Hours after death with rigor mortis already setting in and the body beginning the long process of final decay, some of them returned to themselves with a hard gasp. They flailed at the air as if fighting off avenging angels that would carry them to a bower of rotted meat and maggots watched over by things with hungry teeth.

They couldn't talk, couldn't walk, sometimes could not even move, just suddenly opening their dead eyes on their assembled loved ones gathered for the wake. The mourners would scream and beat their breasts and make the sign of the cross to ward off this sudden, inexplicable invasion of evil. The dead should not return. The dead should not open their eyes and rise up to walk.

It was not as if this had not already been going on for thousands of years. The first apelike human to stand on his two legs had lived in South Africa a hundred and fifty thousand years ago. Mentor believed the genes in those people held the precursor of porphyria and the mutation that would manifest into vampire. But the people among whom Mentor was born and raised knew nothing of those vampires who lived in other lands far away, too far for even tales of their debauchery and murder to travel. So when it happened to Mentor, who was a young man in his prime, though shriveled on his frame from the debilitating disease, his family ran from him into the streets of the medieval city of London. They cried out that the devil had come to Earth, walking now in the guise of their beloved dead son and brother.

Mentor had fled, climbing from a window into an alley filled with bawling cats and scurrying hordes of rats. He elbowed aside two inebriated men who tried to halt him, feeling his strength return, gaining more strength than he'd had before becoming ill. It was as if molten energy coursed through his body, giving him the strength of ten men and ten wild horses.

He hid himself from mankind, going down into the cellar of an abandoned brick building, closing the broken doors behind him and shutting out the world. That world now abhorred him and thought him the master of hell. He wanted nothing to do with people if they were that ignorant. Didn't they know the misery he was in? Didn't they know he'd had a dream that would make any man appear mad? In that dream he had embraced . . . something cold . . . something older than the world . . . something eternal. Since his family could not embrace him back into the bosom of their love, he would hide away from them until they came to their senses.

But after a short time down in the dark of the old building, the hunger came. It was like a fire in his gut and in his brain and in the very tips of his fingers. When his hunger pushed him past all endurable limits, he crept back up the lichen-covered, slippery stairs to the city night and went on a hunt. He knew what he needed and he would have it and no thought of the death it might bring could deter him from his mission in the slightest. When a man is hungry, he will eat, he reasoned in his mad way. He will kill an animal, tear up a vegetable from the soil, and he will even turn on his brethren if circumstances leave nothing else upon which to feed.

And so he did. He loosed his hunger on the populace. For no meat or vegetable now could he imagine going into his mouth or stomach. He turned to men and women, with their rich red blood, and he took them with abandon, some nights just dropping one horribly drained and bloody corpse onto the muddy street before grabbing another victim to fulfill the cold, driving need.

It was months before this madness abated and Mentor sat in the twilight darkness of the cellar, alone, the bones of victims strewn about him like so many sticks of kindling. He seemed to come to himself, the self he'd been before the illness and the pain and then the strange death dream, which came to make him into a Predator vampire.

Who am I? he wondered. *What has become of me? I am not an animal. I am not a man. I am a new creature under the sun and as God made all creatures, I am one of them. But if that is true, then for what purpose have I been made? Need there be a purpose? There must be,* he wailed to the heavens. *I must have a purpose!*

He knew instinctively that it was not just to maraud among London's poorest, taking life wherever it presented itself to him. Why, he'd even killed a child, a little boy no older than five who had wandered too near the cellar steps chasing a small carved wooden ball. And he had taken him gleefully, laughing uproariously afterward at the hot sweet taste lingering in his mouth and the feeling of bright steely energy flooding all through his sleek body.

For now, yes, after feasting so long and so well, he was sleek and beautiful, his gaze bewitching to male and female alike. They did not appear to notice his tattered and bloodstained clothing, or his tangled, uncut hair. They were captured in an instant by his gleaming eyes and his smile, that hauntingly beautiful smile that held out such promise.

He had murdered too many to remember. Old, young, male, female, crippled, virile. He had done it because it was his nature to do it and until he was completely satiated, he had not been able to think about the consequences to his soul.

Once he did, he was appalled. He had been studying religion before his death, stealing books and parchments from the rich by invading their homes when they were away or when they slept. Early on, he had found someone to teach him to read, lying in her bed each night in his fifteenth year, resting after his sweaty service, bending close to the letters and struggling with the words.

His lover was not a good woman and only gave him the lessons because he would do her will for nothing else. She was heavy, a woman whose fat rolled from her belly and her thighs as he climbed on top. She was always perfumed, but beneath the fragrant scent she still reeked of scorched potatoes and of goose dripping yellow fat, these items being among her favorite dishes.

He had been a man in search of holiness, despite what he'd had to do in order to learn to read and in order to find material in the ancient texts he wanted. At least in his own regard he believed he searched for perfection of the spirit and a rapport with God. His family thought him overly ambitious from the beginning with his crazy hope to rise from the class into which he'd been born.

"Nothing good will come of it," his mother said, brandishing a wooden spoon about his head and whacking him on the ear when he least expected the spoon to descend. "You need to find work, to find work and feed us before we starve, that is what you need to do! Why don't you have your stumpy woman in her fine costumes give you a handful of coins, for pity's sake? Does she not love you enough?"

No, she did not love him, but she loved his finely tuned and exquisite abilities lavished on her in the private quarters of her great mansion. Though she would tire of him before he tired of learning, he would no more asked for coin than he might have begged for a morsel from her overladen table. Hunger at that time did not drive him, as it did most of his family. They worked and sweated and went into servitude only to fill their bellies. Love did not drive him, as he had never loved yet and knew nothing of the glory of it. What drove him was his quest for God, as if he were God's bridled prize stallion and all he wanted to do was to find a way to slip from the meanness and degradation of his life into the robes of the Holy Church.

His mother understood none of that, nor did any of those who lived around him. Love God, yes, believe in His righteous anger, yes, but to think one of their kind could ever hope to attend a place of higher learning or don the robes and bear the chalice, no, never, ever, never.

So it was when he came to himself and remembered God's holy edict against taking life, and he found himself surrounded with the brutal evidence of his bloodthirst, he cried out piteously and buried his head in his arms. He was lost, dear God in heaven, he was set for the furnace of hell, just where his misguided family believed he'd come from when he returned from the dead. Perhaps he *was* possessed by demons or his body and mind were substance to clothe the devil himself. How else had he caused such great destruction and suffering without guilt until now, this moment months into the mad bloodletting rampage?

He could not bear to be alone with himself. He could not stand to hide like an animal in the burrow of his dank cellar stinking of corrupted flesh turned gray and falling from bones. He rushed up the stairs, sprawling a time or two as he went in his haste, yearning for the sky and clean, fresh air not redolent with his misdeeds.

He came out into the sun, shading his eyes. He saw people shy from him the way they did when he was ill and showing all the outward symptoms of his dread disease. Women spoke to one another behind their hands, clutching their market baskets to their breasts. Children hushed and clustered together for comfort, seeking an adult for protection. Men opened wide, frightened eyes at him and hurried along, almost running to be away.

He must look a monster. No longer lit from inside with the power that produced a beauteous gaze to entrance his prey, he was now simply a wrecked creature deep in the mire of guilt, fearing for his soul.

He slunk along the side of the buildings, shading his eyes, hiding his face until he came upon a dirt path leading from the city. He took it gratefully, hurrying now with all the preternatural speed he possessed at this point in his vampiric development. He hurried headlong into some oblivion away from humankind where he would not do them harm; where they would not stare at him and see him for the terrible, blasted revenant he had become.

He hurried for days uncountable, haunted by despair that he, a man questing after God, had done such despicable things against men, women, and even children. He wept and let the blood drip and dry on his ragged shirt. He slept where he fell, whether it was a ditch or a hummock off the road, and woke in a frenzy to get away, *get away fast.* He didn't know where he was going. It didn't matter. He hadn't the insight to realize he ran from nothing less than the shred of human conscience which still beat quietly as a tiny bird fluttering within the iron cage of his vampire body.

He might have been on the road wandering for a month or longer before one day, beside himself with recriminations that kept sweeping over him like a filthy ocean on a ruined shore, he came to a place in the road where a footpath led into the forest. The gloom called to him, whispering of darkness and surrender. That was where he belonged, he thought. With the wild animals he so much resembled.

He sped down the path, embracing the pinpricks of pain sent through his arms from bramble bushes growing close to where he walked. His wounds healed quickly, he noted with surprise, but the pain lingered with phantom twinges.

Low limbs swatted him in the head and bounded back again to knock with bony hands against his fleeing back. He didn't bother to duck or to move aside, welcoming the pain. As he plunged deeper into the forest gloom, a clarity began to steal over him like none he'd had before, even when human.

He was a killing creature and must face it. The world was full of murderous beings, whether animal, fish, fowl, or human. All of recorded history spoke of the monstrous acts men had perpetuated against men. In South Africa when the dawn of man brought forth a thinking being able to feel some small remorse for his actions, he, too, must have felt something akin to regret about the beasts he murdered.

That he had turned to feast on his own kind was not so remarkable. There might even be some way to avoid it, as he'd done during his days of forced march away from London. He had taken small furtive animals and drained them of their blood, but he had not tossed the lifeless shells. He had buried each and every one, every muskrat and weasel, every wild pig and cat and horny goat.

He had not even been tempted to touch another human, horrified at his past senseless actions that drove him now from the madness of murder to the madness of flight.

He stumbled on and noticed the gloom giving way slowly, by tiny increments, to sunlight. First it dappled the pathway through the forest canopy, and finally it shone with brilliance straight down between the rows of trees bounding each side of the path. He slowed and looked around, noting the brambles were gone and in their place grew heather green and low to the ground, tiny bluebells nodding within taller grass, and wild peace lilies with their striking white heads bending down in prayerful solitude.

Where was he and what sort of place was this? He had lived all his life amid the hovels and streets of London where the multitude clogged the arteries during the day and crawled back to their miserly tenements in the dusk. There they cooked cabbage and ham bones with precious little meat still fastened to them, cuffed their children about the ears, made noisy love, and snored into the new dawn.

He had not seen a lily except in the flower stalls in the better part of London. He had heard of bluebells from country kin, but never spied one. He marveled at nature and the wild profusion of beauty it had created in this lonely wood.

As he walked softly now over velvet sod, he came to a

clearing that spread out from the meager path to encompass an almost perfectly round pond fed by an underground spring. Rocks ringed the pond and the forest stood back, drooping limbs over the pool so that the reflections of green were deeper than the pure, sweet aqua green of the water itself.

Mentor, known then by another name, came to a halt. He sat down on a stone and stared into the pool's depths. It burbled slightly in the center, and he knew if he were to dive deep down into the water and open his eyes, he would see the source of the spring—a fissure in the earth, out of which the pond flowed. On the other side of the pond he saw a small creek, barely more than a rivulet really, easing through the forest and going . . . he did not know where. To a river, perhaps, or another pond or lake or stream.

He firmly believed he'd arrived at a sacred place. A place meant to house him until he could return to the world. The place itself was peaceful and beautiful, yes, but it wasn't just that. It was set off from the world, brighter than it should have been, quieter than the tomb. A place to find relief. A place to drop the burdensome rock of guilt and the baggage of past sins.

This was where he stayed until he was sane. He came to understand that there were mysteries in life, untold thousands of mysteries, of which his existence, against all usual understandings of nature, was but one. He believed when in future times of agony, remorse, or need of redemptive balm he would find places on Earth like this, where he could lay down his pain and go on. Not as he had before, but better, with more purpose and a surer footing.

Just as he thought, so it was. Over years and tens of years and hundreds of years. He might not know where the sanctuary lay hidden, but if he set out boldly and with faith, he knew he would find it, and he always did.

That is how the monastery in Thailand, their prison for the unquiet monsters, came to be. He had been searching for something after his wife's death and thirty years of desolation in a cold Swedish fortress. He yearned for a sacred place to give him some reason to go on, and he had come upon the crumbling cells and chapel and underground corridors of the monastery, long abandoned by its earthly order and fully forgotten. The jungle had overtaken it, vines wrapping around towers to bring them tumbling down. Doors were riddled with wormholes and soft sodden spots that gave way at a touch. Stones in the halls and cells had been pried and lifted out of place, taken for who knows what purpose—maybe to build a hut or to top a grave.

But . . . it was sacred. He could feel it like a silken cloak laid upon bare skin. It was a place that enveloped him and stilled his frantic, tortured mind. It had been made sacred three hundred years before Mentor happened upon it and, though abandoned, it held that sacred peace in trust for the next weary traveler who needed to find succor there.

There were other places, too; some hidden away like the spring-fed pond in the English countryside and the jungle-entombed old monastery. Some were open to the public, people tracking through these places daily with little Japanese cameras and notebooks and pens. They fondled the stone or glass, leaving behind their imprints, their oils that could corrode. On occasion they unavoidably passed gas, made lewd remarks or gestures, drank from secret flasks, slipped illicit and spellbinding pills beneath their livid tongues—never dreaming they were in jeopardy of desecration. Sometimes couples stole kisses and made promises they'd never fulfill.

One such public place was the Taj Mahal, the grand monument built by one man to one woman, a magnificent expression of depthless love. In there, in the dark when the place was closed and quiet and tomblike, Mentor could sit and ponder the hardest questions and confirm the best actions to take. Or he could just rest, as he needed—and he needed rest almost as much as he needed blood.

Some public places he'd found to be sacred were surprising, even to him. It was easily understandable if he found a pew in New York City's St. Patrick's Cathedral to be a place of rest, but who would have imagined that the ward in a children's institution in Athens, Greece, was another? He'd happened on it by chance, as he did all the best havens.

He'd been summoned by the strident plea from a child halfway across the world. It was the millennial year, 2000, and he had been sitting quietly in his own home, reading. He seldom interfered in matters off his own continent, but this cry for help was heard around the world, and other vampire mentors—for there were a few more—were too engaged to take leave from their stations. By telepathic means they all urged Mentor to go to the young vampire screaming for someone, anyone, *Help!*

The child was a boy, around eight years old, who had been mercilessly taken as he hobbled along an Athens street at night. The boy, Justin, had a clubfoot and some slight mental retardation. His family had left him to die. Unable to keep him when he was much younger and displaying an inability to walk because of his misshapen foot, they took him out into the arid lands bounding the city. It was such a disgrace in Greece to have borne a handicapped child that engagements were broken on the basis of a baby born with disability to anyone in the family. Most of these babies were given away young to institutions, but some, like Justin, were dumped on the mercy of the world to die beneath the harsh elements.

This heartless treatment seemed alien to Mentor. Men had progressed for two thousand years, their sins too many to number, but for a family to throw out a child as if he were garbage in these modern days was unfathomable.

However, Justin proved resilient and lived. He never prospered, but he became cunning at survival. That is until the fateful night he was making his way past the closed doors of vendors' carts in an old marketplace, looking for some safe place to sleep. He was snatched by a rogue vampire, one of the scruffy, half-mad beings who, like Mentor when newly changed, didn't stop to consider the age of a victim. But something went wrong, the murder was interrupted, a policeman having come around a corner and spied the adult vampire latched like a leech to the young child's throat. When Justin fell to the street, his attacker having absconded, his heart still beat, and he was already recovering from the attack. Even as he had survived the pitiless abandonment in the desert as a younger child, his tremendous will to live now drove his heart to fill anew with blood and take up a slow, irregular rhythm.

As he struggled, as his heart beat erratically, the cavity filling with the last of his blood, his will came to the fore and forbade him to give up. Unbeknownst to him, a minute amount of blood left behind was tainted with the vampire's own, and it was already working the magic of transference, the sickness of infection. It was even now sending him straight into the hands of the Predator-Maker in the death dream. Had he died, he'd have been spared, but living out to the end, he teetered into the world of vampire.

There he was at the moment of his greatest despair, lying in the arms of the policeman in the real world, dying, but in the supernatural world he faced the giant Predator who swooped down through a dark wood, a full bloody moon at his back.

Justin's cry echoed and found Mentor's ears. Mentor swiftly took to the skies, traveling so high that below him the Earth turned. He came down again in Greece, in a sultry Athens night, and speaking to the policeman in a mesmerizing tone, took the dying child from the other man's arms. Together they disappeared, or so it would have seemed to the officer, who woke disoriented from a small trance.

Mentor had Justin firmly clutched to his chest, moving rapidly down moon-bathed stone stairs and into a crypt in the shadow of an old pagan temple. He went immediately into the nightmare world where each of them died to the real world and woke into the new. He was with Justin in the dark wood, advising him to *run*, run away from the Predator-Maker, if his soul allowed it. Did his soul truly wish to rise again into a life of murderous intent? Or did he wish to be nearly his human self again? Or at the very least, did he wish to listen to the Craven Mistress and embrace a life of darkness and sickness?

Justin was but one of the many thousands Mentor had given this same advice, offering counsel about the choices involved, but the fight never failed to give him the fright of his life, each and every time. He and Justin could *see* the Predator, large as a comet approaching landfall, rushing down on the boy in fiery glory to make him into one of his own. The struggle went on for hours on that other plane, when in real world time only minutes might have passed. Had anyone seen them, the old vampire with the white unruly hair, head bowed as if in prayer, holding a dead child in his arms, they could not have guessed the two were in serious combat with the Predator-Maker and the ancient Mistress of the Craven.

Justin, as Mentor had hoped, disavowed the eternal life

of a Predator, forgave the Mistress for hoping to convince
him to be born again as a Craven, and turned into Mentor's
arms, choosing at the last to be a Natural when he returned
to life. He would from then on live as man lived and he
would pass as human, doing no harm, spending all his many
lifetimes in service to, and for the benefit of, mankind.

When Justin, having chosen his way, woke from the
death dream, Mentor laid him gently on the stone floor in
the near darkness and said, "I'll leave you, but don't fear.
In a while the paralysis will wear off and you'll be able to
leave this place and find the Master of the Blood here who
will supply you on credit until you can pay."

All this Mentor said without speaking, mind to mind, and
saw the boy's now open eyes increase in understanding. He
could leave him and not worry for his soul or his future.
But there was something Justin wished to tell him, so Mentor paused at the door and listened quietly.

Again, mind to mind, the boy said, "Thank you for saving me."

Mentor nodded and was about to continue on his way
when Justin said, "There is a place you need to go to see
about little children."

Curious, Mentor turned and retraced his steps. He stood
over the boy, looking down on his still face and vibrant
eyes. "More children like you who need me?" It was
astounding to think there might be a whole slew of little
vampire children, newly made, awaiting him in Athens.

No, not vampires, Justin said, projecting his thoughts
quickly now. *They're like me. They were abandoned because
they're different.*

Mentor's attention was drawn to the small boy's deformed foot. He couldn't fix it. It had been formed when
Justin was a fetus, and now it was a permanent disfig-
urement.

*Yes, like my foot. Some of them have something wrong.
But most of them have something wrong in the brain. You
know how my brain is not as good as yours . . . you were
in it . . . you know it's . . . broken.*

That was how Mentor came to cross Athens and find the
sacred place no one would ever have thought existed.
Going by Justin's directions, he found the building, a
square, squat place made of white stone, the windows dark-

ened for the night. Entering an open window, sensing already how full the building was of children, feeling their soft breaths and hearing sounds of muffled weeping, he found them congregated together in a ward of metal cribs with tall sides. Standing stock-still, frozen in place, Mentor gazed around the big open ward and his heart sank within him. Hundreds of children, all of them imprisoned in their cribs, tied with white gauze by ankle or wrist. The ages ranged from one year to a full-grown man of thirty-five, but most of them were under twelve.

They'd all been put here by their families. They'd all been given up as no good. Mentor knew all about them in an instant. Why they had been put here and forgotten. Why their poor mothers gave them up. Why they were crowded this way and kept in cribs, kept bound so they wouldn't crawl out or fall to the hard tiled floor. They were all to some degree or other mentally diminished. Some also had physical handicaps added to their problems, as did Justin, but for the most part it was their minds which were in disarray rather than their bodies. They received no comfort or personal attention, as there were not enough staff people to care for so many abandoned children.

Mentor moved swiftly to a crib and reached in to take the hand of a little girl, four years old, who lay awake, sensing him and beginning to cry, frightened of the intruder. She calmed and the tears dried. She looked up at him, smiling sweetly.

For one terrible moment Mentor imagined himself leaning over the sides of the crib, taking the child's slim neck into his hand and lifting it to his mouth. He could vanquish this life for her, he could steal it from her and release her from bondage.

But no. It was not what she wished and not what he wanted. She'd been given life, as lowly as it appeared to be, and it was hers to live, however small and circumscribed.

It was then Mentor knew this place, as horrible an institution as it was, filled with as many tortured souls as the eye could see, was as sacred a place of peace as any he'd ever discovered in his global travels. There was no hatred here, no remorse, and no ego. Ambition had never existed, lies had never been uttered, and these little ones had never meted out pain to another.

The children knew on some level they were in a small prison that measured no larger than the sides of their metal cribs, but they hadn't the capacity to hate their caretakers or even the parents who abandoned them. They did not know what hate was or how to muster it. They knew no vanity and when despair came, it vanished just as quickly, the shells of their minds rejecting it as easily as a bovine will shake off the flies on its swinging tail. They were as perfect in goodness as any newborn, untouched, unsullied by the vagaries of the world.

The girl, now quieted, let go of Mentor's fingers and tucked her hand beneath her cheek, shutting her eyes and drifting into sleep. Mentor slid down to the floor and sat with his own hands folded together in his lap. He soaked in the love that permeated this large populated room. The love came from the children who projected it, having no other emotion to give. They were lost children, pitiable in their tiny prisons, but they had made this place a haven, a sanctuary. To one another they communicated with their glances, with their sighs and grunts. None of them possessed a language, so they were rather like the vampires, able to project their simple thoughts to one another over the distance, mind to mind.

He heard a child with a deficiency in understanding ninety percent of the stimuli that came into his mind cooing to another child in a crib next to him, cooing that said it was okay, it was all right, he was not alone, never really alone.

He heard another speaking in thought symbols that only roughly translated to human language, yet it seemed to Mentor it was as pure an embodiment of the emotion of love as any thinking creature could distinguish. Everywhere Mentor turned his intelligence, he picked up the myriad mind sounds coming from the children, like susurrations of warm wind through palms, and it was like being led through a fantastic land where lollipops grew on trees and gingerbread cottages sprang up along strawberry lanes.

I am so happy here, Mentor thought, falling into meditation that drew him away from his life and the world he lived it in. *These babies are imprisoned and alone with no mother or father or sibling to care for them,* he realized, *but they whisper about love and dream of heaven.*

Often, the institution for children in Greece was where Mentor headed when he needed reminding of how precious life was, the bare breath of it. No matter how mean or distressed an existence a man or child lived, it was still imbued with a beauty untold. If, as the Buddhists believed, a man, a child, a stick, a leaf, a bird was not separate from one another, that all was one while being singular, then that was the complete reason for the children's survival. They were part of the whole. They served some purpose not even Mentor could decipher, but knew instinctively existed. He would not fall into the conceit that they existed solely to comfort *him*, but they did exist for some reason kept secret from him and he was sure of that.

So it was here, in Dallas, Texas, as he sat beneath the willow in Bette's small, enchanted garden that Mentor had found another Good Place. Without these places to retreat to, he thought the deep fire of his Predator nature might resume and become such a bonfire it would consume innocent and evil alike, child and mother, saint, Madonna, and demon. It was the garden—the pond in England, the monastery in Thailand, the children's prison in Greece, the Taj Mahal, St. Patrick's Cathedral and so many others he'd found over the centuries—which saved him from real destruction.

Here, in the dimming of the moon and the deepness of the night, he could release the fires which burned in him. He could let himself be no more than the white island rocks in the great shining sea of white gravel.

He didn't wonder if the woman recognized what she had created in the midst of an urban rundown minority neighborhood. He didn't wonder because he knew Bette Kinyo Star was a naturally gifted psychic. Guided by innate abilities Mentor did not understand when they were demonstrated by human instead of vampire, she had carefully carved out an oasis of peace with nothing more than shrubbery, small trees, rocks, and gravel. She'd done it for herself initially, and now, having found it, he shared the perfect magic with her.

* * *

Bette woke the moment she sensed Mentor entering her garden. She came from sleep to wakefulness in an instant.

Her eyes were as wide as they might have been if she'd just been slammed around inside of a car broadsided by a big diesel semi-truck. She lay still for some time, thinking about the great vampire who visited her garden. She always knew when he came. He always came at night when she slept.

She and her husband Alan had made a pact with Mentor. They knew another great vampire controlled one of Dallas' largest blood banks, and that he shipped much of that blood out of the city to other towns all over the southwest. Bette was the hematologist who supervised the testing of all blood supplies leaving Dallas, and she had come upon the discrepancy with Strand-Catel. That's when Mentor first came to her. He'd meant to wipe away her memories of the discrepancy, and then, when she was able to recall those memories, he made a pact that she and Alan never tell anyone what they knew.

What they knew for certain was the fact they were dealing with supernatural creatures who could tear their heads off their shoulders at a whim. They knew more than any other humans in America about vampires. And they had promised to keep that knowledge to themselves. If they didn't, they would have died long ago.

For more than three years the two of them harbored the dread secret. It wasn't hard to remain silent. The threat of quick and bloody death went a long way to insure it. Sometimes they talked about it in whispers, turning to one another in bed and entangled in one another's arms. Often Bette shivered uncontrollably, and Alan had to hold her tightly, soothing her with words of love. Knowing that thousands of vampires moved among mankind was like knowing there was a silent plague stalking the land, yet they had sworn never to speak of it to anyone else.

As Bette lay quietly in her bed, eyes open, senses all raising flags of alarm that assured her the vampire was nearby, she wrestled with the urge to go to him. It was not as if he called to her. He never did that. No, it was as if a strange, wild need rattled around within her brain, unwilling to be stilled until she went to him.

This happened every time he came, yet she never gave in. She feared Mentor, of course, but, more, she couldn't deny a deep yearning to know him more intimately. Here was a creature who had once been human and yet had lived hundreds of years beyond his natural death. His wisdom had widened over those centuries until he became the repository of a world history not gleaned from the dusty pages of textbooks, but from experience earned in the midst of human events. There was so much she could learn from him if she could get him to speak of his past.

This night, as on all nights when he appeared, she struggled to stay in bed next to her sleeping husband, and away from the vampire. For long minutes she won against the urge.

And then she sat straight up in bed, flinging the covers aside, and swung her feet to the floor. She found her bathrobe lying on the end of the bed and slipped into it. She got her bare feet into the white satin slippers. Before she let herself rethink the wisdom of her actions, she had crossed the darkened bedroom and was halfway down the stairs. In the kitchen where her back door led out to the garden, she paused, hand on the lock. Did she want to see him? Did she really?

She threw the dead bolt and turned the knob, knowing she couldn't stop now. She stepped out onto the concrete stoop and slipped down the three steps to the scattered stone path that led to the bench beneath the willow tree. She saw him as soon as she was clear of the door. He sat like a large black bird perched on the bench. He hunched over his knees, hands folded and supporting his great shaggy head. At her approach he turned slowly and even in the darkness she saw the glow of his steady gaze.

"Do I disturb you?" he asked.

She was at his side now and taking a seat next to him on the bench. She stared out at the white gravel sea she'd created in the center of the garden. Shadows and moonshine undulated across the surface, shifting as the light breeze moved through the branches of the willow. "I wake up when you come."

"I should not come, then. I didn't mean to cause you trouble."

Bette reached over and took hold of one of his hands. She didn't know whether she meant to comfort him or to comfort herself. He was cold. She held the hand of a dead thing, but it did not frighten her. "Don't let me force you away. This garden is . . ."

"It's sacred," he said.

"Yes. It was made in a prayerful attitude and reflects my love for Buddha."

They sat without speaking for a few minutes. He had closed his other hand over hers, so that she felt her small, warm hand encased in the hard cold box of his flesh.

"Do you always wake when I come here?" he asked.

"I can't explain it," she said, "but I always know. I've been wanting to see you, but until tonight I never acted on the impulse."

"You're not afraid?"

She looked at him. "Of course I'm afraid."

Mentor hung his head. "I would never harm you, Bette. Not in a million years."

She knew her small smile was hidden by the shadows. "I know. We share more than the secret of your existence, don't we, Mentor?"

He sighed heavily and did not respond. Finally he said in a sad voice, "You know how I love you, don't you?"

She took back her hand from his and folded it into her lap. "I think I must. And I don't think it's wise."

"When was love ever wise?" he said. "I loved another mortal once, my wife, Beatrice. It may have been a mistake in the eyes of others like me, but even now I know it was destined I love her."

"Was it long ago?"

"Yes, a very long time ago. I met her when she was just eighteen, a girl on her father's farm in the Scottish countryside. I'd been traveling alone, staying away from the cities, agonizing over my self-enforced loneliness and my need for . . ."

"Blood?"

"Yes, my need for blood. I'd already abstained from taking humans at that time. I couldn't live that way anymore. Though my nature is that of a Predator, I fought my nature and won over it, but I was always starving, always waging the fight. I had been living on the blood of animals when Beatrice appeared in the lane, a basket over her arm. She was going to the house of an ill relative. I saw her and my first thought was to kill her, God help me. As she saw me and shyly smiled and nodded her head, the thought fled. I was as captivated as the proverbial fly in ointment. I stopped and asked directions. I said I'd been on the road a while, and she invited me to her home where her father would give me food and a bed for the night.

"I hurried to her father's house and, just as she promised, he invited me to stay and rest a bit in my travel. They received few visitors and were happy to have someone give them the news from the cities. Beatrice returned that afternoon and the rest, as they say, is history."

"You never wanted to make her like you?"

Mentor smiled and Bette saw his large incisors slip down and then slowly retract. She forced herself not to move abruptly at the sight. *Be calm,* she told herself, *he does not murder humans.*

"Often I wanted to take her so she'd live with me forever. But I knew her wishes, and they were that she never give up her humanity. I watched her age, grow frail and, finally, sick. Simply said, I loved her enough to let go when death came."

"You've never regretted that decision?"

"I've always regretted it. But I would have despised myself so thoroughly if I'd done it, I'd never have been happy again. Beatrice would never have forgiven me; she might even have lost all love for me. It was the best decision."

"Why do you feel love for me now?" She really wanted to know. If he'd loved his wife so much and had been alone all those intervening years, why her? Why now?

"I wish I could say. Why did I fall in love with Beatrice? I may know many things, but I know nothing at all about why we fall in love—even when we hope not to. It's a mystery."

Again they sat quietly, sharing the cool night and the vista of the miniature Japanese garden. A few clouds floated across the face of the moon, dropping them into an inkier darkness. Bette shivered. When the clouds passed and the moonlight once again gleamed over the yard, she felt prompted to break the silence. "Do you believe in God? Do you think He watches over you? These are questions I've wanted to ask for a long time."

"I do believe in God," he said firmly. "Before I was

vampire, I had aspirations to join the Catholic church and become a priest. The Church then was the most glorious institution. It held hope of redemption from a sinful world. And it was the most powerful entity in all of England, even stronger than the king. Since those days, so many things have happened. Now I have no confidence God even knows I live or had anything to do with my . . . condition."

Bette thought about his answer. It had to cause him to constantly fight off despair if he thought God had deserted him forever. She thought he had been an evil creature at one time, as he admitted, but believed now he was not. This feeling couldn't be logically explained; it was something she knew, the way she knew when he was near her home. Also, she felt he wouldn't have found peace in her garden had he been evil and corrupt. He wouldn't have recognized the sacred heart of it.

The sound of the back door opening brought both of them to attention at the same time. Mentor possessed all the supernatural qualities of his kind, but Bette had been born with a natural telepathic ability that she accepted as a birthright. Her ability was almost as strong as the vampire's. Bette stood, knowing it was her husband. Mentor remained seated, only his head turning to take in the interruption.

"Alan?" Bette took a few steps toward the house. She had never meant to wake or worry her husband.

"What are you doing out here?" Alan stumbled a little as he came down the path to meet her. His hair was mussed, and he knuckled his eyes, wiping sleep away.

She turned to the side so she would not block his view. When he saw the vampire, he stiffened. The look in his eyes was one of primitive fear. She took his arm and said in a gentle tone, "I knew he was out here. I wanted to talk to him."

"It seems I've upset your whole household," Mentor said, rising to excuse himself. "I'll go now."

"But why are you here?" Alan's voice was unsteady.

"I think your wife knows why. I never meant to bother you, however. Please forgive me."

"He feels at peace in my garden," Bette said. "He's been coming for a long time."

"Has he?" Alan's face reflected his confusion. Bette

could see from his expression that he wondered at it all. She needed to reassure him in some way. She turned to Mentor only to find he was gone. She shouldn't have been startled, but was. She flinched at finding him absent before turning again to her husband. She walked with him to the house, her hand still clasped on his arm.

"He's gone," she said, knowing she spoke the obvious. "Let's go back to bed."

"He comes here all the time?"

She laughed a little at his amazement. "Yes, sometimes a few times a week. I don't know how many times he's been here over the past three years."

"Why didn't you ever tell me?"

"It might have ruined your sleep."

He shut the door behind them once in the house, shot the dead bolt, and tried the doorknob. "You're right about that. I don't think I like the idea even a little bit."

"Alan, he's not here to hurt us. He's a tortured soul. He discovered my garden makes him feel at peace. I wouldn't want to take that from him."

"What about my peace? How will I sleep knowing he might be out there and you might go to him?"

"Oh, Alan, you're not jealous, are you?" She snuggled against him, wrapping her arms around his waist. "You know how much I love you. I could never love a . . . a . . ." She couldn't say it. Of course she could never love an un-dead creature such as Mentor. The very idea made her feel a fear that crawled along her hairline and made her lips twitch. It was not love, but kinship, which drove her to his side this night.

"I don't think it's jealousy," Alan said in his defense. He hugged her close. "I just worry about your safety. I mean, I've *seen* what they can do. They're no more human than a fire truck or a . . . a . . . doorknob."

"And that's what's so pitiful about them, Alan. Because Mentor once was a man, just like you. He loved a wife, just as you do. He hasn't forgotten his life, you know."

"Well, I think you have more empathy for him than I do," he said. "Let's go to bed. We both have to be up early for work tomorrow. You won't go out there again, though, will you? When he comes back?"

"If you prefer I don't, then I won't. I'm not sure why I

did it this time." She followed behind him up the dark stairs, careful to hold to the railing. In their bed she drew close into the circle of his arms. It was only then she regretted saying she would not go out into the night to see Mentor again. Didn't her husband understand there was so much they could learn, there was so much to know, so many more secrets she could discover? How many humans ever had the chance to interview a vampire about his life?

She sighed into her husband's chest and breathed in his scent, loving it, loving him. She never wanted to cause him any worry. She should stay away from the old vampire; she knew Alan was right. He had watched one of them murder two women, ripping their throats with fanged teeth, taking their blood as they fought him. She must keep their lethal thirst foremost in her mind. She did not think Mentor killed, as had the vampire they called Ross who ran the blood bank and whom Alan had witnessed killing without remorse. But Mentor *was* vampire, and who could know what he might do one midnight in the garden, a warm, human subject at his side.

She really shouldn't tempt a creature of such fierce strength without knowing what he might do. It was like trusting the tiger in the cage or a sleeping bear in his den.

She drifted into sleep, remonstrating herself for her actions. She should do nothing to put herself or her husband in jeopardy. She would stay in her bed, in her house, and away from the dark hunched silent figure who frequented her garden. She would. She really must . . . she knew . . . she had to. . . .

*   *   *

Mentor moved so quickly in the garden that the humans never saw him leave. He flew across the sky, a darkness against the darkness, until he reached Ross' large double-winged ranch home on the outskirts of Dallas. He did not knock on the door, knowing Ross was aware of his arrival. He opened the door and entered, finding Ross sitting on a very uncomfortable-looking silver metal Eames' chair. Ross put aside the book on art history he was reading and looked up. "I'm glad you could make it," he said.

Mentor sat on the bright orange sofa with a figure-eight

back. He could not understand Ross' love for strangely-
shaped modern furniture. He was never comfortable with
Ross anyway, thinking him impulsive and murderous, but
when he had to visit Ross' home, he felt he was in a future
world where he did not fit. In his old-fashioned, rumpled
black suit and white shirt with his windblown, unruly Albert
Einstein white hair, he might as well be a homeless person
at a White House reception.

"I know you called for me an hour ago, but I happened
to be busy," he said. He'd rather not tell Ross he spent
some nights in Bette's garden. It might be taken the wrong
way. Ross knew he had some affinity for the young couple,
but he had no idea the depth of Mentor's feeling for the
woman.

"What if I'd summoned you because of something momentous?" Ross raised one eyebrow in his arrogant way.

"Then you would have told me." Mentor disliked sounding impatient, but Ross drove him to it.

Ross stood and went to a glass-topped table to retrieve
a cigarette from a silver box. He took his time lighting it
with a silver table lighter. He exhaled and said, "I love the
idea that it doesn't matter what I do to this body with
cigarette smoke. It gives me such freedom because tobacco
is an exhilarating substance, don't you think?"

"I don't know since I never smoked. You have to know
it *does* stink, though. So, come on, Ross, the night is late.
I need some rest."

"Upton." Ross blew out a cloud of smoke in Mentor's
direction before moving back to his chair. "He's onto
something."

"What?"

"He got hold of some kind of cards, cards that I've been
told might help him discover a way to escape the
monastery."

Mentor almost laughed at the thought but suddenly remembered how there had been things in the world before
which held magic. Once Beatrice had found a stone at the
edge of a creek and the stone glowed, as if there was fire
locked inside it. Mentor took the rock and buried it deep
in the forest. He did not know what manner of thing the
rock was, but it wasn't a normal rock composed of normal
minerals, and he didn't want it around his wife. He ex-

pected even today, a hundred years and more later, the buried rock still glowed with sinister heat.

Another time, many years in the past, he had gone to the aid of a young vampire who claimed he was cursed. No matter what he did, it all turned out wrong for him. He was a Predator, and every time he stalked a victim, the human found a way to slip from his clutches. He could not even take a drunk, without losing him in some debacle or another. He was about to starve, he told Mentor, and did not know what to do.

Mentor searched his house and found an antique brass hairbrush on the vampire's dresser. The back was stamped with a lion standing on its back paws, and there was a coat of arms on the brush handle. The young vampire, a dandy who loved velvets and lace, used it every day to brush his long, luxurious blond hair. Lifting it in his hand, Mentor felt a surge of evil power, and knew whoever had owned the thing before had infused it with a sort of evil magic. After learning the vampire had bought the brush months before in a Venice market and his fortune had gone downhill soon afterward, Mentor suggested he take the brush, melt it down, and bury it in the ground. It held something from its original owner that gave it the power to affect anyone who used it.

There were other objects in the world which seemed to possess an unnatural power that could not be disputed. Mentor did not know how these things came to be, but he realized it was foolish to disbelieve his own experience.

"Where did he get the cards?" Mentor asked. "And who told you about them?"

"The monks gave Upton the cards when he asked for a deck to play with. Madeline sent me a message saying she saw the cards, she held one, and she thinks they're possessed in some way. She knows how much you want to keep Upton imprisoned for the good of all of us. She thought we should know about the cards so that we could investigate, just in case Upton could really use them to free himself."

"Well, I've never run into magic cards, though Gypsies have claimed for centuries some decks have the power to tell them the future," Mentor said. "But Madeline's not talking about fortune-telling cards, is she?"

"No, not quite. She says they look like tarot cards, but

she felt an electrical surge on touching them. Upton immediately snatched the card from her hand, but for the few moments she held it, she saw a knave holding a cup move on the card. It stepped back from a table and stared at her, as if the figure was alive. Then it lifted the cup and drank from it."

Mentor decided he must go to Upton and take away the cards. Whether they could free him or not, he couldn't let Charles Upton have any advantage, even if it were but a mental one. The man was a genius and incredibly passionate about changing everything about the way vampires had lived in the world for hundreds of years. Given his way, he would rule the Predators, first in the United States, and later in the rest of the world. He would cease supplying the Naturals and Cravens with life-sustaining blood. If that happened, Naturals would be forced to prey, reverting to their most base natures, and Cravens, too ill for the most part to prey, would starve and turn into dusty skeletons. It would create true chaos, disrupting societies and even governments.

"I'll go to the monastery and take care of it." Mentor rose from the hard sofa. He added, "Though you could have done this small thing yourself. I guess you're too content to leave your home."

"Don't act like a peeved child, Mentor. You know I'm needed here to watch over Strand-Catel. Now I have the blood supplies in Arizona and Oklahoma to see about, too. You act like I never do anything when I'm the one who does *everything*."

Mentor sighed, seeing the argument would not be won this night. Ross liked business. He liked numbers and accounting sheets and, lately, computer tracking system software and computer electronic mail to keep in touch with his minions. He thought dealing with anything at the Thailand monastery a real imposition. No matter that Mentor was in charge of hundreds of new vampires who had to learn how to live in the world again, or that he had Dell's young *dhampir* to monitor, or the Craven, Dolan, to train. Let Mentor do it, that had always been Ross' position. Let Mentor handle the people and Ross handle the business, the money, and the blood supply.

"All right, keep your shirt on, Ross. I'm leaving now. If Madeline contacts you again, tell her to stay calm."

"That woman? She's like a nuclear warhead with a hair trigger. There's no telling her anything."

Ross was right. Dealing with Madeline was precarious. One moment she was reasonable, the next she was a maniac.

Ross did not bother to rise and see him to the door. Mentor stepped outside and stared into the night sky. He sensed the sun creeping toward the horizon like a yellow claw reaching around the face of the globe. Dolan, like all Cravens, would have to retire to Mentor's basement and sleep in darkness. Mentor and Ross and all the Predators and Naturals were blessed to walk in the sunlight, the porphyria that killed them having been burned away in the change they made on the brink of their deaths. Cravens, essentially still suffering many of the characteristics of the human disease, were painfully burned if they braved the sun's light, just as they had been when alive. He would have to do something about that for Dolan if he wanted him as a helpmate.

Mentor should hurry; however, as it was already day in Thailand and there was no telling what Charles Upton was up to with the unusual deck of cards he had in his possession. It was imperative he not have anything to further his ambitions, at least not as long as Mentor lived.

Spreading his molecules thin until his Earthly body transformed into a thick, black cloud, Mentor rose into the sky and sped toward the upper stratosphere, there to wait for the turning of the planet Earth.

5

"Hello, Madeline." Mentor closed the cell door behind him. She sat at the desk, writing on sheets of white paper with a long turkey quill. She had been offered more modern writing materials over the years and had snorted in dismissal. She had grown up using a quill and she saw no reason to change now.

She did not turn at first. Mentor thought she was finishing the sentence she had been writing. When she did turn, he saw her face was ravaged with tears. She had cried so long her cheeks were red with blood, as was the whole front of her dark dress.

"What's wrong?" Had she been in a rage, he wouldn't have been surprised, as she was often in high spirits, but to see her brought so low with weeping took him aback.

"Is anything right?" She put her hands over her face and wept harder.

Mentor went to her, touched by her pain. He tried to pat her on the back, not knowing what else to do, but she twisted away and he saw the old Madeline resurface beneath the tears. She glared at him and said, "You dare lay a hand on me!"

"I'm only trying to help. Can't you tell me what precipitated this?"

"You know, Mentor, you've known it for a hundred years. I can't live without the man I loved so much. I've done it so far, but I don't know why I've even tried. I was writing my memoirs and came to the time when I met and married Ian. I broke down the way you see me now. I can't go on, Mentor, it's too hard."

Again she buried her face in her hands, her shoulders shaking. Mentor thought the retelling on paper of her life had brought her loss to her all over again and he feared for her mind now as he hadn't before. He realized with a sudden insightful shock that if he were to sit and write a close personal account of his love for Beatrice, he, too, might be filled with such misery it would block the sun. He had told Bette very little about meeting Beatrice, but if he tried to re-create their long days together, their every joy and shared burden, it might drive him mad.

This time he did not try to comfort Madeline by touching her. This time he approached her mentally, speaking in her mind with soft loving words from one equal to another. He was buffeted by her great pain, but stayed, letting the hurricane of grief sweep over him. He spoke to her quietly, with feeling she knew to be true, for now he commiserated with her mind to mind. He told her that he had known love, too, and had lost it. He thought she should not try to write about it. She should wrench her mind from the past that could not be changed to the present, where she could find some hope of getting well.

It was some time, the shadows lengthening in her cell, before the weeping trailed off and Madeline found a folded napkin and cleaned her face. She said, "Thank you, Mentor. You are very kind."

He thought it best to divert her attention to the matter at hand. "Ross told me you sent word of a problem with your neighbor, Charles Upton."

Madeline's eyes narrowed, and he could almost see the intelligence behind them focusing. "That man is more dangerous than you know." She turned the chair at her desk and faced Mentor. "The cards he has possess some kind of power, whether you believe it or not. I held one. I saw it. He said Joseph gave them to him, and I cannot fathom why. Didn't he know what they were?"

"I'll speak to Joseph and find out, but obviously he didn't. Do you think they really might help Upton?"

"If they wish to, they will. It's hard to explain, but I think there might be some sort of presence behind them."

"Is it vampire?"

"I don't know. Perhaps. It's powerful, that's all I could discern."

"I'll take them away," he said, going for the door.

"If you don't mind a little advice?"

He turned at the door. "Yes?"

"Confronting him to take away the cards will cause a tremendous fight, I think. His powers have really grown. You'd do best to go in when he's sleeping. He stays up most of the night, deciphering their meaning, and when he sleeps, he's so tired he falls over where he sits and even a gong striking next to his ear wouldn't wake him."

Mentor thought her advice salient. Ross had made Upton. He had had the human condition of prophyria and was dying of it. He did not have their mutated strain of that same disease, and would never have been vampire had not he tricked Ross into making him one right at the last moment before death. Having been made by one of the great Predators, he possessed some of his Maker's power and strength and ability. He had not been trained, as Mentor trained new vampires in their powers and responsibilities, so he could not perform as well as Ross or Mentor, but the potential was there for destruction if it came to a serious confrontation.

"I'll wait," he said. "Thank you, Madeline. I hope you'll put away your memoir as I advised."

She glanced toward the pages covered with her fine script, and her face fell into sadness. "It's all I have left," she said. She turned back to him. "Go now, leave me be." She fluttered her fingertips in the air at him. "Go, I say, go away."

Her mood had changed, as it was wont to do, so Mentor hurried out the door so as not to be in the path of her irritation. He slipped down the corridor away from Upton's cell, hoping the other vampire had not sensed him there.

He must find Joseph.

*   *   *

Joseph, confused and wallowing in guilt, told Mentor how the prisoner had asked for a deck of cards to play solitaire. Joseph remembered he'd seen cards wrapped in old velvet lying on a bookshelf in the library. It was on a top shelf and undisturbed, having lain there for years. Brother Hadeem told him they hadn't been touched since the vampire monks took over the abandoned monastery.

"I didn't really look at them," he said. "I knew they were cards, that's all. I took them to the cell." He hung his head guiltily.

Mentor said, "Don't despair, it's not your fault. I'll get them back."

As Joseph left the chapel where they had been talking, Mentor scooted back on the oak pew, shiny from use, and draped both arms along the back. The monks had not taken down the old large Buddha above the altar. It reached from a stone base into the high rafters, larger than life-size, and crudely carved. Afternoon light filtered through high stained-glass windows, casting a rainbow of colored shadows. On the altar, incense burned in shiny brass coffers, the scent permeating the whole room with sandalwood.

The monks prayed here, just as human monks had in the past. The vampires who chose the monastery as their home held to the old religion, even adopting the orange robes and leather sandals and shaved heads. They were vampires who, like Mentor, had come to the decision they must control their hunger and rid their hearts of the evil that drove them. They were pious, but still lethal if provoked by their prisoners. Most of the monks had been doing this for so long their strength was honed to a quick and deadly measure. They were mainly guards but also religious suppliants, dedicated to keeping order in the world. Without them, and other devoted men like them in other places in the world, Mentor thought the vampire nations would be completely out of control by now. They would have formed sects and splintered off, one from the other, battling for territory, taking down mankind without thought to the future.

And that is what Charles Upton wished to create, giving no thought to what chaos and suffering he would inflict on the world. He was shortsighted, his ambition blinding him to how wars between the vampire clans would loose great evil and destruction. Left to their own devices and inflamed with hot rhetoric, some of the Predators could be talked into taking down leaders of state, heads of corporations, the rich and wealthy, celebrities, churchmen, and the intelligentsia alike. These were the men and women who kept the world on an even keel. Such devastation would send financial and political institutions into a turmoil from which none could recover. All would be anarchy. All would be lost.

Balthazar would be such a leader, his thoughts of war very close to those of Charles Upton. Balthazar, however, hadn't been heard from in decades until he showed up in little Malachi's dreams. It hadn't really been a dream, but a dimension created by Balthazar from a distance, invading the child's mind and speaking with him as if there in person.

The difference between Balthazar and Charles, though, might not be in their aims, but their resources. Balthazar hadn't had much luck in gathering together an army. Upton, set free and given sufficient time, could command a much greater army because of his higher intelligence and resolution.

Mentor had lived long enough to know which vampires to fear and which to merely watch. He had also seen how humankind could cause warring periods of history and knew the long-term ramifications on both land and commerce. It took decades for order to resume and the populace to recover. A vampire war would portend even larger destruction. Bombs, warheads, snipers, and attack helicopters were nothing to what a large number of supernatural beings could do.

Men might do these things, but if Mentor could help it, a vampire would not. Certainly Charles Upton would not get free and begin that destruction because of damnable cards accidentally given him.

Mentor sat listening with his preternatural hearing to all the sounds in the monastery. He heard the sounds of the jungle that surrounded it, and farther away still, the sounds of nearby villages where life went on without a hint midnight creatures lived so close they could reach out and pluck any man or woman or child from life at a moment's notice.

Twilight came and the bells rang, calling the monks to prayer. Mentor slipped from the chapel to allow them privacy. He walked a path through the jungle, hoping the night would hurry and Upton would tire soon of playing with the cards.

He was hungry, but kept that hunger dampened as best he could. Failing, he spied a chattering monkey in a tree.

It was dark gray with lighter gray splashed across its wide chest. Its animation resulted from the excitement over a stranger passing through its territory. Mentor's mind fell back and his need drove him as he mindlessly climbed the branches in a wink and reached out, his hand clamping around the small monkey's neck. He bent his head to the snarling animal's velvety throat and sank his fangs in, taking life as quickly as he could. He sat on the limb, the dead monkey in his hands, and suddenly his eyes blurred and he dropped the little body to the ground. He climbed down slowly, his heart dark as outer space.

He picked up the monkey, holding it in his hands, the arms, legs, and head hanging down in limp death. Mentor could still feel the warmth of the skin through the fur. He looked away, infuriated. He didn't *want* to do these things. He wished to God that he wasn't driven to killing this way. In Dallas he took his sustenance from the blood bags he got from Ross' operation. Charitable humans willingly gave the blood. It was paid for and put into refrigerators for shipment. Mentor did not have to take animals this way when in the city. And he hadn't murdered a man in ages.

But in Thailand or when he was on some trip out of the country for other business, he sometimes found himself turning to the animal world to sustain him. Each time, as now, he hated himself with a hate so bright it was like the interior of a minor sun.

He dropped the monkey into the brush along the path and turned back. He was no longer hungry, but he was no longer content either. The monkey's blood roiled inside him, infusing his organs, giving them life. It also suffused him with unhappy guilt he was not going to outrun by merely returning to the monastery's shelter.

He broke off a large leaf as he passed by a bush and crushed it in his fist, his fingernails digging into his palm.

I am vampire, he thought.
I am unholy and commit murder against living things.
I am doomed, always doomed, there is no escape.

*   *   *

Midnight came and went as Mentor waited for Upton to release his hold on the cards and sleep. Around three in the morning, Upton finally keeled over like a mechanical doll that had wound down.

Mentor appeared in the cell and saw the cards spread in a large rectangle across the floor before the sleeping Upton. With a wave of his hands around the surface of the stone flooring, Mentor gathered the cards into a deck and tucked them into the breast pocket of his jacket. He left the cell as silently as he had come, moving rapidly down the corridor into the monastery and out into the compound. In mere minutes he had left Thailand and had returned to his modest home in Dallas.

There he sat down to examine the deck of cards. At first he thought Madeline had been duped or her mind was so confused with her madness that she'd misinterpreted what she saw. *These are just old tarot cards,* Mentor thought, relaxing. But as he shuffled and fanned the deck, the cards grew warm in his hands and he paused, startled. Inanimate objects did not possess a way to generate heat, he knew. In some way the cards truly were supernatural. He leaned forward to the coffee table and spread them out, faceup. The side table lamp was still lit, having been left that way by his houseguest, Dolan.

Peering closely, Mentor saw the magic begin. The figures on the old cards began to waver and finally to actually move about the face of each card as if there was a separate world, a completely different dimension of reality within each individual card.

So this is what intrigued Charles so, Mentor thought, watching the cards carefully. *Madeline was right, after all.*

Suddenly a bolt of understanding rushed through his mind as if the cards had sent the lightning across the space between them. Mentor looked at each card in turn, placing them in the same sort of rectangle he'd seen in Upton's cell. He ran his fingers over each one, as if blind and reading Braille. Just as a book opens and the pages reveal knowledge through printed words, the cards began to reveal their own esoteric knowledge through figural scenes.

A war will come between vampire clans, they whispered to Mentor's mind.

The imprisoned one will free himself and lead it.

There will be much destruction in the vampire nations; death meted out without mercy, and blood running in rivers.

Your life hangs in the balance.

Mentor's mind was freed, going blank for just a moment and then returning him to himself. He sat back, mouth agape and eyes wide. The card figures had stopped moving now. The cards lay immobile, just pieces of old cardboard and artist renderings in paint.

Mentor rubbed his brow and hung his head. He sighed heavily. He had no doubt about the veracity of the cards' prediction. The cards had shown him scenes of Upton standing before an army of Predators somewhere deep inside the Earth in tremendous vaulted caves. He had heard Upton's persuasive voice, his words powerful and inflammatory. He had seen Predators preying on the helpless Cravens, killing with fire and with polished steel. He had seen blood, the Life Giver, taken away and spilled on open ground.

"My God," Mentor whispered.

He knew, though, that the cards were not an item that could be used to free Upton from captivity. They foretold the future for the one who possessed them just as they had done for the original owner. That and no more.

Furious with the prediction, having hoped the clans would never decide such a fate for one another, Mentor grabbed the scattered cards, swooping them into his hands with the same speed he'd used in the monastery. He crushed the deck in his hands as he stood and approached the dead fireplace. There he stooped and drew back the metal mesh curtain. He placed the deck on the grate and reached for a box of matches lying on the hearth.

You'll tell no more tales, he thought, striking a match and setting fire to the edges of several of the cards he pulled loose from the deck. Once they were aflame, he stood and stepped back. He watched until all the cards caught and were consumed to ash.

He sensed someone at his back and turned to face Dolan.

"It's early in the season for a fire, isn't it?"

"I had to get rid of something," Mentor said. "I'll tell you about it later."

Dolan didn't respond, but stood quietly, hands at his sides.

"Have you been lonely here?" Mentor asked. "I haven't been gone too long, have I?" It seemed to him he'd been away from home for days, when in reality he knew it was not more than a few hours.

"I'm all right," Dolan said. "I still have no idea how I can be of any use to you, though."

It came to Mentor how Dolan could help. An inspiration. "Have you ever been to Thailand?"

"No. I know it's odd, but I've always stayed in this country. I think I was too depressed to think anything would be better anywhere else. Isn't Thailand where we have one of our prisons?"

"Yes, in a monastery I found abandoned many years ago. I need you to go there. I want you to stand by and watch someone for me. His name is Charles Upton, an American businessman."

"I've heard of him. He runs a big company down in Houston, doesn't he? A multimillionaire?"

"He used to. His operations were moved to Dallas. He's vampire . . . Predator. Made by Ross."

Dolan let out a low whistle. Few of them were changed to vampire by being infected and given the blood of another. The made ones were usually superior and became clan leaders, sons and daughters, as it were, the inheritors of ancient blood.

"Why do you need me to watch him? Can't you do that from a distance? And what about the monks? Don't they do that?"

"They do, but sometimes they make mistakes," Mentor said, thinking of Joseph giving the cards to Upton. "And I do monitor Upton from the distance, but I worry one day, just at the moment I'm enthralled by the Predator-Maker in the death dream, one day when I'm trying to guide someone through it—my concentration focused on death—that's the exact time Upton may find a way to escape. I'll never know it and won't be able to prevent it."

Mentor glanced at the heap of ashes in the grate before saying, "He may be a threat to all of us one day if he gets free. He doesn't know his powers or how to use them, but when he finds out, someone needs to tell me. I want you to be there to do that. I can't go there and devote myself to him, Ross can't go, and you'll be doing me a great favor."

"Of course, I'll do it. I need to be of service."

"Fine. That's what I wanted to hear. You see? There is

a need for you, Dolan; you're vital to me. But be warned. Charles Upton is no fool. As a man, he was devious, vindictive, and vicious. As a vampire, he has grown cold and deadly, his nature only intensifying. You must not let him see you or even sense you nearby. Ask the monks to give you a room far from him and just keep me posted." He wasn't sure Dolan would be that much of a help, but it would keep the old vampire busy and give Mentor a break before he had to train him for some other job. Besides, he really did need someone besides the monks to keep an eye on Upton. Cravens were especially telepathic, spending most of their long lives turned inward and alone. Dolan could monitor Upton easily enough without sending any signal he was doing it.

Before the sun rose and Dolan had to hurry again to the safety of the basement, they went over Dolan's duties and the seriousness of his post at the monastery. They arranged for his departure, Mentor taking up the phone and calling an airline to reserve a ticket for Dolan. As a Craven, Dolan possessed weaknesses and limited powers, except for telepathy. He could not transmigrate the way Mentor did so easily and hadn't even a clue how it was done. He would travel conventionally, aboard an airline, and be at his destination by the next night. He would interact with humans and must be coached to pass among them without comment. Mentor would provide him with papers, with a passport and money. Dolan was excited at being granted such a momentous task.

Just before he left Mentor's living room where dark night gave way to the gray dawn of morning, he thanked Mentor for trusting him.

Mentor waved away the thanks. "Just do this job right, and then we'll see about training you for other responsibilities. I can't tell you how long this might take, however. Be prepared to stay at the monastery a while."

"I have time," Dolan said, smiling.

When Dolan left, Mentor sat back and let his head rest against the sofa. He wasn't going to have time to do something about Dolan's sensitivity to the sun. The Craven would have to outfit himself to protect his skin.

Mentor dozed and woke with the sun full in the sky, light streaming through the windows to warm his home. He immediately looked to the fireplace to assure himself the cards were gone. He was startled to see that the ashes had vanished. He rose to investigate, glancing at the coffee table only to see the cards stacked there, whole and untouched.

He should have known. Cards that could come alive and portend the future could also preserve themselves as long as they wished, just as a vampire could. He found the tattered velvet and wrapped the cards in them, then turned one way and then the other, thinking where he might put them away. No one should consult these cards, that's all he knew. Not even himself, ever again. They would never foretell good fortune. They were a divination method for chaos.

He finally put them into a steel box where he kept mementos from his life with his wife. He locked it with a padlock and replaced the box beneath the loose floorboard in the kitchen under the table there.

He might not be able to destroy the cards, but at least they were no longer in Upton's possession.

6

When Malachi had been fed and dressed for dropping off at the day care center, Dell rushed around to find the keys to the old Toyota she drove. She found them beneath a heap of bulk mail on the hall table. "Hurry, Malachi, we're late."

She had her hand to the center of his small back, pushing him just a little toward the front door. He often dawdled and today wasn't the day for it.

Suddenly he stopped in his tracks, unmovable. "What are you doing?" she asked. "We have to go."

"Aunt Celia is on her way. And Carolyn."

"Aunt Celia?" Dell had been in too much of a hurry to open up the channels of her telepathy and precognition. She now reached out with her mind and saw her aunt driving down the county road toward their home. Next to her Carolyn dozed, her head laid against the seat and slumping toward her shoulder. Celia was driving with one hand and drinking coffee from a Styrofoam cup with the other. There was a deep crease imbedded between her eyes. Something was wrong with Carolyn.

"Oh, no, we don't have time," she said, moving past Malachi to the door and opening it.

"She has a problem with Carolyn. Carolyn's sick. Aunt Celia's afraid."

Halfway out the door, her foot stepping onto the porch, she turned to her young son. He had alerted them before when someone was coming to the house. She usually knew before he did, but he played the parlor game for his father's amusement. Yet he'd never told them what was in the minds of the people who approached.

This new ability had to do with his fever and near-catatonic state the night before when she'd called for Mentor, she knew it. Malachi would be changed, Mentor had told them. He'll be true *dhampir*—human with vampire abilities.

While Dell stood looking at her son, he vanished before her eyes. Her heart stuttered in her chest. "Malachi?"

He reappeared, or seemed to, holding the cordless telephone out to her. "I guess you'll need to call work and the day care center. To tell them we'll be late."

He had moved so quickly that, while she was lost in thought, he'd sped to the living room to retrieve the telephone. This was new. He had never done anything like it before.

She took a deep breath. She realized getting used to this change was going to take some time. "Thank you, yes, I guess I better call in."

Aunt Celia, Malachi's great-aunt, was not vampire, one of the few members of Dell's family who had been spared the disease. Her daughter, Carolyn, had not been infected yet either. Unless the sickness Malachi spoke of was the beginning of it.

By the time Celia arrived, Dell had made excuses to her boss at the library and alerted the day care center that she'd be bringing Malachi in late. When Celia stepped from the car, waving a bit, Dell had already moved her mind across the distance from the house to the car and to her cousin, Carolyn. A year younger than Dell, Carolyn always seemed much younger, especially after Dell became a Natural. Nevertheless, in the past few months Carolyn had fallen in love and she was engaged, planning her wedding for the summer. The whole family was involved, happy for her.

Dell carefully sensed Carolyn's being as if she were a dog sniffing a bone. Carolyn dozed in and out of a fever much like the one Malachi had suffered the night before. At first Dell stiffened, fearing the worst. For Malachi the fever meant he was becoming more fully what he already was as a *dhampir*. But Carolyn was human and a fever could presage the beginning of porphyria and death and rebirth as vampire. Dell probed her mind, looking for the dread dream place where the soul decided if it would return as Predator, Natural, or Craven.

She found nothing but wisps of regular, human-inspired dreams. Carolyn was ill with a form of pneumonia. Treated with antibiotics she would be fine again. Dell was so glad she felt light all over.

Dell hurried to the car and stepped into her aunt's embrace, returning to herself. She smiled and said, "Carolyn will be fine. It's only pneumonia. With medicine, she'll be good as new."

Celia, used to her vampire relatives possessing advanced knowledge, still showed surprise that Dell had discovered her fear so quickly—even before she'd said a word. She slumped a little in relief. "Oh, thank you, Dell, thank you."

"Come inside. I haven't much time, but it's been so long since I saw you." Dell led her indoors and asked if she wanted coffee. They decided to leave Carolyn sleeping in the car, as sleep, Dell told her aunt, was exactly what Carolyn needed right now. "Coffee?" she asked.

"No, I just had a cup, thanks. I was so worried I just lost my mind. I tried to call you, but no one answered."

Dell wondered why she hadn't heard the phone. They lived so far out in the country, the phone was on a trunk line that sometimes proved unreliable. Often people reported they'd tried to phone when she'd been home and she never received the call.

"It's my phone, I guess," Dell said. "Sometimes my calls don't get through."

"Well, when I couldn't reach you, I was in the car with Carolyn and driving here before I could stop myself. I drove past your parents' house and they had already left for work. I didn't know where else to go, who to go to. I almost called an ambulance, but Carolyn stopped me. She refused to go to the doctor. She was afraid . . . well, you know . . ." Celia ran out of steam, her voice trailing off.

Dell understood her cousin's reluctance. What if she'd been dying with the dread disease that would turn her to vampire? What if she died in the eyes of the world, and then while it looked on, she rose, ravenous and splendidly lethal?

Celia looked at Dell and continued, "But I don't mean to keep you." She sighed, releasing the pent up emotion she'd bottled on the trip. "If it's pneumonia, I can get something for her. I'll call a doctor right away."

"There's a big lump. Right here," Malachi said, walking

slowly to his great-aunt and touching her just above her
right breast.

"Malachi!" Dell was flabbergasted the way all parents
are when a child does something discourteous. What was
he saying?

"A . . . a lump?" Celia placed her hand over the top of
her breast, and her face blanched. She turned her gaze
upon Dell. In a small, weak voice she asked, "Is it true?"

Dell sat next to her aunt and moved her consciousness
until it left her body and hovered around Celia's torso,
enclosing it as a blanket would, pressing against the flesh,
seeking disturbed cells. She jerked back into her own head
and closed her eyes.

"Dell? Tell me."

"He's right. It's not really large, but it's . . . growing."

"It's mean," Malachi said. He frowned and then
amended himself. "Not really *mean*. It's . . . hungry. Very
hungry."

Dell wished Malachi hadn't said that. He was too young
to know the impact his words might have on mortals. She
admonished him on a mental level to keep quiet. He must
not spout every fact he discovered. He must hush *now*. He
glanced at her, confusion in his eyes and then a slight dawn-
ing of understanding. He put his hands behind his back and
looked at the floor.

"I didn't know," Celia whispered. "There's no pain."

"There are things they can do," Dell said. "Go to your
doctor right away. When you take Carolyn, see someone
yourself."

"I will, most certainly." Her voice was stronger, the terrible surprise wearing off quickly. Dell decided she really
must have suspected something might be wrong. "I'll be all
right. I'm too tough to kill off yet." Her laugh was a nervous trill escaping uncontrollably.

She reached out to Malachi. "Come here, sweetheart.
You didn't do anything wrong. In fact, you told me a very
good thing and maybe you've saved my life. Don't be
upset." She hugged Malachi and kissed him on the cheek.
He looked into her eyes and smiled back.

"The hungry lump will go away," he said. "Someone will
kill it dead."

Now Celia's laugh was natural and hearty. "I'm very glad to hear that, dear." She turned to Dell. "Aren't we glad?"

Dell put her arm around her aunt's shoulder. "Of course we are. I have to tell you Malachi's had a . . . change, of a sort. He doesn't know yet how to control all the stimuli assaulting him. He's so . . . young."

"I understand," Celia said, standing and clutching her handbag to her soft round belly. "Don't scold him. What he's told me is important. No matter how shocking it is, at least now I know how to protect myself. And I'm so relieved to know Carolyn's going to be all right. Thank you so much, darling."

Once Celia had left, Dell took Malachi onto her lap and said, "I'm glad you told Aunt Celia she had a lump, Malachi, but it might have been better if you'd told me first so I could check things out and then I could have told her. Some things you know can scare people. You have to be careful about what you say. Do you understand?"

"I think so, Mommy."

"I'm not scolding you. I'm just afraid you'll say things to other people, people who won't understand. If you scare people too much, they'll get suspicious of you or they'll get really afraid. You don't want to scare anyone, do you?"

"Uh-uh." He shook his head and his naturally curly hair fell over his brow.

She brushed his hair back and set him on his feet. "All right, we'll talk about this more later. Right now we have to get going."

Once she'd dropped off her son, Dell hurried to the town library and took her position behind the check-out desk, apologizing again for being so late. All day she mulled over what had happened that morning, wondering if her admonition would stick. What if Malachi began telling his playmates things about them he shouldn't know? Or what if he mentioned something odd to his caretaker, odd enough to cause her alarm?

Dell could see how the whole situation could get out of hand. Malachi's friends might stop playing with him, instinctively knowing he was not like them. He could be made an outcast, a pariah. The adults coming into contact with him might discover his predictions were true and bring the news media into the secret. Then what?

All day long Dell worried, watching the clock until she could pick Malachi up and question him. She must really impress on her son the seriousness of all his actions, no matter how innocent they appeared to him. He only wanted to help, she knew, but he hadn't the maturity to realize the ramifications of the news he carried.

What am I going to do, she wondered. *Can I really control how a three-year-old behaves when I'm not with him?*

The hands of the clock crept toward two in the afternoon, each second a decade, each minute a lifetime.

* * *

Charles Upton woke, coming from deep sleep without any residue of cloudiness. He saw immediately that the cards were gone. He flew to the cell door in a rage, raising his thunderous voice. "Madeline! Did you steal my cards? Give them back!"

A faint voice floated along the corridor and to his ears. "I don't have them. Leave me alone, you simpering beast."

Upton knew she spoke the truth. "Where are they, then? Who took them? I'll take his head and crush it to pieces."

Madeline did not respond. This caused Upton's rage to spin out of control. He shook the iron bars in the grate until Joseph came running, his leather sandals flapping noisily down the long corridor.

"What's going on here?"

"The cards you gave me are gone. I want them back!"

Joseph kept his distance from the door. He put his hands behind his back and glared at the other vampire. "I was remiss in giving them to you. They belonged to a priest who asked for them back."

"Liar!"

"Stop this racket. It won't get you anywhere."

"I'll howl until your ears bleed, you lying bastard. Give me back the cards."

Joseph turned away and was gone in an instant.

Upton beat his head against the bars between his hands until his forehead bled. As he'd threatened, he howled like an animal, furious he'd been lied to. He had to have the cards. Already he'd been able to discern some of their vital message. They told him he was to be a great being, a vampire that would go down in history as infamous as any historical figure in the past. He'd been about to question the cards about how that event would come about and ask for advice on escape when he'd fallen asleep from exhaustion the night before. He'd been on the very brink of knowing everything he needed to get out of the monastery and be free.

How could they do this to him?

Violently, he flung himself away from the door. He struck the opposite wall and rolled around the walls of his cell four feet above the floor. He twirled so fast the world blurred to a dark cylinder. All the while he screamed at the top of his voice.

So violent was his spin around the walls that he never knew when the cell door creaked open and six large monks entered. The first he knew of the intrusion was when strong, cold hands clamped onto his head, shoulders, arms, and legs, throwing him to the stone floor with a tremendous thump.

"Let me go," he shouted, struggling mightily. He bit at his captors, teeth sinking into sinew and bone.

He heard Joseph's voice. "We will enter you now and bind you for your own good."

He hadn't an inkling what that meant. He continued struggling, throwing the whole bunch of them who were clasped to his body around the room.

At first he felt a chill, as if ice had formed to circle his brain. His thoughts diminished to a tiny glow, held deep within the innermost part of his brain. He had stopped moving and gone limp in the hands of the monks. He struggled now with silent voices which whispered, *Be still. Rest now. Be not afraid.*

He tried to curse and could not. He tried to move, but his limbs would not obey. There were presences inside him, milling about, standing guard, arms crossed. He could not see them, but he sensed them and knew the individuals would not leave until they were ready to do so. His brain seemed dead to him. All light was extinguished. His fury remained, but it was so small that it could not send out a signal to react against the beings who held him. He was as helpless as a babe, his consciousness bound as firmly as if it had been roped and dragged into an eternal pit.

He sat in his mind, crouching in the darkness, nursing his fury, waiting for release. He did not care how long it took. Time meant nothing to him. It meant nothing at all. He would sacrifice a thousand years if he had to.

Time stoked his need for revenge and revenge was a cloak in which he wrapped himself. He would throw it off so that it took his enemies into a whirlwind. Just as soon as he could manage it, that is.

Until then he would wait. He had no other choice.

* * *

Dolan sat in the chapel listening to the tolling of bells. It was midday and he was alone. He could walk around during the day in this place as it was as dark and shadowy as night inside the massive stone walls. The night before the monks had let him into the monastery on his arrival, bowing as he passed. He had never been treated with respect before. It produced an astounding feeling of well-being. He was thrilled to be on a mission of importance for Mentor and to be treated like a prince.

On the bumpy bus ride that brought him from the city airport to the small village, he soaked in the new and exotic sights and sounds of the night-shrouded Thailand country. He knew that once it was called Siam and the people called Siamese. No matter what they called it, he thought the country extremely beautiful. Even the signs of poverty, the shacks and huts, the roadside altars made of mud, the throngs of poor in their tattered clothing, children barefoot and hollow-eyed, could not lower his esteem for the land. He knew he was being romantic and he might have felt the same had he flown to France or Greece or Spain. He knew he was acting like an awed tourist who has never experienced the world. But he couldn't deny he had fallen helplessly in love.

As the bus left the village, stopping to let off passengers along the route, the long green fields and thatched huts gave way to a dense, emerald-green jungle that pushed in from each side of the ruddy road. From the open window Dolan caught glimpses of monkeys swinging in tall trees, looking for a branch fork to make into a bed. He wanted to get out and walk beneath the canopy and lose himself in the wild. He saw the mountains rising all around as they drew nearer to them.

When the bus slowed, gears grinding, he saw he was at his destination. He took up his bag and stumbled for the door. Far from any other habitation, the monastery rose from the floor of the jungle like a stone vision from antiquity. It was ringed with a high stone wall with a wide-open gate. Beyond the gate lay a courtyard, the pale moon-washed ground brushed clean and still bearing the marks of sweeping. In the center of the courtyard was another ring of gray stone blocks setting off a twelve-foot stone tower from which was suspended a set of three engraved brass bells.

Dolan was met near the bell tower by a monk in the traditional orange Buddhist robe. "Welcome," he said. "We have a room ready for you."

Dolan thanked him and followed his guide into the deeper dark of a portico where earth gave way to cobbled floor. They passed through massive wood doors, propped open with brass statues of temple dogs that caught and reflected moonlight.

Dolan lost himself in contemplation of the high ceilings where ancient, rough-hewn beams held up the roof. Along the several corridors they took, there were niches in the walls with various Buddhist figures surrounded by candles dripping fragrant wax.

"I could live here forever," Dolan said.

The monk leading him did not turn, but replied in a reverent tone, "We love it, too. It's very special."

Dolan was put into an austere cell on the ground floor.

"If you require anything, please let us know." The monk bowed and backed from the room, leaving Dolan alone.

There was a bed made from a slab of stone that projected from the wall. It held a burlap bag filled with straw and then covered with white wool bedding, a crisp white pillow propped at the head. Across the room was a gorgeously carved rosewood chest to hold his clothes. A small writing table stood against the wall beneath a window looking out over the courtyard, the shutters thrown wide to the night's passing breeze. On the desk was a pewter pitcher of water and a washbowl made of carved wood. Heavy round candles set in saucers of brass gleamed on table and chest.

There was no ornamentation other than these simple utilitarian objects.

Dolan put down his bag and went to the open window. He leaned out, his arms resting on the wide wood sill. If Mentor had wanted to send him on a vacation, he could not have found a more restful place.

Of course, this was no vacation, he reminded himself. He had been given a sheaf of papers to take with him on the plane. The information gave him a picture of Charles Upton that any fool could see meant the vampire was a risk. He read about what sort of man Upton had been in life and what had transpired since his change to vampire.

It seemed to Dolan that Mentor might have made a strategic mistake in not calling for Upton's death. They probably should have taken him out into the West Texas desert, burned him to ashes, and scattered him to the wind. Neglecting to do so meant they were stuck watching him, the way a mortal might watch a hooded cobra.

A vampire had not come along who voiced such demented ambition before now. Upton wanted to murder the Cravens and throw the Naturals upon their own devices to obtain the blood they needed. He would have the world turned upside down, mortals slaughtered far and wide to quench the ravenous thirst. He cared not at all if the world discovered they walked alongside beasts bent on their destruction.

Dolan shivered with the thought. Anyone who had been born of woman could not think this way. Yet Upton had been a man, but obviously one of those rare men without a shred of empathy.

The jungle forest infringing on the compound resonated with birdsong and the raucous chatter of monkeys. Though it was night, Dolan could still feel the day's warmth rising from the wood beneath his hands. He smiled and turned to unpack his things.

This Upton would not get away from him. He'd do a good job and make Mentor proud. He was a Craven, but he was not useless. He was not a blight and a burden. He'd been given an important task and he would not fail.

The night sang with life outside his window and the moon rose above the canopy to shine down on the courtyard, its light soft and silver and without menace.

7

Malachi learned early not to interfere in people's lives. He had done it once when he'd known his great-aunt Celia had a lump growing in her breast and from that time forward he was very careful about what he told people. There were *secrets,* he thought, and people didn't want to know them. Some of the secrets had to do with illness and some had to do with other things, like accidents about to happen, bad luck on its way, the loss of an expensive object, the betrayal of a loved one. Secrets came in all permutations, as unpredictable as the shape of the clouds in the sky.

He just couldn't tell anyone anything anymore, that's what his mama said, and he knew she was right. He'd known it was a mistake to speak out the minute he'd seen his great-aunt's stunned face. He'd shocked her. He'd scared her. He shouldn't have told her the secret.

It didn't matter that he thought she already suspected the lump wasn't a good thing. He never told his mama that, how Great-aunt Celia knew. In a way. She knew and she didn't know. She didn't want to know. Then he'd told her and messed everything up.

So the day he went to day care and his friend, Stevie, came in looking all gray and sick, Malachi couldn't help but put his hands on the other boy's shoulders. He did it as a gesture of friendship, one boy to another, but he had other reasons, besides. He had to know what was wrong. He couldn't stand not knowing. Upon touching Stevie, he knew everything. It was not a hungry, growing lump deep in his young flesh. It was something hungry in Stevie's blood. It was something that ate up some of his blood cells, one after another and another and another. He imagined it as a Pacman monster, hurtling through his friend's bloodstream, gobbling everything in its path. He knew immediately what it meant: Stevie was dying.

Malachi didn't say a word. He looked into Stevie's eyes and knew he shouldn't. Stevie wouldn't understand. He was too little to understand something invisible and painless was gobbling him alive.

But he was dying, that was irrefutable.

That night Malachi went to the porch and sat with his mother after dinner. She sensed his distress and asked if he wanted to talk about something. He felt her presence not only outside himself, but creeping now into his mind.

"Don't do that, Mama," he pleaded.

She withdrew, sitting quietly at his side, waiting.

He thought it over. She'd get mad at him again, he feared. Though he hadn't spoken aloud his misgivings about Stevie's future, she could still find something wrong with him knowing and she'd get that look on her face again—the one she'd used on him when he'd blurted out the news of the hungry lump.

He finally shrugged and said he didn't have anything to talk about. Nothing at all. Nothing.

It proved to be a terrible burden. When he was older, he realized if he'd confessed to his mother that night all his fears for Stevie, it might have helped. But he hadn't told her. He just went to day care every day and saw Stevie dwindle little by little. He watched the light in his eyes dim. Helplessly, he stood by and watched.

Stevie stopped playing with Malachi, stopped playing with anyone. He'd sit for hours with blocks in his hands, staring at the carved letters on their sides as if they contained a message, hardly moving for long minutes. He'd watch television, but never show any real interest in the cartoons.

Stevie didn't cry or complain. He just got grayer and smaller and quieter, like a gray mouse sitting in a corner, starving slowly. Then one day he didn't come to day care and Malachi never saw him again. He didn't have to ask the teacher where his friend had gone. He knew.

It was that way for many years. The secret keeping.

When he was eight, he watched as his elementary school teacher, Mr. Golden, walked in front of a speeding car that hurtled out of the student parking lot. Malachi had known for hours it would happen. It was like a movie running over and over in his head. Mr. Golden had an armload of books. He was looking to his right when he stepped from the curb. He was about to turn his head to look to his left when the red convertible driven by a high school boy who had come to pick up his little brother, sped toward him like a tornado.

Malachi hung back on the playground, covering his eyes. He was crying when they found him. They took him to the office and called his parents. His father came to pick him up and Malachi hunched his shoulders and cried all the way home. Once there, his worried parents made him talk.

"I knew my teacher was going to walk out in front of that car," he said finally. "I knew since I got to school this morning. I was passing Mr. Golden in the hall before the bell rang, and I had this . . . flash. I saw everything." He wiped his teary face. "You told me not to tell." He sobbed some more. "And now he's dead."

His parents held him close and absolved him of all sin. He was a child, they said. He didn't know it would really happen. It wasn't his fault.

"I'll keep all the secrets," he said.

His mother took his tear-stained face in her hands and made him look her in the eyes. "If you feel something bad like that again, you call me. Okay? Maybe I can stop it from happening."

"What if I don't have time? What if I can't get you?"

His mother frowned, realizing the logic of his protest. "Let me think about this, Malachi. I just don't know what's right yet."

Later that night when he'd been sent to bed she came to him. "I've talked this thing over with Mentor," she said. "He wants you to start seeing him once a week so he can teach you how to block these feelings out. We both think it would be best if you . . . well, if you don't even know about bad things."

He didn't know how he could stop it. How could he not even know? It would be some kind of miracle.

Malachi was bereft for the rest of the night until he fell into an exhausted sleep. How was he going to stop knowing the secrets? How could he block them out? And if he did, how would he feel when something bad happened he might have prevented?

During the next year, under Mentor's tutelage, he came to understand the gravity of his gifts and the responsibilities they conferred on him. If he could sense impending disasters, they could haunt him every day of his life. He couldn't always prevent them. Life, in some ways, was predestined, and souls, Mentor said, walked individual paths that might have been laid down for them even before they were born. If he interfered in the lives of others, he was in effect rewriting destinies. And no one should have that responsibility, least of all a child trying to tune into his human nature so that he could live a natural life.

It was a long, slow process, but Malachi came to love his time with the old vampire. He wasn't like anyone else in Malachi's life. He was stronger and smarter than anyone. He was wiser. He had lived many more lifetimes than Malachi's mother or anyone in her family. He was ready to admit he was fallible and made mistakes, but, to Malachi, it seemed that was impossible. Mentor knew everything. He knew Malachi's mind and heart. He knew what would keep him safe and sane. He knew how to help him.

By the time Malachi was a little over nine years old, he had learned the valuable trick of neglect. He simply did not make any effort to know what he could have known had he tried. He developed ways to keep from putting his hands on his classmates, even during playtime. He became a log in the stream, letting the water of life rush past. He did not move, nor did he seek out secrets ever again. Not only did he not touch his classmates if he could help it, he kept his mind closed to stray visions that sometimes streamed from others. He ran from involvement.

And after a while, a peace descended on him that he hadn't known before. He grew calm inside, and it translated to a quiet, reserved exterior personality. He was able to love his classmates without fear he'd learn of their imminent deaths or disasters which might befall them. He loved them as he should have—in the moment and without reserve.

The knowing of secrets and then the not knowing changed the boy, advancing his maturity beyond his years, and increasing his compassion. Mentor finally patted him on the back and sent him home that last day when Malachi was nine, his lessons at an end.

"You're a good boy," Mentor said. "An apt pupil. You'll be all right."

Malachi smiled all the way home in the car with his father who came to Dallas and Mentor's house to pick him up. He was as proud as he could be. Mentor did not hand out compliments casually. Mentor had been a stern task-master, admonishing him to do as he was told. If he didn't understand the reasons, that hardly mattered. "When you're older," he'd said, "you can make your own decisions, but until then you must do what your parents and I tell you to do. Is that understood?"

Nevertheless, Malachi grew to love the old man and to trust him.

Mentor, by teaching him restraint, had granted him his freedom. He could be like everyone else now. Unknowing. Dumb, deaf, and blind. Swept, just as humanity was, by the whimsy that was his fate.

Until the night of the nightmare when the wolf came and lured him astray.

It was a summer night soon after he'd finished his in-struction with Mentor. He had been working on a model truck, a 1955 Ford with a short bed. He was painting it cherry red, lying on the floor on his stomach, screwing up his face as he concentrated. Like his father, he enjoyed tinkering with vehicles, but he was too young to help his dad out in the garage, so his father had bought him model kits. It was after ten at night when his parents told him to put his things away and brush his teeth and go to bed. He carefully set the unfinished model truck on a shelf in his room. Tomorrow his painting would be dry and he could attach the decals. He brushed his teeth, picked up his fa-ther's electric razor and pretended to shave his soft, bare cheeks, and left the bathroom finally, grinning. One day he'd shave, just like his dad. He'd be a man, a big man like his dad, and he'd drive the old truck his father had re-stored. In his room, he slipped on his pajamas and climbed into bed. Within minutes, he was asleep.

The wolf came padding across the bare, coldly lighted plain, its thick silver fur shimmering like a sequined blanket from the pale moon overhead.

Not you again, Malachi thought, trying to push aside the dream world.

"Come with me." The wolf's lips never moved. His mouth was closed, and his nose pointed up at the boy's chest as if sniffing his scent. Malachi stared into the wolf's golden eyes and felt mesmerized. He tried to tear his gaze from the wolf's eyes and could not.

"I can't, I have to go home." Malachi backed away, his bare feet sliding in gritty sand. He looked down and saw he wore the pajamas he'd put on before going to bed. He needed to get out of here. He needed to sleep in his safe bed, in the security of his warm home.

He needed help.

"I won't hurt you," the wolf said in a satiny voice. "Come with me, and I'll show you something."

He turned and trotted away. Malachi's feet began to follow against his will. He cried out, but the wolf ignored him. He couldn't stop himself. He was following the wolf.

And meantime . . . in the reality of the world where he lived when conscious . . . Malachi slipped from the covers, stood beside his bed, and started from the bedroom. Barefoot, he padded quietly through the house to the front door. It opened for him before he reached it, and he glided onto the wide front porch. He was in the yard now, dew wetting his feet. He went toward the back pasture, and looked beyond it to the woods . . .

The wolf took him a long distance. There was not even a breeze in this world of sandy plain and moon. From one horizon to the other emptiness stretched. A great fear seized Malachi's heart, and he tried in desperation to halt his feet. He didn't know where they were going, but he knew he should not go there. Where could it be? There was nothing, nothing in this whole world but the malevolent moon overhead, uncaring of his destiny, and the wide, empty, featureless plain of flat sand.

He thought he protested, but nothing came from his lips. In his mind the wolf hissed, "Shut up. Follow me. All will be revealed."

. . . and in the world of his parents, Malachi strode across the open land where the cattle rested, bunched together, swiveling their heads at his passage. The moon overhead was not pale at all, but gold as egg yolk. At his back his mother

called, "Malachi! No! Come back!" He heard her, but some-
thing waited for him in the woods and he must go there . . .

The silver wolf stopped, and Malachi's feet halted as if
he were merely a puppet being moved by strings. "Watch
this," said the wolf.

From out of the floor of the plain rose a mound, the
sand shifting and falling all around. There was a groaning
as the earth buckled and heaved. The sand fell away from
the rounded back of a vampire and then the beast rose up,
straightening, the sand still falling from his naked shoulders
and long wavy hair. He had no body hair and no genitalia.
His body looked as neutral as the body of Malachi's G. I.
Joe dolls. It was obvious this was no real vampire, as Malachi knew vampires lived within human bodies. No, this
was a dream monster and he could be anything, he could
be any dimension and wield any sort of power he wished.
He was there to punish Malachi. He was there to take
his head.

. . . Malachi reached the edge of the woods and plunged
into the darkness without hesitation. The yellow moon's light
was sucked into this black void, disappearing. He no longer
heard his mother at his back, calling to him. He heard a
great sound of wind coming from within the thick stand of
trees, wanted to see what made it . . .

The vampire seemed fiercer in its nakedness than if it
had been clothed. The skin looked stretched to a straining
point over the great muscles of the body. The face was
disfigured, a distorted image of human mixed with animal.
The mouth was too wide for the face, the eyes too huge.
The teeth it showed Malachi were exaggerated in size, large
enough for a crocodile, each one glistening in the moonlight
with pointed ferocity. This beast opened its mouth and
roared, filling the plain with rumbling sound so loud it
flooded Malachi's ears and caused him to fall to his knees.

. . . in the woods Malachi sought the great wind and found
it came from the throat of a beast half as tall as the massive
oak trees it stood beneath. The wind was breath, foul and
stinking of decay. Malachi bowed his head under the force,
gagging. He turned his back to the vampire, hoping his
mother still called to him and that she had come to his res-
cue, but everything behind him was blurred to grayness, as
if he had stepped through a doorway in the woods and left

*the real world behind. He began to cry, tears running down
his face. "Mama," he called softly. "Mama, please . . ."*

The roar faded across the open night plain. The wolf
trotted to Malachi's side and sniffed at his face. "He wants
to eat you," he said.

Malachi's heart almost stopped in terror. He could imagine
those giant crocodile teeth sinking into his body. It
would shred him like cabbage and leave him in strips under
the pale moon. "I want to go home," he cried.

"Go home then to your Maker," the wolf said.

The great vampire took steps toward them. With each
footstep the earth shuddered. Malachi lifted his head, a
cold light coming into his young eyes. "You are nothing,"
he said, choking back tears. "You're just a dream, that's
all you are. I can beat you if I want to."

The beast faltered, threw back its great shaggy head, and
roared with laughter until Malachi's ears rang again. He
came to his feet. He reached out and struck the muzzle of
the silver wolf who had made this monster to scare him.
"Make it go away," he commanded. "It doesn't scare me."

*. . . the vampire bent from its great height, breaking apart
massive tree limbs as it neared the ground. It hovered over
the boy and cocked its head at him, eyes glittering with red
sparks. "I will eat you," it said. Malachi straightened and
wiped at his tears with his fists. He could hear his mother
now, at his back, calling for him again. She was frantic. He
felt the fabric of the grayness that blocked her tearing as if
it were a curtain on a stage. "You can't eat me," Malachi
said, given courage by the closeness of his mother. "I'm
stronger than you." The vampire threw back its head and
laughed, and only then did Malachi note that the beast was
undressed and that it had smooth, pale skin, hairless and
without gender. "You're made up of smoke," Malachi
said . . .*

"You're made of smoke." That's what Malachi told the
great beast hovering above him and the wolf on the moonlit
plain. "The wolf made you. He thinks I'll let you eat me,
but I won't. He'll have to do that himself." And then Malachi
turned to the wolf and stepped forward, rapping the
animal on the head with his small knuckles. "Eat me," he
said bravely. "Go ahead, try to eat me, you mean old wolf.
You can't hurt me, and I'm not afraid of you."

And suddenly he woke, drenched in fear sweat, and he was in the woods at the rear of the ranch. He ran toward the moonlight, his feet pricked by sticks and acorns so that he began to hop while he ran, hopping, running, tearing apart the gray veil to reveal his mother. He made for the opening to the fields. He found his mother waiting there at the woods' edge, her arms open for him, the look of alarm on her face. At first he thought she was the beast from the woods, from the plain, and in disguise, but she spoke and he knew he was saved.

"Malachi!"

He rushed to her, hugging his head into her belly, wrapping his arms around her waist. "Oh, Mom! He wanted to eat me."

She took him home, holding onto his hand tightly as they crossed the field. She led him to the bathroom and washed his sweaty face with a cool cloth. He sat on the side of the tub and let her wash his dirty feet. He put on clean pajama bottoms as his others had wet, soiled cuffs. Then his mother took him to the kitchen table and sat him down while she prepared hot cocoa. She was calm now and spoke to him softly so as not to wake his father. "The wolf tried to lure you away," she said. "I saw him, too."

Malachi didn't want to talk about it. It was too real and too fresh in his memory. He laced his fingers around the cup of hot chocolate and brought it to his lips. He loved the tiny marshmallows floating on top. He'd always loved marshmallows.

They didn't talk about it anymore. He returned to bed and his mother sat down beside him, her hand on his chest until he slept. He didn't know if she stayed there all night, but he suspected she had because she was in the same spot when he opened his eyes to the morning.

He dreamed and wandered the plain no more that night.

• BOOK TWO •

THE *DHAMPIR* COMES OF AGE

1

The years after his lessons with Mentor passed without crisis for Malachi Major until the summer of his eighteenth year. At the age of three he had come into his own as a *dhampir* and for the next fifteen years he had been protected and guided by his parents, and, on occasion, Mentor. Now and then there were minor jams, like the night the dream wolf lured him into the woods far from home, but for the most part childhood flew past without mishap.

As his powers grew, he began to understand even more deeply the responsibility that came with supernatural ability. Though he could read minds, he refrained from doing so except when absolutely necessary to make his life run smoothly. Though he could move so fast it appeared in mortal eyes he had vanished, he rarely indulged in the ability around strangers. Though his hearing was acute and his eyesight enhanced, he worked hard not to let anyone know. He wanted nothing more than to embrace his mortality and lead a normal life. Most of all, he wanted to be like his father. Strong, hard-working, and peaceful. A man dedicated to those he loved.

By age eighteen, Malachi stood six feet four and weighed two hundred and sixty pounds. He played football in high school, hailed as the best running back the school ever had. He was president of the honor society, his memory being phenomenal and studies easy for him. He felt like a fraud having so much knowledge gained so easily, but his mother said, "Malachi, many people are born with gifts. Treat all your abilities as gifts and don't waste them. You're competing with students who are also gifted. Don't fail just because you think your gift is unfair. God doesn't make mistakes."

"Do you believe in God, Mom? Did God make you immortal?"

He saw her features at war as she struggled with the questions. She said finally, "I do believe there's something greater than we are. I call it God because there's no other name for it. I don't think He made me . . . what I am. I think that's some quirk of evolution, just as being human in the first place is a quirk. If we came from warm salty waters, crawling first, and then learning to breathe on land, why can't we also become vampire by accident? Without plan or reason. Yes . . . evolution. It's the only thing I can think."

It was the first time she had spoken to him about how she felt and he could hear the confusion in her voice. Mentor had told him nearly the same thing. They all struggled with unanswerable questions.

On the subject of his gifts, however, it was true there were other intelligent students, some of them with IQs that were going to make them leaders in commerce or politics or academia. There were guys on the football team who were the best receivers in the state, always in the right place to catch the ball when the talented quarterback threw it. These tremendously skilled athletes would be picked up by pro teams. There were girls with so much charm and real beauty they were going to sail through life on their physical assets. There were teenagers with so much computer expertise, they started up their own companies, raking in millions before they ever turned twenty.

Finally, he decided his mother was right. He wasn't exactly a fraud. He was just someone born with gifts he had no right to squander. If the world knew the *extent* of his gifts, he'd be a freak they'd want to study, but in the end he began to believe he was hardly more gifted than other superior humans.

Because of this humility he was well-liked. He kept aloof, however, fearing too many close friends might lead to the discovery of his secret. And he never forgot the loss of his little friend in day care. He feared ever experiencing that loss again. If he got to know someone and care for him, what if he lost that friend, too?

Instead of hanging out with friends, he spent most of his free time riding his horse, Harley—he was better than a motorcycle, after all—or reading books deep into the nights.

When he was sixteen, however, he met Alex Bradner on the football team. Alex was naturally outgoing, friendly, and persistent. He didn't live far from Malachi. He began to drop by on weekend afternoons to invite Malachi out for pizza or for fishing at the river. Alex, like Malachi, was a running back on the team. When he got the ball, he was quick as lightning and resembled a bull as he plowed through the opposition, heading for the goal line.

The two youths began to go out after the games, visiting the local fast food joints where other high school kids hung out until midnight. Malachi invited Alex over to ride horses, and sometimes he took him up on the offer of fishing trips. They sat for hours, fishing rods dangling from their hands into the wild Trinity River that was not far from their homes. Sometimes they filled coolers full of catfish and climbed a bluff to the pier jutting out over the river where a cleaning station had been set up. They took turns having their mothers fry the catfish fillets, eating whole platefuls, laughing easily and talking about school and football and girls.

Alex wanted to be a pediatrician. He wanted to help kids. He came from a large family of seven siblings. Being the eldest, he'd been called upon to help out with the little ones. He had an affinity for his brothers and sisters that flowed over into the wider world of all children. Malachi had seen him with his family and grinned at his childlike joy as he took a younger brother on his back for a horsey ride, or as he pushed his sisters in a tire swing in the yard. He saw his gentleness as he wiped a young brother's face free of grime or tied the bow at the back of a little sister's dress. His element was childhood. He became as innocent as his younger charges when around them. He hadn't any of the aggression Malachi had seen in him when playing football.

"Alex, I think all those kids would get on my nerves. How do you stand it?"

Alex, tall as Malachi, and even heavier, grinned showing large square teeth and the tip of a pink tongue. He looked like a country oaf in his oversize coveralls and big lace-up boots, but that impression was deceptive. Behind his round brown eyes lay a first-class brain. He was an honor student and had already won a scholarship to Baylor College of Medicine. He'd make a fine doctor.

"You're just an only child," he said to Malachi. "That's your problem. It spoils you, makes you think you're the center of the world." To make sure Malachi didn't think he was being too critical, Alex banged Malachi on his arm with a balled-up fist. "Brat," he said.

Malachi banged him back and laughed. "Don't call me spoiled. You're the brat, not me."

"Hey now, I didn't put the Mountain Dew and pickles in the water bucket." Alex referred to their last game of the season when the championship was on the line. After a narrow win, a bucket that should have held ice water was dumped over the coach. Malachi had earlier poured twenty cans of Mountain Dew into the container of ice and added fifteen jars of sweet gherkins. The coach, expecting his crew to douse him with ice water, got a surprise when the Mountain Dew spilled over his head and the pickles cascaded around his shoulders. He hopped around sputtering and licking his lips.

Malachi just about laughed his ass off. Alex stood aside, pointing at his friend, until the whole team jumped him before Coach could see who was being accused.

"You've got to admit, the Dew and pickles were a stroke of genius," Malachi said.

"You know Coach hates that stuff. He's a Dr. Pepper man."

They laughed easily together. It was always that way. Alex was like a brother. He was a rock, always there on the field when Malachi needed him for protection. He was Malachi's excuse when Malachi forgot the time and was late on a date. "He was at my house," Alex lied easily to Malachi's parents. "We were playing a computer game and forgot how late it was."

Now they were going separate ways and that saddened Malachi. Alex was working two jobs during the summer, saving for college. From early morning until early afternoon he worked as a clerk at Walmart. After washing up and gulping a quick meal at home, he waited tables at Sholinger's Restaurant until it closed at eleven. They hardly got together anymore for fishing or horsing around. Alex told Malachi he was making a mistake by not applying to the better colleges, where he'd be admitted easily. But Alex didn't know Malachi really hadn't a clue about his future. He had no all-abiding passion the way Alex did. He didn't know what he should do with his life. Everything appealed to him, but nothing gripped him to the point he wanted to pursue it. He thought he could farm or ranch and never go to college at all and it would be perfectly all right with him, though he knew his parents had higher ambitions for him.

His mother liked Alex a great deal and thought he was a good influence on her dreamy son. "Why don't you go to medical school like Alex?" she asked. "Or what about veterinary medicine, like your father? You need *something,* Malachi. You can't just drift."

Well, he didn't know about that. Why couldn't he drift? Was drifting a sin and would he be punished for it? He couldn't help it if he had no focus. He liked football, but not enough to turn pro even though a scout had quietly offered him a beginning spot on the new Houston Texans team. He loved books and reading, like his mother, but he hadn't any ambition to teach or write or become a librarian like his mom. Mostly, he loved riding horses, helping his father with their growing cattle herd, and being out in the open, feeling the changing seasons on his skin and in the roots of his hair and in the depths of his soul. What kind of degree did he need in order to do that, he wondered? Where was the money in it, unless he tried ranching? He teetered on the edge of feeling like a bum.

To please his parents, he took up the many college catalogs he'd brought home from the counselor's office, and began to study them in a half hearted way. He was late. He should have already made up his mind about where to go and what to do years before graduation, but before then he just couldn't manage to get excited about it.

Danielle never gave him grief about his lack of direction. They'd been friends since elementary school, and he was more serious about her than he found comfortable to talk about to anyone—even Alex. And he certainly wasn't ready for his parents to meet Danielle, though he knew he should bring her home soon.

Danielle Orlena, a Mexican-American, with parents who had both migrated to Texas from Mexico, was a small, dark girl with the silkiest black hair and sweetest smile this side

of the Pecos River. She was hardly five feet three inches
tall and did not weigh more than a hundred pounds. She
possessed a tremendous sense of true justice, always cham-
pioning the underdog, the poor, and the outcast.

When he was ten he had witnessed her in a school yard
brawl during recess. She rushed in to defend a smaller girl
from bullies, rescuing her and facing down the cruel attackers. Malachi stood nearby in a group of boys, watching, and
he'd admired the plucky little Mexican girl for her courage.
She was as fierce as a tiger, wading in against three larger
girls who had their victim pinned to the ground, rubbing
dirt on her face.

As she'd helped the smaller child to her feet and began
to lead her to the bathroom to wash her face, Malachi
broke from the boys and fell in beside them. "That was
great," he said, gesturing, "what you did."

Danielle spared him a glance to see if he was mocking
her. When she realized he was sincere, she smiled a little,
and his boy heart did a triple pitty-pat that made him stumble over his own feet.

After that, he watched and admired her from a distance
in grade school, and by junior high had fallen into puppy
love. She was smart, pretty, and dignified. By high school
he could think of no one but Danielle.

Now that they'd both graduated, his thoughts had turned
to some kind of future with her—he couldn't imagine one
without her in the picture. But when should they become
an *official* couple? Danielle knew and accepted his slow
resolve, her patience another trait he found attractive. She
often said, "We're young, Malachi. We need to take our
time. I've seen what happens when people get in a hurry
and make mistakes."

She referred to classmates who, because of early preg-
nancies or just from high passion, made commitments before they'd really had time to grow up and experience life.
Though both their parents had married young, she wasn't
sure youthful relationships were right for everyone. He
agreed, though if he were truthful, he'd have to say he was
as crazy about Danielle as a man could be about a woman.
For the past year they had been having sexual relations,
something that had brought them extremely close together.

He was devoted to her, utterly, even if he couldn't fully express that devotion.

Everyone in school saw Malachi and Danielle as a couple, but in every other area Malachi was considered a loner—a quiet, reserved young man, though not withdrawn. He did have Alex as a friend, after all. Others thought Malachi serious, reflective, a perfect gentleman who loved his parents, stayed out of trouble, minded his own business, and was destined for a bright future.

Soon after his eighteenth birthday, when the world had just opened to him with a million opportunities that he recognized, but did not know how to acquire, it all came tumbling down.

For months he had been having dreams that interfered with his waking life. The dreams were essentially the same, the only difference being the intensity of each. In the dreams a wolf came to him beneath a silver moon. It had never tried to lure him away from his house with sleep-walking again, but it still came prowling through his sleep like the predator it was.

"Malachi, have you changed yet?" the wolf asked in the first dream he'd had in many years.

Malachi stood silently, fear a freezing cold hand around his neck. He remembered this place, the silver moon, and the wolf. He'd dreamed of it all before in some dim past when he was a child. The wolf was a magician, changing to vampire and back to wolf at will. It drew him from his bed that long-ago night, intent on letting him be a snack for one of its voracious minions.

"You're a man now. What are your plans?" the wolf asked.

"I . . . I don't know what you mean. I don't have any plans."

"I left you alone for years. I really wasn't going to do you harm the night you walked into the woods. Your mother promised you'd never threaten us, so that was just a test. Now I've come to find out if you are the one from prophecy. If you are, the promise means nothing to either of us."

"Threaten who? What prophecy?"

"It was prophesied a *dhampir* would be born who would turn on Predators. All of us. Will you? Are you my future killer?"

"I . . . I . . ." Malachi glanced around. He wondered how he could get out of the nightmare. He tried to wake himself, but couldn't. He concentrated, trying to change the dream if he couldn't leave it. But no matter what he tried, the dry, open plain was as real as life, and he was trapped in it, at least for now. He straightened his shoulders.

"Who are you?" he asked, finding a steely center in his being.

The wolf transformed into a man, evolving from four feet to two. The man was a vampire, a large, menacing beast now revealing tremendous fangs. Malachi believed he made himself look that way, manipulating the dream however he wished. In reality he was probably a vampire trapped in a small human body. However, if he merely wanted to scare Malachi in the dream world, he was doing a good job.

"I asked your name," Malachi repeated.

"My name is none of your affair," the vampire said. "I want to know your intentions. I want to know your plans."

"I have no plans. I don't even know what you mean. I'm . . . I'm not your enemy."

The vampire nodded as he contemplated Malachi, looking him up and down from head to feet: "This may be the truth. If it is, I warn you not to take any interest in the world of your mother. If you disobey me, I will return and not in dream. Do you understand?"

Malachi woke from these dreams that came night after night sweating and trembling, the reality of the dream world so strong it seeped over into the reality of his room. For moments after waking he imagined the silver moon was in the corner of his room, shining brilliantly down on his bed. He saw his bed standing in the center of a sandy stretch of ground, the wall at his back as transparent as smoke. Only gradually did the dream world recede, leaving him sitting up in bed at home, eyes wide with anxiety.

"Jesus," he whispered, wiping his brow.

He lay down. He punched the pillow beneath his head, trying to relax. Once asleep again, either the same dream would repeat itself or another one played out in his mind. In this one there was a vampire in chains, an old man skinny of frame, with a twisted mouth and evil intent in his gaze. This vampire was being held somewhere against his will, but just as Malachi tried to decipher why he was watching the old vampire in a dark cell, the scene changed and suddenly, with no transition at all, the vampire was free and on the run.

In the dream Malachi followed him, invisibly pulled along by a thread of consciousness. He was an unwilling spectator, watching as the old vampire killed his way through a dozen victims. After the bloodshed, the vampire went into a wilderness area dominated by high stone cliffs. From there he called Predators to him from all over the world. He sent out a call to the renegades, the loners and misfits, the most desperate and dangerous of the entire vampire nations.

Malachi thought he knew what the dream meant. If he were to believe it, there was going to be an uprising and resultant war. Mortal man hung in the balance. If vampires fought, and it got out of hand, men would die.

On waking a second time, Malachi shook uncontrollably and his nerve endings tingled as if he'd just come from an electric bath. He was unable to move for long minutes while the wisps of nightmare were burned away in the morning light of reality.

He had not spoken of these recurring dreams to anyone, not even to Danielle. As much as he loved Danielle, how could he ever tell her about the supernatural nature of his mother and the talents he'd inherited from her? How could he ever admit there were real vampires, for Pete's sake? In the first place, she wouldn't believe him, and in the second, if she did finally believe, what if the whole notion scared her off? He just couldn't chance losing her.

His mother suspected something was wrong, but waited for him to talk about his troubles. She had long ago promised she would not poke around in his mind, whether he was awake or asleep. She would grant him the privacy all humans expected as a right. Some mornings he almost spoke of the nightmares. He would be sitting at the table with his mother, and she would be carefully watching him, as if waiting. But each time he tried to speak, his tongue knotted and his throat tightened.

Malachi knew many things about the vampires from his mother, but he didn't know if the great vampire in chains from his dream existed or if he was just a fantasy produced by the dream wolf that haunted Malachi's nights. He also didn't understand the connection between the wolf vampire and the renegade on the high cliffs. No matter how he pondered these dreams, knowing they were trying to tell him something, he could not decipher their meaning beyond the distinct feeling they presaged a vampire war.

A week later, at a family gathering for July Fourth, he realized he'd not kept his nightmares secret at all.

Everyone came. At least everyone from the maternal side of his family. They had never thrown the two sides of his family together. He couldn't imagine his father's people standing around waiting for hamburgers from the grill while his mother's people stood nearby, hungering for a glass of blood taken neat.

Great-aunt Celia and her daughter, Carolyn, had come together, holding hands, walking from beneath the shade of the giant oak. Carolyn's husband, Andrew Greer, a lanky computer programmer with a lock of silky blond hair falling over his gold-rimmed glasses, followed just behind. It was known he was not vampire, not part of the clan, but he knew the truth and it made him skittish at these gatherings. Malachi's grandparents were there, holding hands, and smiling contentedly as they sat in the swing. His great grandparents were there, too, bopping a volleyball over a net to one another and laughing. They did not look as old as his own father, for they, like most of his relatives on his mother's side, were vampire and had not aged physically.

Even Uncle Eddie showed up, coming into the back pasture from out of the woods like a wraith, his twelve-year-old body disguising the adult vampire he had become.

Malachi was happy to see him. He hadn't talked with Eddie since he was just a boy himself. On that first meeting he had taken his uncle for a child at first, someone to play ball with. He had run to him, hugging a football to his chest, about to ask this boy to throw it to him. The minute Eddie spoke, however, his voice deep as that of a grown man, Malachi knew he was no child. "I'm like your mom," Eddie said in that surprisingly adult voice. "I'm not human anymore. I'm really in my mid-thirties. Damn shame, isn't it, boy? Give me that ball and run out there and see if you can catch it."

They threw the football back and forth a few minutes and then Eddie said, "Let's go for a walk, kid." They walked off together that first time, away from the family, and Eddie talked about growing up with Malachi's mother, and how they'd all hoped, he and his parents and the entire family, that Dell would never be stricken with the malady that would turn her into vampire. She'd escaped it until she was in high school and they'd all been lulled into believing she'd been spared, like Celia, like Carolyn.

"But few of us are spared," Eddie had said. "I sure wasn't. I changed when I was twelve and left home three years later. I couldn't finish school. I couldn't live in the neighborhood. I had to . . . go off."

"Where did you go?"

"I went to Brazil and stayed for many years."

"Why Brazil?" Malachi asked.

"There were whole gangs of children in the cities living on their own, scrounging through the dumps, living without adults to care for them. I sought their company. I was still a child, but I'd never grow up. No one noticed in Brazil, except the children. And they didn't care. Most of them were feral, more like animals than children, so we had something in common. That suited me fine for a while because I felt like an animal too. Then I saw how it really was for the gangs. They sniffed bottled glue out of paper bags for cheap highs. They couldn't live in the world, so they sought another, a fantasy one. They grew cold and hard, committing worse crimes than theft to fuel their habits."

"Did you leave them?"

"After a couple of years. I couldn't really find my place. The glue didn't affect me. I couldn't escape what I was and what I faced in the future the way they could. I grew so depressed I went outside of the city and away from humankind. I spent several years in the jungles, living like a lost explorer or a native. Living like Tarzan."

"Tarzan. Ha." Malachi laughed uneasily.

Eddie ignored him. "It was silent. That's what I remember. The silence, broken only intermittently by jungle sound, by bird or frog or the antics of monkeys. It took me some time when I came back to civilization to even speak. I hadn't spoken a word in years."

"What did you do then?" Malachi was fascinated. His mother rarely talked about her brother. He didn't know any of these details of his uncle's life. Being a boy himself at the time, it sounded exciting and adventurous to live in Brazil, to go into the depths of the jungle and live with the wild things. Had he swung from vines and bathed beneath waterfalls? Didn't all boys dream of such heroic adventure?

Eddie continued, "I went back to the city. All the children I'd known before I left had disappeared. They'd died or moved on or were kidnapped or they'd just managed to reach adulthood and were assimilated into the crowds on the streets.

"I wandered South America until I got to Buenos Aires in Argentina. It was different from the other cities. It was clean and prosperous. Urchins didn't pick over dump heaps and I never saw the homeless lying in gutters or doorways. I began to think about living again, like a human. I found a . . . a patron. Or he found me."

Malachi vaguely understood the word. He'd read that word in Dickens, but he wasn't sure the meaning was the same for Uncle Eddie.

His uncle must have read his mind. "A vampire patron," he explained. "I was half starved, having come into the city after traveling. I was skulking in a park, hiding in shadows, when this tall, thin man appeared. He came down a path wearing, of all things, a bowler hat and sporting a cane. I remember sneering at him. Did he think he was in London? Was he lost? And why was he walking this dark path when he could have taken a better lighted one?

"Before I knew it, he'd left the path and he had me by the throat, lifting me straight off my feet. I fought him, but without a prayer. I knew then he was like me. Vampire."

Malachi shivered, imagining being taken off guard and threatened that way in the darkness.

Eddie grinned suddenly. "He knew what I was. He was just teaching me a lesson. He said I was a rat, hiding like that in the shadows. Rats were brainless and not predators at all. They were *scavengers,* he said. Was I a little scavenger?

"He let me go and made me walk with him all through the park. He made me tell him where I'd come from and what I thought I was doing. That very night he took me in and told me I could stay with him in his villa on a slope above the city. His servants were closemouthed and loyal, they'd never betray us. He had money and interests he could share with me. He could teach me all that I'd missed from my abruptly ended school days. He had a great library, he knew the famous writer, Borges, he could take me to the opera and the museums. He knew painters and artisans. He was a patron of the arts and highly regarded. He had nothing better to do, he said, than to bring me into that rarefied culture where he would make me an educated gentleman." Eddie laughed harshly.

"Is that where you live now? In Buenos Aires?" Malachi asked.

"I live in the house still," Eddie answered slowly. "I no longer live with the patron."

"Why not?"

Eddie grew agitated and stopped walking. They were miles from the house and surrounded by thick woods. "He died."

Malachi was shocked. Vampires did not die. He never heard tell of a dead vampire. It just wasn't possible, was it? The body gave out, he had heard, but not the spirit. It went on, taking another body. "Died?"

"He asked me to kill him." Eddie had been staring at his shoes, a pair of fine leather sandals from Italy. He was dressed in gray slacks and a gray shirt with a pinstripe of red around the edge of the short sleeves. He looked like a miniature man. He glanced at his nephew and saw his consternation.

"Malachi, life is not as easy for the Predators as it is for Naturals, like your mother. If you're a Natural, the way I was, and you go off on your own, away from ready supplies of blood, you sort of . . . revert. You become more Predator than Natural, more vampire than human. That's what happened to me.

"Many Predators do away with themselves. My patron, my . . . teacher . . . admitted he'd taken me in purposefully to train me as his little assassin. I never knew that, of course. If I had, I would have run away from him as fast as I could. He first did all he promised, furthering my education about the world. He introduced me to intelligent people and taught me to hold my own in conversations with them. He made me read most of the books on his library shelves and then questioned me about what I'd read. He had me write essays and put forth opinions, then defend

them. Finally, satisfied I knew enough to pass in society as
a precocious young man, he showed me all the details of
his finances and how he handled money and made it grow
for him so that it hardly diminished as he lived on it. When
he was sure I would be all right without him, he made me
promise I would take his life and release him."

Malachi thought he'd never heard anything so awful.
"How could you do it?" he asked.

Eddie grabbed him suddenly by the shoulders. He looked
at Malachi face-to-face as they were nearly the same height.
Malachi dropped the football he'd been carrying, and it
rolled away from them. "Look into my eyes, Malachi. Read
what you see there if you want to know the truth."

Malachi tumbled down the corridors of his uncle's wide,
fiery eyes. He fell into visions that rushed into him and
transported him through time and space. He stood with
Eddie in a beautifully appointed room where the only light
came from tall mullioned windows open to the breeze. It
was night, the air scented with summer blossoms mingled
with the exhaust of vehicles on the crowded streets. Neon
lights reflected from the shops below, turning the night
vivid. Voices and traffic sounds floated from the city three
stories below.

An old vampire sat in a high-backed leather chair stud-
ded along the wide arms with brass nails. He spoke roughly
to Eddie. "Do it! Don't make me get up from this chair
and turn the sword on you."

Malachi looked at Eddie and saw he held a long broad-
sword in his right hand. It hung limply from his hand at
his side, the tip almost touching the floor. Light danced
from the blade. The hilt was thick and heavily ornamented
with scrolls worked in silver. It was a very old sword, possibly ancient. Malachi marveled, having never seen anything
like it.

"I don't want to do this," Eddie said. His voice was not
that of a grown man yet. It had the high squeaky sound of
a frightened youth.

"You have no choice now, Eddie. I will die this night . . .
or you will."

"Don't make me do it." There was revulsion and sadness
in Eddie's plea.

"Lift it over your head, swing it wide, do not make a

mistake!" the old vampire bellowed. "You're not a coward.
You are vampire and the recipient of all my knowledge.
I've given you everything. In return, I command you to
kill me!"

Malachi knew the second the sword began its upward
arc, and he turned his head away, turned his body to the
side, and refused to watch. If he were in a dream, it was
too real to endure. He did not want to see the beheading.
He would not watch it. He wanted to go home, find his
mother, and bury his head in her lap. He wanted to forget
he'd ever talked to Eddie and come to this foreign place
of murder and death.

He blinked and felt Eddie's hands fall from his shoulders.
He fell to his knees, his eyes tearing. He was back home
again, the woods he loved so well all around him. His uncle
stood above him, his fangs lowered, his eyes ablaze.

"Dell got off easy," Eddie said. "So did you. Now you
know a little of what it is to be trapped in a boy's body
and commanded to murder someone you love. I didn't do
it because he might have killed me. And he would have,
don't mistake it. I did it because he begged me and he
wanted it more than he wanted another moment of this
life, and because there was no other way. I owed it to him."

Malachi never forgot the scene that had been projected
into his mind that day. He understood his uncle's agony
and his tenuous hold on his humanity. He realized how
different the Predators were from all that he knew. He felt
a fear of them he had never felt for his mother or her
vampire family before this.

He knew murder. Sacrifice. The depth of despair. The
loneliness of separation.

On this July Fourth gathering, Malachi went across the
pasture to meet his uncle, remembering the day of the confession in the woods. He hadn't seen Eddie in over a year
and hadn't really expected him to come today. Eddie
looked the same, of course. Boy size. Fragile wrists at the
end of long arms. A thin, freckled neck. Ears too large for
his head. But in his eyes resided boundless experiences and
more knowledge than Malachi at eighteen could imagine.

Eddie smiled, taking Malachi's hand to shake. "You've
grown into a big man," Eddie said. "Are you a line-
backer?"

Malachi laughed and fell into step beside him. "I played runningback."

"Bet you bowled the opposition over. Going to college now?"

Malachi sobered. "Oh, I don't know. I mean, yeah, I guess. I just don't . . ."

"Knowledge is power, Malachi. Get all of it you can get. That wolf in your dreams? You can keep him at bay with knowledge."

Malachi turned to him in surprise. "You know about that? The wolf?"

"We all do. Dell told us. We keep a watchful eye on you, didn't you know?" He paused and then said, "No, I guess you didn't."

So they all knew. For how long? Why hadn't his mother told him?

"How long have you known?"

"Since you were a toddler."

"What? Oh, man."

"You had these nightmares when you were very small. I don't know if you remember. Your mother contacted the dream walker and found out his name. She made a deal with him. But she didn't trust he'd keep it. She made sure all of us knew of him and his threats. Even from Buenos Aires I've kept in touch with your mother, just to see how you were doing. I even know about that time when you were nine or so and Balthazar lured you from you bed into the woods."

"God, I don't know what to say. I . . . I didn't know."

Then they joined the family in Malachi's yard and Eddie went to embrace his sister, Malachi's mother.

Later, Malachi questioned his grandparents and great-grandparents. Did they know about the silver wolf from his dreams? Yes, certainly, and they were on alert, always, for any message from his mother. His great -uncles and -aunts, his cousins, all of them knew, all of them had kept a quiet vigilance.

He felt greatly loved, but also in some way violated. He had thought his worries his own. Maybe his whole life was an open book and nothing belonged to him, no secret or privacy. He felt invaded, even if for good reason. He must speak to his mother when the celebration ended and the family scattered for their homes. Had this all been necessary? Was the threat so real she had to divulge it to everyone?

That night he and his parents talked. Since graduation he had been at loose ends, and they left him alone. They went to their jobs, they didn't bug him about making a decision. They let him do what he did best—drift.

But now they talked openly, and he learned many things. How worried his mother had been all his life. How she had called Mentor and found out the dream walker's name— Balthazar. Her reasons for telling the family had been out of love and concern. She was sorry it felt like an intrusion to him. "I had to do it," she said. "Malachi? Don't you see? We're part of a clan. As *dhampir,* you're one of us." She glanced at her husband and smiled a little "At least half, anyway," she amended. "We can't let something happen to you. We had to be ready. I had to know I could count on help if I needed it."

In the end they weren't. Not ready at all, any of them. Perhaps Balthazar had taught his assassin to cloak himself so he could not be detected until too late. Perhaps Malachi's family sensed trouble and thought it another dream plaguing him. Whatever left him open that day for assault, it came as a total surprise, just as Balthazar wanted it.

The day was in August, a very hot and bleached white cloud-hazy Texas afternoon that sapped the energy and left everyone drained and lethargic. It hadn't rained in two months. The grass in the fields had turned brown, and the cattle had to be given extra hay in bales in order to survive. They clustered beneath the sparse shade of trees, rubbing their flanks together, their tails swinging to swat away green-backed flies.

Malachi still hadn't decided where to go to school or what subject to pursue there. He was home on the ranch alone, studying a college course catalog and trying to decide what direction he would take at Sam Houston University that fall. He might as well go to Sam Houston. It wasn't a great university or widely known, but it was close by and it wouldn't change his life very much if he went there.

Unlike his parents, who had always known where their interests lay, he had trouble centering on a major field of study. He knew he didn't want to stay at home and take

Internet classes like his parents had done. He also didn't want to move to Bryan-College Station, Texas, and go to A & M. Huntsville's Sam Houston was good enough for him, he thought, it was absolutely fine. Besides, his mother worked there in the university library. She'd be near if they ever needed one another.

And he'd still be close to Danielle, who he couldn't imagine not seeing regularly. She had already enrolled at Sam Houston State and had urged him to join her. They might even share an apartment, help one another study, and split expenses. She was a thrifty girl and would have to work her way through college. It was too late for him to apply for scholarships. Together they could work it out. And wasn't it time he told his parents about her, she had asked him with a crooked smile. Would they be so disappointed?

He had wrapped her in his arms and denied he was keeping her from his parents for any nefarious reason. They would love her, just as he did, he swore. How could they not?

He thought of Danielle now and then as he read and reread the course descriptions in the catalog, his head resting on sofa pillows, sneakered feet propped on the sofa arm. The air-conditioning buzzed in his ear, relaxing him so that he dozed a little, the catalog slipping from his legs to the floor with little noise. He held Danielle against him, their bodies intertwined on crisp, white sheets. He slipped his hand over the swell of her buttocks and pulled her closer. His lips sought hers and . . .

Suddenly he was wide awake and tensing. He came up from the sofa, swinging his long legs to the floor. He kicked the catalog out of the way. He had sensed a presence approaching the house. He turned his head and stared in front of him, getting that hundred-yard stare his parents recognized as a state of mind where he had disengaged from the world and was in touch with something or someone at a distance.

He knew the person approaching was not human. Predator, then. And not a Predator Malachi knew. Not Mentor or Ross, not the Predator-like Eddie. Not any of the Predators who delivered his mother's blood and took her money.

Malachi rose from the sofa. He walked softly to the door

and opened it. Waiting. It wasn't a delivery. This wasn't the day for it. It was no one he knew. A stranger, then.

A sense of alarm rushed through him, leaving him jangled and breathing unsteadily.

His mother was at work at the library and his father at his small veterinary clinic in a town twelve miles distant. Malachi wished all of a sudden he had one of his parents beside him. He hardly knew fear, except in his dreams. Possessing many of his mother's vampire talents made him immune to most ordinary accidents or bodily harm, relieving him of normal anxieties that plagued other people. Yet, now, as he stood at the door staring across the ranchland, he felt a palpable fear creep up the back of his neck and over his head like a large hand enclosing his cranium with icy fingers.

The fear kept coming at him like an arrow aimed at a bull's-eye. He recognized danger all around, like a force field holding him at its center.

He saw no one, but knew he did not have to see an enemy to know he was near. Mentally, he scanned the land around the farmhouse, searching for any hint of where the Predator might be hiding. He went through the house to the back door and looked out from there, nervously expecting the intruder from any quarter.

Seeing nothing out of place, he was about to send a telepathic message to his mother when he knew the Predator had entered the house and stood at his back. He whirled, his hands tightening into fists. He felt his adrenaline surge until his heart thudded with resounding thunder loud as a hammer pounding an iron rail.

Before him stood a Predator of about his height and size. He was dressed in soiled slacks, a torn and dirty gray jacket, and a faded plaid shirt open at the throat. He would be taken for a homeless man on the street. His wrinkled face was layered in grime and his eyes were red-veined. He opened razor-thin lips and said, "I was told you need to be sent to the devil."

Malachi thought he should try to first engage the vampire in conversation. His first instinct had been to attack, but all his life his teaching had been against violent action as first recourse.

"Why would you want to kill me?"

"Because you're the *dhampir*."

"I'm not the only one. I've heard there are others like me, maybe as many as a hundred scattered across the globe."

"I was sent to *you*."

"But how can you be so sure?" This rebuttal gave Malachi time to send out the alarm to his mother. His father was strong, but mortal. His mother was the only ally who could battle another of her kind.

"I'm sure." It was as if the vampire was a robot, his speech simple and delivered in a dull monotone. In his eyes Malachi saw the hunger and knew the beast hadn't supped in a very long time. He'd come on his mission on the brink of starvation. It gave him stronger motivation to kill and to drink the blood of an enemy. Never was a vampire's blood taken unless he was dead, that's what his mother had told him. One vampire did not feed from another, unless there was combat and hatred involved.

"Who sent you? At least tell me that before you take my life," Malachi said.

"The silver one. The Wolf."

So his dreams were precognitive. The time had come. The wolf in the dream was carrying out his threat in the real world. He hadn't believed Malachi had no plans to hunt down Predators. He must be mad.

Malachi saw the deadly resolve in the vampire's eyes a moment before his muscles bunched and he moved. Malachi sped away, walking backward up the door to the ceiling, down the wall behind the vampire and then through the door and rooms of the house.

He was caught before he reached the front door. Clawed hands took him by the shoulders and threw him across the room where he struck the mantel, knocking photographs and candlesticks to the floor. A sharp pain shot down Malachi's back.

He was up in an instant, slightly stunned, but feeling his strength growing. As a small child he had pretended he was Superman. He climbed walls, leaped from any high furniture he could find, and ran through the house so quickly mortal eyes could not detect him. Holding down his exuberance had been a chore for his parents, who were always afraid he would hurt himself.

Now he felt stronger than the fictional Superman might ever have been. Playing at being a superhero as a child hadn't been as impertinent as it had seemed at the time. Feeling immutable and untouchable gave him an iron will to win over the insanely hungry vampire following on his heels.

Suddenly Malachi laughed, throwing back his head and holding out his hands, palms up, from his sides. This reaction would throw off the vampire, confuse and weaken him. Malachi knew the beast was an underling. A ragged, starved thing sent out to test him. If he got lucky, the vampire might bring him down and sink his fangs in Malachi's throat after murdering him, but unless he was able to throw off the stupor Malachi sensed clouded his mind, his strength would betray him.

The vampire attacked again, rushing in and grabbing for Malachi's throat to pin him to the mantel. Malachi stepped aside again, turned and caught the other around the throat with his arm. He took hold of his wrist with his other hand and began to haul back, lifting the vampire off his feet and throwing him to the floor. Malachi could feel his strength as if it were steel wire running from his shoulders down into his arms and hands. His heart beat so hard he expected the vampire could feel it against his back before he was thrown down. Malachi straddled the prone beast and reached out his hands for the throat.

"Oh, Jesus." It was his mother at the door. Then she was next to him as he pinned down the snarling vampire. Malachi had his knee on the beast's chest, his hands wrapped around his throat. Dell commanded, "Let him up."

Malachi glanced at her. He had never seen such fury on his mother's face. He protested, "But . . ."

"Let him go!"

Malachi drew back, his hands falling from the vampire's throat. He stood next to his mother, watching as the vampire rose slowly to his feet. His eyes bulged, and his lips were pulled back from his teeth. He spoke in a rage-choked voice. "Get out of my way, woman."

Dell did not bother to respond. She flew at him, wrapping her arms around his neck and pushing her face toward his throat. His head bent to the side as he howled, struggling to free himself.

Malachi's heart stopped in his chest in fear. He didn't know what to do, how to help. If he got near the two of them, he was afraid he'd get in his mother's way.

The vampire began to spin, trying to throw off the woman biting at his neck. His scream rose louder and louder, the sound ricocheting all around the walls.

Malachi heard his mother's command in his mind. *Get the machete.*

Of course! She wasn't going to be able to kill him with her attack. He'd be weakened if she could manage to take some of his blood, but he wouldn't die.

Malachi hurried to the mud closet by the back door where they kept their boots and slickers. They also kept a machete there to use on rattlers and moccasins during the spring when the lethal snakes crawled out from beneath the porch.

He came toward the spinning couple, the machete raised, still unsure what he should do. He couldn't just hack his way into the melee, for fear he'd strike his mother.

A small pale arm reached out and plucked the big knife from his hand. Malachi stepped back, feeling impotent and afraid. *Mom*, he thought, *Mom be careful.*

The spinning ceased and now blood spurted from over Dell's shoulder. She drew back, hacking at the monster, her arm and the machete blurring with dizzying speed. Wounds opened on the vampire, his flesh rending with each flash of the machete. Flaps of muscle hung from his shoulders and arms. Swinging with a sudden arc of her arm, his mother separated the terrified vampire's head from his body, and he fell to the floor.

Malachi turned away, unable to look at the body twitching and jerking in death, blood pumping from the headless torso.

He felt his mothers' hand on his forearm. He couldn't look at her. He knew she was covered with blood. Her eyes would be wild from battle. She would not look human. Instead, she would look too much like the beast she'd murdered.

"Malachi?"

"I have to go out," he said, pulling away from her and making for the door. The carnage in their living room sickened him. He had been more than willing to throttle the life out of the intruder, but he didn't know if he had the will to hack a person to death. "I just can't look at it," he said, his back to her.

Once outside he drew in a cleansing breath and began to tremble. He wondered if the dead thing in his house was just the first victim. He thought there would be more vampires coming. They wanted to kill him, but he didn't know why. What had he ever done to call this upon himself? He wasn't even vampire and there were others like him, *dhampirs* as they were called, so why was he singled out for death and no one else? The dream world told him he was the one prophesied. He didn't know how that could be or why. He was just a peaceful guy who wanted to go to college, if he really had to, and marry Danielle, and have a ranch and a family like his father. He only wanted to live a normal life and forget his vampire heritage.

It was nearly an hour before his mother, clean and fresh from a shower, her hair hanging in wet strands around her face, came to him. He sat in the glider beneath a locust tree.

"It's all cleaned up?" he asked.

"Yes, pretty much. I'll take him later and burn his body away from the house."

"Where is he now?"

She pointed toward the garage where his father kept an ancient truck he tinkered with when he had free time.

"Mom, I . . ."

"You don't have to say anything. I know it's brutal to witness murder. But it had to be done. We couldn't have rid ourselves of him any other way, unless there'd been a fire."

"Why are they coming for me this way?" Malachi asked.

"Some of them think you've been chosen to lead a holy war against them. They created a myth a very long time ago and began to believe you were part of it. I promised Balthazar you'd never be a threat."

Malachi said, "I told him I don't want to hurt anyone. I told him in the . . . the nightmares. Can't you make him believe me?"

Dell came to sit by him on the glider. "I can try. Until

now I didn't really think he'd do anything like this. After that time he lured you away from the house, I sent word that if he tried that again, he would have to fight me and everyone connected to me. We had a pact. He'd left you alone so long after that attempt. Something's happened, something's changed. He doesn't trust either of us anymore."

They sat in companionable silence as the afternoon waned and a sliver of white moon hung in the daylight sky. When Malachi's father came home from work, they finally joined him in the house to tell him about what happened. Soon afterward his parents went to the garage and slung the wrapped corpse over the back of one of the horses. Then his parents mounted their own horses and rode off across the land toward the back pasture and the dense woods that skirted it.

Malachi found himself spooked, looking around at shadows, watching for danger, checking and rechecking for anyone approaching the little farmhouse sitting out in the middle of a wide green field.

He didn't know if he'd ever feel safe again.

*   *   *

Charles Upton spent fifteen years in volcanic struggle. He never got the magical cards back to help him. For months he raged, trying to convince his captors to return them. He knew how the monks would come into his cell and possess him, mind and body, if his temper flared out of bounds, so he was careful not to try their patience. He still made everyone's life miserable by raving in his cell for hours each day. At least he could do that much.

Madeline came into his cell once during that time, lecturing him, but he laughed in her face. "You would tell me how to conduct myself in this place? A woman often restrained because of a vile temper? Please. That's ridiculous," he said, using her favorite word.

Insulted, Madeline retreated to a corner of the cell and pressed her lips together in an unforgiving line.

He asked, "Why is it you can come in here and the monks don't stop you? Every time I try to leave, they catch me before I get far."

"You try to escape, that's why. I just come into this cell. You try to leave the monastery. They have placed a spell over the windows in our cells and the outside walls and the ceilings. We can't get out. They always catch us when we try, as you well know. Combined, their strength is overwhelming. When I come in here, I'm not escaping. Why should they care?"

When Upton retreated into silence, thinking how long Madeline had been kept in the monastery, she began to shimmer. He glanced at her and smiled. He wouldn't beg her to stay. He would be indifferent to her. She didn't know any more than he did about how to escape. Until now he hadn't known the cell windows and outside walls, and even the ceilings were impenetrable. He'd just thought the monks came to possess him every time he tried to shimmy out the bars or through the chinks in the exterior stone walls, that being their only recourse. But the monastery was a more formidable prison than he'd ever imagined, wrapped in supernatural spells.

Upton didn't care if Madeline never came back. He had come to relish his solitude. Only in solitude could he fashion some means of escape. He'd made attempts nearly every year, a total of eleven times, with eleven failures. Not knowing how to use his strength and cunning in the beginning, he had been determined to learn how. It was a slow process, as he had no one to teach him, but eventually he learned to transmorph himself into mist. He had entered Madeline's cell without her knowing, watching at her back as she sat at the desk and scribbled furiously. He'd even slipped in when she slept, standing right at her head, close enough to touch her if he'd wanted.

He had then slid outside of the prison cell, slipping through the bars in the door leading into the interior corridor as easily as a puff of wind. He was free mere seconds, however, before one of the monks caught and bound him, and he woke to find himself in the cell again, lying like a block of wood on the cold stone floor.

It came to him that the monks used some sort of inner radar system to monitor him. They didn't have to be near or watch him with their eyes.

Usually it was Joseph who came for him. Joseph, surely,

was his personal keeper. Of the eleven escape attempts over the years, Joseph alone had returned him to the cell six of those times.

Upton had learned many tricks, but immunizing himself from takeover by Joseph was not one of them. No matter how strong his will or how swiftly he moved, Joseph or his comrades caught him.

Once Upton sensed another nearby vampire presence that watched him closely. This one was not a monk, but an outsider residing in the monastery. All his probing told him was the vampire's name. Dolan. Where he came from or why he was there remained a riddle.

Dolan was not always there either. Mentally searching for him did not turn him up very often. But just when he was sure Dolan was gone for good, he'd sense him creeping down the halls or pacing in the courtyard or lost for hours in the jungle, taking paths the monks used to approach the far village.

Dolan's presence confused him, but he finally decided the vampire was one of Mentor's lackeys, sent there to help Joseph keep an eye on him. This meant Mentor feared him and could not altogether trust the monks. Good! That meant there must be a crack in their system; it wasn't infallible. Just because Madeline had never discovered it didn't mean he wouldn't. She was a woman who did not devote all her time toward finding the crack through which to slither away, whereas it was all he ever thought about.

Besides, he was glad Dolan was often in the monastery, giving evidence to Mentor's fears. He wanted Mentor unsettled. Foremost, he wanted Mentor to die, but to keep him unsettled was as much as he could hope for until he broke free.

Upton had also learned how to change himself into another kind of living thing. He had transmorphed into a tiger, but when Joseph showed up at the cell door, the old monk just smiled enigmatically and went away again. He had changed himself into a little brown bird, lighting on the sill of the door's small barred window. Again Joseph appeared and before Upton could fly into the safety of the cell, he was trapped in the monk's first, strangling.

"Hello, little bird," Joseph said. "I could feed you to a starving villager for dinner, boiled, with carrots and rice."

Then he let Upton go and went away again, proving once more there were no tricks worthy of his time.

Day after day Upton tried out his powers, honing them and discovering just how far they would take him. Already it was harder for the monks to possess his mind when he went into a rage. He was able to fight them off for several minutes before they could shackle him into the dark pit of his brain, making his body go limp.

One day, Upton thought, *I will outwit them. One day, Joseph will turn his attention away just at the moment I make my escape attempt, and I'll skitter away in the guise of a mouse, or fly into the jungle as a colorful parrot, or be taken by the wind in the form of a cloud of mist.*

That he'd not done it yet might have defeated a smaller, more fragile intelligence, but Upton would not give up hope. He would *not* live in a dank, cold cell for eternity. He would *not* give up his entire magnificent vampire existence to talk with insects and vermin that came to invade his sleep.

When he'd first been made vampire, he thought the world was at his feet, there for his personal amusement. He could have women, wealth, all earthly pleasures, and even fame, if he desired it. He would live forever and eventually he'd rule over every living being and every vampire on Earth. He was not so megalomaniacal to think he'd own the world and everything in it all at once. It would take work and time. It was in a future where Mentor and Ross were both dead and out of his way. But becoming a god was worth the years it might take and any amount of effort. He wasn't made to live eternally only to waste away within the confines of four stone walls.

It had come to him in the last couple of years of his incarceration that he had been trying to use the wrong skills. Rather than perfect the art of changing into mist or another living entity, he believed his greatest skill might be in invading Joseph's thoughts. If he could know where Joseph was and what he was doing as easily as Joseph knew the same about him, he might find a way to use the information to his advantage.

The first time he tried it, Joseph had been at prayer. He was standing before an old worn prayer wheel, spinning it with his hand, mumbling beneath his breath. He was lost in his meditation. Yet Joseph knew instantly when Upton touched him. His hand paused, his words ceased, and he turned his head to look out at the open courtyard.

He smiled.

Upton hurriedly pulled back with a jolt into his own skull, silently cursing. He hated Joseph, his malice toward him as hot as the center of a live coal. How had this old monk developed such superior skill? Tiptoeing into his mind without notice might be impossible. God *damn* him.

Nevertheless this did not deter Upton from trying. He would pester the old monk until he wore him down or caught him unaware. Some way. Somehow.

He never dreamed his chance would come on a late June day in the nineteenth year of his imprisonment. Though he thought himself ready to snatch any opportunity to wriggle away into freedom, when it came, he was so elated he almost missed it.

Joseph came down the corridor alone. He had in his hands a small bucket swinging from his right hand. Sloshing within was the blood to feed Upton, his daily ration, just enough to keep him from starving.

Upton sent out his probe to the monk's mind, tickling him with his presence, hoping to torture him into submission. He'd done this every time the monk was near and each time was rebuffed and thrown back as easily as tossing aside a bone to the floor. He expected it to happen again, as always, but something was different. He discovered Joseph's mind was dim and his thoughts scattered and as indistinct as faded photographs. He had never been this way. Touching his mind before had been as dangerous as reaching into a tangle of thorny locust trees.

Upton probed deeper with his telepathy. He spider-walked into the monk's brain in amazement. The farther he went, the more his mind turned into the flesh and finally he realized what was going on. Joseph's old body was dying. He had kept it too long. In mortal years, the body he inhabited was over one hundred years old. It had served him well, but he'd grown too fond of it and had held onto it long past the time he should have let it go. He should have found another body to inhabit many years ago.

All this information came from Joseph's dying thoughts that flew about in a maelstrom of disarray.

Stunned and hopeful, Upton, probed deeper. He hadn't

known that vampires changed bodies. He had no idea that once the mortal body gave out, the vampire soul could transfer itself to another. All in a flash he knew everything he needed to know. Though his body stood immobile in his cell, his mind began to glow with excitement as it slid about on the slippery slopes of the monk's brain tissue fighting against imminent physical death.

Joseph stopped at his cell and set the bucket on the floor as if in a trance where long routine kept him performing old tasks. He fumbled for the keys at his waist to unlock the grate on the door, fighting to finish this one duty before seeking safety to deal with his failing body. All the while he forced the flow of blood in his rapidly deflating veins. It was as if he knew what was happening, but just couldn't believe it. Refused to believe it.

Even as he struggled in this way, the blood flow to his brain diminished, slowing the way water in a pipe does when a faucet is being closed by a slow, weary hand. He hadn't the strength to ward off Upton's probe. He might not even know the prisoner was there, watching through mental eyes the rapid deterioration of the elderly brain.

Suddenly Joseph dropped the keys and clutched at his chest. Along with him Upton felt a sizzling pain slice down his left arm and paralyze it. A greater pain squeezed his heart, a physical pain so devastating that not even a great vampire's supernatural abilities could ward it off.

No! Upton knew these symptoms. As president of his corporation before his change to vampire, he'd been present when a colleague at a corporate meeting had fallen from his chair, the victim of a heart attack. The colleague had died before the paramedics arrived.

Joseph was dying. Right now, this very minute. Upton realized the truth. Though a vampire's heart did not beat, the intake of daily blood suffused it. That fresh blood kept the heart supple. Now, as veins and arteries closed down, depriving the heart of life-sustaining blood, the organ had suddenly spasmed, mimicking the heart attack a human would suffer. Joseph would have to slip from the body and find another quickly or be doomed to wander like a haunt, lost to the real world.

Upton knew all this just as Joseph knew it. The two of them, locked in the dimming brain, panicked.

Joseph's thoughts raced to find a body nearing death he could take over. He could not take over a living person. Upton knew this, too. He knew all that Joseph knew—and it was terrifying knowledge.

Hysteria gripped Upton so strongly that he almost withdrew. Every instinct screamed that he leave the monk's person and return to his body to save himself.

Yet, if he left the old monk, his one real chance at escape evaporated with the departure. *If only I can hold on,* Upton thought. *If I can stay while Joseph flees, and if I can animate the dying body, I can leave this place forever.*

Joseph had no thought for him. His salvation lay elsewhere. He could not battle the prisoner and at the same time save himself.

The body they both occupied fell to its knees. The bucket was knocked over, blood spilling along the floor in a messy red stream. Joseph was on his hands and knees, head hanging down almost to the cobbled floor.

Go, Upton urged the monk. *Go now. Leave the body while you have time.*

Suddenly the monk's brain was as empty as a dead planet circling toward the scalding center of a red dwarf. Upton found himself alone in the center of a brain where the lights were going out. All around him the sparkling neurons died, blinking out silently and without fanfare. The body keeled over onto the floor, the head striking stone with a resounding crash that echoed inside the skull. Upton didn't know where Joseph had vanished to, but he was gone, leaving behind the husk that had sheltered him for a lifetime. Upton did not believe Joseph had obeyed him. He'd merely fled the body because he had no other choice.

Upton wondered what would happen to him if he were trapped inside the dead body. But he hadn't time to worry about it. He had to find some way to get the body to its feet and to stumble away from the monastery. He had to *move* this body. The other monks would not even imagine it was Upton's spirit which animated the revered Joseph's form. He could pass by them without suspicion. They'd never think to probe or test the spirit animating their brother's body. It was Upton's one chance to be free!

They left it to Joseph to alert them when he escaped. Only then did they rush to come together and bring him back. With Joseph frantically searching for another body, he could spare no attention for his prisoner. This meant *no one* knew he was now the monk, Joseph.

He was Joseph. Completely.

He felt no thread of connection at all to the body he'd left within the cell.

All Upton had to do was infuse Joseph's old body with enough life to take him away from here. If he could do it . . . if he could only do it. . . .

He was fully inside the body now, feeling the pain increasing inside it, suffering the earthquake that shook the foundation of the old, failing heart. *Hold on,* he cried. *Hold on!*

Unused to the new shell of flesh, he lost precious seconds trying to sense the hands, arms, and legs. When he did, they were wooden and unruly. He sent thought impulses to them and managed to get the hands to press against the floor, raising his upper body from the stone. He looked out of the dimming eyes and saw all peripheral vision was lost. He could see only round porthole tunnels of vision so that he had to turn his head to observe more than a few feet around him.

He forced the trembling legs to draw up and raised himself to his knees. Pain racked him and made him grimace fiercely with every small effort.

I can stand this pain, he told himself. *I won't suffer long. I have to get away and then I can discard this old flabby shell.* He despised the body's odd scent and the unfamiliarity of the muscle and sinew. It was like walking into a smelly old house that had been lived in by a family of untidy strangers.

By taking hold of the door handle of his cell, he was able to pull himself to his feet. He leaned against the barred grate in the door and with astonishment saw his old body inside the cell lying on the floor. The eyes were open, staring opaquely at the ceiling. There was no hint of life left in that body.

By fully leaving it behind, his entire spirit gone from it, the body must have died for good. When he'd become a bird or mist or a tiger, the molecules that made up his body came with him. But when he'd fled into Joseph's dying form, his former body had been totally vacated. He had taken another body, just as they all did when their housing grew too old. *So this is how it was done.* You had to want it badly enough, want it with all your being. Only no one, he would wager, had ever fled into a body near the brink of death. No vampire would be insane enough to do such a fatally foolish thing.

He mourned the familiar body on the floor of the cell for only a moment before remembering his important task at hand. He owned the monk's body now. It was his. He must move it or he would be trapped inside it. He did not know what might happen if he did get trapped. He knew he wouldn't die. His spirit could not be killed that way. He didn't yet know exactly *how* he could be truly killed, but he didn't think a heart attack would take away his consciousness.

Still, he didn't know for sure. He must hurry. He must be quick. Even now the cells of the brain were dying off, millions of them winking out and going dark and utterly silent.

He fought against the anvil that was the inert body. The heart had gone into sudden fibrillation, flapping like a wild bird against the ribs. Though it did not beat in the undead, it could still leap into movement and cause the death of a body too worn to be replenished by blood. He had not known this. There was so much he did not know, he felt like an ignorant peasant.

His vision dimmed and brightened, light and dark alternating in rapid succession. Fear ripped through him like a madman banging a big bass drum.

Upton stumbled away from the cell door, leaving behind his aged body, and angled down the corridor to where he saw stairs leading up to shifting sunlight. He could hardly think. The mad drumming of panic bore him step by step away from his old cell. If he could get out here, he'd leave the prison behind. He must take it. He had to, even if it took every ounce of strength he'd ever had in all his life.

He reached the stairs without passing anyone, ignoring the vampire hisses from other prisoners when he moved past their cell doors. They thought him their captor, their jailer. He shrouded his real persona from them by keeping his thoughts focused only on putting one foot in front of the other as he went toward the light. He got his hand on the wooden stair rail and saw the flesh of his hand was gray, the color of death. His extremities were leaden and difficult to animate. His feet were pails of cement, his hands cold and numb as if they'd been frozen solid.

His teeth were showing, his lips having pulled back in hard effort and savage pain. He took a step and then another, pulling himself up the steps, his face held up to the light. A second attack shook him, the heart spasming. It caused him to halt, his left hand clawing up and his heart sending out an excruciating radius of pain. The heart was treasonous, working now when it hadn't worked for years, trying to bring the body to the brink of real death.

He had never known such physical suffering. He had never been so hurt, even when he was mortal and living with the disease of porphyria. His vision went black and again he panicked, the fear of entrapment in the decrepit body causing him to want to leap from it as from a furnace. Yet he held on. The very real threat of physical death and entrapment forced him onward. The pain slackened only for moments and he could see again, though even less than before. It was as if his eyes had blinders on them, shutting out everything but one tiny pinprick circle. He was about to collapse, he knew it. He had to get up the stairs and out of the dungeon prison. Had to . . . had to . . . the sun up there . . . the air . . . he had to reach it.

He grabbed at the railing and pulled himself up the steps one at a time, silently screaming against the dimming of the light. He finally reached the top and staggered into the open. None of the monks were here either, as it appeared the passage had led to the back of the monastery. It was too early for the order to be working in the small garden where they grew herbs for seasonings and medicinals they sold in little packets at village markets. He had learned all the herbs' names as he'd watched from his cell window while they worked the gardens. Here was rosemary, tansy, and the nodding yellow heads of feverfew flowers. He stumbled across a bed of bright, fragrant lavender, broke through tall plants of spearmint and peppermint, crushed the ground-hugging pennyroyal. His feet dragged through the herb beds, crushing their tender leaves and stems as he staggered, and the air filled with pungent, green scent.

Would the monks notice his bedevilment of their precious garden? He didn't know, but he was very glad they weren't here now and that the garden was empty.

Through a nearby gate he could see a path leading into the jungle lying at the base of a forested mountain. Upton made for it, spilling forward like a drunk, the world turning above and below him. All his senses were on the precipice of being extinguished. He could hardly see where he was heading. He couldn't hear, his ears as closed as the door of a bank vault. He couldn't feel the warmth of the sun overhead. His feet were blocks that he painfully force-lifted to make the steps necessary to reach the path.

He gritted his teeth, his head splitting with pain now that narrowed his eyes to slits. He found himself on the path, still not pursued. This small freedom gave him greater impetus to press forward. He went on in his stumbling, shambling way, sheer desperation guiding him. What will I do now? He screamed silently to himself. *What can I do? Oh, God . . .*

Before he knew it, a young man was at his side, propping him beneath a shoulder, babbling in a dialect that made absolutely no sense to Upton. He was a native of the country, a Thai, trying to help what he saw as a fainting monk.

Upton tried to speak, but his tongue was lax and his throat would not move even to swallow. Thin streams of blood filled and dripped from his slack lips. He felt himself being lowered to the jungle floor, while above him the dark young man still spoke to him rapidly, but now he could not hear a word. He saw the lips moving, but the world was hushed and silent.

As Upton felt the last of the body's strength deserting him, his lids lowered and his gaze fastened on a leather pouch at the young man's waist. From it protruded the carved bone handle of a knife. With all his remaining will, Upton lifted up a hand and touched the other man, letting his hand slide with gravity's help down the broad chest to the young man's waist and to the knife's handle. He had to kill this man in order to take his body.

He had to . . . had to . . . if he wanted to live, he had to.

There was a look of surprise in the man's eyes as Upton withdrew the knife and pushed it with all his remaining might through the mortal's rib cage. The Thai hovered above Upton, his hands going to his chest and the knife embedded there. He looked down at himself in disbelief. He looked back at the monk, and then his eyes rolled back in his head and he fell headlong to the side of the wide satiny umbrella leaves of a large elephant plant.

Upton gave in to the dying of the body he possessed. He willingly let it go, relaxing all effort to keep the pain of this death at bay. He closed his eyes and turned all his consciousness inward, gathering himself to leave.

He would be young again.

He would be free.

He would be undetectable for long enough in Thailand to flee to the far ends of the Earth.

Mentor . . . Mentor would never find him. . . .

*   *   *

Dolan, tuning into the corridor where the special prisoner was jailed, knew suddenly something was wrong. He felt the hairs on the back of his neck rise. He walked to the corridor door and held onto the roughly hewn wood facing, his head cocked as if listening to a distant tune. He was listening with his mind to the unrelenting silence in the far cell. Too silent. No sound of movement. No electrical charges from anything living. Nothing occupied the cell but inanimate objects.

Dolan had kept his distance from the place where Upton was held. On his visits to the monastery over fifteen years he had never approached the old vampire, knowing that to do so would put him in jeopardy. Now he rushed back down the halls and took the stairs leading to the underground corridor of cells. He saw ahead of him a spilled bucket of blood.

He's gone, Dolan thought wildly. *Upton is gone!*

He hadn't any fear the vampire was playing a trick. Though a Craven, Dolan had grown more and more like the Predator species—strong, powerful, full of supernatural instinct. He could walk in the daylight now. He could go in Mentor's place to guide new vampires as they tried to fit back into the world again.

He knew what he'd find before he reached the cell and peered inside. Upton's body lay there, its spirit fled. Had the body died and trapped him in it, Dolan would have sensed it. This body was as dead as any mortal who had died. It was empty and cold, nothing but a fleshy container.

Dolan turned around, hearing a woman's voice calling him. "Did he try to get away again?"

Dolan strode to the adjoining cell on his left and saw the woman there at the window. She seemed amused. She'd evidently seen Upton attempt escape many times before.

"His body's here. He's not here with it."

The woman put a hand over her mouth. She whispered, "Oh, no. How could he do that? That's never happened, not in the nearly twenty years since she'd been here. I heard Joseph the monk outside his door. Where is Joseph? Why didn't he stop him? For God's sake, call Mentor, call him right away."

Dolan went back up the stairs at a heady speed, his mind reaching out and sending the alarm that would travel over half the world to his master. "He's gone!" went the alarm. "Upton's gone!"

Dolan ran into a monk coming his way and grabbed him by the shoulders to keep them both from falling over. "Charles Upton has escaped. You must find him."

The monk's expressionless face changed, evolving before Dolan's eyes. It became a mask of hatred, the eyes darkening, the brow lowering, the lips drawing back so the fangs could lower into place. "We will find him, then," he said. "Please release me."

Dolan dropped his hands from the monk's shoulders and watched as the Predator monk rushed away. All over the monastery he felt the monks turn from their work and speed toward the underground prison cells.

Where were they when this happened, Dolan wondered? He returned to his room and tried to throw out his net of consciousness to pick up the missing Upton, but he caught nothing but the fearful coming together of the monks as they set about to share what information they had and give orders for the search.

"Jesus," Dolan whispered, staring out at the hot summer evening casting lengthening shadows over the courtyard. "I can't believe he did it."

Mentor had told Dolan the maniac Charles Upton did not understand his vampire powers or how to use them. He had never changed bodies until now.

Upton must have changed bodies. If he was not present in his own body, he must have taken . . . the monk's. Joseph. But how?

Dolan, like any vampire who had lived beyond a normal life span, had transferred from one body to another. No one had to really explain it to him or teach him how. The pure necessity and urge to survive helped draw him from a dying body toward a live one. After the first time, usually an abrupt event where one's body gave out suddenly, a vampire tried to be aware of his host body so as not to be taken by surprise and without a plan.

Had Upton's body been dying? It shouldn't have been as Upton hadn't been more than eighty-three. A powerful, strong, vibrant eighty-three at that. His disease had been healed and his body appeared to be near optimum health. Had he simply left his old body when it wasn't dying at all? Had he taken the monk's body just to escape?

Of course he had.

Since Dolan had never abandoned his own human form until it was of no further use to him, he couldn't imagine how such a thing was done. He imagined it would take a very powerful entity to do it. Someone so determined he could jerk away his consciousness from one body and enter with it into another.

Then what happened to the monk? Had he been thrown out of his own body by force or had he fled it for some reason?

It was all a mystery, but one Dolan hoped would be cleared up when they caught the monster again.

The monster who walked now in the robes of a vampire Buddhist monk.

*   *   *

Upton straightened from the ground and reached down to pull out the bone-handled knife from his chest. Blood gushed at first, but the flow lessened as the edges of the slit skin came together, and then beneath the skin, the muscles mended, the organs that had been pierced by the knife's point healing in scant moments.

He was truly vampire.

He had a brand new body, whole and strong and brown as a walnut.

As the young man, Upton stared down at the carcass of Joseph and kicked at it until he could get the body rolled off the path and into the cover of the jungle. He looked behind him and saw no one in pursuit. But he knew they would be coming soon. Someone would find the spilled blood in the corridor, or one of the monks would casually look for him in his cell and find his old dead body.

Upton didn't know where he was going, but he knew he could move faster if he were a low, sleek animal and not a man. Even a fast young man could not outrun some of the faster jungle predators.

He closed his eyes and focused his energy, changing rapidly into a black jaguar. He found himself on four paws, his vision at ground level. He could smell the scent of hot blood left back on the path during the stabbing. His nostrils flared at the smell of death from the old one who had been kicked and prodded away from the path. A long pink tongue snaked out and curled around his lips. He would like to eat the dead man. But he hadn't time, no time, no time.

He leaped up the path, bounding forward and then into the jungle, running as fast as his strong animal body would carry him. He noted monkeys racing away from his passage, screeching madly. Birds fluttered from branches into higher cover and small furtive animals made for burrows, but Upton ignored everything. He must put distance between himself and the monastery. He thought a village lay in this direction, but wasn't altogether sure. He relied on his animal sense of smell to lead him toward where men lived.

Within a half hour he was many miles away from the monastery. He lay on his belly at the edge of a clearing. He had run faster than any man could have followed. He could see ahead of him a small, thriving village where people moved about in a natural manner, unaware of his presence. He slithered back on his jaguar belly, digging into the soft ground with sharp claws and stood when he was in the shelter of cover by a wall of thick green foliage. He focused again and his molecules spun, whirling into a dark cloud first and then forming the outline and finally the solid body of the young man he had possessed. Energy remembered the matter it came from, returning to the same form it had left. He marveled at this, at how much power he'd been granted by being made vampire.

Upton did not know what he looked like except that he was rather tall, with long limbs and large bare feet. His skin was dark, his face and chest hairless. His hands were finely formed with slender fingers. He wore a pair of beige shorts streaked with dirt and a striped polo shirt stained with rusty droplets of blood. He did know his vision was perfect, his teeth all present and whole, and the internal organs that supported the frame were as healthy and vital as could be. He could not have asked for a healthier body, but he didn't know what the face looked like and because of that went into the village shyly, holding his head down as he walked. For all he knew he was an ugly creature with a deformed face, a face only a mother would love. But at least he was Thai and wouldn't stand out the way he might if he had been entering the village in his old white man's body.

He found a worn bench carved from a tree trunk and sat in the shade of a crumbling building that housed both a tea shop and an old watchmaker's shop. He sat on the bench, watching life stream around him. The people of Thailand were beautiful to him—slim, small-boned, dark-haired. They smelled of spice and sesame oil. The women, especially, drew his attention. For the most part they were short and small breasted, with shiny hair twisted into intricate buns at the back of their delicate necks.

Watching the women, he realized he was ferociously hungry and also sexually excited. Being in a young body that had never tasted blood increased his appetite tenfold. It also had reawakened his sexual appetite. He waited for dusk and for darkness to fall so he could snatch a victim. He would take care of his sexual needs later, when he felt safe, but he didn't think he could go much farther from the monastery until he fed. His stomach seemed rolled over onto itself and his intestines all tangled.

He kept his mental energy high to watch for enemies who might enter the village searching him out. They would know him, know his true spirit, despite the disguise of a new body. Vampire knew another vampire, that was certain.

The day waned quickly, though not quickly enough to

suit Upton. However, he was practiced in patience. He sat immobile, watchful, head down, making himself as invisible as possible.

A little boy approached, a ragamuffin living on his own, or away from his parents for the day. Upton turned his head on his neck stiffly and glared at the youth. He hissed at him and rolled back his lips to show how he could cause long new fangs to slide down from his upper gums.

The boy froze and caught his breath.

Breathe not a word, little man. Upton whispered to the boy's mind. *Take yourself away from me and hide if you have any wish to live beyond the setting of the sun.*

The child blanched, going pale through he was normally the color of toasted coconut. He turned on his heel and beat a path away and into the throng of villagers until Upton lost sight of him. Upton smiled, thinking what a tasty morsel the boy might have made.

What a really tasty morsel, fine and tender enough to make a hungry man smack his lips in anticipation.

*   *   *

When daylight left the sky and night descended, the village emptied of commerce and workers and shoppers. Only a few men strolled the dry dirt streets, going and coming from the two bars. One of the bars boasted the only neon in the village, a gaudy pink sign that Upton could not read, though he did recognize the liquor bottle outlined in purple neon that hissed like a perpetually alarmed snake.

Unable to wait any longer, he moved toward the darker bar, the one without any electric sign to splash light around the entrance. There Upton lounged against the wall outside the door, waiting. He did not have long to wait. A smaller, older man, stumbling and mumbling from drink, came from the bar and turned down the lane. Upton stalked him until they were near a small opening between one-story buildings. He was upon him in an instant, taking him from behind, twisting his head to the side so he could get at his throat.

He had sunk his fangs in and was taking the old man's blood in great draughts until his mind warned him of another vampire—a Predator—nearby. He brought his mouth from the drunkard's neck, holding the comatose body around the waist so he wouldn't fall. He listened with his preternatural hearing and heard the footsteps passing the bar and coming toward where Upton stood holding onto his burden.

He dropped his victim immediately and sped away down the opening between buildings. When he reached the rear, he turned right and rushed on, heading for the edge of the village and the jungle beyond. He would change to jaguar again and disappear into the leafy camouflage.

He didn't know who the Predator might be, afraid to probe him to find out, but he suspected it was one of the monks, sent to search the village.

Having reached the road leading out of the village and the jungle that pushed against it on both sides, he changed into the big cat and padded on all fours into the deep emerald greenery. He hurried, beginning to leap and bound, jumping over low bushes and tall grasses and fallen limbs on the jungle floor.

He sensed the Predator now on the road, but he hadn't yet left it to come into the jungle.

I've lost him, Upton thought exultantly, moving even faster, his paws hardly touching ground. In a moment he would give up all his personal hold on the animal he had become and let the animal body and mind take over as it raced away from danger. No Predator would track him as a jaguar, if he cleared his mind.

Even as he began to let go of his own thoughts, and as he outdistanced the vampire at his back, his hunger returned, never having been satisfied. He could still taste the liquor-polluted blood of the old man he'd had to let go. *Don't think of that,* he scolded himself. *They can track you if you think of blood and feeding.*

Damn him, Upton thought, a snarl escaping his cat lips. *Damn the monk who chases me, and may he fry in hell along with Joseph.*

* * *

Mentor paused on the road in the darkness, bending his head slightly in thought. He tried to pick up Charles Upton's intelligence again. Without warning, he'd lost it all of a sudden, like a lightbulb going dark.

Mentor kept completely still, sure he could find the other vampire again if he tried hard enough. Surely Upton had not learned how to evade him. He'd learned many things—how to change into a cat, how to leave his body and become Joseph and then leave Joseph's dying body and finding another body to inhabit. But how had he discovered the trick of cloaking his mind so no one could detect him?

Mentor could hardly believe it. He mentally searched the area again, feeling his way slowly and meticulously around the jungle on both sides of the road. Where Mentor stood had been the last place Upton, in the form of a jaguar, had passed. He'd fled in some direction off the road, but which direction?

This would not do. Mentor sent out a call to the monks wherever they were in their searches. *Come to me,* he commanded. *He's where I am, but I've lost him. Come and help me.*

It wouldn't take the monks long to reach him outside the village, but every minute gave Upton a chance to move even farther away. Mentor tried to search out every large cat in the area, but knew that would take a while. He had to test each one, entering into each mind to find the alien presence of a vampire.

Still, he was not too upset at Upton's disappearance. No matter where he went, he'd find him eventually. He'd track him until he found his lair, and there he'd bind him and haul him into a private place where he would set him on fire. This time they would not imprison him. They'd held off killing Upton over the years because of Mentor's reluctance, and his hope Upton might one day mature into a vampire with a conscience. Now he knew he had been wrong. He should have listened to Ross and the others. Upton grew in strength and cunning with each year that passed. He saw now it had only been a matter of time before Ross' protégé escaped.

Several monks pressed around Mentor, touching him to find out what he knew. Wordlessly, they spread out into the jungle, going in opposite directions on each side of the road. They would cover as much area as possible, seeking contact with every animal in the vicinity in case Upton changed from jaguar to something else.

Mentor chose to enter the jungle closest to where he stood, thinking he had at least a fifty-percent chance of finding Upton. He moved rapidly, focusing on every leaf and stem for evidence of recent passage. He picked up the scent of a large cat, possibly the jaguar, and followed it.

He spent hours searching, losing, and retracing his steps, seeking to find the jaguar's path again. He received mental reports from the monks, who had no better luck than he did.

Morning rose and many of the monks returned to the monastery to help the few guards they'd left behind. They must attend to the prisoners' feeding and take care that someone else didn't escape.

Mentor doggedly trekked on, hope dwindling. He searched all through the day and into the next night without pause. At some point in the day he lost the jaguar scent altogether and thought Upton had changed again, either to man or another animal.

He didn't want to admit it, but Upton had outsmarted them all. He feared he was gone, at least for now. He'd had too much of a head start and his incentive to be free was strong. While imprisoned, he'd been an annoyance, but set free, he was a formidable problem. He'd had nearly two decades to form a plan to take over the Predators. All their clans were loosely governed; their only true sin was to turn renegade. It was Upton's ambition to give all the Predators freedom to do what they wanted to in their dread hearts. Like him, they might start to believe they had a right to kill off the Cravens and a duty to release the Naturals from their reliance on blood banks.

If that ever happened, Mentor shuddered to think of the upheaval it would create. For years the vampire nations had lived in a civilized way, keeping their secrets, doing as little harm to mankind as possible. Upton would change all that. He would lead vampires against man, proving to them the invincibility of a supernatural blood feeder.

Mentor found himself entering another village, emerging from the jungle with a weary tread. He cast about, searching for Upton, but could not find him. He probably hadn't even been here, Mentor thought. He would have left a trace of his flight.

Just as Mentor moved to leave for the jungle again where

he could take flight and return home to the States, a child appeared from behind the wall of a small house near the jungle wall. He called Mentor's name.

Mentor halted, turned, and waited until the child came near. He inspected the boy and saw nothing distinctive about him. He was barefoot and dressed in poorly fitting dirty clothes. His face was small, with a pointed chin and a firm set to his lips. He appeared to be about twelve.

"It's me, Joseph," the child said in a low, sad tone of voice.

"Oh, no. Joseph?"

"I'm sorry, Mentor. I didn't know my old monk's body was on its last legs. I paid more attention to my prayers than to monitoring my health. I'd been in that old body so long . . . more than a hundred years. I just didn't notice. And now look at me. I've made one mistake too many." He spread his hands and looked down at his feet.

"I'm sorry too, Joseph. Upton's disappeared. He hasn't been found, not yet." Mentor hesitated before saying, "The child's body you possess—he died?"

Joseph nodded. "When I had to leave the monastery, I was disembodied for a while, panicking to find a new form. I was so afraid I wouldn't have time, I'd be lost and wandering forever, looking on while others lived out their lives. Only now do I know what ghosts suffer." He frowned and began to press his hands together as if from memory of prayer. "This child lay dying in that house you see behind me. I crept into the room and waited over in a corner, away from his parents. It didn't take long. The boy had been ill with malaria for months and the fever . . . took him. So far none of his relatives suspect I'm not him. They don't know he died."

Mentor could imagine the scene, and it made him want to lie down in a shady spot, shut off his mind, and rest his head on his arm. He wanted to be far away from the newly made vampire boy who was trapped now in the tiny body, destined to keep it until in some distant future all the organs failed, once again setting Joseph free. To spend a normal mortal lifetime in the arrested physical body of a child was a torment.

He was reminded of the child he had helped in Greece.

Separated from life, wandering in death, always a boy. And Dell's brother, Eddie, who had fled to South America.

"Don't feel bad for me," Joseph said, sensing his distress. "I'll soon ask my new parents to let me study with the monks. The pay they receive when I got to the monastery will compensate them enough I won't be missed at home. They have many children and not enough to feed them. I'll find . . . something . . . to do for the monks. I am, after all, still Joseph."

Mentor put a hand on the child's shoulder before turning away. He heard Joseph say, "I'm really sorry about Upton. I know it's my fault. I've been the only one who ever made a mistake around him. And now I've made the worst one of all."

Mentor shook his head slightly to let Joseph know he did not blame him. After all, he had kept the man prisoner for nineteen years. Glancing once more to Joseph, he plunged into the jungle, leaving the village and his old friend behind.

He must go home. He was doing no good here. He'd be told when or if anyone found Upton. He'd turn up, Mentor was sure of it. Probably sooner rather than later.

He sent word back to the monastery to his indispensable friend, Dolan. His frequent visits to Thailand were finally at an end.

2

Charles Upton moved through the night streets of Sydney, Australia, like a snake cautiously testing the air for scent of humans. It had taken him days to make his way out of Thailand. He could move swiftly along the ground, but he could not sail the skies as he knew other Predators were able to do. He had to rely on boats and the rails to get him away from the country. Once in Australia he migrated to the edge of the country and the bright lights of the metropolitan city. There he expected to find Predators who would listen to him, who would join his cause. He'd found only three in crowded Bangkok and was told that except for the monks, few vampire clans lived in Thailand.

It took weeks to seek out Sydney's strongest vampires. At first he thought Australia might be another country the vampires regarded as hostile, but eventually he began to sense the lone Predator stalking the city streets, and it was the loners he wanted most of all.

He stalked the first loner he found, following at his back in the shadows. Finally, sensing him, the Predator turned, scowling. "What do you want? Who are you to watch me this way?"

Charles came from the shadows, showing himself. "I'm your friend," he said. "Perhaps we could talk?"

They went to a wharf and perched on a piling side by side. Below them water slapped around the piling bottoms. Charles could smell the mingled scents of salt water, mussels, the slime of green growth on the slick pilings.

"All right, Friend," the Predator said. "What do you want to talk about?"

"Are you happy?" Charles asked. "Are you living the life of a god the way you rightfully should?"

The Predator laughed. "Happy? Am I supposed to be happy? Are *you* happy?"

"I will be," Charles said. "As soon as we rule the world. I can do that with your help and with the help of others like you. We're the same, you and I. We need more respect. We need power. Everything that belongs to us has been taken away. We need to take it back."

The Predator stared at him, then a ghost of a smile came over his face.

It took so little to charm the lost ones. He appealed to their buried feelings of discontent. He painted rosy futures where they would be rulers rather than skulking beasts.

Each night he found more. He went to them individually, calling himself Charlie, never speaking of his imprisonment or his connection to Mentor and the distant continent of the United States. Some asked in reply, "How else would we live, if not hidden, shrouded by the night?"

Charlie had a lot of suggestions for them. He spent long hours in deep philosophical discussions, carefully pointing out to his comrades how they hadn't tapped even a tenth of the possibilities an immortal existence offered. Why should they curb their natural Predator instincts just to keep order in the world? Whose order was it? The secret they shielded so determinedly was for the benefit of whom? Who cared, he asked, about mortals or how human civilizations prospered? Why should such majestic creatures hide from man's notice and conduct the boring and tedious business of blood banks and secret repositories when all they had to do was to let themselves prey, the way it was ordained by their nature? What leader in the dark past had ever decreed they must work in conjunction with mortals so that history never knew of the existence of the vampire?

There were a few Predators who turned aside Charles' offer. These Charles dispatched without warning. He fell upon them, slitting their throats with a knife and then ripping their heads from their bodies. He wanted no one reporting back to a clan about his entreaty to join him.

He knew some of his Predators were going to leak their thoughts enough that Mentor would pick up the change taking place in Australia. Charles didn't even care if Mentor knew it was him. He never told his followers where they were going. If Mentor came to Sydney to investigate,

Charles would simply flee, taking anyone he could with him. Once away from Sydney, he'd have his Predators shield their minds from Mentor's probes. This was something the first recruit taught him. They had been together only days when the other said, "You're wide open, a vampire transmitter."

"What do you mean?" Upton asked.

"Your mind. A vampire can feel it coming from miles away. Don't you ever shut down?"

It was explained to him what was meant. Charles discovered he could retreat with his thoughts deep into his mind and put up a block that kept others like himself from reading him. It made it wondrously easier to stalk enemies and it would help keep him safe from Mentor, too. It was the same trick old Joseph had used when he hadn't wanted to be bothered by Upton's intrusions in the monastery.

So much he hadn't known. So much. But he was free now, and the other Predators could teach him what he needed to know. Once he learned a trick, he was able to perfect it quickly.

Charles worked each night rushing through the Sydney streets, building his army. He'd give Mentor no time to find him or stop him. With diligence and cunning, Charlie, the Thai man with the large feet and the artistically gesturing hands—the foreigner with the dark, brooding eyes and regal presence—convinced many of his kind to join him in some far-off place where a whole new world order could be planned. His charisma was palpable. His words struck a chord in both the Predators who walked the fine edge of civility and those who in their hearts had always longed to be outlaws. Their ingrained timidity fled and the frustration they'd harbored for years found an outlet in Charlie, their new leader. They awaited his command, grouping in clusters around the great city, supernatural ears tuned for the instruction that would lead them on an exodus.

Once Charles made a mistake and approached a lone vampire on the streets who happened to be part of the hierarchy of the Predators in the city who supplied blood. When gently probed, the vampire seemed to be a loner, a renegade. Yet he had turned on Charles, speaking rapidly and with a hard tone. "I've heard someone was gathering the loners. What is it you're up to?"

Charles carefully concealed his plans for the future, and also his plan to murder this vampire who dared question him. "I'm harmless," he said instead, assuming a submissive manner. "I'm doing nothing wrong."

"Is it true you came from Thailand? Why did you leave there? What do you want with your own group of Predators?"

Charles hung his head like a scolded child, but all the time he was sidling closer to the other vampire. "I've been lonely, that's all," he lied.

The second he was within reach, he flew at the Predator and clasped his hands around his throat. He roared in his face, his mouth wide, his fangs exposed. Their battle lasted long minutes, for this was a powerful creature, one much older than Charles. At one point he thought he might be defeated, but their fierce engagement aroused the attention of other vampires in the area, luckily the same ones Charles had won over to his side. They joined with their leader and, together, they tore the enemy apart.

When it was over, Charles stood in the empty street, the torn body at his feet, and thought: *Mentor won't be hearing from this one, at least.*

After two weeks, the night came to take his motley crew of loners away from the city. Before morning dawned they would be elsewhere, having left the city for good. Until he had enough vampires to lead his crusade, they needed a secluded place where men wouldn't interfere with them. They must be a secret society until they could defeat Mentor and gather more Predators into their way of thinking.

Charlie paused in his walk and glanced up at the starry night. He felt as brilliant and invincible as the almond moon that rode across the sky. He wore a suit of black raw silk made by the finest European tailors and walked in the most supple and expensive leather shoes. He loved his new body and draped it in appropriate style. He hadn't yet gained control over the vast funds of his lost corporation, but money had been easy to come by. He simply took the cash and the credit cards from his victims, using them at the best boutiques in the shopping district. He feared no law enforcement in the world. As he told his followers: *There is no law. We make the law. Gods do not obey man's decrees.*

He'd almost finished his work in the city. He'd taken two victims tonight and was as flushed and pink as a cherub. He passed by Sydney's waterfront where great sailboats bobbed languorously in the slips. He spent time admiring the elegant lines of these spectacularly rich ships, their prominent brows, and their pristine hulls glistening from tiny lights strung along the pier. He walked down one long pier, his footsteps ringing softly as waves lapped beneath the pilings. It was almost time to take his apostles inland to an isolated, wild place where they could plot an uprising.

It would start in Australia and then move to the Americas. Once he had an army behind him, no one could stop him. Not Mentor or Ross, not any president, king, or premier. Military organizations with advanced weapons and warfare technology would be ineffectual against them. They would hide, they would strike in the night, and even the world's armies would not find them or be able to stop them.

You can't kill a dead man, he thought darkly, laughing to himself. *You can't even threaten a dead man.*

Charles turned around and retraced his steps. He'd researched the topography of Australia and decided where to take his Predators. They would go into the Blue Mountains just two hours inland from Sydney and the sea. In that inhospitable terrain of mountainous cliffs made of stone and ringed by thick forests, man would not detect them. Down in the valleys were small villages, surrounded by tall grasses, crocodiles, emus, and kangaroos. When his followers hungered, they would find ready prey. From the Blue Mountains, Charlie could make forays into the other cities and gather more Predators to his cause, bringing them together until there were enough to leave the country and invade other continents. Strength would lie in numbers. When he had a multitude at his command, they would advance on the States.

Lately he'd been getting telepathic messages from vampires in Europe, begging to join him. They were tired, they said, of living the genteel secret life. They wanted to rule, to destroy. They wanted to live free and unconstrained lives. No one, until now, had listened to their appeals. They felt like bugs pinned to corkboard, flapping their wings and crying for release. Charlie told them to come. Hurry. Delay not a moment.

They arrived daily, taken in by Charlie's groups and tutored in the plan of annihilation. Charlie went to meet each and every one, shaking their hands, putting an arm around their shoulders, and assuring them they'd made the right decision.

He also asked them, "Has Mentor heard of me? Have the vampire nations been talking of us?"

"No," they assured him. "We have been circumspect. No one has heard from Mentor, not a word."

Charlie expected the other Predators probably knew something was afoot. So many couldn't disappear from favorite hunting grounds and not be missed. He had some doubts about Mentor knowing, too, but it was all right as long as Mentor didn't find out where they were gathering. Charles realized he knew no fear now that he'd found so many who believed in him. If Mentor knew something was up, the information was surely too scattered for him to follow up. Charlie hadn't felt so free and powerful in all his eighty-eight years walking the Earth. He had procured the loyalty of the fiercest vampires he could find, vampires with excessive supernatural talent and murderous intent. They would protect him if Mentor tried to take him back to the monastery. No one would ever imprison him again.

*   *   *

Mentor spoke with Dolan of his worries.

"I think Charles Upton's gathering an army."

"Where is he? Let's go get him." Dolan had just finished bathing and now stood at the sink, combing his hair.

Mentor moved down the hall and knew Dolan followed at his back. "I'm not sure yet where he is."

"You don't know?"

"He's . . . I think he was in Europe. Maybe in Australia. All I'm getting are vague impressions. He's being careful. But he's contacting Predators."

"Are they going with him?"

Mentor stood before the dead fireplace, staring into the dark depths. "I think they are. I've spoken to the clans in the major cities overseas. They suspect a Predator is gathering the renegades. Everywhere they're missing, renegades from all over, some in Europe, some in Asia, others in

Australia. Charles must have them cloaking their minds. Once they do that, I can't pick up anything else."

"Should I go there to search him out?"

Mentor thought about it then shook his head. "You won't find him. He would have closed down all the channels."

"Damn!"

"It's all right. He can't stay hidden forever. If he's got a lot of renegade Predators with him, sooner or later one of them will slip up and I'll know where they are."

"He must be pretty good if you can't find him."

Mentor smiled. "You think I'm infallible, don't you? If I were, he wouldn't have gotten away to begin with. No, I'm afraid I fail, just like everyone else."

"Not like anyone else," Dolan said. "You're not like anyone I've ever known."

Mentor sent Dolan on an errand to calm the fears of a new vampire, a Natural, who had come into the vampire life only days before. Dolan had learned how to make his touch calm the ruffled spirit. Over the years he had grown until he was able to handle some of the pressing affairs that took so much of Mentor's time.

With Dolan out of the house, Mentor sent word to Ross to join him. An hour later Ross came through the door. He was agitated. "I had to leave a meeting. How can I run Upton's corporation if I have to keep leaving when you call for me?"

"You have David to handle it for you."

"Who do you think my meeting was with?"

Mentor gave him a dark look and Ross settled down. He took a seat on the sofa. "All right, what's this about Upton and an army?"

"I don't know for sure, but I think he's gathered quite a few to his side."

"Let's go bust him."

Mentor almost laughed. "You've been watching cop movies, haven't you?"

Ross shrugged. "Well? Why don't we? Where is he?"

"I don't know yet."

Ross stood up. "You don't know? You called me from a meeting to tell me you don't know how to find him? Then why am I here?"

"Ross, I've been picking up some communications overseas. Italy, England, and in Australia, too. Sydney. Upton's finding renegades to join him."

"Well, which is it? Which country is he in?"

"I can't pinpoint it. No one knows."

"If you figure out where he is, let me know. I'll go take care of him."

They spoke a while longer about Upton Enterprises and how to funnel the profits from them into different accounts. Ross took a good portion of these profits, but in deference to Mentor's wishes, and to keep the peace, he let some of it be used to support Craven houses.

When Ross left, Mentor caught himself pacing the house, worrying again. It hadn't helped much to unburden himself to Dolan and to Ross. The scant information he had just didn't give any of them enough to go on. But they all knew Upton was up to something. If they could only find him.

If they could only stop him in time.

* * *

They just kept coming.

Balthazar's assassins.

Dell had to take vacation time from her job to stay at home to watch for them. Some days her parents missed work, too, and stayed with Malachi on the ranch. Sometimes her uncles and aunts came, milling around the yard like dark crows in their muted clothes until she sent them away again, hoping the next hours would be quiet.

Now she sat in the living room with her son, her mind lost in thought. Malachi sat on the sofa, morose as he'd ever been, watching her. At eighteen he should have a mother nearing forty, a woman showing a little age and maturity. But his mother looked no older than he. She had died at seventeen, a year younger than he was right now, and since then she'd never aged a day. When she readied to go out of the house for work or shopping she wore makeup that disguised her youth, magically creating the mask of an older woman. Malachi's father was thirty-nine, his fortieth birthday coming up next week. He still looked younger than his age, but much older, of course, than Malachi's vampire mother.

Dell realized with a shock that one day her son would be as old as his dad and his mother would still look seventeen. She'd look like his daughter.

She couldn't imagine it. And worse, one day he would be an elderly man, humped over and shrunken, maybe bald, definitely wrinkled, and she would *still* be a girl.

She shook her head to clear it of the vision and Malachi noticed. "You'll have to tell me what you're thinking," she said, seeing he waited for her to speak.

She meant she wouldn't read his mind, because he hated it.

"Oh, it was nothing."

"Not true," she said. "It's these renegades. They're beginning to get to you."

He nodded. "It's them, too. How long do we keep killing vampires and burning them on the back forty?"

"We don't have a back forty."

He smiled. "It's just a stupid expression, Mom. The back *one hundred,* then."

"I don't know how long they'll keep coming. Mentor said he was going to try to talk to . . ."

"The silver wolf?"

"Balthazar. He's not a wolf, you know he isn't. It's just how he likes to appear in dreams."

"Balthazar." Malachi rolled the name around his tongue like a marble. "Balthazar is such a strange name."

"He was originally Turkish."

"In the time of the Huns, I guess."

"I don't really know," she said. "It's probable he's very old, but maybe not that old." She tried to smile.

"Mom . . ." He hesitated.

She had a feeling she wouldn't like what he might say. "Go ahead, say it," she said, as if she knew.

"I have to leave, you know that. They might hurt Dad. Or you. Or all of us. I can't take that chance."

He wouldn't look at her. She'd give him that Mother Frown, the disapproving look that could make him hunch his shoulders if he did and he probably knew it. She softened her gaze. "You don't have to," she said, her voice a little strained. "I told you Mentor will talk to Balthazar. He'll get him to stop this. I don't know why he's doing it. For years he left you alone."

"I don't think he'll stop."

Dell didn't think so either, but she'd never admit it. She would go herself to Balthazar if she had to. She'd make him leave them alone.

She and her son sat quietly for another hour, both lost in their thoughts, and then Ryan came indoors from the garage. She went with him to bed, leaving Malachi alone in the living room.

"Good night, son," Ryan called.

" 'Night, Dad."

Dell merely kissed him on the top of his head and wandered through the house to the bedroom, following her husband.

*   *   *

Malachi lay that night on top of his covers, his arms flung wide. He couldn't get comfortable. He couldn't be still. He kept turning and tossing, sleep out of the question. Just when he thought he'd be awake all night, he drifted off into a troubled sleep.

He woke at the sound of a muffled voice. He sat up in bed, the sheets gripped in his fists. "Mom? Dad?"

No one answered him. He left the bed and padded down the hall to his parents' bedroom. The door stood ajar. That was unusual. They always kept their door closed at night.

"Mom?"

When he opened the door, he saw the bed was empty. His heart lurched and he turned, hurrying down the dark hallway toward the center of the house. He knew they weren't there. The place was empty. He really had heard something, a voice, but now that voice was gone.

He found the back door open to the night. He stood on the threshold looking out at the land. There was no moon.

He breathed in deeply and smelled the scent of Predators.

"Mom!"

He sent out a signal of distress and alarm. His mother answered in his mind with a vision. She was running as fast as she could. Ahead of her, Predators fled with Malachi's father.

Malachi leaped from the threshold of the back door to

the ground, clearing the steps. He raced across the land that was open fields until he came to the edge of the woods where he knew his parents had gone.

He hurried through dense forest, flying past shadows of tree trunks and limbs overhead. He came upon his mother leaning over her knees. He caught her by the waist and swung her around to face him.

"Dad?"

"They took him. They were too fast. I couldn't catch them."

Malachi took off again, his mother's voice calling at his back. He moved like a laser through the woods. He couldn't let them hurt his dad. He was going to leave just so this would never happen.

He saw them ahead, silhouettes moving through the trees. Two vampires and his father. They had him by the arms and they weren't even touching the ground. Malachi screamed and they turned, snarling at him.

"He's ours, boy," one of the Predators said.

Malachi raced forward, both his fists blasting into the faces of the vampires holding his father. They dropped him, but came back strong to attack Malachi. He felt them on his back, dragging him down. Suddenly one was jerked off him so that he was able to turn and get his hands around the throat of the other. He saw his mother battling a vampire, the two of them falling and coming to their feet again to fly at one another.

Malachi knocked the Predator away and saw from the corner of his eye a small flame. He looked and saw his father lighting debris with his lighter. Where had he gotten the lighter? And then he remembered his father was dressed when he'd found him with the vampires. He must have been up in the house, unable to sleep, when they came. If the fire took . . . if it got big enough . . .

He fought on with the Predator, the woods filling with their death struggle. The fire caught and rose, licking up the bark of a pine, crackling as it caught the limbs on fire. Firelights danced all around, lighting up the woods.

Malachi caught hold of the Predator and threw him with all his force into the fire. His clothes caught flame and he went running away into the forest. A scream sounded, and

Malachi turned to see his mother had pushed the other Predator into the flames.

They all watched as he was consumed, twirling around, his arms out, his mouth open in a soundless scream.

When it was over, when the Predator was dead, Malachi put his arm around his father's shoulders. He could feel and smell his fear. He left him to help his mother put out the flames around the burning tree before the fire spread to the whole forest. Once they had the fire out, they walked together toward home. None of them spoke until they reached the house.

"That settles it," Malachi said. "I'm leaving. I have to."

"Why don't I leave?" his father asked. "I'm the one most vulnerable."

"You can't, Dad. I won't let you run. You have your vet practice and people depend on you. The vampires won't come here if I go."

"But, Malachi . . ." His mother saw his face and didn't finish her protest.

"You just don't change the mind of a fanatic. Balthazar's been dogging me since I was little. He'll keep sending them for me. There'll be more and more of them. They'll be stronger ones. Or he might end up coming himself. What if one of them catches Dad here alone or out riding his horse—kidnaps him when we're not around?"

Dell looked away. "I won't let that happen."

"You might not be able to stop it. Look what they did tonight."

She didn't reply, but her frown was answer enough. She felt guilt she hadn't been with Ryan to stop the attackers before they could seize him. She still wore her sleeping gown, a thin cotton slip with an embroidered top. She was dirty and her hair was wild.

"I'm just going to go until this is over," Malachi said.

"You need me," Dell said quietly.

"I'll be all right."

"You're my . . ."

"Son. That gives me your powers, or most of them. I'm not defenseless. Didn't I handle the last two?" He meant the two vampires who'd come as a team only days before. He'd gotten the machete and this time wielded it himself, his rage a frightening thing. He was like a tornado, spinning and striking deathblows with precision. No matter how fast the Predators moved, he stayed with them, backing them from the house into the yard and then across an entire acre, spinning and striking, the machete like a silver saw blade separating bone and flesh, tendon and muscles. When it was over, Malachi stood over his handiwork, not even breathing hard, the bloody machete hanging from his hand at his side.

His mother had approached him and touched his shoulder. He turned to her, his eyes blank and cold. He had killed, and it wasn't as traumatic as he'd thought it might be. He just felt empty, his emotions as quiet and removed as distant galaxies in the sky.

"You did fine. And tonight, too," Dell said. "But what if Balthazar sends more? Three, six, a dozen at once? You'll need me."

"I'll find a way to survive," he said. "Maybe I'll stop waiting for them and go to the source."

"No!" Her eyes widened, showing fear. "I mean, no, please, listen to me. You can't think of doing that, Malachi. Balthazar isn't at all like these . . . these things he's been sending to us. He's . . . he's . . ."

"I don't care, Mom. If this doesn't stop, I won't have any choice."

"Never do that without calling for me," she said, taking him by his arm. "Do you hear me? Never attempt something like that alone."

"All right."

"Promise me."

He promised. That night while his parents slept and he kept vigil in the living room he struggled to write a goodbye note. His mother knew as well as he did that he had to go. He had to lead the enemies away from his home, away from his father.

They wanted him, Malachi. They cared nothing for his parents. He'd lead them far away from the ranch, and he'd battle on alone. His mother had taught him many things over the past weeks. How to fight. How to move and feint. How to appear and disappear with rapid movement, creating confusion. And how to fight to the death, shutting out everything in the world but surviving the dance.

He didn't intend to die for a very long time. Once Mentor had told him that he would be as strong as any Predator one day. This was that day. He could take care of himself.

He would settle this eventually and return to enroll in college. He would propose to Danielle and marry her. He would have a normal life, just like anyone else. All he had to do was rid himself of this specter who had haunted him for too many years.

He stared at the blank page. He hardly knew what to say. He didn't yet know where he was going, except he must go far away. He would miss his parents, but he couldn't write that. He loved them more than anything, but he didn't know how to say it. He was sorry his mother was a vampire and he had inherited vampiric abilities. He wished the world was the way most mortals thought it to be—untouched by the supernatural. He dreaded sleep, his dreams stalked by Balthazar in the guise of a wolf. He wanted only peace, and yet he must employ violence.

Finally, he wrote none of what was in his heart, but just told them not to worry. He would be back one day. It wouldn't take long. He or Mentor or someone would make Balthazar stop this insanity.

He folded the paper into thirds and propped it on the dining room table. He bent to take up a small airline bag with his clothes in it. He had savings in the bank to draw upon, so he would be fine out in the world on his own. Since he was twelve, he'd raised calves for sale through a local 4-H program, all the profits going into his own account for college. It wouldn't take much to keep him while he worked out this problem.

He looked around the darkened house once more before turning for the front door. He had already called Danielle and tried to explain his leaving without alarming her.

"I'll wait," she said. "No matter how long it takes."

"I'll be back," he promised, whispering into the phone. "Just as soon as I can. I wish I could tell you what this is about, but I can't. One day, maybe . . ."

"Don't worry," she said. "Do you hear me, Malachi? Don't worry about me."

"Danielle?"

"Yes?"

"I love you, honey."

He didn't know about destiny. He didn't know anything for sure, not even if he'd be the victor against Balthazar's assaults. But he was willing to try. He had to *try*.

At the door he thought he felt his mother's intelligence gently reaching out to touch him, like a finger at his back. She did that at night sometimes, making sure he was safe. He did not turn or respond in any way to her probe. He would not be stopped.

He turned the knob and let himself out into the cool night. He kept still, taking in all the scents that reminded him of home. He would take these smells and this place with him in his heart until he could return to it. He could detect the horse manure in the riding path, hay bales in the barn made from rich Texas coastal grass, and oiled tack from the horse stalls. He could smell the midnight sweetness of the red-and-yellow trumpet flowers his mother called four o'clocks. Where they grew up a trellis near the house, intertwining vines with flashes of color, he could smell white roses with their hint of clove and red damask roses with their perfume of honey. He could smell cedar and hackberry, daylilies and blackberry flowers and yellow jasmine. In the distance he could see the leaning shadows of the split rail fence, the pale winding road that cut across the pastures to the back woods, the shiny metal cattle guard gate that met the highway.

This was his place, his Shangri-la. And he would return to it.

He stepped off the porch and turned away from the ranchland that was the only home he'd ever known. There was no point in lingering. He might change his mind. And he couldn't change his mind.

He meant to take a bus to Austin. From there, he didn't quite know what direction to head. Maybe West Texas, somewhere into those open dusty plains so reminiscent of the moon-washed landscapes of his dreams, there to meet the wolf. For he knew eventually Balthazar would tire of sending poor assassins and come himself.

Malachi must be ready to battle alone.

3

Balthazar chose the black volcanic island of Lanzarote in the Canary Islands as his home. It appealed to him because of its isolation, of course, but more so because of the four-mile deep caverns which bored down through the island. Lanzarote, covered with volcanic ash for centuries, was inhabited by descendants of a tribe called Guanche, who had come to the island in the fifteenth century. Since then Spain had owned the island, but the natives remained, intermarried with the Spanish invaders, and now hardly remembered their ancestors. Just eighty miles across the sea lay the African coast, but the sudden blasts of winds which swept Lanzarote came not from that emerald continent, but rather from the chain of islands called the Azores.

Three hundred volcanoes, the Mountains of Fire, had created Lanzarote, but now they'd been dormant for a century. The climate was so dry the people had to dig pits in the volcanic ash in order to grow grapevines. During the night they covered the depressions with plastic that helped condense the night air into precious droplets of water to feed the vines. From the grapes, the people made and exported wines that were as fragrant and full-flavored as any Parisian spirit.

The tunneling caverns had been made by volcanic action over many hundreds of years. Deep in the earth the caverns developed sheer drops and gaping chasms. In a few places there were small openings to the sky and in other places the darkness was deep enough that it spooked mortals so much they kept away.

They called the caves the Cueva Verdes, the Caves of the Green Man. The few tourists who visited Lanzarote were taken on brief camel rides lasting but fifteen minutes, and they were shown the white-washed buildings in the town, none of them more than four stories high. Most tourists left unimpressed and more than slightly depressed from spending time on such a black, infertile island where nothing flourished and the Azores' wind swept down with such suddenness it would snatch hats and glasses off the head.

Balthazar had lived in the very bottom of the Cueva Verdes for nearly a hundred years. At first he lived alone, creating a bone palace in the wide earthy depression he found. Taking victims not only from Lanzarote, but from the other Canary Islands, he would let the carcasses molder and decay, waiting for the death beetles to finish their grisly work of stripping the flesh from the bones. Once the skeletons were as clean as fine, spotless china, he fashioned chairs, a bed, sofas, and tables from the bones. He used the skulls, sitting upside down, to hold thick candles so that light poured from the empty sockets and gaping mouths. He was perfectly at home in his macabre palace, until his mind began to slip and betray him. It happened slowly, so slowly he hardly knew he was growing demented.

Mentor had come to this place once, seeking him out, sensing his mental health teetered toward madness. Mentor counseled him to leave his bone palace and come up from the caves into the light of the world. Ross would put him to work in the States. He could find a society of Predators who would take him in and keep him company.

Balthazar laughed and laughed, his maniacal laughter ringing over the domed roof of his cave. "What work would I care to do?" he asked. "Why would I want to subject myself to Ross, who cares about nothing but money and acquiring wealth and earthly goods? What use do I have for fine palaces and expensive baubles when I have *this*?" He then swept his arm around the room of skeletons and smiled broadly. He said, "What would I do with the company of other Predators?"

"These skeletons are . . ."

"They're what?" Balthazar asked. "Evidence of my misdeeds? And I suppose you never killed a single soul. You never drank the blood of an innocent. You, a Predator, never preyed."

He sent Mentor away, holding more critical comment from his acid tongue. He could have berated the old vampire in an even meaner way if he'd let himself go. After-

ward he sat in a bone chair that resembled a throne,
rubbing his palms along the smooth thigh bones that made
up the chair arms. He was meant to be alone, hidden miles
underground, didn't Mentor understand that?

These bones that made up his furniture held the memories of his hunts. They were the repositories of the mortal
souls that had once animated the living forms. The thigh
bones he caressed had belonged to a statuesque woman
from the African coast who had thought herself immune to
aging and to death. Like most mortals, she believed she
would live forever in her large house with her fine silks
and abundant food and servants who were at her beck and
call. When he'd taken her, she had fought like a wildcat,
clawing at his face and neck with long nails, shredding his
skin with her hands. He could still recall the taste of her
blood, the taste of her fear as she fought and died.

He had made a mausoleum of the dead to always remind
him of his place in the natural world. He was meant to
kill. His role was to take life without compunction, without
remorse, and he *loved* murder. He loved the stealthy hunt
where he stalked his victims. He loved the surprise in their
eyes, the taste of despair in their souls when they accepted
their doom at his hands.

If that meant his mind was warped beyond repair, fine.
Fine!

But then things got worse, and he finally realized Mentor
had seen in him something more than murder.

Many Predators walked alone, taking blood from mortals
at will, keeping apart from the clans. They weren't bothered unless they got very sloppy, the bloodletting so out of
hand the police grew suspicious. Then they risked not only
a visit from Mentor or another leader like him, but a visit
from a whole gang of Predators who gave an ultimatum.
Cease and desist or we'll send you into the wind from fire,
they would threaten. *We will not be found out,* they said,
because of your reckless thirst.

So it was not Balthazar's murders that pointed toward
madness. He was not taking too many mortals or taking
them too young. He was not leading authorities to search
for a beast who tore the throat and drained the blood. He
was a careful hunter, arranging his victims in a way that
made men think they died natural deaths, prompting no

autopsy. Even their puncture wounds were carefully healed over before Balthazar left them. It was not the victims, then, that Mentor and the others worried about.

It was his complete and utter separation from his kind. His solitude.

It was his cavern full of carefully styled bone furniture that flickered in the shadows of candlelight.

It was his obsessions with Malachi Major.

The isolation and the bones did not especially disturb Balthazar. Of course not. Or why would he make the Cueva Verdes his home? The vampire nations knew he was eccentric, so what? He was not like them. Who cared?

But when he began to believe he'd found the *dhampir* who would eradicate his kind and when, as the years passed, he grew into the firm conviction that his very future depended on killing that *dhampir,* he knew vampires like Mentor would think him truly out of his mind. They might try to stop him.

Why was he so convinced he had found the one *dhampir* who had been prophesied as the leader who would hunt the Predators? Because he had been graced with a vision.

It had come to him almost twenty years ago. On a winter night he lay in his bed fashioned from bones. The Azores' wind whistled around the mountains of Lanzarote, the openings into the caves singing with deep tones as that wind drove across the mountaintops. Balthazar dozed, reality fading in and out as he flirted with sleep. He was convinced the vision appeared when he was awake, but even if he'd fallen asleep, he believed the vision was prophetic.

His consciousness hovered above a city. The people on the ground in the streets ran around wildly, screaming. Vampires fought one another while humans fled the scenes of carnage, their minds incapable of witnessing the supernatural. Peering closer, Balthazar saw Malachi, the *dhampir,* at the head of a gang of vampires who were Naturals. He led a rebellion. One by one they sought out and found the Predators, setting them afire with torches. Burning Predators twirled like dervishes, screaming in agony. Balthazar knew the killers were Naturals and the victims Predators because the vision told him. The vision said to his mind, *A war. He leads them. Naturals are murdering Predators.*

In an incredibly old scroll found in a crumbling Belgium castle, it was written that a *dhampir* would be born who would change the world of the vampire. Studied by vampire scholars of the region, the scroll was determined to have been written by a seer of the Predator nations living in 900 AD. A ripple of unease went throughout the world, and vampires everywhere spoke of the scroll and the prophecy.

Now Balthazar believed that dead old seer, murdered by a nobleman soon after writing the scroll, had spoken to him from the other side of death. He had been granted a vision of the future.

It had definitely been Malachi. He was the one.

Balthazar went to the child in dreams and tested him. He found no malice toward vampires, so he did not act against the boy. Could he be wrong about him? When the boy's mother, Dell, came into the dreamworld and begged for mercy, making a promise to him, Balthazar decided to wait. He might be wrong. He could be wrong. He had once had a mother, too. He understood how evil it would be to steal away the life of a child if that child was innocent.

For years he monitored the boy and still never found the murderous intent he expected to find. It was all so curious. If Malachi was the villain from his vision, why could Balthazar find no indication in the child's heart? Once he'd even traveled halfway across the world and lured the child from his bed and into the woods. He thought he'd test him in person, in reality. If he found the evil he expected, he'd dispatch the boy right then. But the boy stood up to him. Both in dream and in reality. He was scared, he was terrified, actually, but he was brave and it was his bravery, finally, that convinced Balthazar to wait. Wait just a while longer. He left the woods. He let the child return to his mother.

It went on this way for years, his checking on the boy and then withdrawing. But the closer the boy came to adulthood, the more Balthazar believed he was a threat. For one thing, Malachi was stronger than other *dhampirs*. His supernatural inheritance from his mother surpassed what any *dhampir* had ever been granted. Malachi was almost a god. He was as impervious to wounds as any advanced Predator. He was as fleet as the fastest vampire.

His bodily strength was immense, his intelligence superior, his resolve unshakable. Surely only the best *dhampir* would be the chosen one.

It had to be him.

Balthazar castigated himself for having waited. It would have been simple to dispatch a child. Out of sentimentality, he'd waited, and now the *dhampir* had grown in ability to the point he would be hard to kill.

As a lone Predator, Balthazar thought he hadn't a chance of success. Mentor, who felt no fear of Malachi, knew about Balthazar's obsession with the *dhampir*. Mentor knew where Balthazar lived. He knew his preferred hunting grounds on the Canary Islands and the coast of Africa.

Over the years, then, Balthazar began to put a plan into play merely for his own protection. He gathered others to him, those lone vampires like him who refused to come into the natural world and live alongside man. If he had his own sect, Mentor and the others would be loath to attack him.

His first follower was a female Predator he'd found riding one of the camels among the tourists on Lanzarote. From deep in his cave he sensed her presence above him on the island and came out to see her. A vampire passing as a tourist. Too bizarre.

He hid behind volcanic outcroppings and watched from a distance, sending her a mental invitation to join him after the tour.

Her name was Sereny and she was from Italy. She'd been traveling many months disguised as a tourist, learning of the world out of boredom and some despair. She'd been alone a long time, he discovered when they met in his chamber and talked. She was not an extremely old vampire, but had gotten sick in her thirty-fifth year, the only one of her mortal family who had been so afflicted. She'd run away from them, afraid she'd be tempted to make them like her.

She had left behind a husband of eighteen years and four children she adored. Within twenty years of her disappearance her husband had died and in another thirty years, her children were dead, too. Bereft, she began to migrate from country to country, walking with tourists, living like humankind. Except at night when she hunted and fed. She was emotionally unattached and spent long hours every night contemplating suicide.

Now and then, she confessed, she stalked children. Not to kill them, but to kidnap them. She wanted her family back. She hadn't finished her mothering. She missed her past terribly.

"What do you do with kidnapped children?" Balthazar asked, puzzled. "Are they human children?"

She nodded, then continued speaking in her low, husky voice, "Human. Little children who weren't afraid of me. I'd take them away and keep them in a house outside of the cities where I found them. I'd . . . care for them." She sounded ashamed. "When they began to beg for their real mothers, I'd begin to feel so guilty I'd take them home again."

"How often have you done this?" he asked.

She shrugged. "Five times. Six. I never hurt them, not a bit. I fed them good food and cleaned them and played games."

"Then you took them home."

"Yes."

She told Balthazar all this, lounging on one of his bone sofas covered with thick brocade cushions and silken pillows. She was not at all astonished by his lair. It was as if nothing could touch her anymore, except perhaps children; nothing was important enough except playing at motherhood to lift her from the depths of her despair.

Balthazar commiserated with her, presenting an understanding, fatherly figure. She was but a half century old as a vampire and already lost unless someone rescued her. As she spoke in her low, husky voice, he rose from his chair and approached her. He reached out slowly, cupping her chin and lower face in his hand. He raised her face to his and said softly, "How long has it been since a man loved you?" When he'd said that, he didn't know what possessed him, what made him want her so badly.

Tears sprang to her eyes and she blinked at the red film of blood blinding her. He leaned down and kissed her lips. He kissed her cheeks, each in turn, ran his tongue along her cheeks, tasting the blood tears and finding them precious as rubies. He moved his kisses to an earlobe and down to her neck. He felt her body shiver and although he had come to her with selfish intent, hoping to seduce her to keep her with him, he suddenly wanted her to love him in return. He wanted her at his side forever. Without her, eternal life would truly be longer than he could ever hope to manage. No one had ever affected him this way.

He took her into his arms and carried her to his bed, placing her carefully on the soft goosedown mattress and stacked pillows. She wrapped her arms around his neck and whispered into his ear about how long it had been since she'd turned vampire and since her husband had touched her.

Balthazar ran his hands over her breasts and down her slim ribcage to her waist. He found her extremely exciting. Though approaching middle age when she changed, she was as svelte and luscious as a girl. Her flesh was firm and responsive to his touch. She arched her hips and he pressed down on her, burying his face in the crevice of her neck. She smelled of olive flowers and the bark of old trees. He wanted to drown himself in her.

He twined his hands now in her long dark hair and kissed her hard, taking her tongue into his mouth. They fed from one another and, finally, when their blood lust was satiated, they mated in an animal frenzy that would have been revolting to a human observer.

Sereny became his lover and faithful companion. She came to believe with him that Malachi was the *dhampir* prophesied by the seer as the one who would go against their kind and bring ruin to the Predators. With Sereny's help, Balthazar went into Spain, looking for other disgruntled or lonely vampires who would join them in the Cueva Verdes on Lanzarote. They found a few lost souls in the Azores, more on the African continent, and still more in Sereny's Italian homeland.

For fifteen years Balthazar and Sereny worked ceaselessly to gather a group large enough to implement their plans. Sereny did not stalk children during this time, nor did she speak of wanting to. He kept her as busy as possible, sending her out to recruit. It was very slow going and some nights Balthazar despaired, crying out with his arms flung heavenward.

Sereny always soothed him, taking him into her arms and placing his head upon her breast. "Listen to me," she would whisper. "After the *dhampir* is dead, we'll convince other Predators they should break way from the clans they belong to and join with us. We're all born into the unnatural world. We have no need for secrets and hiding. Let the mortals know they're just food for superior beings. Food for gods! Let the world belong to the vampire, not the mortal. Let the world end in death and blood, Balthazar. Let it die away in darkness."

Now, as the caves filled with his followers, Balthazar began to send emissaries out to kill the dangerous *dhampir* who would threaten all their futures. He had walked in the young man's dreams and was sure he was the one.

When, one by one, his minions failed their missions and never came back to the caves, never answering his telepathic queries, Balthazar raged how the prophecy was already coming true. No one could kill the boy. Why couldn't they kill him?

Sereny suggested he send out their people in pairs. If that didn't work, send them out by the dozen, send whole murderous groups. Surely a half-vampire could not defeat a dozen true vampires?

Balthazar neglected to tell her what he knew about this particular *dhampir*. How he was superior to other *dhampirs*. How it was going to be much harder to kill him than it might have if he hadn't waited so long.

While Balthazar struggled with all the politics of dealing with the hundreds of vampires he'd gathered, keeping them happy as they built lairs inside the deep caverns, he heard from a new follower about a very great vampire Predator who called himself Charlie. A totally simplistic and stupid name, it seemed to Balthazar, but then not every vampire wanted a powerful name.

Like Balthazar, this Charlie was gathering together the loners, the outcasts, and the eccentrics. Not only did Balthazar feel these Predators belonged to him, but it was said Charlie wanted to do the same thing Balthazar hoped to accomplish. He wasn't interested in the *dhampir,* Malachi, but he thought the Predators should disentangle themselves from the Naturals and Cravens, and take over the mortal world.

"Ask him to come here," Sereny advised. "We don't want more opposition, do we? Invite him to join us. Together, we'll be indomitable. His force combined with ours will be enough to begin the war. We won't have to wait any longer."

Balthazar thought it over. He shut himself away in a small dark tunnel where he retreated when he couldn't take contact with his followers any longer. He pulled a stone over the opening, lifting it as if it were a feather. All light was extinguished and the dark was deeper than any night.

After so many years of solitude he had been having a difficult time with all the voices and personalities vying for his attention. He needed to hide from his followers more and more often, shutting himself away in the tiny tunnel. He sat on the cold earth, knees up, his arms wrapped around them, and his head down.

Sereny was right, he finally admitted to himself. Charlie, whoever the hell he was, wasn't a threat. Charlie was a godsend. Together they could effect the change among the vampire clans that should have come long before now. All he had to do was convince him to join forces. And why wouldn't he?

Charlie was said to live in Australia's Blue Mountains. Balthazar would send Sereny to ask him for a parley on Lanzarote. He would sit him upon his most elegant bone-encrusted throne and talk reasonably of how together they could bring about the new order.

And if he refused, Balthazar would kill him.

It was as simple as that.

*   *   *

Mentor sat on Ross' patio in a violent green-and-purple-flowered lounge chair that would have given him a raging headache had he been mortal. "This is an extremely ugly patio set," he said. "Even your pool looks psychedelic with all those zigzag blue stripes painted on the bottom. Who's your decorator? For that matter, has you architect been prosecuted for lack of taste yet?"

"Did you come here to *in*sult or *con*sult?"

"All right. Let's get to it. Upton's still free. No one's talking. I can't find anything out about where he's gone."

"He'll surface."

"It might be too late when he does. We need to find him, Ross."

"Screw him."

"There's no call for that kind of talk. You know I don't like it."

"Screw you."

Mentor sighed. "Balthazar's got more than four hundred Predators in those caves of his now."

"Good for him. Do they all sleep on those monstrous bone beds?"

"What would it take to arouse you from this sick stupor, Ross?"

"I'm just relaxed."

"If you were any more relaxed, I'd have to get a shovel and cover you with dirt. I think you've been spending too much time opening up clinics and running corporations. You act like the chief of a reservation, everything you see, you own."

"What do you want me to do?"

Rather than answer him, Mentor said, "Balthazar ran Malachi off by sending so many assassins. We don't need innocent blood shed."

"I know that. The kid skedaddled. But he should have. Balthazar's insane."

"Certainly he's insane, but now he's caused trouble outside of his little island. He's got that kid on the run. Malachi's parents are frantic."

"You don't know where the boy went either? You're losing it, Mentor. I always thought you would one day."

"I *know* where he is. I'm keeping a watch on him as often as I can. That's not the point."

"What is the point, then?"

"The point is Malachi's running away isn't going to stop Balthazar."

"Then put Balthazar out of his misery."

"You forget he has a clan of his own now."

Ross raised his sunglasses and peered at Mentor perching uncomfortably on the lounge chair. "You can't handle that?"

"Why don't you quit being so impossible?"

"You need help, is that it?"

Mentor hung his hands between his knees and stared at his feet. "There's something else."

"What's that?"

"My sources tell me Balthazar's interested in joining with Upton."

"Screw that."

"Come on, Ross, cut it out. Be serious for once in your life. Don't you see where this is heading?"

"War. That's where it's headed."

"We can't have war," Mentor said carefully.

Ross sat up, ripping his sunglasses off his face. The muscles along his cheekbones tightened and his lips thinned as he grimaced in sudden fury. "Why not? Because some ancient, some ancestor of us all decreed it? Who was that, Mentor, can you tell me? Was it Moses, for Christ's sake? How far back were the rules made? How many hundreds or thousands of years have we mindlessly followed all the rules? Don't you know we're entering a whole new age? The world changes from day to day faster than it used to change in a twenty-year span. Time's speeding up. If Balthazar or Upton or both of them together bring war, then we'll go to war. That's all there is to it, Mentor. Face it, this is no longer the Old Days. Some of the Predators are as young in vampire years as small children. There are only a few of us as old as you and me. The mutation's spreading. There're more and more of us. How long did you think we could control it; how long could we hide out?"

"As long as we have to."

"No." Ross stood and threw the towel off his shoulders. He stood at the poolside in swimming trunks, his back to Mentor. In the bright sun he looked like a bronze god. He stood six feet six inches, his body as strong and toned as a professional athlete's. He wore his hair long to his shoulders. An errant breeze blew it away from his neck like a black sail. "No, we can't control it anymore, Mentor. Balthazar is only the beginning, Upton just a symptom. This has been coming for a long time. It's a miracle it never happened before now. The clans are too loose and disorganized. There are too many of us. A lot of Indians and not enough chiefs, as you put it. If it takes war, then . . . that's what it takes."

He turned to glare at Mentor. He said, "You'll have to

lead us. You need to prepare. I don't think you can stop this. All you can do is get ready."

"Christ." Mentor again looked down and now he shut his eyes.

"Screw him and the cloud he rode in on," Ross said and then he laughed. "What'd he ever do for us?" He turned and plunged into the pool.

Mentor stood and without looking at his host in the water, went through the house and let himself out the front door. Ross had an ugly mouth lately. He'd been watching too many gangster movies. And he was getting as moody and tense as everyone else Mentor had to deal with these days.

But Ross was probably right.

War was inevitable. The strange, indestructible tarot cards had predicted it. Upton's escape had signaled it. If someone didn't stop him, Balthazar would initiate it.

Was Ross right? Was it all getting out of hand? Were things changing so that the old rules didn't apply anymore?

Mentor walked down the long empty highway away from Ross' ranch house and turned his attention to Malachi. He was just an old man out for a walk. When people passed in their cars and SUVs and trucks, they waved to him and he waved back. He kept one wavelength open just for the boy, but he couldn't always monitor it. His intelligence had a boundary, his abilities a stopping point.

Dell had made him promise to watch over Malachi. He was her only child, probably the only one she'd ever have. It would tear her apart to lose him.

Mentor no more believed in the old prophecy that a *dhampir* would come to destroy the Predators than he believed there was a man in the moon. But if Balthazar and all his clan believed it, that's all it would take to make prophecy reality.

And isn't that how it usually worked, he asked himself? Someone predicts the future. And someone else makes sure that particular future comes to pass.

He touched Malachi's mind lightly and knew he was all right for now. Soon he wouldn't be. Balthazar would find him, just as Mentor had. Then all hell would break loose and Mentor knew he'd have to get there to protect the boy.

Would it precipitate war? Would Predators rise up and

fight one another because of his decision to protect an innocent *dhampir* from a mad and obsessed Balthazar?

He didn't want that. He dreaded it. He was too old in
both mortal body and vampire years to withstand the pain
and blood of extended battle. Every day he remembered
how old the body he inhabited was. He should find another
any day now. He didn't want to find himself suddenly
trapped in a dying body, as Joseph had in the monastery.

He wished, hoped, and prayed an upheaval would not
come. But if it did, if it couldn't be prevented, then as Ross
would say in his vernacular tongue: To hell with it.

Bring it on.

                    *   *   *

Malachi stayed only days in Austin. The western plains
called, and he answered by packing his small bag and leaving the rooming house where he'd hidden himself. None of
the assassin vampires had come for him since he'd left
home. Perhaps they'd given up. He hoped so.

He took a bus to El Paso, a city with a true Old West
feel to it. It sat on the edge of Texas and bordered Mexico.
At night the lights of the city stretched out like a sparkling
necklace of lights lying at the foot of dark mountains. Once
there he bought an old Yamaha motorcycle with dents in
the gas tank and black clotted grease along its silver chain.
He cleaned it up, tinkered with the old engine, and got it
in running order. He drove north out of the city, following
a highway that used to be the main artery west until super
freeways were built. Now travelers rarely used it.

He could see for miles in the empty distance, the sunlight
ricocheting off flinty stones embedded in dry mountain-
sides. Miles of speckled and patched tarmac rolled beneath
the bike's tires. It seemed this was the end of the Earth,
all human habitation having fled these dry, hot, sandy flats
between distant mountains. If Malachi squinted as he
drove, he was able to create mirages of water standing on
the road ahead.

In his imagination he could see history unfold across this
desolate land. As he raced his noisy little motorcycle down
the long road, he could see Plains Indians riding bareback
on their ponies, dressed in breechcloths of animal hide,

feathered arrows hoisted on their backs. He could see campfires, cattle drives, and wagon trains desperate to cross the valley floors to be free of the brooding bald mountains surrounding them.

This western land was indeed wild and lonely, the vegetation sparse, and the sun scorching. As inhospitable as it was, Malachi came to like it very much. It possessed a wild natural beauty that made him feel free. The farther he drove, the more he became part of the landscape of desert and sky. He might have been a tumbleweed rolling down the highway, lost in the clear golden light.

One of the reasons he liked it so much was because the landscape was so completely different from his ranch in Southeast Texas. There were no trees here, when they were abundant at home. There were no rivers or streams, when at home he couldn't ride a mile on his horse before coming upon water. Except for the dry mountains, there was nothing here to relieve the gaze from the long stretches of desert. He thought it amazing how Texas possessed so many varied landscapes, from desert to forest, from seashore to hill country.

A dot in the distance grew as Malachi raced toward it. The closer he got, the more curious he became. When close enough, he realized it was a house or a store with a large billboard. As he closed in, he could read the billboard above the ramshackle building, which he saw now was indeed a store or service station. Faded red lettering announced a rattlesnake farm. HOWARD'S RATTLESNAKE HAVEN, it read.

SEE THE DEADLIEST SNAKES ON EARTH.
RATTLESNAKE
SANDWICHES & DRIED RATTLERS FOR SALE.

Malachi smiled as he slowed the bike. Someone had a great sense of humor. Who would want to buy both a snake sandwich and a rattler as a souvenir all in the same place? Or in any place, for that matter?

In front of the building stood one ancient gas pump that appeared to still work. It had a red insignia of wings on a clear upper tank, the bottom being faded white paint spotted with rust. Malachi stopped beside it and pushed down the kickstand on the bike. Before he could lift the gas pump handle, an old man in worn, dusty overalls came from the shadowed porch and approached him.

"Howdy," he called, smiling like a fool. "You're lucky to find us. Not another gas station for a hundred miles any direction."

"Then I really am lucky," Malachi said. "I was nearing empty."

As Malachi pumped the gas, the old man leaned on the pump watching. "We've got cold soda pop inside," he said. "Only a quarter a can. I get cases of off-brands in the Walmart when I go to El Paso."

"That sounds fine to me." Malachi replaced the pump handle and screwed on the gas cap. "What about a place to wash up?"

"Oh, we got that, too. Running water and everything." The old man laughed as he sauntered back to the deep porch and a screen door there. He paused on the first step and Malachi stopped at his back, waiting to enter the little store.

"Dottie, you and Jeremy come on out," the old man called to his right.

Malachi looked and saw the flash of a little girl's blue dress before it disappeared behind the corner of the store.

"Dottie? Jeremy? You hear me now. We got a customer. Y'all come on out and show some manners."

Dottie was a child of nine or ten, thin, barefoot, wearing a blue dress made of some kind of shiny material. She looked like a little princess who had forgotten her slippers, for her feet were bare and dusty. Her hair was brushed and shining like spun gold as it cascaded around her face in thick curls. Her face was made up with pink lipstick, rouge on her cheeks like round red moons, and even mascara on her long lashes. A silver purse dangled from her arm. Behind her a boy appeared looking over her shoulder. He was the same age and wore a white T-shirt and overalls. He, too, was barefoot.

The two children came up another set of steps at the end of the porch, keeping their gazes down.

"Dottie, Jeremy, say hello to the nice young man. What's your name, son?"

"Malachi."

"Say hi to Malachi. See how it rhymes, hey? Say *hi* to Mala*chi*."

"Hi," the little girl said shyly.

"Hi," said the little boy.

"This sweet little gal and this big boy are my grand-babies. She's Dottie, he's Jeremy, and I'm Howard Clemmons. Come on in with us, kids. We're going to have a soda pop."

The children fell into line behind Malachi as they went through the screen door.

Inside more surprises waited. The darkness was broken by long cords holding tin-shaded lamps dangling from an open-beamed ceiling. Along one side of the big open room loomed a waist-high glass case. Inside were shadowy objects that drew Malachi to them. He put his hands on the glass countertop and leaned over, looking down inside at boxes of rattlesnake tails lying on squares of cotton. Farther down the case he saw carefully constructed rattlesnake skeletons held by steel pins attached to pieces of driftwood.

"I got the live ones back there." Howard pointed to the back of the room.

"Thanks, but I like to steer clear of rattlesnakes. We had them around our ranch every spring. I don't much like them."

"Not like them? Why, the rattlesnake's the King of Texas, don't you know that? They been here longer than the Apache. They're God's only creature really equipped to live in the desert. We're just strangers here. The rattlers, now, they're the ones own the land."

"I can't dispute that."

"They sing."

Malachi turned around to the little girl who had spoken. He wasn't sure he'd understood her, she spoke so low. "What?"

"They sing. The rattlesnakes."

The old man said, "She means when they rattle their tails. It sounds like a song."

Malachi shook his head. What a weird family. Singing rattlesnakes. Oh, man. But what did he expect to find out here in the middle of a desert? The old man and little kids were so isolated they probably made up stories for one another just to stay sane.

"Uh, how much do I owe you for the gas?"

"Here, have a cold soda pop first. We don't get many travelers. You're not in a hurry, are you?"

Malachi didn't know how it happened, but after sharing Cokes with the old man and the children, the four of them sitting around a square table covered with slick red oilcloth, the gloom of the shadowed store drying his sweat, he started talking about where he'd come from. East Texas was like a foreign country when compared to West Texas. The old man had never been east of El Paso. East Texas piney woods was like a fable to him. Trees and whole forests growing in Texas sounded like a lie God made up to entice folks away from the west, he told Malachi.

"Not only have I never been across Texas, but I ain't been any farther west neither. I hear there's rain forests up in Washington State and streams so clear you can reach out and touch fat, sassy bass in Colorado, but all I know is my place here. That's why it suits me. That's why the King Rattlers let me stay. I was born and raised and guess I'll die and get buried right out back behind the store when my time comes."

"You can't ever die," Jeremy said, his face serious as a car wreck.

"Oh, no, uh-uh, not for a long, long time. Don't you fret about that, boy."

"What happened to their folks?" Malachi asked, chugging down the cold Coke.

"Their momma was my girl, Sherry Ann. She left here with a Marine who came one day for gas, just like you. Sherry Ann had been telling me she was going with the first available looker stopped in. She wasn't lying. Bill—that was his name—Bill gave her a smile and a wink and off she went, everything she owned already packed in her ma's old suitcase. She didn't come back until over a year later, tiny little Dottie and Jeremy in her arms. They're twins." The old man smiled indulgently at his grandchildren. "Dottie's five minutes older, aren't you, Sugar?" He waited for the little girl to smile and nod before he continued. "Not long after Sherry Ann was home, she got sick. I drove her all the way to El Paso to a doctor, but they said it was too late. She had septa . . . septa . . . ."

"Septicemia," Jeremy said, pronouncing the word carefully. "Poison in her blood."

"That's it! Septicemia. Jeremy here is a smart kid. Anyway, they said she hadn't never healed right inside her from the cesarean she had when the twins were born.

"So it's been me and these two scamps ever since."

"Don't you ever get lonely out here?" Malachi asked. He thought he'd go batty living such an isolated existence.

"Let me show you something." The old man stood and Malachi followed him to the back of the store and through a door into a darker room. He could make out a full-size bed with an old metal frame and a doorway leading into another bedroom farther back in the darkness. On the other side of the living quarters was a small, apartment-size gas stove, a sink and drainboard, and next to it, a yellowed refrigerator. There was a sagging sofa and two cane-bottom chairs facing a TV on a metal cart.

"Come on." The old man gestured him across the room to a back door leading outside.

Malachi stepped into the sunshine and had to wait a moment for his vision to adjust. A dozen steps beyond the door sat wire cages on wooden frames. Hundreds of cages. They stretched the length of the store building and behind them were three more rows of cages. All filled with snakes. Big, little, and gigantic snakes. Rattlers lay like languid scarves across bottom wire, other rattlers were curled so tight their heads had disappeared, and many of the snakes slid like dreams across one another in silky, smooth, gliding motions.

"Jesus," Malachi said. "That's a lot of snakes. I've never seen so many snakes."

"I breed 'em," the old man said proudly. "I milk 'em, too. For the venom. There's this lab in El Paso pays me high dollar for that stuff. It's more precious than gold. As you might guess, we don't get too many customers." He laughed in a jolly way that made Malachi grin.

He walked behind the old man as they passed behind the first row of standing cages and into the second. When they reached the last row Malachi thought his skin was actually shriveling from the creepy feeling brought on by so many rattlesnakes.

Then he saw they'd come to the front of a small cabin. It seemed to be one room, with a shake-wood roof and a barn-wood door.

The old man turned to him. "You may be a drifter, I can't tell. I don't know you, I admit that. But if you're just looking for a place to wait something out, this is it. I've rented this little cabin out before. I don't ask much for it 'cause it ain't worth much. You can eat with us. I always cook more than we can eat anyway."

"Why would you take in a stranger?"

"Well, son, there's people come by here and they don't know where they're heading. You can see it in their eyes. You can tell how they hold themselves kind of stiff, like they might break into a thousand pieces if they move too fast. And they wouldn't even be on this highway if they really knew where they wanted to go. Why they'd be taking the freeways and bypassing this place. People who come here need a little time to get all straightened out where nobody's gonna bother them. It seems to me you got that look. You can stay, if you need to. 'Course, nobody's gonna twist your arm," he added.

Malachi was astonished the old man had sensed exactly what he needed. He couldn't keep driving across the country. He had to stop somewhere and this was as good a place as any. He didn't think anyone would ever find him here. It wasn't a main highway. Hell, it wasn't even a minor highway. More like a lost one. He bet not more than two vehicles a day passed by.

But the cages of rattlesnakes made him hesitate. He didn't have a phobia about snakes, but he wasn't enamored of them either. Rattlers were like cold alien things that went where they wanted and killed anything in the way. They could swallow a rabbit whole, their jaws opening incredibly wide. They were swift and, when they were as large as some of these were, they were deadly, able to cause a man's heart to stop dead under a minute after a strike. Though they couldn't kill him if he were able to heal himself of the poison's toxin fast enough, he still didn't like them at all.

"Well, that sounds like a good offer," Malachi said, eyeing the snakes. "But these things don't get out of these cages, do they? I mean, they're pretty close to the cabin."

The old man laughed and struck him on the back, guiding him to the door of the little house. "They won't hurt you none, son." He laughed again. "That rhymes, hey? None? Son?"

An hour later, after he'd showered the road dust off himself, Malachi stored his bag in the cabin and walked a wide circle around the rattlesnake cages to the store. He'd paid for a week, the old man charging him just twenty dollars. He thought he could hang out a while, no problem. He liked the old man with his silly rhymes and the serious little twins with their sad eyes and silent ways. People who lived so alone seemed strange at first, but while in the cabin cleaning up, he had listened in to their conversation about him. They were in the store, at the red table. Malachi's hearing was so sensitive he could pick up their voices through the walls of the cabin, the walls of the store, and across the distance, even while shower water sprayed over his head.

The old man said to the children, "He's in some trouble or other. We got to help him."

"He's not a bad man," Dottie said.

"No, he's not. He's just a boy. He needs a place to stay a while. We'll treat him right and take care of him good as we can, and maybe he'll go back to his momma and daddy then."

"He can read my mind," Jeremy said.

The old man guffawed. "He can't do no such thing, Jeremy."

"I think he can."

"Come sit in Grandpa's lap," Howard said. "You just need a big ole hug."

"I love you, Grandpa," Dottie said, joining her brother in Howard's generous lap.

There was a small silence, and Malachi turned off the water to listen for the old man's response. When it came, it was a loving, fatherly voice.

He said, "I love you more, Sugar. I love you more than the moon."

4

Charles Upton had formed his own clan. They lived atop a stony plateau where a narrow white-water stream fell off the cliff two hundred feet to a tree-circled pond. The Australian Blue Mountains had opened their arms to him and to his followers. They couldn't have all come together in a city. Even if they'd taken over a large building, some nosy human would have come sneaking around, inquisitive about them.

Once in the mountains, the Predator's were dispatched for supplies, each bringing with him a load of new material for creating small geodesic-domed shelters. They were made of lightweight panels, but proved strong enough to withstand the wind and rain. Most vampires were used to creature comforts of some sort, and living openly in the wild wasn't something many of them would have liked.

To keep the area manageable, the Predators lived two and three in each shelter. At night they gathered around bonfires, the flickering shadows transforming them into silent and ghostly apparitions.

Below them in the valleys lay scattered small villages where the Predators fed, careful not to take too many victims. Some complained they were starving; they had never had such poor pickings. But Charlie made it a strict rule there should be as few deaths as possible so as not to arouse the populace. Any Predator who could not comply would be banished. "Take the wildlife," he said. "No one will miss a kangaroo."

However, few Australians ventured into the mountains once the vampires came. Anyone who approached was taken down or turned away, their minds disoriented as they stumbled down the mountain paths back to the villages.

Rumors abounded, frightening the villagers so that even the courageous feared walking up the slopes after sunset.

More and more vampires gathered, sent for by "Charlie" and promised the world. They were getting anxious now, coming to Upton too often to ask about his plans. When were they going to be allowed to kill the Cravens? Oh, they wanted to kill them, they abhorred them, why must they wait? When could they take control?

When they pressed him too much, Upton could feel the bones of his face melting and rearranging. It always put his petitioners on edge. Since he'd become a jaguar in the jungles of Thailand when he'd escaped the monastery, he had felt more and more compelled to change his head into that of a feral cat.

Who said he must look like a man? When his emotions raged, he let his face go all liquid and then reform like soft putty. His cheekbones rose. His chin receded. His nose pushed out from his face into a snout. His eyes changed to an elliptical shape and became amber with fiery red pupils. His forehead slicked back into his black hair and his teeth, all of them, sharpened to diamond points.

Finally, Upton stopped performing the trick for the followers who harassed him and began to let the cat features of his face remain once the petitioners left his central dome shelter. He looked at himself in a hand mirror and grinned like the Cheshire cat. He could still be thought a man, but one who was deformed, or maybe one whose face had been misshapen in an accident and fixed badly.

He knew what his clan said of this transformation. That he was truly deranged. That he might not be able to deliver what he'd promised. If he wanted to be a jaguar, why, what other manner of weirdness would he want and how would it affect their future they'd so hastily placed into his hands?

He called them together one night under a new moon. He stood before the bonfire so that his face was cast in shadow. "If I frighten you," he shouted, "you need to leave here. You need to return to your solitary haunts, living depraved lives on city back streets and alleys. If I can put the fear of God into you simply because I choose to be part animal, then what possible need have I of you? I will tear you apart with these teeth and drink you dry! Bring me the weaklings!"

None stepped forward. Some cowered, and Upton took notice which ones feared him most. That night after the clan had settled in uneasily, he went around to the ones who might betray him one day because of their cowardice. He brought with him a bejeweled scimitar he had procured before leaving Thailand. The deaths were not easy, nor were they prolonged. One by one, in utter silence, the weaklings struggled against their attacker until they succumbed, their blood left on Upton's long rough tongue.

When the killing was finished, Upton's shrill cat cry thundered out over the clan and rang off the stony plateau. No more would they mock him or speak of his eccentricity in whispers. A few deserted him the next day, slipping from the camp and making their way through the long valleys and back to the port in Sydney. The ones who were left were his kind and devoted to him. They looked on his deformed face and smiled. They went in search of other Predators to replace the missing and the dead, vowing their allegiance to Charlie, Jaguar Charlie, Cat Charlie, the greatest Predator they had ever known.

He kept the cat face permanently after that. He let go of all semblance of a human face. It made him happy to scare the life from his victims even before he ever touched them with his dripping fangs. His power grew and his supernatural abilities increased by substantial leaps. It was as if by letting go, by embracing his true self, he was more vampire than ever, more truly the creature he had always hoped to be.

By the time Balthazar sent Sereny to him, Charlie had more than two hundred and fifty followers. The plateau was crowded with shelters, and at night the many bonfires lit up the sky like an erupting volcano. Villagers in the valleys pointed to the Blue Mountains and the faint yellow light there. They cringed behind closed and locked doors. Whole communities packed their things and left their homes, heading for anywhere but the mountains. They went on foot, on donkey, crowded together in rusting buses and broken-down cars.

Upton knew of the exodus and didn't care. He would leave the Blue Mountains before anyone came to investigate. He would take the battle to the enemy. It would begin on American soil before spreading throughout the world, and the destruction of Mentor would be his first victory.

He knew before Sereny said a word why she had come. He silently rejoiced, shielding his emotions from her. He had heard of Balthazar and his caves. He had heard stories of Balthazar's underground bone palaces and crypts. He thought these things were an extravagant and ostentatious display of evil, yet pleasing to the mind, like the remembrance of rich chocolate melting on the tongue. A Predator should live and *look* just as he pleased.

It seemed to Charlie that the great Predator in Lanzarote would make a fine commander in Upton's army. He could be his right-hand man if he was not too proud to take a secondary position of power. On the other hand, if he wanted to give Charlie orders, there would be no joint endeavors whatsoever. Charles Upton had built a billion dollar conglomerate through sheer cunning and intelligence. He hadn't taken orders from anyone since he was a child. Not even the monks.

Upon being brought to him once she climbed the high cliff to his lair, Sereny paused a long time at the door staring in at him. He sat on a woven grass mat, his legs crossed before him. A mellow light from the overhead sun suffused the dome so that the panels glowed around him like a burning orb. He looked like Buddha in the center of a golden altar except for his inhuman face. He stared back at her, his oddly shaped eyes sleepy and amused. His lips pulled back and revealed two rows of fangs. He spoke in a slow, seductive voice. "What is it you want with me, dear woman?"

Sereny feared him. He could see it in her face, feel it radiating from her body. It was a good sign. Had she not been full of natural fear, he might have been tempted to reach out and take her by the throat, slitting the artery with one long fingernail.

She took a tentative step inside the glowing dome and sat down before him, crossing her legs in imitation of him, her hands lying in her lap with the palms up. She was a beautiful woman, Charlie thought, her hair long and so lustrous it seemed to carry the sunlight indoors with her. She had fine, keen eyes and lips as red as the juice of a pomegranate. She had not been a young woman when she became vampire, he could see that, but over the years her face and body had responded well to a diet of fresh, young blood. She was flushed with health, her skin radiant.

Charlie reached out one hand and stroked her cheek. "You belong to Balthazar. He's a lucky man."

She turned her head into his palm and pressed her lips against his flesh there, surprising him. All her fear had fled and she turned doting eyes on him. "Will you come with me and meet with him?" she asked.

"I think I would go with you into hell if you asked," he said, almost meaning it. He spread out his arms and she came into them as naturally as if they'd been together as a couple for a hundred years.

That night they mated over and over and over again, Charlie crying out with each orgasmic release like an alley cat with a bitch in heat. When morning came, they stepped outside of Charlie's small domed shelter and there stood before them all of the Predators, waiting, knowing they had been summoned.

"Take down every shelter and burn all evidence of our life here," Charlie said, his arm around the waist of the woman. "We're going with her to Balthazar. We're going to join together with his clan and then we're going to war."

Shouts rose up and the vampires raced one another to tear down the temporary structures while others built up several fires on the plateau in which to burn all indication of their habitations. The sky filled with smoke; it filled with wild laughter and gleeful dancing.

Charlie stood by, fully satisfied, his cat face turned sharply into the blowing wind, Sereny at his side.

His mind slipped away from the chaotic scene and found a pivotal moment from his past. He was fourteen and visiting home from his private school in Connecticut. He hadn't thought of his youth in years, and the memory pleased him.

His parents lived in the exclusive River Oaks section of Houston, Texas, but it seemed to him they'd sent him as far from home for schooling as they could manage, into a prep school in Virginia. He had not developed the dread porphyria yet, so he was not ill or deformed. He was, however, a willful, impertinent child, his intelligence probing and intuitive. He made his parents nervous. He asked questions that revealed hidden truths, picking holes in deception. He was so full of disdain for adults, none of them had a chance to like him. But, of course, he didn't know that. He never really understood why adults were so uneasy around him.

He sat at the breakfast table with his mother during summer vacation. His father had already left for the office. His mother, a society maiden who had brought money to the marriage, had little use for her only son and didn't bother to hide her feelings.

Charles decided to tear away her polite mask so he could see the mother monster beneath. He had known it was there from a young age. Today he was determined to force it into the open. "You don't even like me, do you?" he asked.

His mother put down the society page of the newspaper and smoothed it carefully. "What would make you ask such a horrible thing, Charles? Where have you learned such beastly manners?"

"Oh, stop sounding like a damned Brit. You were born and raised in Texas, who do you think you're kidding? And you're evading the question. You don't like me. Father doesn't trust me. The fact is, I know you both think I'm a mistake and you wish you'd never bred. You must have done it because it was expected of you. All that money . . . and no one to spend it on but your silly selves. You didn't want to appear *too* self-centered. But you know what, Mother? I don't care. Do you understand? I don't care that my parents hate me. It frees me from having to pretend I love you back."

His mother stood from the table, keeping her gaze from him. He could see he'd hit a raw nerve, which was always what happened when he scraped down to the nugget of hideous truth. "This is a stupid conversation. You're being too ugly. I have shopping to do."

Charles stood abruptly, flinging aside his napkin and with the other hand sweeping his place setting to shatter on the polished marble floor of the dining room. A servant ran in to see about the commotion, and his mother waved the girl away. "Leave it," she said.

She turned to her son. He saw real fury in her eyes for

the first time in his life. Mostly she presented a stolid and brittle exterior. She was not simply a cold woman. She was an ice floe.

"Those dishes were imported. They cost more than one semester of your school. I do not appreciate your destructive nature, Charles. Please contain your temper tantrums until you're outdoors where you can set fire to forests or . . . or . . . run a motorboat into a bridge piling."

"You'd like that, wouldn't you, Mother? You'd like to see me put into prison or drowned in a boating accident. Well, guess what, it's not going to happen. I'm going to be valedictorian. Did you know that? I'm smarter than anyone in that fancy prep school you sent me to. I'm going to Yale. I'm going to inherit your money, Mother, and I'll turn it into a great fortune. You'll be rotting in your grave and I'll be stomping the ground, singing Hallelujah, the bitch is dead, thank God, the bitch is dead."

He had been going for the throat and saw he'd succeeded. Her expression crumpled just shy of a fit of weeping. But he knew even her tears were crocodile, for her heart was stony flint.

Steel came into her demeanor. She said, "Not if we change our will, Charles. If you persist in this type of behavior, I assure you not one penny of our money will be left to you. I'll give it to the Salvation Army before I give it to you, you ungrateful little bastard."

Then she stomped from the room and that was the last time he saw her. She never had the chance to carry through with her threat to disinherit him. Later that evening she met with her husband to tell him of their argument. As they drove from a parking garage at a downtown hotel where they'd dined on salmon with wine sauce, a speeding Ford Explorer ran a red light and slammed into the side of their Mercedes, sending the couple into the arms of death.

Charles was taken in by his paternal grandfather who died in his bed one night just when Charles was about to go off to Yale. Charles took a sixty-million-dollar inheritance and within ten years turned it into six hundred million. Before he was thirty-five, he owned the world's largest shipping company and controlled two major Texas oil companies. He shipped oil around the world in monster tankers. The money rolled in until it was impossible to say just exactly how much Upton was worth, but it was safe to say he was a billionaire.

It was that day, though, the showdown day with his mother, the day she threatened him and died for it, when he knew he didn't give a fig for other people. If they served him well, he let them alone. If they got in his way, he savagely ruined them.

And if they threatened him, as his mother had done that morning, he hired a suicidal maniac with an extreme coke habit to ram a Ford Explorer straight into the side of a Mercedes.

*   *   *

Charles sent his followers in small groups into the other Canary Islands outside of Lanzarote to reconnoiter areas ripe for taking victims. For his first meeting with Balthazar he wanted to be alone.

He was surprised when Sereny came with him and stayed at his side. She took him first to a small opening in one of the island's volcanoes and told him this was where they'd enter the caves. Using their supernatural ability to defy gravity—an ability that now came as naturally to Charles as breathing to a human, because of the time he'd spent practicing in Australia—they floated through the black volcanic rock opening into a narrow passage that plunged straight down for two miles. Descending into the darkness, smelling the close, pungent scent of damp clay walls so close he could reach out and touch them, Charles thought of Stoker, and Dracula's coffin filled with earth taken from his homeland. How could Balthazar enjoy living like this?

The sun was shut out, the opening above them dwindling to a pinpoint of distant light like a faraway moon over a dark planet. The air grew heavy with moisture. The darkness turned to a chill slab of black so dense nothing could be seen with the mortal eye. Had he not been vampire, Charles would not have been able to maneuver.

After the descent, Sereny gestured him down a winding horizontal passage lit with lanterns. It seemed this labyrinth went on forever and that it was on an incline, so they were still burrowing deeper and deeper underground. Finally they came to Balthazar's lair beneath the island. An arch served as an entryway. Burning torches stood sentinel. The arch opened into a cavernous room roofed with stalagmites, some of which were as large around as tree trunks where they were attached to the ceiling. This gave the whole chamber a sense of impending disaster and for some minutes Charles fought against hunching his shoulders and glancing at the tall ceiling.

The room was furnished, as Charles had been told, with bone furniture. It was obviously an act of contrition for murder, though he was sure Balthazar didn't understand that. The bones were reminders of his sins. Or, on the other hand, reminders of his pleasures.

There were chairs, sofas, tables, shelves, all of them made with human skeletons. Here and there a skull sat peering in accusation out into the smoky gloom, while in other skulls, used like saucers, candles burned, giving off the stink of paraffin. Near the wall stood Balthazar, his back to them. He filled three silver goblets with blood from a glass pitcher whose contents gleamed like a ruby in the lamplight. He handed each of them a goblet and said, "I'm glad you came."

Charles thought Balthazar a handsome vampire in a wild, untamed way. He had strong features, almost rough, as if his ancestral line had been nearer Neanderthal than modern Turk. Yet his eyes were remarkable—blue as the ocean that surrounded Lanzarote and as clear. His lips were finely sculpted and full, with a deep indentation in the center of the lower one. He was tall and trim, his shoulders wide and hips narrow. He wore expensively tailored black silk slacks and shirt. The cloth draped his frame to give him a nonchalant elegance. Were it not for the paleness of his skin, he could have passed for a craggy prince.

On his right hand he wore a ring of gold holding a large sapphire with diamonds flanking it. The unusual sapphire caught the torchlight and shimmered like a chip of dark blue flame when Balthazar gestured with his hand.

Sereny stood at Charles' side when they first took the drinks, but now she moved toward Balthazar. She wrapped a languid arm around his neck, pulling his face down to hers where she kissed him for a long time, her eyes closed, her thick lashes lying like dark butterflies on her white cheeks.

Charles expected no less, but couldn't help feeling a twinge of jealousy. He had coupled with Sereny so many times in one night that he had tricked himself into believing she might belong to him. She did not, of course. She was Balthazar's partner. He didn't suspect Sereny used sensuality to persuade him to join forces with Balthazar. He suspected Sereny loved the one she was with. And now that they were back in Lanzarote, she was with Balthazar.

Sereny unwrapped herself from Balthazar's embrace and took a seat on a sofa covered with cushions made of ivory brocade. She smiled over at Charles as if to say, *You see how I am? No one owns me for long.*

"How can we help one another?" Charles asked his host.

"Sit down. We'll relax and drink together." Balthazar sat next to Sereny and watched Charles with immense blue eyes that had turned piercing. Charles realized he'd known immediately his woman had coupled with him. Balthazar surely wasn't surprised, but he was also not happy about it.

Charles took a chair opposite them. He sipped at the blood that even now was coagulating and creating a rim along the inside of the glass. It was disgusting. He only drank it so as not to appear discourteous.

"How many Predators have you gathered?" Balthazar asked.

"Around two hundred and fifty. And you?"

"Four hundred and fifty."

"We're not a great army," Charles said, "but there would be enough of us to begin changing things."

"I agree. If we move as one, we can be as powerful as an iron fist. So what's your thought on our first move?"

"I'd like to go to America. There are two Predators in Texas who had dealt me a terrible wrong."

"They imprisoned you."

"Yes. For years."

"And they should be punished," Balthazar agreed. "I know who you mean. Mentor and Ross. And I have a problem in Texas, too."

"You do?" Charles was suddenly afraid Balthazar wouldn't go along with his plans. He had his own agenda.

"Yes, I do. There's a *dhampir* . . ."

"Excuse me, what's a *dhampir*?"

"They're half-breeds, half vampire, half human, born

from that ungodly union. Not many of them live beyond infancy. The ones who do are usually outcast and never taught how to use their vampire abilities. But this one I speak of is eighteen and strong. He's also an adept fighter with enhanced physical senses. He's the one the prophecy said would come and help destroy many Predators. I want him killed."

Prophecy? What on Earth did Balthazar mean? Also, Charles didn't understand the problem of doing away with the nuisance, no matter how enhanced the *dhampir*'s abilities. "Then just send someone and . . ."

Balthazar raised one had to interrupt him. "I've sent twenty-six of my clan."

"And that many couldn't kill the *dhampir*?"

"They didn't go as a group. That's where I made my mistake. I sent them one at a time for a while, and then in pairs. The *dhampir*'s mother did away with most of them. She's a very powerful Natural and her mother instinct is resolute."

"Send a group, then."

"I've just done that. The boy left his home and is away from his mother's protection. I sent eight of my men today. They've found where he's hidden."

"That should solve your problem," Charles said. "If not, we can all go and take care of him, along with Mentor and Ross—the two Predators I owe my revenge."

"It's Mentor who imprisoned you?"

Charles nodded. "And Ross who made me."

Balthazar sat quietly, deep in thought. He said finally, lifting his gaze to Charles, "Mentor won't be easy. He's well liked, and many of our kind would come to his aid. Ross, on the other hand, is universally hated. He's arrogant, abusive, and domineering. If we were to attack these two Predators, it would have to be a sudden strike. But we have another problem."

"What is that?" Charles was growing weary with Balthazar's mounting problems. What was wrong with just going after what they wanted? To hell with all of these reservations.

"Mentor monitors us," Sereny said, answering before Balthazar could speak. "He knows we've sent out assassins for Malachi."

"Malachi?"

"The *dhampir*," Balthazar said.

Irritated in the extreme, Charles rose from the chair and began to pace the room, his hands locked behind his back. "Mentor knows all about you? He knows of this place?"

"I'm afraid so," Sereny said. "He even visited once. It was years ago; it was a while before I knew Balthazar."

"So what are you saying?" Charles asked. He had stopped pacing and faced Balthazar. "Are we going to combine forces or not? Are you going to help me change how things are run or not?"

Balthazar stood and refilled his glass before responding. With his back to the room, he said, "Of course we're going to work together. You help me with my problem, and I'll help you with yours."

"And if Mentor knows what we're up to?" Charles asked. "If he knows we're coming?"

Balthazar shrugged. "We'll find out what happens when it happens, won't we?"

He held out his hand to Charles, and they shook. Sereny showed Charles to a chamber that had been furnished for him. The bone thing got on Charles' nerves. What was wrong with a stone slab or a normal bed frame?

"When your followers show up, they'll be met and taken into the caves and shown niches where they can rest," Sereny said, turning to leave.

"Tell me about this prophecy." He grabbed her arm to stay her.

"It was foretold more than two hundred years ago." She pried his fingers from her arm.

"What was?"

"A *dhampir* would be born who could not be vanquished. He would be the downfall of the Predators."

"You don't believe that, do you? Prophecy is . . . it's . . . old wives telling tales."

She gave him a shocked look. "I do believe it. Balthazar said it was Malachi, and I believe him."

"How does he know?"

Sereny turned her back on him and went to the door opening. "Ask him, why don't you?"

Charles impatiently circled his chamber, worrying. Balthazar sounded to him like a man obsessed. Who cared about an old prophecy that probably meant nothing in the real world?

Oh, God, he needed to get out of here and into the open air where he could think. He needed to find a human and feed. Balthazar's cold blood offering had done little to sate his hunger.

*   *   *

Sereny knew Balthazar had spoken to her, but she hadn't heard the words. Her mind was in some place where it rested while her body performed the repetitive routine of housework.

"What?" she asked, turning with a dustrag in her hand from where she'd been giving the shelves a once over. She had not been a wife and mother for nothing. Now that she was back in her home, she felt the need to clear it and make it her own again. *I'm nesting,* she thought, *like a damn mama hen.*

"What do you think of him?"

He meant Charles Upton, of course. Since becoming vampire Sereny had given up habitual lying. People lied to keep society running smoothly. Without all sorts of lies, from little white lies to whoppers, society would fall apart overnight. She said, "I think he'll prove a dangerous partner. You don't really understand one another."

"Why do you say that?"

She returned to her dusting. "He can't be trusted. He's like his Maker."

"Like Ross?"

"Yes. But worse. He's even *more* arrogant. He expects to rule the whole world—just him. Not the two of you together. Later on, he'll turn on you. He has vast appetites. He's like some evil ancient king looking to fill his coffers, beat the servants into submission, and pillage the towns of all their women." She wished she hadn't said the last. Balthazar wasn't stupid.

"You slept with him, didn't you? He's already pillaged his competitor."

This was why lying was forbidden to her. Lies only complicated what was simple. It covered the truth with the mud of deception and then truth was never clean again. If she lied and said she didn't sleep with Charles, Balthazar would slip into her mind one day and discover the truth. If he hadn't already. He wasn't jealous, as where would jealousy get him? He couldn't own her. But he hated guile. "I slept with him. It was . . . his face."

"His face? You mean that cat thing? He thinks he's a jaguar. That made you want to have sex with him? I don't understand you, Sereny."

"I don't understand myself," she said. She couldn't explain the weird attraction that had come over her when she met Charles. It was his face, yes, that wild animal staring at her from the body of a man. But it was much more. In their first meeting he had attracted her like a magnet drew metal filings. If she didn't know better, she might think he had mesmerized her, but he hadn't. He just possessed an animal eroticism that made her weak-kneed with lust for him. Had Balthazar appeared and gotten between them at that moment, she would have fought him. She would have gone over or through him to get to Charles. She'd wanted his touch all over her body, wanted him to run his long tongue along the curve of her breast. Now that she'd gotten what she wanted, she had no feeling left for him at all.

Except maybe suspicion.

She put the past from her mind, knowing Balthazar had probably tapped into her memory lapse. She returned her thoughts to the chore of dusting. She took out armloads of ancient texts Balthazar loved to read and dusted each one with care before returning it to the high bone bookcase. What she did understand perfectly well was how she loved to tidy a house. This was no house, naturally; it was a cave chamber littered with skeletons, but it served as a living space, so it was her home now and she made do.

When human, she had loved housework so much she found ways to make herself indispensable to her husband. He came to cherish his clean home and had pride in it, though they were of the poorer classes. He began to adore the food she cooked with such meticulous care, the clothes he wore that were so carefully washed and pressed, the feel of the softly ironed sheets upon which he slept. Her children were the best-dressed in their school, not because her husband could afford good wardrobes, but because Sereny taught herself to sew and became a master seamstress. She could imitate haute couture clothing so well no one could tell the little dresses and suits her children wore hadn't come from an expensive boutique.

She learned to make soap and lotions and facial creams from herbs. She took rags and hooked rugs. From scraps she make quilts. Her domesticity knew no bounds.

The secret of her homemaking skills lay in the peace it afforded her. When dusting, washing, pressing, vacuuming, sewing, or cooking, she lost herself in the simplicity of the task and entered a heavenly trance. When things shined from her cleaning, she stood back in awe at their beauty—whether it was a china cup or a wooden floor. When she walked through a completely orderly home, she loved herself. With pure ingenuity and love, she had created an oasis in the midst of squalor.

Most of the world was filled with filth and chaos, especially the small Italian city where she'd lived and raised her family. She made light and beauty out of honest handiwork. Her thoughtful arrangements, from a vase of wildflowers to an old armoire stacked with handmade quilts, gave her such pleasure that it didn't matter whether anyone saw or enjoyed them other than herself.

It was more difficult to reach her peaceful, mindless haven by doing housework inside of a large dark earthen cavern four miles below the surface of an island, but she didn't cease trying. She hoped once the coming vampire war was finished and Balthazar in a position of power, he would let her pick out a European castle and attend to it by herself. Oh, what she could do with a castle and unlimited funds! Think of all the art and sculpture and silver and glass she could care for and make shine. What peace she would enjoy.

She might even kidnap a child again, maybe a vampire girl or boy, to keep as her own. Neither of them would ever grow old. She could be its mother forever.

Here, to keep busy until that fabulous day, she dusted shelves, arranged pillows, made beds, and swept the dirt floors with careful movements that kept tiny debris from accumulating. At first Balthazar protested, wondering at her strange energy and why she would misplace it in this way. When she explained it was the only part of her that was still human, and that she needed the work to make her happy, he let her alone.

She moved on from the book shelving to the sofas and took each pillow in turn, plumping and fluffing, arranging them again in just the right positions across the sofa back to please the eye. She knew Balthazar understood her mania for housework, but the others, his followers, often found her down on her knees picking up tiny rocks or they'd interrupt her scrubbing soot from the glass globes of the lanterns, and they would stand around laughing and making fun of her.

Look at the washerwoman, they jeered. *Look at the lowly servant.*

She simply shut them out and continued with her work until they tired of their mean-spirited taunts and wandered away.

The "Bone Palace," as they called it, might have little to offer but dark passages, dirt floors and walls, and bone furniture, but it would be a clean place. It would be neat and polished.

And this above all gave her satisfaction.

*   *   *

The deep caverns were so dark, damp, and cold, they depressed Charles. He was used to the open blue sky and warm sun of Australia. Even his cell in the monastery hadn't been this close. Already he felt suffocated in the confined spaces, menaced by the looming ceilings, and hemmed in by the unrelenting darkness. When first landing on the island and seeing the vista of land covered with black volcanic rock, he had shivered deep down inside with dread. It was such a dead place, like an abandoned black ship nodding in the center of a great, wide sea.

He just had to get out of here, he thought, moving anxiously for the door. He left his chamber and traipsed the long passageway until he found the shaft that rose to the top of the volcano. He sped up the tunnel toward the opening and the sky beyond. It was dusk when he exploded from the caves, hovering over the volcano like a cloud of dusty brown smoke. He was so happy the other Predators had taught him this trick.

"It's not difficult," they said. "All matter is energy. We can control our own matter, the way you do when you change into . . ." They let the words trail off, not wishing to remark on his cat face.

He had spent days trying to change his body into dancing molecules of energy until one day he succeeded. He could point his energy cloud to the heavens and go there. He could rise above the ozone and look down at the Earth in amazement.

Now he stared far out at sea and imagined the African shore. He could be there in minutes if he wished. He was like a new god with the world as his playground. He could go anywhere. He could do anything! If only he had known of this in the monastery. Why hadn't he understood that's how the monks entered his body, entered, for that matter, into his mind, and bound him from escape? If he'd studied what they'd done, he might not have spent nearly two decades under their power.

The dark cloud changed rapidly to his Thai body as he stood on the precipice of the volcano. He thrust out his face, his cat features sharpening, his eyes closing down to slits. He pushed out his mind before him, pulling the physical body in its wake until it broke up for a second time and became nearly transparent. He moved through the sky and across the waters, heading for the Dark Continent. He would not return until he was gorged with fresh blood and the taste of the cold liquid from Balthazar's goblet was erased from his palate.

Perhaps by that time his depression would lift and he'd feel more like working in tandem with the cautious Balthazar. He could tell already their methods were different and they might clash over them. Charles wanted to do things quickly, in a rush of passion. Balthazar wanted to go carefully, thinking over each move from several angles before committing himself. It was said he had spent years gathering together his own clan when it had only taken Charles a few weeks.

Then again, if he wanted the power of another four hundred and more Predators at his back, he needed Balthazar. He couldn't afford to irritate him right now. *Later,* he thought. *Later, when I possess the power and the army I want, Balthazar will have to go.*

Charles laughed to himself in joy at the thought of running the elegantly dressed vampire back into his deep dark caves. Why would any of the followers want to stay with the eccentric Balthazar when they could join with Charles and enjoy all the spoils of triumph?

The coast of Africa rose out of the ocean like a green-knuckled giant thrusting up from the sea floor. Not far into the interior, Charles came down gently, molding his face back toward its original Thai human form. He loved "going cat" once he had a victim under his power. Until then he didn't want to frighten them any more than was necessary. Fear drove them to flee, and he'd never enjoyed the physical chase, despite how easy it was to catch a victim.

He moved down a jungle path, feeling as if he were back in Thailand again, and came upon a little town shrouded by night. He smelled the heady scent of meat roasting in banana leaves and a whiff of shredded coconut and spice mixed with a white starchy tuber. He could hear voices speaking softly in the night and the crying of babies. He slipped into the first thatched-roof hut he came to, slithering through an open window. He startled an old woman sitting in lamplight, weaving a reed basket.

She began to speak in her native tongue, but Charles didn't bother to understand her, though he could have if he'd wanted. He knew the gist of her queries. *Who are you? What do you want?*

He came close slowly and reached out one hand to encircle her throat. She dropped the basket work and clawed at his hand. Her eyes bulged as her air was cut off.

Now Charles let his cat self out, his nose lengthening into snout, his eyes narrowing, his cheekbones sliding back while his skull flattened and elongated. He looked down into the woman's horrified eyes and smiled his cat smile.

And then he ravaged her, ripping the jugular vein from her throat and closing his wide mouth over the wound in order to catch the flow.

She was old and frail and skinny. She tasted of dust and resin, of bone marrow gone dry and musty. She was hardly an appetizer. She hadn't lasted seconds past the opened wound in her throat, her terrified gaze falling dead and her eyes turning back in her head.

Before the night was over, Charles had stalked and taken

six victims in the little African town. On his way back to the caves on Lanzarote Island, he glanced at the yellow moon in the sky, and inside his mind he howled like a victorious beast on the first night of a ravenous rampage.

Soon, he told himself, *soon I will have my victims brought to me bound and shivering. Soon I will make both vampire and human tremble when I pass by. Soon I will control the world and every living thing in it.*

5

Days passed without incident for Malachi in the little cabin behind the country store. He took his meals with Howard and the twins, careful not to complain about the old man's cooking, despite the fact it was frequently inedible. The dinners ran to beans and franks, beef stew filled with more potatoes and peas than beef, and tomato soup served alongside bologna sandwiches. Breakfast was better, since there wasn't much Howard could do to eggs that could ruin them. The days he cooked oatmeal, however, was another story. Oatmeal Howard's way turned out thick as tar and so salty Malachi could hardly eat it.

Dottie and Jeremy took to hanging out with Malachi during the day. He tinkered with his old motorcycle, and Jeremy liked handing him tools. Dottie enjoyed fetching cans of cola for him to drink. As he got to know the twins, he came to admire their genuine sweetness. Though their grandfather doted on them, they were as unspoiled as a peaceful summer day.

"What will you do if something happens to your granddad?" Malachi asked one afternoon. He hadn't meant to get involved, but he really liked the old man and his grandchildren.

"I'll take all the money from the register, call my great-aunt in Plainview, Texas, and have her come get us," Dottie said.

"So you've already thought it all out. That's good."

"Grandpa helped us," Jeremy said. "He gave us his sister's phone number."

"I keep it in my purse," Dottie said. She lifted the glamorous little silver purse from her side and shook it a little.

Every morning Dottie put on a new dress, some of them much too large for her so that the skirts dragged on the

ground. Malachi suspected these dresses came from her
mother's closet, left there when her mother had died so
many years ago. After putting on a dress Dottie carefully
applied makeup. But shoes weren't in the picture. "I hate
wearing shoes," she confided. "I have lots of shoes cause
Grandpa keeps buying them for me in case I change my
mind and wear them, but I won't."

"I don't like shoes either. I don't even like *underwear*,"
Jeremy said, not to be outdone.

Malachi laughed. "Why don't you like shoes?" he
asked Dottie.

"They pinch my feet. When they're new, they rub blisters
on my heels. I'd rather go barefoot. I *really* like it when it
rains and I can squish my toes in mud. But it don't rain
much here." Dottie gave him a wistful smile.

"They pinch my feet, too," Jeremy echoed.

Malachi glanced at the boy before looking at Dottie
again. They sure were twins, all right. "Why do you wear
makeup, Dottie?"

"I just like it," she said. "Like going barefoot."

"Don't you want to wait until you're all grown up to
wear lipstick and stuff? Little girls don't usually wear
makeup because their faces are so pretty anyway. You have
a pretty face."

"Thank you," she said, preening, "but I just like it." She
reached up and patted her rouged cheeks.

"You don't wear it to school, do you?"

"Makeup? Oh, no. When school starts, I only wear real
light pink lipstick. They'd send me to the principal's office
if I wore mascara and rouge."

Malachi forced himself not to smile this time. "Hand me
the wrench," he said to Jeremy, turning to work on the
bike's chain.

It was the eleventh day Malachi had been staying at the
cabin when the vampires came. He thought he'd escaped
them. He thought they'd lost him and after a couple of
months they would give up the search.

Due to his naïveté they caught him unaware, bent over
his bike as he worked. Dottie was inside getting him a soda
and Howard was busy concocting another inedible stewed
or boiled supper. Jeremy stood faithfully at Malachi's side,
a dedicated assistant.

The first Malachi knew the vampires were there, they had him by the scruff of the neck, hauling him backward to the ground. He saw them then, surrounding him, and there were more than he'd ever seen before. His heart quadrupled in its beating and he found it hard to breathe. He thought of home, the ranch. He thought of how his mother had so often known before he did when the assassins came for him. She'd been like an early warning system.

"Go inside," Malachi told Jeremy. The boy, rooted to the spot, began to back away slowly and the vampires let him go.

"Where's your mama, half-breed?" one of them asked as if reading Malachi's mind.

"Don't talk to him. Let's get him out to the desert and get it over with," another said.

Malachi began to struggle, throwing off the hands that grasped him. He stood quickly, his heart still beating furiously. He backed away just as Jeremy had done. He needed a weapon, some kind of weapon. *Oh, God,* he thought, looking at them as they advanced, their fangs showing as they snarled. *There are eight of them. How will I . . . ?*

At that moment Dottie came from the back door of the store with his cold drink. She stood riveted to the steps, her eyes going wide in terror. Jeremy reached the steps and ran up them to his sister.

"Run, Dottie, go inside and lock the doors!" he said.

She dropped the can, cola spewing across the dry ground. She turned, opening the screen door and rushing inside with Jeremy. Within a minute the children emerged again, this time trailing their grandfather.

Malachi saw the old man had a shotgun. He pointed it at the group and said, "What the hell do you think you're doing? Leave that boy alone and get off my property."

"Go back inside, Howard," Malachi pleaded. "Take the kids, lock the doors."

"Yeah, go away, old man," one of the vampires said, turning his head to show the intruder his fangs.

Howard stared hard at the vampire, taking in the fangs, and now his eyes widened as Dottie's had earlier. "What are you?" he whispered. The shotgun trembled in his hands, the barrel wavering. Both children slipped behind his legs, holding onto the denim of his overalls.

"I can show you." The vampire began to approach the steps.

"Jeremy! Get me the shovel, hurry!" Malachi danced away from the Predators, speeding so fast only the vampires were able to see his movement. He had moved closer to the store.

"You go to hell, whatever you are," Howard said, and pulled the trigger on the double-barreled shotgun. The vampire had nearly reached him at that point. The blast took off the vampire's head, knocking him backward and to the ground. He didn't move. Two more vampires changed direction from where they stalked Malachi and came toward the old man, hissing.

Howard fumbled with shells he withdrew from a jacket pocket. He got them socked into the chambers and snapped the gun shut, raised it, and said, "I wouldn't if I were you."

Dottie had hurried back into the house with her brother. Jeremy ran through the building to the front door. He slammed it open and flew across the porch, racing around the house away from the killers in the back. He hit the door of the shed, knocking it open and went straight for the shovel leaning against empty snake cages. He hurried out with it again, going around the store in the opposite direction now, hoping to get close enough to Malachi to hand the shovel over. He'd heard the shotgun blast, and tears sprang to his eyes, but it didn't slow him down.

Howard shot one of the vampires coming for him, turned the barrel and shot the other. Both of the creatures fell back to the ground, but even as Howard chambered two more shells he saw the two vampires he'd shot rise up again. Miraculously the middle of their bodies were as untouched as if they'd never been shot. Shirts hung in shreds from their bodies around their middles, revealing unblemished skin.

"My God," Howard said, talking to himself. He was sweating now and fumbling in his pocket for more shells. "What do I need? I need a stake, I need a silver bullet, I need a crucifix . . ."

Malachi was in a fight for his life, unable to give his attention to the old man. He threw off three vampires who were attacking, all of them biting at him on arms and chest and face. He screamed, the pain shooting through him like fire. He, too, would heal quickly, but not nearly as quickly as a true immortal.

He saw Jeremy coming, running as fast as his feet would carry him, the shovel held across the front of his body. He had to get the Predators off him so he could take the shovel. He could use the shovel's blade to slow down his attackers and when he got the chance, he could use it to lop off their heads, thereby rendering them dead forever.

He turned, beginning to spin so that the vampires couldn't latch onto him. His mind fell away, and he was simply flesh intent on survival. His movement was so swift that he looked like a blur. The vampires fell back a step or two, taken off guard. They never expected a *dhampir* to employ such ability. Balthazar had told them Malachi was unusual, that he was formidable, but they hadn't believed him. A half-breed as fast and deadly as they were? It had to be a lie.

Malachi leaped toward Jeremy just as he neared the melee. He took the shovel from his trembling hands. He stood still now, feet apart, the shovel held before him. He said, "Hide, Jeremy. Run and hide. Now!"

The two vampires Howard had wounded reached him on the store's back steps before the old man could chamber the next shells. The shotgun was ripped from his hands, causing him to wobble on his feet. He cried out in surprise and fear, but his cry was cut off by a roundhouse knock to the head with the butt end of the shotgun. He fell where he stood, crumpling to the ground unconscious and bleeding.

The vampire who had struck him dropped the shotgun, leaned down, and pierced the side of the old man's throat with one long fingernail. Blood welled and the vampire went to his knees, his face closing on the puncture. The other vampire turned back to Malachi.

Malachi began to fight in earnest. He knew one of the Predators was feeding on Howard and if he didn't get to him soon, he would be dead. The vampires surrounding Malachi backed off, wary of the sharp spade end of the shovel, their gazes following the rhythmic swinging motions as it sliced back and forth through the air.

Malachi advanced with such speed his attackers couldn't retreat. One by one Malachi took them down, slicing off the head of one, shoving the blade into another's midsection to slow him, striking another against the shoulder to knock him off his feet. All around Malachi the frenzy rose, the death-dealing so fast a mortal couldn't have followed it.

Malachi knew he was only able to outwit and outfight the vampires because he drew on the inner reserves that belonged to his own vampire heritage. He did not know how he had been so blessed with strength and agility, and he had no time to question it now, but it was obvious to his enemies he was no ordinary *dhampir*. He was no weak half-breed. In fact, he was as awesome in warfare as a monster killing machine. Despite the Predators' fearsome abilities, Malachi was superior to them.

With five of the eight mortally wounded or dead, Malachi went after the vampire kneeling over the old man, taking his life from the jugular in great draughts. He knocked him aside and buried the shovel blade into the vampire's stomach, withdrew it and used the spade as a hammer, swinging it high above his head and bringing it down with tremendous force on the enemy's neck, severing it from the convulsing body.

Six down, two more to take care of, Malachi thought frantically, swinging around to attack the remaining vampires. He saw he was alone, and panic filled him. He glanced down at Howard and realized the old man's eyes were open and fully dilated. He was gone. He'd been too late to save him.

What about Dottie and Jeremy? Was he too late for them, too? Jesus.

He sped across the yard, looked in the shed, found it empty. He scanned the rows of rattlesnakes and saw many of the cages had been knocked from their stands, the latches holding the cages closed having come undone. All around him on the desert ground swarmed the rattlesnakes, some fleeing into the nearby desert land, some curling, ready to strike. He backed away from them and turned. He rushed around the house and saw no one in front of the place. Up and down the long straight highway the lanes were empty.

Inside. They must have gone inside.

He flung open the door and entered the dark store, his vision adjusting immediately from his adrenaline rush. He saw nothing moving, no hint of the vampires. But he could feel them. He could sense their cold presence.

He ran into the back rooms where there was a kitchen and bedrooms. He heard voices and followed them, the shovel raised. He couldn't let them hurt the twins. He'd fight to the death for them.

He pushed open a bedroom door and thought he was hallucinating. Could he be dreaming?

It was the twins' bedroom, obviously, decorated with cartoon wallpaper. On one of the twin beds lay Jeremy stretched out on his back. On the floor two vampires lay dead, decapitated, blood from their mortal wounds spreading in wide puddles across the hardwood. Between their bodies lay Dottie, her dress soaking in blood, her throat torn open. Calm, dead eyes stared unseeing at the ceiling. And over the bed stood Mentor and Ross looking down at the male child, their backs to him.

Malachi dropped the shovel. His whole body went weak, and he caught the doorjamb to keep from crumpling. He couldn't stand this. Couldn't. It couldn't be true. He had fought so hard, he had taken down the enemies with as much speed as he could command. How could they have killed the children? Even monsters should hesitate to take the life from a child. "Mentor," he whispered.

Mentor turned and came to him. "I came as quickly as I could," he said. "I'm afraid it wasn't quick enough." He lifted a sheet from the unmade empty bed and walked over to the girl on the floor. The sheet billowed out and floated down to cover her. "We knew you could handle the others. We tried to get in here before the children were taken."

"Oh, God." Malachi hung his head, his heart breaking inside him. He moved to the bedside where Jeremy lay. "Is he . . . ?"

"No, he's not dead," Ross said quietly. "We interrupted the attack. He's in the dream of the red moon."

Malachi sank onto the bedside. He took the boy's limp hand. There were sores on his bare arms and face. He'd been bitten by one of the vampires, but not killed. He'd been infected.

"Oh, no." Malachi knew what it meant to die to the world and enter the dream Ross spoke of. His mother had told him about it. How the soul chose there what sort of vampire he or she would come back as. Jeremy would be vampire. Jeremy would live again eternally. He'd be destined to walk in his nine-year-old child body for a hundred years, trapped in childhood though his mind would mature into an adult's.

"There's nothing to be done about it now," Mentor said, as if listening to Malachi's thoughts. "I'll try to help him."

Ross moved and Mentor knelt by the bed, taking the boy's dead face in his hands. While Ross and Malachi looked on, Mentor closed his eyes and mentally entered the death world with the child, hoping to guide him.

*   *   *

Malachi tied his bag onto the back of the motorcycle. It was morning, the sun only just risen. Jeremy stood at his back, waiting. He was still barefoot and dressed in overalls, but he no longer looked like the innocent child he had once been. His face was as white as cooked rice, the eyes too intense and otherworldly to be human. When his lips twitched, as they did constantly now, his small fangs showed. Despite Mentor's advice and guidance during the dream of the red moon, he had chosen to be a Predator. Mentor said he'd been so full of the loss of his sister and grandfather that he'd been incapable of choosing otherwise. He'd been motherless and fatherless, and now had lost the only two people left in the world who had ever loved him. Knowing how alone he was, he had moved toward the Giant Predator Maker with sure resolve, inviting the immortal change that would give him the most power.

"I want to be like them," he had told Mentor in the death dream. "Like the ones who came to the store. I want to be exactly like them. I don't want to live as human anymore. I want to hunt and to fight. I want to kill."

He would soon possess more powers than Malachi, such as the power to change form and to fly. He would learn more as he lived the life and perfected the supernatural arts granted him.

"Where will we go?" he asked now, watching Malachi secure his belongings in the saddlebag on the motorcycle.

Malachi paused and looked at the far dry mountains of

West Texas. "I don't know," he said. "Anywhere but here." They would wander. Stay on the move. Keep out of cities and away from other people so this would never happen again. He'd left home to save his father and instead had made Jeremy into a victim. He felt so heavy inside, like a bag of rocks was fastened around his heart, weighing it down.

Ross had buried the old man and Dottie. Then he'd disposed of the vampire corpses out on the desert plains. They'd locked the doors of the store, set loose the remaining rattlesnakes, and put the CLOSED sign in the window. They just didn't know what to do with Jeremy.

Malachi had insisted he come with him. He felt responsible for what had happened. If he'd never stopped at the store, never stayed, both children would have been spared. It was all his fault. Who was going to teach Jeremy how to live again? Who cared enough to protect him until he found the right way to exist as vampire? Mentor had too many responsibilities. Ross had no interest in fledgling Predators, especially one who was under four feet tall. So Malachi would take the boy and he would teach him how to survive. No matter how long it took.

"Get on the back," he said once he'd straddled the bike. "Hold me around the waist."

With the boy mounted and his arms encircling him, Malachi rose up on the starter pedal and turned the motor over. He sat down once he had the engine revving and, without giving the bike gas, turned the wheel first one way down the highway and then the other. He turned his head this way and that, trying to decide.

Jeremy let one of his pale hands fall from Malachi's waist and pointed. "That way," he said.

"Okay." Malachi put the bike into gear and let out the clutch. They were headed east again, but he wouldn't go home. He'd go somewhere else.

Somewhere safe.

Somewhere to hide.

• BOOK THREE •

THE UPRISING

1

Dell sat on the porch thinking of her son. It was Saturday, and Ryan was in the garage tinkering with his old truck. He was unaware of her worries and even if she'd told him, there was nothing he could do to help. As lovable and good as he was, his mortality kept him from being any help when it came to vampire troubles.

Dell tried to keep her mind at home, but Malachi was all she could think about. Mentor had told her what had happened. Now her son was not alone, but had a child in his care. He had no idea what he was doing, it seemed to Dell. Eddie, Dell's brother, had been infected and changed when he was just a child and it had been a sad event for the whole family.

Today Eddie was a wanderer. She might see him once a year, if she were lucky. He couldn't stay home, living as a Natural, and continue going to school while never physically maturing. They'd all known the day was coming when he would go away. It was put off as long as possible, but two years after Dell's marriage to Ryan, Eddie came to her to say good-bye. They had wept together and hugged. He would live a lonely existence, wandering the world, never fitting in anywhere for very long. He had heard of a colony of children, he'd said, living in Brazil. Perhaps he should find them.

"Oh, you don't want to do that," Dell had said. "They hang out on the streets, abandoned, wild. They aren't vampire, Eddie."

"The kids in Brazil are no wilder than they have to be. At least they'll take me in."

The Brazilian band was separated from their families, making one another brothers and sisters, creating their own families. The Brazilian public and the government thought they were scabby little runaways or orphans, sniffing glue and rummaging city dumps for food. No one cared about them. No one knew what to do.

Eddie didn't know what to do, either, unless he kept on the move, all alone, until his body finally gave out and released him so he could take the body of an adult. He didn't want to be so alone, he'd said, for so many long years. He'd rather be with children.

Dell had let him go, standing on the porch, watching him vanish. His molecules danced like a storm of light and then swept upward into the sky until no hint of his existence could be seen. She mourned him for many months, worrying about how he was doing. He would never tell her, she knew. None of the vampire nations liked to admit their youngest members were doomed to live such a hellish nightmare.

Now her son had taken on the burden of watching over a child who would one day have to leave him. She wished Mentor had taken the child away, but he said Malachi wouldn't let him. Her poor son, with his heavy guilt, had insisted the boy go with him. Maybe she should find them and try to protect them both. But then what about her husband? How could she leave the one person she loved with all of her heart? If Balthazar sent more assassins out of revenge, Ryan wouldn't have a chance. They'd kill him, killing her soul. She couldn't leave him and had to hope her son, who had proved so far that he could care for himself, might continue to survive the attacks.

*   *   *

"Tell me a fairy tale," Jeremy said.

They were camping in a dry gulch off the lost highway. Around them loomed the deep night, the sky overhead shining with an array of stars. Malachi lay on his side on a spread sleeping bag, supporting his head on one arm. A campfire made from fragrant sagebrush and small dry sticks flickered nearby. The smoke spiraled into the sky like deep gray ribbons sailing to heaven.

"I don't know any fairy tales," Malachi said. It was the truth. His parents had never told him stories, and the books they read to him were about cars or trucks or farming. It seemed his childhood had been so immersed with night-mare and dream that fictional tales weren't needed. He didn't even know if his mother knew any fairy tales.

"You don't know any?" Jeremy asked.

"Afraid not."

Jeremy sat cross-legged before the fire, staring into the flames. "I can tell you one, then."

"All right."

"There were two little kids who lived in the woods," Jeremy began. "They were named Hansel and Gretel. There was also a mean old witch who lived in the woods . . ."

Malachi listened to the child's tale and realized it was similar to what had happened to Dottie and Jeremy. Two children, a boy and a girl, menaced by something evil. When the boy finished, Malachi sat up and poked at the fire with a stick until sparks flew skyward. He wondered why anyone would tell a child such a terrible story.

"That's pretty awful," he said, adding more brush to the fire.

"Not so bad. It's just a pretend story."

"Yes, I suppose so." He wasn't going to ask for another fairy tale. He didn't think he liked them.

After a companionable silence, Malachi said, "Are you hungry?"

"Very. Really really hungry. My stomach hurts."

Malachi nodded, knowing it wasn't really the child's stomach that was involved. His whole being was deprived of sustenance. Soon he'd be moaning, unable to go on, starving for blood.

Malachi stood from the campfire and said, "I'll be back in a few minutes. Stay right here and you'll be all right."

"Where are you going?"

"To find gingerbread and gumdrops."

Jeremy smiled and his fangs showed. "Okay."

It took under fifteen minutes. Ever since he was small, Malachi had been a superb hunter. He could smell the prey before he saw it. He could sense the slightest movement, the blink of an eye, the whisk of a tail. It was clear to him that he was in no way ordinary, not for man or for vampire. He had fought off a whole cadre of vampires. He was be-ginning to feel changes taking place inside that he couldn't understand. He wondered at this, finding it curious and bizarre. He thought he should try to find out why. Mentor might know. When he returned home, he'd ask him.

A tiny sound interrupted his thoughts. He spied a prairie hen waddling through brush and cacti, swooped down on it, and plucked it from the ground before it could take wing. He wrung the hen's neck as he sped back to the campsite in the distance. When he entered the circle of firelight, Jeremy looked up surprised.

"You didn't hear me coming?" Malachi asked.

"Uh-uh. You're real quiet."

"Don't worry, your instincts will kick in soon. You'll be able to know where I am even if I move far away from you."

"That would be good," Jeremy said in a suddenly serious tone of voice. "I want to know everything. I want to find out who sent those bad vampires to my house."

Malachi could have told him, but thought now was not the time.

"Here," he said, handing over the fowl. "It's dead, so you have to hurry. It won't taste so good once it's dead too long."

Jeremy took the hen into his lap and stared down at it. He began to brush the feathers smooth. He lifted the limp head and looked at the glazed eye.

"What do I do?" He peeked up at Malachi, a lock of hair falling over one eye.

Malachi stooped and took the hen back, snapping off its head with one quick motion. Blood immediately welled and slid over the neck of the bird onto its back. He pressed the bird toward Jeremy's face.

"I can't do that," the child said, scooting backward on his haunches, holding his hands up to ward off the bloody carcass.

"You have to." Malachi waited, holding the bird out.

A look came over Jeremy's face, a wild and feral look never seen on the face of human children, even those who were starving. He blinked, staring at the blood coming from the bird's neck.

"I don't like that," he said. "I can't . . ."

"You have to, Jeremy. You need it. You'll starve."

With a movement that was like the strike of a snake, Jeremy leaped forward and jerked the bird from Malachi's hands. He buried his face over it in his lap, the sounds he made causing Malachi to turn away.

This is a terrible thing, Malachi thought. *This is a terrible thing. He might be better off dead.*

Jeremy's voice came from behind him. "I'll never die now," he said. He had read Malachi's mind.

Malachi turned and saw the boy standing there, the dead bird hanging from one hand at his side. On Jeremy's face the blood was smeared across his lips and cheeks and chin in scarlet streaks.

"I'll ever die." He dropped the bird and kicked it away from the camp. He wiped his face on his shirtsleeve and went to his own sleeping bag and lay down on his back, his face to the sky.

"I'm so sorry, Jeremy." Malachi stood over him.

"It's not your fault."

"Yes, it is. If I hadn't come to . . ."

"I'll make them pay one day," Jeremy said, never looking at Malachi. "When I'm stronger and can do what I want, I'll make them pay."

The quiet little boy who had followed behind his twin sister like a shadow was beginning to come into his own. He had drunk his first blood. He knew the depth of his true nature. He knew he would live forever if an enemy vampire never vanquished him.

Jeremy was Predator, and Malachi mourned the long future that lay before the child. He didn't know it yet, but the uncountable years ahead were like a nightmare from which he would never wake.

2

———————

Mentor sat beneath the breezy willow limbs in Bette Kinyo's garden. He knew the new child vampire had just feasted for the first time on warm blood. He tried to keep a channel open to watch over the wandering pair on the Texas plains. He'd been too involved in local affairs to do it before and look what had happened. He and Ross had been too late to save the little girl and her grandfather. And the assassins had made the boy into a Predator.

The woman was at the door.

Mentor turned his head to look at her where she peered at him through the back-door window-panes. She was pale and wan in the reflected moonlight on her face. He rarely came to the garden anymore because it disturbed her. She knew when he was there. But this place was one of his sacred retreats, and right now he felt he needed it.

When she saw he had noticed her, she let herself out the door and came to join him on the concrete bench beneath the willow tree.

She looked toward the white gravel sea and the great stones there that represented peaceful islands. "You're worried about something," she said.

"It's getting easier for you to read me," he said.

"Maybe my psychic ability is getting stronger."

He remembered once when she'd called his name and he'd heard it more than two hundred miles away. She was almost as talented as any vampire in knowing of his where-abouts. It was a mystery to him when he found humans with such skill. As a human, he had never been able to do such things. He was as closed and unknowing in the world as an unopened book.

"Yes, I'm worried," he said. For the vampire nations— he was the one they came to for advice and help. He found himself hoping Bette might serve as his adviser and was surprised to realize he truly needed one.

"Do you want to talk about it?"

"I think so."

They sat in silence for a time, the woman showing no impatience. She knew him well enough to know he must speak in his own time, at his own rate.

Finally he sighed and said, "I might as well be honest with you. All this might affect you and your kind."

"Humans." It was a statement.

"Yes, humans. The world you know."

He stared hard at the gravel sea and imagined himself in a small boat drifting there, the rock island so far away that it seemed but a speck on the horizon.

He said, "There's threat of war in the air. An uprising from a large party of Predators who want to come out and let the world know we exist." He had once explained to her all he knew about the vampires. How their affliction came from a genetic disease that had mutated and left him immortal. How they chose to become Predator, Natural, or Craven. How he had walked the Earth for hundreds of years and had chosen the role of moral leader and adviser, guiding new vampires and binding each nation, one to the other.

"Why do they want to come out of secrecy?" she asked.

"They're a band of misfits and loners who have never felt wanted. They were left alone to do as they wished only if they didn't try to upset the balance between men and vampires. Now they have leaders who are megalomaniacs—greedy and thoughtless Predators who don't care what happens anymore. Simply put, they want to rule and they'll do anything to get what they want."

"Would they rule us?"

Mentor put his arm around Bette's shoulders to soften the truth. "In the end, yes, they would." He felt her shiver and held onto her tightly.

"Can you stop them?" she asked.

He decided not to lie. "I don't know. They've gathered a great many followers and when they come here, they'll find more who'll want to join them. It'll be war. And it'll start here."

"They're coming now?"

"Yes. Soon."

There was another silence until Bette said quietly, "You have to stop them, Mentor. First you have to believe you can."

Mentor removed his arm from her shoulders and stood. He looked down at her, a small woman wrapped in a brightly printed silk Oriental dressing gown. Her short black hair was swept back from her face as she looked up at him.

"Do you believe?" she asked.

"I have to, don't I?" He reached down and stroked his fingers along her cheek.

"I couldn't live in a world that belonged to the vampire," she said. "A world of the hunter and the hunted. Don't let that happen, Mentor."

He promised to do his best. To give his immortality, if it came to that, in order to prevent a split in the vampire nations. He stood perfectly still when she rose and kissed him on the cheek. He didn't trust himself not to wrap his arms around her and take her away from her husband and her home. He was afraid if he moved to touch her, he'd want to spirit her away and hold her captive where he could love her as his own forever.

When she'd disappeared into the house again, he lifted his head to the night sky and rose into it above the lights of Dallas. In minutes he was in his home, having summoned Ross to meet him there. When he arrived, Ross sat on the sofa with Dolan perched nervously on a chair across from him.

Dolan looked relieved to see him. Mentor pressed him down in the chair when he tried to rise. Dolan would never be truly like a Predator. He possessed too much humility.

He took another chair and faced Ross. "You know we have to do something," he said without preamble.

"I know we should have killed that bastard Upton in the beginning." Ross glared at Dolan to remind him he hadn't been any help when Upton escaped from the monastery.

"Well, you were right," Mentor said. "I should have let you kill him. But we have to deal with the problem he presents now rather than rake over the past. And it's not just Upton. It's Balthazar, too."

"A defector from Balthazar's group told me Upton's there now," Ross said. "On the island."

"So that is where he is now. Then they're close to combining forces. I think they'll come here."

"Because Upton wants us," Dolan said.

"And Balthazar wants Malachi," Ross added.

"So who will they go after first?" Mentor asked.

"I think they'll want to get to us first," Ross said, flicking imaginary lint from his pants. "Upton's been waiting a long time."

"Why can't we get some Predators together and go to them?" Dolan asked.

Mentor turned to him, interested. "Yes, why don't we?"

"I'm pulling my clan together," Ross said. "We're getting prepared. Before we could go to Balthazar, I think he'll be here. I think we'll be ready."

Later in the night after Ross had left and Dolan had retired, Mentor sat alone in the dark and moved his intelligence across the globe, searching the Canary Island of Lanzarote and the caves beneath it. While in this trancelike state his body sat immobile, a mere statue waiting for the master to return to it.

He would not be able to pick up conversations, but he would be able to tell how many vampires were gathered in one place. He was surprised to discover the caves nearly empty. He searched for any presence at all and found two, a male and a female. He knew it was Balthazar and his woman. But where were the others? His followers? Upton and his new clan? Where had they gone?

He came back to himself and opened his eyes. Instinctively he moved from the room to the windows and pressed his hands against the glass. They weren't here yet. At least they weren't in his area of town. He'd know if they were out there, near his home.

Ross, who had left for his own home earlier, spoke from behind him. Mentor turned to see he'd come back. "What's wrong? I felt your alarm."

"They're gone. No one's on the island, but Balthazar and the woman he keeps."

"The other Predators are gone? Upton, too?"

"Vanished," Mentor said.

"Then I'll go to the island and do away with the two there. If Balthazar's followers find out he's dead and they have no leader, maybe they'll turn back."

"Be careful, Ross. Balthazar's as old and experienced as you. Maybe I should come along."

"No, stay here. If Upton's on his way, you'll have enough to deal with. Call my clan if that happens. They know something's coming. And, damnit, don't underestimate me," he added heatedly.

Ross shimmered and disappeared. Mentor sank into a chair near the window and tried to find out where Upton might be but after a few minutes realized his former prisoner was still cloaking himself so he couldn't be detected. He was keeping his mind as empty as a dried desert lake. Devoid of personality and emotion, Upton was like a tree or a mountain. He couldn't be penetrated.

Realizing he should do the same so that Upton would not know where he was, Mentor shut down his own mind so that he was operating in stealth mode. Just a few sparks in the frontal lobe allowed him to preserve his thoughts and keep them private. He hated doing it, as it shut him off from any new vampire who called for his help, but he would not let himself be at a disadvantage.

Dolan, noting the activity in the house, came to the living room entrance. "Something's changed," he said. "What can I do to help?"

"Go to the clans and tell them to hide."

"Hide? All of them? Even the Predators?"

"Especially the Predators. If they're found, they'll have to fight. We think Upton's already here. I don't want the clan to fight until we know where the enemy is concentrated."

Dolan didn't need to hear more. If a militant band of Predators had invaded the city, an alert had to be sounded. He swiftly left the house by the door, blending into the night to fulfill his mission.

Mentor stayed behind trying with all his might to find the hundreds of Predators who might have already descended on the city. If he couldn't find where Upton was, he'd have to find his minions. He wondered why Balthazar had not accompanied them and what it meant.

He wondered if he could believe he had the power to stop them.

* * *

Sereny busily swept the long corridor leading into Balthazar's chamber. Her broom left a neat pattern on the hard-packed clay floor. When agitated the best thing to do was keep busy. Otherwise she'd argue too long and hard with Balthazar, and that was always dangerous. He wasn't patient with her temper.

She had known Balthazar was half-mad. Why else would an immortal spend his days deep in the earth surrounded by bone memories of his conquests? It was . . . medieval. People might as well have never walked on the moon or created the Internet or invented fiber-optics for all Balthazar benefitted. He was really a being stuck in a far past.

On the other hand she had known Predators who built crypts of solid gold, Predators who took to the sea and sailed ships without ever coming on land except to replenish their blood supplies with more human seafarers, and Predators who abducted humans and kept them as pets, as slaves. Like Balthazar, they were thought too eccentric to bother with and therefore were left to their own devices as long as they caused no commotion.

She never would have guessed, however, that Balthazar would stay behind when it was time to lead his Predators to the United States.

"Charles can do it well enough," he had said. "Two commanders will only weaken our front."

"But, Balthazar, I thought this was what you wanted. I thought we were going to fight with them. I told you not to trust Charles. Now you've let him leave with the whole army. He may never come back." This really worried her the most. Upton had only joined them to use the ferocious Predators they'd gathered. He cared for no one but himself.

"Why wouldn't he return?" Balthazar raised an eyebrow in question. "Besides, we'll join them later. Once everything's under control."

Sereny didn't believe him. "When? When it's all over?

When the *dhampir's* dead? Are you afraid of the *dhampir*, Balthazar?''

He hadn't answered. She had scowled at him and even pummeled him with her fists in a fit of temper until he winced, but he wouldn't talk to her anymore. When his eyes had grown deadly, she backed away.

She didn't understand him. She'd never suspected he was a coward. She knew he really believed the American *dhampir* was a danger to the Predators, but was he actually scared of him?

Or was he afraid of Mentor? She thought that might be closer to the truth. Mentor had been around forever. They'd all heard of him soon after becoming vampire. He had lived longer than anyone they knew and it was true he possessed terrifying tricks none of them had even imagined yet, but Balthazar would have had over six hundred followers at his back. What could he be afraid of?

One Predator, even one as old and advanced as Mentor, couldn't hope to defeat six hundred. Besides, Balthazar had sent a mole into Dallas months earlier, to keep his hand on the pulse of the city's Predators. He hadn't created a safe place to flee to. Ross, on the other hand, had been holding meetings with the Predators beneath him and instructing them about combat and warfare. It was Ross they should watch, not Mentor, not old, decrepit Mentor.

Now she'd been left behind with her chosen mate, confused, angry, feeling left out of the heart of violent action. At the last minute Balthazar seemed to have betrayed her. What in the hell were they doing here alone, stuck in the center of the Earth beneath a dead volcano? She had never felt so adrift and lonely. She felt like fleeing the caves and abducting a baby from one of the Lanzarote families. She'd hold it near her breast and take a ship away from all this. She'd set up housekeeping in Spain again and pretend . . . pretend her old life had never been stolen from her by the disease that caused her to die and rise again.

She attacked the earthen floor as if it were the enemy, sweeping hard, raising a cloud of dust that would have choked a mortal.

She had her head bent to the task and would have run right into Ross had he not interrupted her train of thought by a very low and menacing growl.

She halted, the broom in her hands, and raised her head.

"Ross," she breathed. His name came into her mind directly from his. Though she knew of him, she had never seen this American Predator. In some ways he was like Balthazar—tall, elegant, beautifully dressed. He wore shark-gray slacks and a gray silk cape that he'd thrown back over one shoulder to reveal a blood-red shirt with long puffed sleeves that gathered at his wrists. He looked like a Spanish prince from the sixteenth century.

"Hello, Sereny. Look at the mess you've made."

She now noticed the dust cloud hanging vacantly in the still air. It would coat everything with a gritty patina and she'd have to get the rags and clean the glass lanterns all over again. She stepped to the wall and leaned the broom there. She faced Ross once more, brushing back the stray hair at her temples. "Why have you come here?"

"Why don't you try to guess?"

She looked deeply into his dark eyes and felt his destructive force boiling near the surface. "You don't have to kill me," she said, feeling an alien emotion. *Fear.* Fear on the cellular level that made her jangle all over, goose bumps rising on her arms. She hadn't feared another creature in fifty years, not even Balthazar, and had forgotten the primeval power of it.

"I think I do have to kill you," he said, stepping toward her. "Where is your lover? He must be drunk on the idea of victory. Why didn't he leave here with the rest?"

The word *coward* leaped to her mind before she could stop it. She looked away.

"I think you've got it wrong," Ross said. "He's not a coward. He's actually more cunning than Upton. He's let Upton take all the risks so that he can reap all the rewards. Hadn't that ever occurred to you?"

It hadn't. Her anger had prevented her from considering that Balthazar might have stayed behind because of secret ulterior motives. Of course Ross was right. Upton would lead the army and risk his existence against a formidable enemy. Mentor would know if he could cut off the head of the snake, it would die. Upton had placed himself in a most precarious position while Balthazar remained safe—or so he'd thought—in the Caves of the Green Man.

"You're going to stop them, aren't you?" Sereny asked.

"You and Mentor will find a way to put down the rebellion. That's why you haven't come before now; it's why you didn't interfere before. Why bring the war to the enemies' land and lose one advantage, was that it? And you want Charles. He's escaped you and you want him back. This way he's come to you—to play in your own backyard."

"What a clever woman you are. But can we do it? Are we at least as ingenious as your lover?"

She expected they were.

Now a smile played at her mouth. While staring at Ross, reading him the way she'd trained herself to read Balthazar, she had picked up one of the most important elements in Ross' life. He enjoyed women. He took human females several times a week, ravishing them sexually before murdering them and taking their blood. He saw himself only reflected in the eyes of a woman. His sleek muscular body. His thick hair and strange dark eyes. He was a hedonist who ceased to exist to himself if he couldn't be admired and loved by the opposite sex. He cared nothing for men or his Predator clan. It was women he needed for his mirror.

She stepped toward him this time and saw the flicker of surprise and interest kindling deep in his eyes. It was her wedge that she'd use to save her own life. She had no doubt Ross could tear her asunder with his bare hands. She had no weapon to stop him. Her strength, compared to his, was as a Lilliputian to a giant. All she had was her affections and vast knowledge of how to please a man. She would use all that she knew.

She moved into his arms like a cloud settling into a spot in an empty sky. She put her hands behind his neck, massaging the muscles just below his ears with her thumbs. She gazed into his eyes so he could read her and know she did not mean to harm him. She brought her face close to his, her lips closing over his mouth. He might let out a roar and bend her head to the side and sink his massive fangs into her throat. He might throw her all the way down the corridor, leaving her broken until he could sweep down and finish her.

Or he could respond on the physical plane as a man to a woman, and fall so profoundly in love with her that her death could be averted. She was not a housemaid now. She was not a mourning mother. Nor was she a devoted partner to Balthazar. She had transformed into the very being Ross believed he needed. The spell she cast was part supernatural, learned and perfected over many years and many liaisons, but on the whole it was a natural physical skill that came easily to her.

She loved the lean strong musculature of men, the rough violence lying latent below the surface of civility, the male member that could fill her with so much joy and sensation that the world and everything in it disappeared. Feeling such immense fascination coming from her, male vampires were able to lose themselves in her, believing they'd found a soul mate.

Ross kissed her back, grabbing hold of her by the waist and pressing her close.

She dared not smile into his kiss. Dared not let her mind rove an inch from the bodily sensations that caused her to tremble and give into him softly. Ross would know the instant she mentally stood back, watching rather than participating.

So she gave of herself wholly, fully, without reserve, melting against his hard body so that she was putty in his hands. Her tongue sought his, her soul turned on the spindle of his desire, and together they slipped to the swept floor, she raising her skirts while Ross unzipped his slacks. Their cool flesh met and warmed with the friction between them. It was the only time Sereny felt warm, the only time, except for her involvement in domesticity, when she felt human again.

They coupled there in the corridor, rolling from wall to wall, her soft sighs rising and falling, filling the cavern with echoes.

*   *   *

Balthazar stood watching Sereny and Ross going at one another like delirious animals in the long corridor.

He had time to slip away again and take the long polished stiletto from the imported monkeywood box in which he kept it. He came back to the corridor, his face set in stone. He had hated Ross and Mentor for years, but this latest betrayal with the one immortal he cared for was the limit.

He did not blame Sereny. She had done what was natural to her, something he understood from the beginning when they'd first met. She had been a lusty woman in a loving marriage when she'd become vampire, and sex was the one thing she'd never given up. She entered into mating with such abandon it could rattle the senses of any partner she chose.

With Ross, she was trying to save herself. It was much less of an emotional betrayal to him than when she had coupled with Upton in Australia.

He stood against the wall, shimmering in and out of existence, so agitated his corporeal body wouldn't obey him. When they finished, he would take Ross' head. He would send it home to America and have it delivered to Mentor's doorstep.

He did not really care that Ross had touched his woman. Sereny didn't belong to anyone but herself. If she ever left him, it would be because she found someone else more vital or alluring. She was a force of nature, like wind or rain, and just as uncontrollable.

He *did* care that Ross had come sneaking into his home intent on killing him. That. Would. Not. Do.

His impatience gnawed at his gut as he waited in the shadows for the act to be consummated. How dare Mentor believe he could send Ross alone to dispatch him. This was what the old Predator thought of him. That he was weak and vulnerable. That he could be taken without a full cadre of Predators willing to sever him from his life.

He shivered and shimmered and winked in and out of reality, his mind brimming with hate. He could hardly wait another moment. If they didn't hurry, he would have to fall on them in the throes of their desire, chancing harm to Sereny.

But, after all, what did it matter?

She had never loved him.

*   *   *

Though the woman made him wild with passion until his place in the world was blotted from mind, Ross had come back to himself moments before Balthazar crept near with a long knife. Never had a woman, Predator or human, bewildered him so thoroughly. Sereny was simply a goddess. She smelled of soil warmed by the sun, a familiar scent that was at once soothing and intoxicating. She might have built this aura around herself deliberately—that of the earth mother—and, if so, it worked. Her skin wasn't brittle and hard like the flesh of most female vampires. It was as soft as a mortal's and covered with silky fuzz like that found on ripe peaches. Her hair was long and slipped through his fingers like sheer chiffon.

Everything about her appealed to his old human senses. To touch her, to taste her, to breathe in her scent, and to plunge headlong into the wild wet of her made him insatiable. If he had not trained himself to monitor his surroundings at all times, even during the most heated of sexual congress, Balthazar might have caught him unaware.

Ross did nothing to change his actions as that would have alerted the other Predator. Instead, Ross continued the motions involved in making love to Sereny yet all the while readying to leap to self-defense as soon as Balthazar closed in.

He did not have long to wait. When the shadow at the turn in the corridor shifted, Ross knew the Predator was at his back and close enough to strike. At that exact second Ross disengaged from Sereny, pushing her with a powerful thrust of his arms against the wall. He heard her wail as he rolled over and away from his position, came to his feet in a flash, and reached into the inner cloth pocket of his large cape to withdraw his own knife. It was not as impressive as the one Balthazar wielded, but it would do the job.

He laughed aloud at Balthazar's utter surprise. It had all happened in the twinkling of an eye so that now they stood facing one another, knives in hand, the woman cringing against the wall. They were equal opponents. Balthazar would have no advantage.

The other Predator read his thoughts. "I do not need an advantage to slit you from throat to bowels," Balthazar said.

"Fatal assessment," Ross said. "You needed every advantage in the world."

Ross flew toward Balthazar as the last word left his

mouth. Engaged, they fought with the fierceness of gods. Knives flashed and drew blood, limbs were slashed and bled, fangs were sunk and flesh bitten away in great chunks.

As they fought, they screamed, the sounds filling the caverns. At some point Ross realized his opponent was not going to be killed in this manner, he was too strong to submit. Mentor had told him to be careful, but it appeared he had really underestimated Balthazar. He would have to defeat him in another way.

Immediately Ross pulled away and flew down the corridor in retreat. On the way he dispersed his molecules, his being disintegrating even as his footsteps sped him away. He cloaked his mind and prowled through new passageways. He noted the many lanterns set into niches all along the paths and in some of the cryptlike rooms. Finally he came to the large chamber that served as Balthazar's home. Taking a burning lantern from a shelf, Ross tossed it onto the cushioned sofa. He took a skull with a candle inside and threw it at the lush fabric covering the bed. Fire spread quickly, taking flame from the spilled oil and wax. Gray smoke changed to black and filled the chamber.

Ross was just as afraid of fire as any other vampire. Just the sight of flame made him so jittery that it took all his willpower not to turn and run from the caves before he knew the fire was taking. But to linger was suicide. He raced away and down a path, knocking lanterns to the ground as he went. He found the passage leading up to an opening in the top of the volcano and flew quickly there. Once in the fresh night air, he looked for boulders and, lifting them without any trouble, moved them over to the entrance to block it.

As he worked, he came from cloaking long enough to check the interior caves for Balthazar and Sereny. He saw in his mind's eye Balthazar trapped between one corridor and the next by fire. He was howling and flinging his arms about. If he were not to panic, he could probably disperse into the air and find some tiny crack in the walls through which he could escape.

Where was Sereny? He hadn't sensed her down in the earth below. Maybe she had fled during the battle. He could still taste her on his tongue and it made him hope she'd got out.

"Is that true?" Sereny asked.

Ross twirled and saw her poised in the air, the wind from the Azores blowing her long skirt so that it was pressed against the outline of her legs. Her fangs had descended so that her red lips were slightly parted.

"I was just hoping you'd got free," he said.

She waited, watching him as he finished piling stone upon stone over the other exists leading out from the caves below. She made no move to help or hinder, as if she had turned to stone herself and none of this had anything to do with her.

Ross knew she could have left and been miles away by now if she'd wanted, yet she'd stayed. He felt no threat from her and decided letting her live was the right thing to do. It was Balthazar the Predator army followed, not this woman. It was Balthazar who had wanted Malachi dead.

Ross finished and sat down on one of the stones while he monitored the vampire trapped below him in the dark smoky caves.

"He'll kill himself," Sereny said, having never moved from where she hovered in the air over the main exit from the caves.

"The fire will kill him."

"Only because he'll let it."

"Why do you say that?"

"You've destroyed his lair. He's lived four miles below ground nearly all his immortal days. You've burned the bones of his victims, scorched the jewels he kept in wooden boxes, and blocked every exit. If he tries to come out now, he knows you'll be waiting. He knows there's no real escape now."

"Doesn't it bother you?" Ross asked. "That he'll die?"

Sereny shrugged, but Ross detected her sorrow. "We all die. Sooner or later." The wind had blown long strands of hair back from her face and she looked like a ghost in the moonlight. Her eyes shone from the sockets like silver nickels.

"Can I go with you?" she asked finally, when he was silent too long.

"I'm sure you can. I don't know if you may."

She smiled a little. "May I, Master, go with you?"

"Let me ask you something," he said. "Has anyone ever

trusted you? Should I trust you to be at my side when I've just separated you from an enemy?"

"I didn't help you stab him or start the fire. I couldn't prevent any of that, could I? You can't betray someone if you never had a chance to save him in the first place."

Ross thought it over. He tested her emotions again and found her sorrow real, and her will to live stronger than any sorrow. How many trustworthy vampires had he ever known anyway? One. Mentor. No one else. There was no point in asking it of Sereny.

"You may go with me," he said, savoring the memory of their brief coupling in the caves.

A long piercing cry rose from deep in the bowels of the volcano. It made Ross' ears prickle, and he hunched his shoulders against it. He imagined the flesh singeing and curling, finally falling from the skeleton. He could almost feel the terrible heat and the cleansing flame that devoured everything in its path, even bone. There was not one ounce of remorse for what he'd done to Balthazar, but he had hoped not to resort to using fire.

"He's dying," Sereny said.

Ross thought regret had crept into her voice. She didn't bother to deceive him now.

"Yes," Ross said. "It's over, isn't it?"

Sereny nodded and floated down, her feet settling gently on the volcanic stone near him. Ross looked into the sky over the vast flat sea, imagining how far he was from his ranch house in Texas. "Let's go," he said. "Let's get out of this godforsaken place."

*   *   *

As Sereny sailed alongside her new mate toward a distant, foreign shore, she let the grief over Balthazar's death enfold her. He had been good to her, and loyal, and understanding. She had not helped him because she could not. If she'd been able, she would have helped him defeat Ross, but it all happened too fast. They were beyond her down the corridor before she ever raised herself to her feet and straightened her skirts. Making love with Ross should have given Balthazar a chance to take his enemy unaware, but he'd waited too long and Ross had been vigilant, even in coitus.

She thought maybe she kept taking male vampires as her own because she was trying to recapture the love she'd had for her husband. She took male vampires and served them as she'd served her husband. In servitude she really wielded the power in the relationship, something she'd known since she was just a girl. In giving of herself, she controlled the man who received her.

No matter what the buried reasons for her behavior, she held no regrets. Ross was just as strong and sexually attractive as her other lovers. She was only drawn to powerful men, powerful vampires. Her lost husband had been just a brick mason, but he had been strong in both body and mind. He studied books in his free time, learning how to manage a business and just before her death, he had taken their small savings and started a little shop of his own. He never bowed his head to another man. He never mistreated his wife and children. He had ambition and loyalty and he had loved her as if she were a goddess. . . .

Now she was speeding across the face of the globe to a new situation. A new world, with a new master over her. She had never been outside of Europe and the Canary Islands. She'd never even visited the African cities though they were so near Lanzarote. She had picked up English and could speak it only because she had been a tourist so long, traveling with vulgar Americans who thought everything in the world was there for their singular amusement. She did not know if Ross really wanted her along or if he'd tire of her and slit her throat.

All she knew was that she was again homeless, without family, and cast out to fend for herself. She'd only survived so far because of her magnetic sexuality and her ability to adjust to change.

She hoped it would be enough this time.

She did not want to die, though Balthazar had always suspected she was suicidal. He had been so wrong.

She really did not want to die.

3

Charles Upton walked openly down the night-shrouded streets of Dallas, recalling landmarks from when he'd moved his headquarters from Houston to Dallas after turning vampire. He marveled at the new skyscrapers raised during his years in prison, the great flowing fountains, and the increased population that meant more freeways and snarled traffic.

He drank in the cardinal scent of humanity all around him. He glanced through windows at the silhouettes of people in their homes, thinking themselves safe behind locked door. They drove past in cars and trucks, going about their lives as if nothing evil might ever befall them. They stood behind store counters, shopped for groceries, drank and danced in bars, and walked hand in hand down sidewalks, oblivious to how precarious their existence was.

Charles reveled in the thought he could take any one of them at any second, ending life so quickly the victim wouldn't even know he was dying. Already this night he'd fed on two men, leaving their bodies exposed so they'd be found, their torn throats as clean and bloodless as his careful licking could leave them.

He wanted to strike fear into men. He would no longer hide away the corpses or heal the puncture wounds before he left them. Let humanity discover they were not alone. They'd been yearning to meet an alien creature for years, discussing the Roswell incident endlessly, looking to the skies for spaceships, devising abduction scenarios and alien encounters. There was a whole cottage industry publishing books and making movies about man's desire, his hidden desire, to bump into something much stronger and more intelligent than he. Charles would oblige, happily. If they wanted monsters, he would show them monsters. His Predators, the most powerful beings in the world, had come from hiding. Nothing would be kept secret any longer.

Ahead of him, Charles saw a small group spilling onto the sidewalk from a downtown dance club. They were young and high on life. They smelled of liquor and tobacco and sex, of acrid sweat and sweet, fruity perfume. They were laughing and talking, unaware of the danger approaching.

Charles neared, meaning to move past so fast they'd never see him, but something about their confident strides and calm voices caused him to slow. They were so arrogant and secure. They hadn't a shred of fear in their minds, and he hated them for their easy camaraderie. His presence was that of a man, they thought. Just a man moving past them, someone on the periphery of their consciousness they could safely ignore.

Charles easily rearranged his human face, the brown Thai skin darkening and sprouting slick black fur, the forehead elongating while his human nose and mouth formed into a snout. His eyes glowed as they slimmed to thin almond shapes. His cheekbones rose. His teeth sharpened.

He growled.

Two males on the edge of the group of people heard him and turned to stare.

Charles came closer. He growled again, louder, the sound coming from deep in his chest and drowning out their chatter.

The whole group paused and turned as one body. They could see him clearly now. He'd stopped not more than three feet from them, his face completely transformed into that of a jungle cat rising up out of the prim white collar of his shirt. More specifically, he had taken on the image of a black jaguar from the neck up.

He turned into their minds.

A cat . . .

He's wearing a mask . . .

What kind of . . . ?

Need to get out of here quick . . .

Oh, God, no, I must be drunk . . .

"Hello." Charles could speak as human with vocal cords though his exterior was perfectly animal. "Would you like to die tonight?"

Two women screamed and one fainted into the arms of her partner, standing at her side. One of the men whispered, "What the hell?"

Another said, breathlessly. "Let's get out of here."

Charles watched them curiously as their reactions evolved from disbelief to understanding. Whether they could have voiced their thoughts or not, their instincts—and their eyes—told them he wasn't entirely human. He was the alien they had always wanted to meet, yet could never really believe existed. He was the childhood bogeyman. He was the fantastic thing hovering just at the edge of their nightmares, the shadow in the open closet door that shouldn't be there. He was the grave and the darkness of the void.

He wouldn't attack. He cared too little about these little people to take their lives. They were the ants working away at the base of a giant tree. They were ephemeral ripples on the surface of a pond.

They were nothing but food. They were blood containers. They were stupid and inferior.

They broke and ran, one of the men carrying the unconscious woman in his arms, staggering with her weight as he made his way across the street with the others. Passing cars screeched as the stunned drivers hit their brakes and bent over their horns in frustration.

Charles let his human face take over his features and then he laughed, his laughter trailing the fleeing mortals like a dark storm.

Once they had disappeared from the street, Charles walked on, a frightening smile on his face. He knew he'd played a parlor trick, but he'd enjoyed the moment immensely. There would be so many more like it. One day he'd transform before television cameras so that even those at the ends of the world could see him go from man to jaguar in milliseconds. They would worship and obey or die. Once his army grew from hundreds to hundreds of thousands, nothing could stop him.

Mankind did not need an Antichrist. They only needed Charles Upton.

Upton's plan to disrupt the natural order of the vampire nations was already underway. His soldier Predators walked the streets of Dallas, methodically decimating the lower level vampires, the despicable Cravens. A few of

Ross' clan tried to intercept, but were quickly surrounded, outnumbered, and taken down.

In his first days as vampire Upton learned of the three distinct categories of vampires and how they lived on the Earth in peace and in hiding. He was repulsed by the Cravens from the beginning. They were weak and useless, creatures that hid from the sun which could scorch and burn them. They were physically ill, suffering the drastic symptoms of porphyria, the same disease that had plagued Upton when he'd been human.

Their very existence infuriated him because they reminded him too much of his last years with the same disease. They were an affront to the supernatural—bottom feeders who drained the efforts of Predators who helped keep them alive. Before his change, he'd believed vampires were not just supernatural beings using human forms, but nearer to gods who ruled the planet. When he'd found out about Cravens, who had no business taking up space, and Naturals, who in their fantasies thought they could continue to function as humans alongside mankind—well, he wanted to protest vehemently. It wasn't at all like he'd imagined. It wasn't at all as it should be. Better that vampires be exactly like the fictional depictions of them than to be so divided and weak.

That it had been this way from the beginning when porphyria mutated to create the vampire meant nothing to him. He thought the Predators should have made it their task to kill off the other nations immediately. They never should have been allowed eternal life, something rightfully reserved only for the creature who deserved the dark gift.

Mentor gave Upton some ridiculous explanation of why Cravens had chosen their path and why none of the rest of them had the authority to interfere. Upton had laughed in his face. "You must believe in a Supreme Being who is able to reason and create life. What a delusion!"

Mentor hadn't appreciated Upton's scorn. He had refused to speak to him of these things again. He warned him, however, to leave the Cravens alone. Leave *all the others* alone, he'd said.

Before he'd been imprisoned, Upton had followed the edict. Now he was free to do things his way, and it wouldn't include mercy for any but the Predators. And not even

them if they refused to join with him. He didn't care how
many vampires died. There were already more than enough
to rule humanity. More Predators were born out of their
human deaths every day. Humans might outnumber them
a hundred thousand to one, but one Predator could bring
a city to its knees if he wished. What were mortals going
to do? Chase a being who could disappear? Fire weapons
at a creature who healed in seconds and regenerated the
flesh without thought or will?

Humans could not get close enough to take their heads.
And if they used fire, they'd have to burn down all of
civilization and still they wouldn't kill them all.

A stray little whirl of wind swept down the street, picking
up leaves and litter from curbs and gutters. Upton glanced
around to see he'd entered a rundown neighborhood. Older
cars were parked along the street and in driveways. Shotgun houses stood in dark silent rows, all of them built fifty
years ago or more and now sagging with age. There were
few streetlights, no patrol cars, and no evidence of guard
dogs.

He had reached his destination. Inside the small white
house he faced resided the woman Mentor had come to
love. He had learned of her from snooping in Mentor's
thoughts one day before he displeased him enough to be
sent to Thailand. Oh, Mentor loved her, all right. She was
like a permanent stain he could not erase. She camped in
his soul like a demon latched onto the devil's tail.

That woman slept now next to her husband, a doctor,
neither of them dreaming their lives were about to end.

The predator cat came forward again, changing Upton's
face into jaguar. He licked his wide cat lips with a rough
feline tongue and moved stealthily toward the door.

4

Detective Lewis Teal was on his way home after a long day filling out paperwork. He had helped lead a task force to round up a crack cocaine ring in the city. All that had been left on the case were the endless forms he had to fill out and file with the correct departments.

He lived near the station in a second-rate hotel called The Swan, named, he presumed, long ago in a better economic climate and a more poetic time. The six-story hotel had once been home to addicts and welfare recipients who ran numbers and prostitutes too old for pimps. When he moved in, the whole place was nearly emptied and another sort of clientele moved in. In order to attract that clientele, the management had painted the lobby and hallways a pretty cream color, fixed the elevator, and put new light bulbs in the hanging sign over the sidewalk where the great, white swan herself floated on a neon strip of blue fizzing gases. Civil servants lived here now, bank clerks, the elderly on pensions, and, of course, a cop.

Teal had never married, not because he didn't want to, but because it just never quite worked out. He was a big, burly sort of fellow with brown suits that never really fit him and big black, lace-up shoes that he bought at a discount in warehouse department stores. His brow overhung his faded blue eyes and his jaw was a couple inches too long for his face. He wasn't Russell Crowe, he knew that. He wasn't even Jay Leno. He wasn't witty. He did not make much money because he was an honest cop and immune to graft. He wasn't anything to speak of, except smart and dedicated.

Those qualities didn't seem to turn women on.

Now at forty-five years old, and three years from retirement, he had accepted the idea he would always live alone. The Swan Hotel suited him just fine.

Tonight the air stank of exhaust fumes and dust, but he drank it in anyway, glad to be out of the office with the piles of papers. He was never happy anywhere but on the street. Paperwork almost killed him, like it did most cops.

A shady character walked toward him on the sidewalk, and Teal mentally froze. He began to wonder. Was the guy a contract killer? Was he a pedophile? A wife beater, at the very least? There was something hinky-odd about him and Teal didn't know what it was. After all, he was just a stranger passing in the night. Without grabbing the guy, handcuffing him, taking him back to the station for a fingerprint run, he had to pass the stranger by.

But he was definitely bad. Something bad about him.

As Teal and the man drew close and passed on the sidewalk, Teal looked into the other's eyes, searching for a telling hint to his character. For a split second he thought the eyes were those of a cat and the face that of a jungle beast. Jesus! They must have slipped something in the station's coffee urn. He was psychotic.

Truth was, he was probably overtired and his brain wasn't hitting on all cylinders. In fact, at this point, it didn't even have spark plugs.

Once the man passed by, Teal forced himself not to glance back. Guy hadn't broken the law. He was bad, but how was anyone to prove it? There were lots of bad guys. Lots.

Let it go, Teal, he told himself. *You're a dead-ass, paperwork-blind cop and need ten hours' sleep. You're seeing monsters.*

And then Teal saw the corpse. He knew it was a corpse. It wasn't moving and it was sprawled all wrong on the edge of the sidewalk, the head stuck under a dusty holly tree that grew just beside the entrance to The Swan Hotel.

Teal took his time approaching the dead body. It was dead. It wasn't going anywhere.

He looked all around and saw no one on the street. The bad stranger had come from this direction and maybe he'd killed this person, but then maybe he hadn't. Who knew? He'd call forensics and let them scope it out.

Maybe the dead guy had died from an overdose or too

much booze and his liver did a fatal flip-flop or he had keeled over from a heart attack.

But it was the way he was lying on the sidewalk that told the veteran cop it was probably murder. It just didn't look good at all. It looked like the result of violence.

As he reached the body, Mrs. Carrie came out of the hotel dressed to the nines. She had on heels, patent leather, white. She wore a low-cut, flowered dress that showed off too much of her aged bosom. A strand of fake pearls dangled in the crevice. She was on her way to the bar two blocks distant, The Rocky Road. Teal always thought of ice cream when he went down there.

Mrs. Carrie hit the place at eight every night and didn't come back to her room until eleven, but she was never really drunk. Slightly tipsy and sweet, yes, but not drunk. Teal liked her just fine. She reminded him of his Polish grandmother, the one with the last name of Tealiski.

Teal reached the body before she saw it and he passed it by, hurrying to take her arm as she came down the concrete steps. "Evening, Miz Carrie. Beautiful night."

She looked up at him in alarm for an instant and, recognizing him, finally smiled to show her dentures, all white and large and as counterfeit as the pearl necklace. "Hello, Mr. Teal. Won't you have a drink with me?"

"Not tonight, but thank you. I'm a little tired. Next time, maybe." He guided her down the steps, careful to stay between her and the body on the sidewalk. He could block a truck when he wanted to. He turned her toward the bar and waggled his fingers at her as she tottered off on the patent leather high heels.

When she was across the street and into the next block, he turned and hunkered down near the body. Dead man. Murdered man. He just knew it.

He carefully moved the short, spiky branches of the holly tree aside so he could see the face. He grew very still, breathing shallowly. His massive barrel chest deflated. "Oh, shit," he said.

The man had a wound in his throat as wide as a wrestler's hand. There were . . . teeth marks. All the tendons and muscles lay bare, sucked or licked or sponged dry of blood. There wasn't a speck of blood anywhere on him. His eyes were open and glassy and looked as if they'd been sucked right back into his skull. The skin of his face was so tight it had pulled his lips back from his teeth, which appeared to be perfectly capable of tearing the hide from a running cow.

Teal let the holly limbs go and stood up. He reached to his waist for his cell phone. He hit the auto dial.

"Teal," he said. "Send the meat wagon and forensics down here to The Swan. I've got something . . . um . . . different here."

It was after midnight before Teal again left the station and headed for home. He had been over to the coroner's office. *Well, not the office,* he thought. *The morgue.* That's where he'd been. Curious, standing around with his big meaty hands behind his back, rocking from one foot to the other. The city coroner said the wound looked like some kind of animal attack. "Dog?" Teal wanted to know.

"Not likely," the coroner said.

"Not even a big dog?"

"Don't think so. This will take some study."

In his hotel room on the fourth floor, Teal got a quart bottle of orange juice from the little refrigerator in the corner, and pulled up a chair to the open window. He sat sipping the good, cold juice and looking out at the night. While he had been at the station, two other reports of dead bodies came in, throats slashed or gashed or . . . torn, hell if they knew. Other detectives were sent out on those cases.

The coroner was busy tonight. He had three mysteries to plague him and he was sorely pissed off about it.

Teal drank and looked at the street and thought he was getting pissed, too. Animals didn't kill people in *his* city. They just didn't.

*   *   *

Bette Kinyo's eyes flashed open as she was aroused from deep sleep by a psychic alarm going off in her head. She was breathing quickly, her heart throbbing painfully in her chest. It was no nightmare that had awakened her. There was something real prowling around her house seeking entry. She knew it was there as surely as she knew the Earth revolved. It was not Mentor. This presence was vampire and Predator, but not at all like Mentor.

She sat up and threw back the covers. She reached for Alan and shook him.

"Wake up," she whispered urgently. "Someone's here."

Alan woke slowly, rubbing at his eyes as he sat up. "Who's here?"

"Someone bad. A vampire." Bette was out of bed and going for the door. "Hurry, we need to get out."

Alan was slow in obeying his wife, sleep still dragging him down. "What did you say, Bette?" He looked at the clock on the bedside table. "My God, it's three in the morning."

She had the door of the bedroom open, her head turned to the side to listen down the stairwell. She put a finger to her lips and shut the door again, the soft click of the lock she turned sounding to her ears like a gunshot. She came to the bed and said next to his ear, "A vampire. To kill us. He's downstairs."

She didn't know what to do. Their escape was blocked. She glanced at the window that overlooked her garden. She knew she should have bought a rope ladder in case of fire, but she'd always put it off.

There was a roof below the window that sheltered the back door. It was small, but they could climb onto it one at a time and drop to the ground from there. It was the only way.

"Hurry," she said, hauling him by the hand from the bed. Her heart was now beating so rapidly she could hardly breathe.

She didn't really believe they'd be allowed to leave the house, but they must try. The vampire she detected downstairs was unlike any she'd met before. It was a Predator with the face of a cat. A very large black cat. She didn't believe it was Ross, the Predator Alan had once witnessed murdering two women. This was another vampire, one with his hatred held before him like a shield. He was heartless and would never be talked out of his murderous rage.

Alan had the window raised and she sat on the sill, swinging her legs out. She turned onto her belly and inched down the outside wall, feet dangling as she felt for the solid roof below.

She cried out mentally, calling Mentor's name. She'd only done that once before, and she'd been able to contact him before he reached Alan in Houston. She hoped he would hear her this time. Their lives depended on it. Fleeing would not take them far from the danger. The vampire in her house was coming up the stairs now and soon he'd be in the bedroom. He could appear and disappear at will if he was anything like Mentor. He wouldn't have to climb, but could fly from her window. A lock on a door was no deterrent for him.

Escape was truly impossible and though she knew it, she hurriedly dropped to the roof and caught herself from toppling to the ground. If they could keep the vampire at bay for just a few minutes more, Mentor might come and save them. It was their only hope.

She glanced back at the window and her husband. She saw he was coming from the window. He had swung one leg over the sill. She turned and leaped to the ground, rolling on the dew damp grass. She grunted from the impact, came to her knees and then to her feet. She looked to the window again, about to hurry her husband along. But Alan had vanished.

"Alan!" Her voice, strangled with fear, was not loud. She called again, "Alan!"

In her mind she screamed, *Mentor! Help us!*

The cat face appeared at her bedroom window. It hissed at her, the lips pulled back in a snarl. Her heart stopped, and she sucked in air to keep from passing out.

"Let him go," she called to the Predator, her voice still weak. "Please. Please let him go. Take me instead. Please, I'm begging you."

The awful face ducked through the window, disappearing. Nightmare images flooded Bette's mind. The cat ravishing her husband Alan's throat torn open and pumping out his life's blood. His eyes closing forever.

She screamed, this time her voice returned to normal. She screamed at the top of her lungs. Lights came on in the house next door and dogs began to bark. She rushed to the back kitchen door and banged on it with her fists, weeping in frustration and mad with grief. It was locked. She couldn't get in. She couldn't get to Alan.

"Mentor, Mentor, Mentor, help us," she wailed, her fists breaking against the wood of the door like thunder against a mountainside.

*   *   *

Mentor had fallen into one of the deepest sleeps of his life. He was exhausted from worry. He didn't sleep but once in every three or four days and only then because the human body he inhabited forced him to it. But this night he lay down on his bed, covered his eyes with an arm, and was dead to the world in seconds.

The cry that woke him was so loud and so fearsome that his eyes snapped open and he could feel his skin drawing tight with dread.

It was Bette. She was on the brink of death or insanity, he could not tell which. He sat up in the dark bedroom and began to shimmer. He must reach her within the next few moments or she would be lost to him.

He shimmered again and he was behind her where she beat wildly at her own kitchen door from the outside. He reached out to take her arms. She turned, flailing at him, her face distorted with tears. He felt sorrow coming off her like heat from a stove. It inundated him and left him senseless.

She finally recognized him and fell forward against his chest. "Up there," she said between sobs. She pointed to the upstairs bedroom window. "A vampire! He's got Alan."

Mentor let her go and rose to the roof and then to the open window. He pushed through into the dark bedroom, but he could see everything as if it were day. There was no vampire, but he felt the presence that had been here. It was moving rapidly away from the house, taking its evil with it. On the floor lay Alan Star, Bette's husband. He had been savaged, his head nearly torn from the body. Blood covered him, covered the floor, the window sill, and the wall.

Mentor sighed and turned away his head. This was not a normal attack. Though every vampire attack was fatal, few of them were this vicious. It was as if the Predator who had done this meant to hurt others besides the victim. He wanted to leave behind enough carnage to damage the mind of anyone who witnessed it.

Mentor could not let Bette see it.

He heard her calling up to him, questioning him. Her

cries were piteous. "Is he dead?" she called. "Is he dead, he isn't dead, is he, Mentor, he didn't die, did he?"

Mentor knelt by the body and took Alan's head and positioned it correctly. He placed his hand over the brutal wound and rested it there. He could make some repairs. He could not bring back this man's life, he hadn't that power, but he could close the worst of the severed flesh so that Bette would never know the horror of what had been done to the man she loved.

When he'd done what he could, he lifted Alan and carried him down the stairs. He laid him on the sofa and went to unlock the back door to let Bette inside. She was again beating at the door, her misery causing her to slip from her mind again. Mentor had learned over the years what made men go mad. The shock and grief Bette was experiencing were enough to plummet her over the edge if she didn't regain control. In madness the landscape changed, the world receded, and the mind sat in darkness, admitting no light.

He took her through the house, his arm around her waist to prop her up. She froze when she saw Alan on the sofa. Her shoulders began to shake. Though she was silent now, he could feel the terrible shock racing through her body. Suddenly, she slumped toward the floor, but he caught her before she hit and guided her to a chair. He found an afghan thrown over the back of the chair, and he took it across the room to cover the body.

There was still blood all over the pajamas Alan had been wearing. Mentor couldn't do anything about that. He wanted the body covered and away from sight. She had to see for herself he was dead and that was enough.

"Bette, I am so sorry. I came as fast as I could." He was not God. He could not prevent every disaster. He could not move instantaneously, covering miles without some time passing.

She couldn't speak. Or she wouldn't. He didn't know and refused to meddle by intruding into her mind. When he'd lost his wife to death, he had been this way. He knew no one could have reached him. He rode the waves of denial and acceptance alone until he could face living again. He must let Bette do the same.

He stood next to her, his hand on her shoulder, and

waited. It might take hours, but she would have questions when she could speak to him and he had to be there to answer them.

The murderer had been Upton. He'd known it when he found Alan. He had detected the scent that belonged only to Upton. Since his escape in Thailand that scent had grown more and more like musk, the mark of the great jungle cat he favored.

Mentor did not have to ask himself why Upton would kill Alan. He had likely been after Bette instead, but she'd eluded him. He wanted to kill Bette because he knew what she meant to Mentor. If he had not fallen in love, and if that love had never been divulged through his thoughts of her, this would never have happened.

Bette might never forgive him. She loved Alan. One love was responsible for the death of another love. Who could forgive that?

He stood at her side, never moving, waiting for the sun to rise and for her to speak to him. This was his self-imposed punishment. Once he told her the truth about why Alan had died, he expected the punishment would be much more serious. She might banish him from her life. He could never visit her garden, never see her again. She would have no idea how that would leech all joy from him. He hoped he was wrong, he prayed she'd realize he couldn't help loving her and he'd had no part in Upton's theft of his most intimate thoughts.

He stood, mourning Alan, mourning for Bette and for himself. There was time enough later to let his fury carry him after the diabolical Charles Upton. For now he must wait, give solace, and eventually admit his guilt.

*   *   *

Dolan had always been a faithful servant to Mentor. If it were not for the great vampire, Dolan thought he would have long since killed himself. Mentor gave him reasons to live. He'd trained him in some of the Predator's arts and just as he'd predicted, Dolan possessed more strength and ambition than his Craven brothers. For years Dolan had gone with Mentor to the bedside of the younger vampires who were going through the red dream of death. He could not enter that fantastic world where the soul departed, returning as vampire, but he grew to have great respect for the crossover they all must make into immortality.

While Charles Upton had been imprisoned, it was Dolan's job to help monitor him. He'd failed miserably at it. he often thought Mentor sent him to the Thai monastery to keep him busy. Given his weaker supernatural abilities, Dolan knew his desire to serve was stronger than his aptitude. As years stretched into decades, time being the vampire's worst enemy, Dolan spent more and more time at the peaceful retreat in the Thai jungle. As those years passed he grew lax and content, his attention often straying from Upton's cell.

Now Mentor had trusted him with another important assignment, and he must not fail this time. He had already alerted three Craven communities, urging them to scatter somewhere away from the city to an open place that could not burn. They should go to ground, digging into the earth and burying themselves, he said, and pray the renegade Predators didn't find them.

He was approaching another Craven communal house when he smelled a hint of smoke in the air. His throat constricted as he hurried, his feet flying over the long expanse of neglected lawn leading to the house. Before he entered, he heard the cries of his brethren. Struggling, Dolan forced open the locked door and a cloud of black smoke engulfed him. He tried to narrow his vision so he could peer into the thick darkness, but it was like looking through murky water. He could make out figures writhing and crawling about, desperately trying to find the exit. He screamed at them to follow his voice. "Here's the door," he yelled, hoping they could hear him through their panic. There was nothing more devastating to a vampire than to be trapped in a fire.

Now he could make out the flames burning through walls and roof, and he heard the crackling as the fire swept through the large old house, consuming it with wicked speed. One or two Cravens made it to the door and stumbled out, their faces blackened with soot, their eyes wild with terror.

Dolan could not go inside. He knew he should. He knew if he were brave, he would. But the heat from the fire even

now crawled over his face and hands like fiery worms and
the smoke blinded him. His instinct was to run far away.
The Predators who had set the fire were gone, and the
Cravens left inside were doomed. Even if he entered the
maelstrom, he might not save a single one.

He pulled one or two more survivors from the doorway
and commanded them to flee from the city. Then he moved
back on the lawn, sirens rising in the distance, and rubbed
at his face with his hands. This was against all the rules
they had once lived by. No one had ever murdered his own
kind this way, heartlessly trapping the weak who could not
save themselves. It was a truly evil entity who had ordered
it. Charles Upton should burn in hell forever for this merci-
less act, he thought.

Before the fire trucks arrived, Dolan left, hurrying to the
next place harboring the Cravens. As the night deepened,
he found more and more houses burning with the Cravens
trapped inside. He saved only two or three out of every
house, sometimes dragging them from the buildings or
throwing them from windows.

It seemed the whole city was on fire, fire trucks wailing
through the seedier neighborhoods where these poorer
vampires lived. Fire lit the night sky while smoke billowed
and hung like storm clouds over whole blocks of houses.
Mortals rushed from their homes, watching the burning of
their neighborhoods, the sparks from the Cravens' homes
dancing through updrafts to fall and take fire again on
nearby roofs.

While hauling a few survivors from one building, Dolan
saw Ross and a female standing in a yard across the street.
He saw that house, too, was on fire, the roof caving from
flame. He hoped Ross would help and send more Predators
to his aid. This was too big for him. It was out of control.
Wherever he went seeking out his kind, he found the renegades had gotten there before him.

This was truly a catastrophe. He estimated hundreds of
Cravens had perished within hours. He didn't know where
Mentor was, but if these events were any indication of the
upheaval the vampire nations faced, it was going to be a
bloodbath. Mentor would face the greatest difficulty putting
down the rebellion.

They had to find Upton and stop him.

Ross crossed over the street, the female at his back. He said, "I've just returned from Lanzarote. What's going on here?"

Dolan didn't know where Lanzarote was or why Ross had been there, but he was tremendously relieved to see him. "The lairs of the Cravens are burning all over the city. I can't get to them in time. Everywhere I go the fire's already burning."

"Where's Mentor? Why isn't he here?"

"I don't know. He sent me. I don't think he knew there would be so many working against us tonight."

"We'll help you," Ross said. "I'll call some others to join us. We must stop this." He turned to Sereny. "Try to call for help from my clan. I have to handle the media and the police. This will be all over television if I don't get to them."

Trusting Ross to handle the big picture, Dolan hurried to the next block just ahead of a fire engine, hoping to find the lair intact enough to get some of the Cravens out. His mission had saved so few, and there were so many more places he had to get to. With Ross' help they might have a chance.

*   *   *

Ross flew above the city in the areas that were burning in order to find the fire trucks and television crews. He came down and went to them one at a time, mesmerizing the reporters and everyone involved. They turned off their lights, their cameras, and filed obediently into their vans to leave, having already forgotten why they'd come in the first place. Next, Ross found the police and, though it seemed to take forever, he implanted in heir minds different memories of the entire night.

This took many hours. Every time Ross approached a human, all he wanted to do was open his jugular and drink. Controlling his blood need took every bit of his effort. But he could not let the fires and the many deaths be reported. It would start a panic in the city—just what Upton wanted, he assumed. Well, he would not get his way.

All through the night Ross tracked down every human he could find who might write, photograph, or report in any way how strange the fires seemed to be and how the targets were all run-down houses full of sick people.

Toward dawn the fires were all out and Ross had reached everyone who might say anything to create a panic. For this extreme aggravation alone, he thought he could cheerfully tear Charles Upton into a million tiny, bloody bits.

When he returned to his house and found Sereny there sleeping already, he crawled in beside her in the bed and put his arm around her body.

He could sleep for a decade, but he knew the night would come quickly and he'd be out again, fighting Upton's forces.

Sereny mumbled in her sleep and turned to face him. He hugged her close, shutting out the war in the city. There would be time enough for all that when the sun set.

* * *

Detective Teal came up to one of the fires that had only been snuffed out. It was almost dawn. He saw a man speaking to a television crew and watched as the crew packed up their van and readied to drive away. The man who had spoken to them seemed to have vanished. Teal looked around and couldn't find him anywhere. *Slick bastard,* he thought. *What's his game?*

Teal hadn't slept at all. The fires started after midnight. He'd seen the first fire glow from his fourth-story room. He made nothing of it, but he didn't leave his chair either. He wasn't sleepy yet, what the hell.

Then two hours later he heard fire engines and saw another fire in the distance, the glow against the bottom of floating clouds. *A big one,* he thought. *What's up?*

When he saw the third fire, he hopped from his chair and made for the door. Something was so wrong tonight it was like being dropped dead smack into some crazy movie written by a screen writer out of his head on crystal meth. Victims with their necks torn open and drained dry of blood. Fires.

It meant something. Maybe it was all connected, though it didn't have to be, of course.

He'd just go see for himself.

He took his car from behind the hotel and drove toward the latest glow in the city. Now he was here approaching

258 *Billie Sue Mosiman*

the television crew. He jumped from his car and hurried across the street. "Hey," he said, flipping out his badge at the blonde woman reporter. *Pretty,* Teal thought, *in a plastic, collagen-lipped sort of way.* "What's the deal here?" He jerked his thumb over his shoulder at the fire that still smoldered. It must have been a big house, maybe an apartment building. It was a shambles now. People must have perished. Big news.

The reporter stared at him like he was a fish.

Teal snapped his fingers in her face. "You," he said. "Can you hear me?"

The woman swallowed. She blinked. She said in a prim voice, "There's no news here."

"I beg your pardon?"

"This is not newsworthy. We'll be on our way now, thank you."

When she turned her back on him, his mouth gaped. "Wait," he called, gathering his wits. He had to rush to the door of the van to keep her from shutting him out. "Look, how many fires does this make tonight? Three? Four? Is there an arsonist loose in the city?"

He swiveled his head, expecting to see a police cruiser. Hell, he'd ask the officers. But the area had emptied. There were no patrol cars. No police. This was as eerie as an eclipse of the sun. Nothing made a lick of sense. If it had been arson, where was the crime scene yellow tape? If it wasn't, where were the families of the victims?

He had his hand on the van window's ledge. "Please let go of my door," the woman said. "We have to leave now. It is imperative we leave."

Teal stepped back, confused. He watched the van drive away.

He looked around and thought again, *this ain't right, this ain't right no way, no how, boyo.*

He returned to his car and, first scanning the city horizon, headed toward the next fire glow reflected off the night sky. He'd hunt this dog until it broke a leg. He jerked the microphone off the dash and called in. "How many cars you got out at the fires?" he asked.

"Fires?" Dispatch asked.

"Am I speaking Armenian to you? Fires, fires! House fires. Apartment fires. Someone's torching stuff all over

Dallas, are you freaking *asleep?* Give me Sergeant Travers."

A cold, white hand covered Teal's fist and crushed his fingers over the microphone. Teal jumped so hard and high his head hit the roof of the car. His testicles crawled up his body, and it felt like a buzz saw had just run over his scalp.

The hand belonged to the man he'd seen speaking to the reporter. He sat in Teal's car now, having appeared there out of thin air. Teal hit the brakes and swerved the car one-handed to the curb. The man let go of his hand.

Teal dropped the microphone. He went for his holster and the gun there.

The hand again, magically it seemed, stayed him. "Uh-uh," the man said.

"What the . . . ?"

Then the world dimmed, and he thought he was floating down the pretty green Guadalupe River in a rowboat. He was relaxed and dreamy, his big belly unencumbered in a pair of loose shorts and his shirt open to the warm sun. A voice spoke softly at his ear and he listened, his head turned slightly to the side.

The next thing he knew it was morning and he was lying in his hotel bed in the same clothes from the night before. He hadn't even removed his big shoes so the sheets wouldn't get dirty.

He was disgusted with himself. He must have had one too many with Mrs. Carrie. He had to stop that shit, even if she did look like his grandmother. He'd be late to work. He had to hurry and take a shower and get his other brown suit from the Mayfair Cleaners. It was going to be a long day.

*　　*　　*

Mentor saw the policeman at the fire.

He saw Ross leave the area after speaking with the television crew, the firemen, and two men in a patrol car. It seemed all was handled. Mentor stood in the shadows, grieving for the Cravens who had died this night. He didn't know how Charles Upton could find it in himself to send out his Predators to do this terrible evil thing. They were all brothers. The Cravens had been infected just as had the Predators. It was not their fault they couldn't contribute to their own well-being or make their own way in the world. They were like mice born blind and helpless. How could anyone wish to stamp them out?

As Mentor pondered these questions, the car came speeding up. The policeman exuded curiosity and anxiety. Mentor saw him approach the television van. The crew was in the process of packing up to leave. The reporter, her mind emptied, offered no answers.

That's when Mentor knew he had to do something about the straggler to the scene. Ross had already left. This policeman represented a complication. He could undo all of Ross' work to quiet the media.

As the man stepped back into his car, Mentor hurried to follow. When he appeared in the moving car's front seat and grabbed the man's hand holding the microphone, he knew he risked causing an accident. He thought it worth that risk.

In wiping the policeman's memory he discovered how worried the man was about bodies found around the city. It seemed to Mentor they weren't going to be able to stop all the information from leaking out. This man might remember his concerns later. He had a particularly strong personality. His mind was like a steel trap, holding all his suspicions with clamped teeth.

Someone in the coroner's office could talk about the murders. A real investigation could reveal the bodies had been dead even before their neck wounds. Dead men, dead again. He would send someone to steal the bodies. They needed to make them disappear. It would be better for the city to get in an uproar about missing bodies than to report on bodies obviously dead before recent wounds were inflicted upon them.

Look what Upton was doing. He was about to let the world know about the vampires. How were they all to function in a world where humans hunted them? And they would. First they'd panic, they'd deny the possibility, and then they would take justice into their own hands and begin to hunt down every vampire they could find.

Mentor left the policeman he knew as Detective Teal lying on his bed in his dreary hotel room. Teal had come along as easily as a child, crawling into the bed upon command and closing his eyes. From the room's window facing out into the city, Mentor placed his hand on the chair that stood there. He picked up Teal's confounded thoughts.

After a moment looking at the brightening sky, Mentor turned and left the peacefully sleeping man. He did not know if he could really stop this human. His mental processes were a maze of connections and not all of them could be so easily erased.

Keeping this vampire war out of the human consciousness wasn't going to be so simple. All he could hope was the reporters, police, and coroner's office personnel never put it all together. The machinery of human detection ground exceedingly slow. It might be months before they released reports pointing to supernatural events. If ever.

Mentor left through the door and took the elevator to the lobby. He stepped from the building just as the sun's first rays breathed life into the slumbering city.

5

Malachi lay dreaming beneath the open night sky. He and the boy had made camp again in the wide open space of West Texas. They had not gone that far from Howard's Rattlesnake Farm store, taking back roads and avoiding towns. They hadn't been accosted again, but this was the first night since leaving that Malachi had been able to sleep.

In the dream Malachi saw fire and smelled columns of choking black smoke. He had seen a flash of the silver wolf howling, his head held high, his long throat extended. Fire brushed his magnificent fur coat so that it curled and blackened. The wolf was dying, consumed by flame.

"Balthazar," Malachi whispered, coming awake at the sound of his own voice. He could almost smell the scent of scorched flesh and hear the howl fading into the night. He brought a hand to his forehead and found he was sweating. The dream was so real. Could Balthazar have died in fire? Would he be sending no more assassins?

The boy's eyes were open when Malachi glanced over at him.

"You're awake, too?" Malachi sat up and scooted to the campfire coals to add some wood he'd gathered earlier. The night air was chilly, though his body was covered with a clammy sheen of sweat from the nightmare.

"I was thinking of Dottie," Jeremy said. He didn't move to sit up. He lay on his back looking at the sky overhead, his arms resting at his sides.

Malachi wished Jeremy wouldn't think of his twin sister. Every time he did, he fell into a morbid mood. Though he was ten, it seemed he had aged since his transformation into vampire. He was often moody and when he spoke, his concerns were not those of a child.

"Do you know why she wore our mom's dresses?" Jeremy asked.

"No, why?"

"Because once Grandpa told her she looked like our mother. She thought if she wore her clothes, she could bring her back."

"Oh." Malachi found that so sad he felt his face collapsing into despair.

"Where are we going, Malachi?"

"I think it's time we went home."

"Your home?"

"Yes. I had a dream, and my dreams have always been prophetic. I saw the man who sent the assassins after me, and he was on fire. He was dying."

"You think he's dead? I thought vampires didn't die. Unless they lost . . . unless someone . . ."

"Decapitates them? That's one way. The other is fire. They can't regenerate if they're burned. It takes them too fast, gives them no time to save the body. Fire consumes the soul so fast it scatters it."

Jeremy was quiet for a long time. Malachi stoked the campfire and looked out over the plains. In the distance were low mountains, but where they camped there was nothing but a flat vista broken occasionally by barrel cactus and the scraggly mesquite tree. He missed his East Texas home terribly. It was nothing like this. There were trees and lush grass, smooth rolling hills, and whole fields of wildflowers in the spring. He hadn't known how attached he was to the ranch until he left it. He missed his horse, Harley, and riding down the long wooded paths. He missed his parents—his mother's soft gaze of love, his father's reserved and respectful care for his son. He missed his bedroom with the east-facing windows where the sun came up and streamed through on late mornings when he stayed in bed.

If Balthazar was dead, it was safe to return home. He'd take Jeremy with him and let his mother help raise him. He'd teach him to ride while she taught him to control his natural urge to kill for blood. His father would teach him about animals and their care and how to work on old cars. Jeremy needed guidance, he needed someone to care about him. He was so young and so helpless yet.

"Do you think Dottie knows I'm all right?" Jeremy asked, interrupting Malachi's reverie.

"I don't know. Maybe." Malachi found it uncomfortable to speak of the spirit. He didn't know what he thought about the soul, though he had just spoken of it to the boy. He believed the soul was real or why else did the vampires battle in death to find the path they should choose? Other people would try to explain it away, saying humans didn't die completely and come alive again as vampires. And if they did, by some fantastic chance, if that could be scientifically proven under lab circumstances, then the vampire's soul certainly could not have entered into a mythological land where he or she chose to be a certain type of vampire. But Malachi knew differently. He believed in the supernatural because he was living evidence of an unnatural human. He could move faster than any person alive. He enjoyed precognition, knowing when something was about to happen. He had extrasensory perception, knowing when another presence was nearby. And he had great inhuman strength and an unnaturally strong immune system.

What he didn't know for sure was why he was the way he was, or why vampires had ever come about. He didn't know if their place in the scheme of nature was an aberration or a leap in evolution of one branch of the evolutionary tree. He didn't know about an all-knowing Creator or if there were many gods controlling human destiny. He didn't know about heaven or hell, about spirits that survived. He just didn't like to talk about it because he had so many questions himself.

Jeremy rolled onto his side and stared at Malachi. "You're sure he's dead? The one who sent the vampires to kill us?"

"I think so."

"If he isn't, I'm going to kill him."

The boy's voice was deep and fierce. In his voice and his words was promise of violence. Jeremy's sorrow had changed to anger. He frequently argued with Malachi or gave him a dangerous look. He was like the newly born viper with a bite as poisonous as that from a mother snake.

"I think he's dead," Malachi repeated.

"I'm hungry," the boy said, changing the topic.

Malachi sighed. Jeremy's appetite doubled each day.

Soon the small animals he slaughtered to give the boy wouldn't be enough. If he didn't get him back to the ranch soon, the young Predator might become so ravenous he'd go in search of a mortal. Or he'd turn on Malachi some night when he was sleeping, unable to help himself.

"I'll go find something for you." Malachi stood from the fire and walked off into the desert. A full yellow moon lit up the landscape, highlighting the animal eyes that shone from burrows and behind brush.

That's my moon, he thought, staring into the sky. *Malachi's moon. It's the first moon of my freedom. Balthazar came into my dreams for years, threatening me beneath a moon like that, but now he's dead. I'll be free to live my life in peace.* He felt his heart soar at the prospect.

He walked on, taking his time on the hunt, hoping to take only the largest specimen. This time he'd let the boy kill the animal himself. Or he might want to drink from the animal while it was still living.

The whole idea upset Malachi, from the hunt to the innocent creature's death, but then he, too, was a carnivore. He and Jeremy might take different nourishment from lower species, but they both killed to live. The difference was negligible when he looked at it that way.

He walked farther into the desert, wide awake and not at all tired. Now the moon was at his back so that his shadow fell long over the desert before him.

He could go on until dawn if he had to.

*　　*　　*

After leaving Detective Teal, Mentor returned to Bette Kinyo's home. He stood close to her again, remembering the long night he had spent at her side.

He had heard the multitudinous voices of dying vampires. They did not call for him, but he should have been there to circumvent their deaths and he knew it. Outside, fires roared, devouring homes not far from Bette's house. The fires hadn't reached her neighborhood yet, but they were on the way if firefighters didn't check them. It had to be Upton sending his Predators to kill the poor Cravens, just as he had promised to do. The night was the best time to attack. Cravens rarely left their communal homes, but at night they always stayed indoors, afraid any strong, criminally-minded human could overtake them.

They moved too slowly to escape if a fire broke out. They were too weak and too debilitated by disease to fight back. They probably put up very little resistance when the Predators came. Killing them as mercilessly as this was an act so evil it rivaled any act ever committed against the vampires.

Mentor had wanted to be out there saving them, but he couldn't leave Bette, he simply couldn't. He had hoped Dolan could reach the Cravens in time, but evidently he hadn't. Then there came a cry so piteous from a trapped Craven in a fiery furnace of a communal house, it caused Mentor to shiver. He had to go to her. It was a female, trapped, dying.

He hurriedly left Bette's house. He found the fire already extinguished and the female Craven near death behind the building. He lifted her up and held her close to his chest. Her eyes rolled back in her head, and he realized he wasn't going to save her; he'd come too late. Her limbs were blackened and shriveled. The flesh of her face was also burned, mottled by fire. He felt her life force leaving her. "Leap to another body," he instructed her. "Go!"

Suddenly her spirit left her and he held merely the dead carcass. She had sped away, trying to save herself, but he wondered if she would find another human to inhabit in time. He placed her body carefully on the grass and stepped over it. It was in front of the hovel of burned timbers and coals that he spied Detective Teal's car speeding to the scene.

Mentor now looked at the light streaming through Bette's windows. He felt bitterness that a day could dawn on so much destruction to the vampire nations. Upton was responsible for murdering most of the Craven population in the city. It was just the beginning. Next, he knew, Upton would try to disrupt the blood supplies to the Naturals. He was intent on throwing all the vampires onto their own devices. This would create a chaotic time that would divide the vampires and crumble the natural order.

He glanced down at Bette. He must rouse her soon. She sat unmoving, not even crying, and he feared for her mind. She needed to call the police and report the murder. She'd have to make up a story about an intruder. Alan's neck wound could have been made from a blow. Before Mentor healed Alan's neck, the authorities would have thought a wild animal had torn him apart, just like the bodies they already had in the morgue from the night's slaughter of Predator by Predator. There was no way Bette could have explained that away.

In the past minutes since his return Bette had not moved or spoken. She sat with her hands in her lap, staring at the covered corpse of her husband across the room on the sofa. Coming to terms with his death would be a slow, painful process.

"Bette?" He lifted his hand from her shoulder. He hunched beside her and took her chin in his hand, turning her face to him. "Bette, I'm back. You have to call the police. I'll have to leave you. Do you understand?"

She licked dry lips and said, "Who do you live to honor?"

Puzzled, Mentor tried, but could not understand what she was asking.

She said again, "Mentor, who do you live to honor? I lived my life in a way it would honor my grandmother. She was a good woman. She never caused harm. She was giving and loving and open. But now I will live to honor my husband."

Mentor understood. Was there someone he tried to emulate? Was there a life he admired so much he tried to live in a way to honor it?

"Bad people live for no one," Bette said. "They have no ancestors or loved ones who can influence them. Like the one who came in the night and took Alan."

Mentor looked back over his long life and realized for the first time that he had also lived to honor someone. He had never thought of it that way, but it was true. His decisions and actions over many decades reflected the sensibility of a Predator he admired. He drifted back in memory to the beginning of his life as a vampire. Early on, he had been summoned to a meeting with what he came to know as one of the oldest living vampires on Earth.

The great Predator called himself Vohra and lived on the Nile River at the edge of the Egyptian desert. Mentor had been wandering the East, trying to find reasons for his condition. None of his family had been afflicted, so at that time he didn't know the disease was usually genetic and ran through whole generations. He also searched for others like him for companionship. Loneliness weighed heavily, causing him to turn inward to such a degree that he felt like a stranger on the planet.

He was like no one else, he believed. He was an abomination.

He would never find someone who understood him.

One night a vampire came to his room where he was staying in a small Egyptian hotel and told him Vohra had asked to see him. Knowing of no reason why he shouldn't go despite the fact he didn't know the vampire who had extended the invitation, Mentor dressed in white linen slacks and shirt, brushed his hair, and followed the servant vampire away from the city and down to the Nile. They were so far from the city the twinkling lanterns from it glowed like a rising sun on the horizon.

Vohra possessed the body of a young man hardly out of his teens, but his eyes belonged to someone incredibly old. He looked to be of Egyptian heritage, with a fine noble nose and full lips. His profile was similar to that of the pharaoh Tutankhamen. He was dressed as a traditional Egyptian, in a white robe tied with scarlet at the waist and leather slippers on his feet. He sat on the sand, the Nile flowing before him. He did not turn his head to acknowledge Mentor.

"I'm glad you've come," Vohra said in a pleasant, cultured voice. He knew many languages and this time spoke in English. "Please sit beside me."

Mentor sat down, hugging his knees and staring out at the wide Nile River. He waited. He thought it would be discourteous to come out and ask this Predator what he wanted of him. He'd tell him soon enough.

"Let me tell you of Bucchus, the divine bull of ancient Egypt," Vohra said.

"All right." Mentor loved to be instructed, and hoped the story would tell him something about the vampires.

"To prepare Bucchus for burial, juniper oil was flushed into his innards and then his entrails were washed and teased out with long instruments. He was anointed all over with sacred salts and more oils and set aside so his flesh would dry. Months later six priests carefully wrapped him in lengths of the finest woven cloth. He was buried in Memphis, Egypt's former capital. One day he will be unearthed by archaeologists and modern man will wonder at such loving devotion given to an animal by the pharaohs."

"That's . . . interesting," Mentor said, noting how Vohra seemed to know the future. And if he knew of Bucchus, he must know of the past, too, since according to him the bull hadn't yet been unearthed. The thought startled Mentor. He said, "You were around when they buried the bull in Memphis?"

"Oh, yes, and before that."

When he said no more, Mentor asked, "How long have you been vampire?"

"Since the beginning."

"When was that?" Mentor had to know. He was excited to think he was speaking with someone who might know all about their history.

"During the time of the dawn of man. At that time I was known by another name, of course. I have been called by many names."

Oh, my God, Mentor thought, exhilarated and a little afraid. He couldn't even imagine how old Vohra might be. "Vampires have existed since man first walked upright?"

The Predator nodded. Mentor believed him. There was no reason to lie. Vohra was what he was looking for in his travels. He needed knowledge and understanding. Maybe the ancient Predator had heard of his need and that's why he sent for him.

"The Egyptians honored the divine bull by mummifying him and sending him into the Beyond surrounded by jewels and companion animals and many vessels holding grain and wheat. They had worshiped him."

"Like Baal in the Hebrew Bible," Mentor said.

"A little. Yes, a little like that. Who will *you* worship?" Vohra asked. He turned his head now and stared straight into Mentor's eyes.

"I . . . I don't know. Must I worship someone or something?"

Vohra faced the river again. "That is your purpose. To find who or what you worship and then you'll know what you should do with the gift of life eternal."

Mentor wondered if Vohra meant *he* was the one who should be worshiped. It might be easy to do if Vohra had really lived as an immortal for so many thousands of years.

Just as he had the thought, Vohra broke the silence. "I don't want your worship. Living longer than you brings more understanding, therefore more peace, but long life doesn't make me a god. You would do as well to worship Bucchus as to worship me."

Mentor thought he talked in riddles, and he could not grasp what advice he was being given. Who, then, should he worship? What should he worship? And then he knew the answers to his questions with a flash of insight. His quest was to find the thing he could devote his life to. He would live hundreds of years or more. Vohra had lived thousands. So might he. He couldn't live if he never found good reasons to go on. He must love someone or something enough to make living worthwhile. He must honor or worship something greater than himself.

Vohra nodded now as if he agreed. The servant who had led him to the river came again and tapped Mentor on the shoulder. He was to leave. His audience was over.

But it was not his last. For many years Mentor stayed close to Vohra in the Egyptian desert lands, listening when Vohra felt like teaching him something, and remaining quietly out of the way when Vohra had nothing to say.

Before Mentor left to go out on his own again, he took with him a vast knowledge of the vampire's history. He hadn't yet found what he should worship, but at least he knew it was his duty to discover it.

Since those years, he had tried to live to honor Vohra. Until now, when Bette asked him, he hadn't known. Vohra was the wisest and most peaceful being he'd ever known. He was a *neutral* being, neither good nor evil, having lived so long he'd passed those artificial boundaries. Even now he knew the ancient one lived secretly in Cairo, passing for an Egyptian gentleman. Leaders of the vampire sects in every country made regular pilgrimages to see Vohra, to listen to his counsel.

"One day, I'll tell you about the person I live to honor," Mentor said, taking Bette's hands and helping her to stand. "But now you have things to do, and I have to leave. There are terrible things going on outside these walls, and I have to try to stop them."

He kissed her on the cheek and walked into the hallway before he vanished. The last thing he heard was Bette's strangled sob as she broke down into tears once more.

* * *

Dell stood around the hospital bed with her mother and her father. The only mortals in the private hospital room were the patient, Aunt Celia, and, standing at the foot of the bed, Celia's daughter, Carolyn. Celia lay in bed, her chest swaddled in bandages. She drifted in and out of consciousness, her body not fully recovered yet from the operation. The cancer had not spread, thank goodness, Dell thought, but it had taken most of one of Celia's breasts. The good parts left they took with the bad, for insurance.

When Malachi had been just a boy, he'd pointed to his great-aunt and informed her of a growth. Celia had taken him seriously and gone to a doctor for confirmation. It was true. She'd had a small tumor in the same breast she'd now lost years later. They'd taken out the earlier tumor and today, more than fifteen years later, it had returned. This time the breast had to be sacrificed.

Celia opened her eyes, and the first person she saw was Dell. She reached out her good arm, the one not bound to her side. Dell held her hand as tears sprang to her eyes. She wiped them away quickly before a nurse appeared. Blood tears would bring a doctor running, and none of them could have that.

"The doctor says he got it all, Aunt Celia."

Celia smiled a little. "I knew they would. I'm going to be all right."

She was using what strength she had to reassure her niece. That touched Dell more than anything.

Celia's daughter, Carolyn, stepped around the side of the bed and bent to kiss her mother on the cheek. "Mama, I love you."

Carolyn hadn't yet gotten the disease that would have turned her into a vampire. She and Celia were the rare family members who had escaped porphyria's deadly mutation. Dell moved aside to let Carolyn nearer the bed. She saw her own mother gesture toward the hallway and said, "We'll be back in a minute, Carolyn."

Standing outside of the room with her parents, Dell's face showed the worry she felt. Not about Aunt Celia. She believed her aunt would gain back her strength and be going home soon. No, it was what was happening in the city. Though Dell lived far enough away from Dallas that it had taken Ryan an hour to drive them to the hospital, she knew about the sirens that wailed across Dallas throughout the night. She knew about the dozens of fires. She knew of the deaths.

"Have you heard from Malachi?" Dell's father asked.

"Not in days. But I think he's coming home." Dell had reached out with her mental ability, connecting with her son, and had found he was heading east across Texas, the little boy at his side.

"He needs to be with you," Dell's mother said. She hadn't aged a day and neither had her husband. They didn't bother to wear the artfully applied makeup they now wore every day in their normal lives in the city. Soon her parents would retire from their jobs and move away from their home to start a new life elsewhere. They'd been in one place, one house, for all of Dell's life—thirty-seven years. It was time.

"I know. There are hundreds of renegades here," Dell said, meaning Dallas. They'd swooped down on the city and set fire to every building they could find that harbored Cravens. It was rumored they meant to disrupt the delivery lines that supplied Naturals like Dell and her parents with the blood that sustained them.

"What's going to happen, Dad?" Dell asked. She saw past her parents down the hall. The elevator door was opening and Ryan had stepped out. She hadn't told him yet of the seriousness of the renegade situation.

Dell's father turned to look at his approaching son-in-law before answering in a low voice. "It's going to get bad, Dell. No one knows how bad. Ross is trying to keep his Predators calm, but there's a lot of fear."

"I heard about some murders on the radio on the way here to the hospital," Dell said. "They called them 'animal attacks.'"

As Ryan approached, she smiled at him. His presence always restored her. She put an arm around his waist.

"The renegades are leaving them where they take them," Dell's father said. "The police haven't put the murders all together yet, the precincts haven't shared their information, but it won't be long. They're going to know the human deaths can't be the work of just one serial killer or something. They're not going to know what to make of it."

"You should come stay with us," Dell said.

"Yes," Ryan agreed. "We have plenty of room."

"No, we'll stay in case we can help do something. We might be needed in Dallas."

That worry Dell had tried to wipe from her face when she'd seen her husband returned. If her parents didn't get their blood delivered by Ross' Predators, how were they to live? How were any of the Naturals to live?

After saying good-bye to Aunt Celia, Dell and Ryan drove out of the city toward the ranch. Ryan had been unusually quiet. Finally he spoke, his worry as deep as his wife's. "Why is this happening? You need to tell me."

"They say it's the Predator called Charles Upton. Remember him? The Houston billionaire that doctor brought to us when I was finishing high school? He was kept prisoner for years. That's why we never heard of him again. But when he escaped, he brought together a small army of disgruntled Predators. He had the help of another Predator who called himself Balthazar. Balthazar . . ."

"I know. He was the one who sent the assassins for Malachi."

She nodded. "Now Upton's trying to hurt Mentor and Ross, who put him in prison. He wants his revenge."

"He wants to turn Dallas into a hunting ground?" Ryan knew the implications of Naturals thrown on their own to find sustenance. All relationships with humans would take on serious complications. When hungry, a vampire of whatever kind would have no choice but to hunt his own food. Many of them would not feed on wildlife. Many of them would track down and kill humans.

"I think he wants more than that. Much more. I think he's just starting in Dallas because of Mentor," Dell said.

"You're saying this could spread? Fires and deaths?"

Dell imagined it all in her mind. First the largest cities

in Texas, all lines of blood supplies breaking down and going undelivered. Every Craven found and burned to ash. Then the surrounding states would be attacked, the war rippling out from the center of the country to all its borders, north and south, east and west. Finally, if Upton was successful and he wasn't stopped, the whole world of vampires might look at the United States and decide chaos should reign everywhere.

Let humanity beware.

Dell said very little of this to her husband. She didn't want to project the problem they had in Dallas out into the world for him. If it never happened, the worry would have been for nothing. If it did happen . . . well, she couldn't think of that. They had to stop Upton. Here. Now.

"Dell?"

She had been staring out the passenger window at the passing scenery, her mind elsewhere. She glanced at Ryan.

"Will you have to leave the ranch? If Mentor calls you? Will you have to go?"

She reached over and placed her hand on his neck, her fingers softly massaging the muscles there. She wouldn't lie to him.

"I'll have to. If they need me, I won't refuse them."

For the rest of the trip home Ryan drove in silence. At the end of the summer they were going to celebrate their twentieth anniversary. After so many years together, their love had woven them into a couple who accepted the silences that came when they shared their worries. She was more human because of Ryan. He had expanded his perceptions of the world, realizing it contained more mystery than most mortals ever admitted. The two of them were bound by love and parenthood.

He had aged, closing in on forty with such grace she hardly noticed the crow's feet at the corners of his eyes or the weathering of his skin. Together they had strived to educate themselves so they could contribute to society. Together they had lived a peaceful, isolated existence, depending on one another for everything while they raised their beloved son.

The uprising in Dallas threw their lives out of balance, disrupting the peaceful flow. Things were changing for the first time in twenty years, and Dell knew it might be a change that lasted forever if Upton had his way. She couldn't even foresee what she and her mortal husband might have to face in the future if life didn't return to normal for them.

"Whatever happens, I'll be there for you," Ryan said, as if this time he was the one capable of reading minds.

She gave him a tentative smile though her heart ached. He was the most vulnerable person in her life. Malachi possessed so many of her supernatural abilities that he could protect himself. But Ryan was as frail and fragile as a roadside bluebonnet under a scorching Texas sun. Without the shade of her devotion and care, he had no real protection at all.

6

With the sun high overhead, Charles Upton wore dark sunglasses that kept anyone from seeing his eyes. He had caught a glimpse of himself in a passing shop window the night before when the city was on fire. Although at that moment he believed he had let his face return to that of the young Thai man whose body he'd stolen, he was stopped in his tracks. He neared the shop window, staring with surprise into his own eyes. They were no longer human. Perhaps he'd changed into jaguar so often his human features were being obscured bit by bit. His eyes were *not* Thai, even though the rest of his features clearly were. His eyes, however, were slanted into the flesh of his face, too long and too narrow to fit the sockets. His eyebrows had disappeared so that the bony protuberances looked naked and abnormally large in proportion to his face. The pupils were vertical and of an amber color never seen in a human being.

He looked out of jaguar eyes. He closed them, the long lids lowering slowly. He tried to rearrange the molecules of his body. Maybe he could force the cat to retreat again.

He opened his eyes to stare into the store window. Cat eyes stared back.

So it was true. He couldn't change himself back anymore. It would make life more difficult as he tried to pass through the cities of man. He'd have to wear the dark glasses and never take them off when he hoped to walk among men without them knowing his real nature.

This was disturbing to him, as he loved tricking men into thinking he was just like them. Yet sunglasses were a good replacement and provided enough camouflage. He thought one day he would simply let the jaguar out and keep it as his true face. He would be like an Egyptian cat god, half human, half feline. Besides, men would fear him even more if he didn't look like them. They'd know beyond any doubt that he was the genuine article—a supernatural being far superior to any of them.

He was on his way to a meeting with Mentor. This was not the time to waste any regret on the shape of his face. His intent wasn't to kill Mentor during this private meeting, or to get himself killed, but he still had to be alert. Mentor had taken him prisoner once before. Upton didn't think he could do it again, not alone, but he couldn't trust him for a moment, regardless.

It was Upton who had called for the meeting. Mentor should know they would never surrender. If Mentor called thousands to his aid, Upton wanted to assure him it wouldn't matter. His Predators would simply fade into the background. They wouldn't go away. And they wouldn't be foolish enough to take their numbers into the open against a vast army.

As Upton went up the steps to Mentor's home, the door opened and for the first time in years Upton laid eyes on his nemesis. Mentor still resided in the old body he'd had when Upton had been taken to the Thai monastery. The body did not appear older but inside it had to be slowly crumbling toward decay. Upton wanted to sneer, thinking of the monk Joseph who had loved his body too much to part with it.

Upton kept on his sunglasses until he was inside the house. As he entered the small living area, he removed them. Mentor turned to face him and when he did, he hesitated before speaking. His gaze fastened on Upton's cat-like eyes.

"Your molecular structure is changing," he said finally.

Upton sat down on a sofa near a dead fireplace. He held the sunglasses dangling between his knees. "So what's your point?" he asked with all the sarcasm he could muster.

"My point is you won't be able to control how you look much longer. The jaguar will mix with the human until you'll be permanently grotesque."

"Oh, for Pete's sake, Mentor, let's dispense with the criticism. If I cared to look like you, I wouldn't have chosen the jaguar."

"You're right. That's not my concern. Turn yourself into a South American vampire bat if you want to."

Upton hissed noisily, his lips raising to reveal the fangs. "You know what I want, and it's not to become a bat."

"You're responsible for killing hundreds of vampires overnight. This has to stop."

"Why did I know you'd say that? As for the Cravens who died last night—they didn't have the right to call themselves vampire. Why any of you let them survive is a mystery to me."

"I told you . . ."

Upton exploded from his position on the sofa, rising to his feet to tower over Mentor. His young Thai body was much larger than the one housing Mentor. "I know what you told me! But you're insane. You and Ross and all the rest of them who let the Cravens live. They should have been murdered the day they became vampire. You're weak, Mentor. You're all weaklings who over centuries of time have convinced yourselves that you're moral and compassionate. Who said a vampire has any duty to be either? Who told you this is as it should be?"

Mentor stared at the floor. He did not look up. He said, "I can see you'll never be taught anything."

"By you? I should think not!"

"Then you'll die," Mentor said, raising his head to stare into the Predator's eyes. "Like Balthazar."

The name was like a punch to Upton's solar plexus. He sank onto the sofa, growling below his breath without realizing he was doing it. He hadn't been in contact with Balthazar. He expected him to come with Sereny once they had control of the city. Balthazar hadn't seen any reason to come until then, explaining it was best and less confusing if just one of them led the hundreds of Predators. Upton was happy to command on his own. It was what he planned to do in the end anyway.

"What do you mean, like Balthazar?"

Mentor now raised his gaze. "He's dead, Charles. Ross went to the island. Balthazar was burned. What's going to happen when his troops find out? Can you get them to follow you then? I think they'll desert you. They'll know we're too strong for them and they're outnumbered. They'll move away from you to grieve for their fallen leader."

Upton was speechless. This blow wasn't expected. He thought he'd armed himself against any surprise Mentor might try to spring on him. He'd never have imagined they'd already reached Balthazar and disposed of him so easily.

Suspicion crept into his mind. "What if I don't believe you?"

"Check for yourself. I have no reason to lie about it."

Upton could have tried to mentally reach Balthazar, but he knew now it was no use. Mentor wasn't lying. Balthazar was dead.

Upton straightened his shoulders. "I don't care if he's dead. I was going to kill him anyway. The Predators will follow me. I'm their leader now."

"And if they don't? Do you think you can take over this city, much less the region, without them?"

Fury rose inside Upton until it came to a crescendo in his brain. He wasn't about to stop the transformation of his face into jaguar. In seconds he was the wild hungry cat whose single imperative was to bring the prey to its knees.

Even as his face changed, Mentor came to his feet. In his eyes glared murder.

"You don't want to test me here and now," Mentor said in a menacing voice.

"I'll bide my time until you're mine," Upton said, edging toward the door. He shook himself, changing his features back to human. He slipped on the sunglasses. If he'd been sure he could have taken Mentor, he would have pounced. But he couldn't take stupid chances and risk the future. In caution waited victory. He would only attack Mentor, or Ross for that matter, when he had other Predators at his side. He wasn't absolutely convinced he could win alone. He must do nothing without certainty of the outcome.

"If you persist in this uprising, most of your Predators are going to die," Mentor warned. "And you're going to pay for going after the woman and then killing her husband."

Upton went out the door and never turned back or responded. It wasn't his business to give the enemy satisfaction. It was humbling enough he'd backed down from a one-on-one pitched battle. But he'd touched Mentor with the mortal's death, that's for sure. He laughed to himself as he remembered the man's death stare, surprise and horror frozen on his face as his blood pumped out. Though he hadn't taken the woman, he'd hurt her, oh, he'd hurt her quite deeply. And through her, Mentor.

That's what mattered.

Even as Upton moved away from the house, he called mentally to his army, dismissing all thought of the mortal's death and Mentor's warning. His Predators were scattered in hiding all over the city. In order to reach them, Mentor and Ross would have had to visit three hundred different lairs.

Upton sent an urgent message directly to his captains. He didn't fear Mentor or Ross intercepting his message when they went directly from his intelligence to the targets he intended to reach. It would have been like trying to catch a butterfly on the wing. He wanted his captains to gather the army to meet with him at a ranch on the out-skirts of Dallas by sundown. It was where Ross lived. First they'd all descend on the vampire leader, burning him along with his extravagant home.

Then they would finish burning and tearing down the blood banks that supplied the Naturals and surviving Cra-vens all over the southwestern part of the state. Already they had attacked the Strand-Catel and taken away all the blood supplied there. Ross was in a frenzy to make up for the loss.

With Ross dead and the routines performed by his clan disrupted, the whole city would fall into Upton's hands. Dallas was only the beginning. Within months he believed he could give over Texas to Predators determined to live as reigning vampires.

In a year, he'd control the middle of the nation, and in five years, the whole country would be quivering in the palm of his hand.

In less than a century he thought the vampires would control the world as they always should have. And what was a century to an immortal? A day before the sun set, no more.

*   *   *

Mentor watched Upton leave, the sunglasses that covered his inhuman eyes incapable of disguising the ferretlike, sloped forehead with the smooth brow and widow's peak of slick hair that seemed to be creeping down toward his face.

He was crazed, of course. Charles Upton had been verging on lunacy even as an industrialist intent on squashing his competitors no matter the cost or how long it took. It was how he acquired so much of his fortune during one lifetime. He had learned to be ruthless and it had served him well. But now his madness was beyond anything Mentor had seen from a Predator in two hundred years. None of them had ever had the audacity to think he could rule over everyone, the way Upton wished to do. The clans in the cities were ruled over by individual leaders. Upton would have to make war against each clan, ripping at the fabric of their organizations.

Mentor turned back into his house and went to the sofa to sit quietly, consoled by the fact he didn't really believe Upton could be triumphant. It was true the Predators were always restless. Until the birth of the New World and Ross' institution of the blood banks, Predators led a more nomadic life, but even then they felt responsibility toward their own kind. They made sure the Cravens and the Naturals got the blood they needed. It was a close fraternity, with brother vampire helping brother, the strongest watching out for the weak. There were fewer of them then and they depended on one another in crisis. Whole societies had been formed across Europe, Asia, and South America, setting up supply lines to service their kind. A Craven or a Natural would have died for a Predator, and vice versa.

Vohra had told Mentor each new birth of a vampire soul who chose the weaker paths put demands on the strong, but it had been that way from the first. It had never been something they *thought* about or discussed, as if there was an alternative. Predators, possibly the least human of them all, still came from woman. They still understood the suffering of death, and the reasons one might chose to be other than Predator. They had all been beneath the glow of the red moon and wrestled with their souls.

Upton thought he could change all that overnight. Mentor admitted Upton might gather some of the new Predators who hadn't been guided long enough. Or he might appeal to the borderline misfits who drank despair like it was a narcotic twisting with need at their innards. But he would never turn a whole history back on itself. He could never convince the majority of Predators to leave the helm and let the ship wallow on rough seas.

This is what made him a lunatic. He was unable or unwilling to see his plan for what it was—a desperate ambition not all of them would accept as righteous.

Nevertheless, Upton was a very large problem and, at least locally, this whole thing had gotten out of hand much more quickly than Mentor had expected. Ross had put his clan though training and had warned them to stay alert. Yet Upton had sneaked into the city and started his destruction before any of them could stop him.

Mentor reflected on the fact that he was godlike in some ways, but evidence of his deficiencies always pulled him down from the high pedestal. The Predators respected him and the new vampires he tried to guide through death even came to love him—some of them. But he could not be everywhere at once. He could not stalk Upton if Upton cleared his mind and made it a blank slate. He could not save the Cravens from a conflagration when evil ones came with the torch.

He hadn't even been able to spare Alan. It bothered him most when a human he'd grown close to was sacrificed with such contempt. Ross had threatened to kill both Bette and Alan for meddling with vampire knowledge. It had taken Mentor months to dissuade him. Now Upton had come along and with apparent ease, destroyed the life of the man Bette loved. Mortals lived such circumscribed live and faced death, for the most part, with enough courage that it put a brave Predator to shame. To snatch a man from sleep and rip out his throat the way Upton had done must be a sin, it seemed to Mentor.

If there were such a thing as sin.

Something Mentor still didn't know and might never find out, no matter how long he lived. If he needed proof he was no god, he had only to remember how little he could do, how few disasters he could avert, and how minuscule his knowledge was of the mysteries in the universe.

7

Malachi turned the motorcycle into the long dirt road leading back to his parents' farmhouse, Jeremy clutching him tightly around the waist. They bumped over the road, the old motorcycle spitting smoke and spewing dirty exhaust that smelled of burned oil. It was doubtful the machine could have taken them much farther. The carburetor needed another overhaul and the brakes were just about shot. He would have to get his dad to help him fix it.

Right away, Malachi knew the house was empty. He turned off the ignition of the motorcycle and kicked down the stand. He slipped off and lifted Jeremy from the saddle to his feet. "They're not here," he said, worry evident in his tone.

"Where are they?" Jeremy asked. Then he spied the horse stalls and stood staring into the dark recesses there. Malachi saw the hunger in his eyes.

"I don't know where they are. Listen, don't even think about bothering the horses. My mom would kill you. *I* would kill you. One of those horses belongs to me."

"I wasn't gonna bother 'em."

"Like hell you weren't. I'll get you something in just a minute. We keep blood in the house."

"In the house?"

Malachi had forgotten the boy knew nothing about the arrangement Naturals and Cravens had with the Predators. "My mom's a Natural. She keeps bags of the stuff in the fridge."

"Bags of it? Blood? Yuck."

"You'll get used to it."

Malachi started for the house. He swung open the yard gate and trusted Jeremy had followed. When he reached the porch steps, he saw he hadn't. "What are you doing? Come on."

The boy was still attracted to the horses in the stall. He hadn't moved an inch.

"Jeremy, you hear me? You can't have the horses. They're pets. You don't kill people's pets."

Jeremy came slowly from his trance and straggled down the pathway. He raised guilty eyes to Malachi. "I was just looking," he said. "They're so *big*."

With so much hot blood in them, Malachi thought with a cringe. He just couldn't get used to the boy's dreadful preoccupation with killing. He had never been around a Predator for any extended length of time. His mother lived like any other human, except for her need for the blood. But she never stalked or killed, the thought abhorrent to her. She'd not chosen to come back to life as a Predator. For that he was immensely grateful. The boy's normal urges that caused him to strike and take small living things was getting on his nerves big time. He was going to have to get some lessons from Mentor. Malachi didn't think he'd be able to control him much longer.

"Just come inside. I'll get you what you need and we'll wait for my parents. They should be home from work by now, but wherever they are, they'll be back soon."

Jeremy trailed him into the house, his small body covered with dust and his clothes ragged and spotted with dark specks of blood. "Why don't you take a bath and I'll try to find some of my old clothes. Mom must have packed a few of them away somewhere."

"I . . . don't think I like water much." Jeremy was hanging back again. He had that bad look on his face, the predatory one that gave Malachi the heebie-jeebies.

"Why don't you like water? It's for washing. You can't go around like that the rest of your life."

Jeremy glanced down at himself. "I'm okay."

"No. You are not okay. You smell to high heaven, and there are probably bugs crawling in your hair. Now come on, I'll show you the bathroom and find you a washcloth and towel."

The boy reluctantly did as he was told. Malachi turned on the bath faucets and adjusted the temperature of the water and left him. But before he had finished rounding up an old plaid shirt and a pair of blue-washed-to-gray jeans that might fit a ten-year-old, Jeremy was out of the shower, standing naked with the towel around his middle. A puddle had dripped onto the wood floor of the hall where Malachi almost ran into him.

"Jesus. Did you wash at all?"

"Yeah."

His hair was plastered to his head so maybe he'd washed it, but Malachi suspected he hadn't done more than a perfunctory job of it. "Okay, fine. Dry off and put these on. I couldn't find any underwear so you'll just have to go without."

"I don't like underwear."

"That's right, I forgot. So okay, put these on."

"Where's the blood?" Jeremy stood holding the clothes, making no move to dress. His eyes were dark in the shadowy hallway, and Malachi couldn't make out his expression. He thought that might be a good thing.

"All right, come with me. Bring the clothes and put them on later." He marched him through the house to the kitchen and opened the refrigerator door. He stood there staring for some seconds before speaking.

"Where's the blood?" Jeremy repeated.

"It's here." Malachi reached in and withdrew the last bag. The box his mother kept her supply in was empty save for the one bag. He couldn't believe it. His mother had never let it get this low. Why hadn't the Predators brought more? What was going on? The empty box was as ominous as a road sign saying the bridge ahead was out.

Maybe that's where his parents were. They never had to go get his mother's supply, but maybe, this time, something unavoidable had delayed the Predators.

The boy stood holding the cold bag and eyeing it with scorn.

"It's not that bad. At least, I don't think it is. Naturals and Cravens drink it that way all their lives. Just try, okay?"

"How?"

Malachi had seen his mother drink only a few times in his entire life. It was something she did in private, as far as she was able. But he knew what happened. How the fangs automatically descended when the bag drew near.

He took the bag from the boy and pushed it up against his face. Jeremy drew back, flinching. Malachi pressed it toward him again. He had to get him to do this. "Look, you can't be picky. I know it's not a squirrel or a rabbit, but it's what you need, so take it."

As the bag neared him the second time, the boy latched onto it like a snake, just as he had with the prairie hen and his first taste of blood. He buried his face in the bag, his hands clutching it so close his face disappeared behind the plastic container.

When Malachi heard the slurping sounds, he had to leave the room. It wasn't that the sight of blood or the taking of it made him sick. It did, for some reason, always produce a sense of sadness in him. To think a creature was reduced to renewing the body only with another creature's blood made him think again and again of becoming a vegetarian. He hardly ate meat anymore as it was. Having Jeremy around for a few days had further diminished his appetite for it.

Not to mention the news of Mad Cow Disease that was spreading around the world. A hundred and fifty thousand cases of it were found in England alone. Another case of mutated cells gone rampant. Protein cells. No DNA. No RNA. One hundred percent fatal to humans. People who contracted the disease died with skulls full of mush, the disease eating away at their brains, leaving it like a hunk of Swiss cheese riddled with holes.

In France there were reports of mad *bees*. Bees so disoriented they couldn't find their ways back to their hives. Maybe their brains were scrambled, too.

My God. Ten years ago he'd have dismissed all these horrors as bad ideas from an old 1950s horror movie. But they weren't. They were scientifically verified facts. One heck of a lot scarier than anything he'd ever seen in the movies. Now that he thought about mad cows and mad bees, he decided he wouldn't be able to look at hamburger or a spoonful of honey the same way again.

While Jeremy drank his mother's last container of whole blood, Malachi walked around the house. He looked for clues about his parents' absence. Unless they'd had to go for a new supply of blood, he couldn't think where they could be. He hadn't been mentally in touch with his mother in the last couple of days. He'd tried without success and wondered at her unavailability. Why had she lost communication with him?

Then a great fear entered him and he stopped dead in the center of the living room. What if Balthazar's last act had been to send eight more assassins to kill his mother? Or twelve? Or, God forbid, two dozen?

No. He would have known if she had been harmed. He put the thought from mind. He stood staring out the window, expecting their car any minute, when Jeremy came up behind him. He knew he was there though the boy hadn't made a sound.

"Don't tell me," Malachi said. "You're still hungry."

"Yeah."

"Well, you're just going to have to learn some restraint. I can't keep going after prey for you."

"Malachi, I'm not at all like you, am I?"

"No. Not much."

"I'm not like your mom either."

"No, not exactly."

"You think I'm bad, don't you?"

He hadn't sounded pitiful, but the question tugged hard at Malachi so that he turned and, stooping to the boy's level, took him into his arms. "No, I don't think you're bad. You just don't know anything yet. You don't know how to control this . . . this thing. My mother can help you. It won't always be like this."

"It won't? You promise?"

Malachi hated to promise when he wasn't sure of what he was saying. He only hoped it wouldn't be like this for the boy forever. His unquenchable thirst was a frightening thing. It was like a dark part of him that drove him above all else. The hunger.

"I . . . I can't promise."

"The man who was in the dream with me . . . you know . . . when I died . . ." Jeremy paused, trying to recall the name. His words were softly spoken against Malachi's shirt.

"Mentor."

"Yeah. He told me not to do it. He said, 'Don't. That

life's not for you.' But I couldn't help it. All I could think about was Dottie and Grandpa. All I wanted was to find some way to get back at those vampires who killed them."

"I know. It's how things turn out sometimes. It's what you were meant to be."

"Malachi?"

"Yes?"

"Will you kill me?"

Malachi flinched as if he'd been bitten or stabbed. He drew the boy away and looked into his face. He hadn't washed all the grit from his face. His eyes looked hollow and sunken. The clothes he'd donned while in the kitchen fit him badly, the collar too big for his little neck.

"Kill you? Oh, Jeremy, why would I want to kill you?"

"I mean . . . if I asked you to, would you do it?"

"Why would you ask me to do that?"

"Because I'm bad. I am. I know it, no matter what you say. I shouldn't be here. I'm . . . cold. I'm always hungry and it's not right, the thoughts I have and what I want to do. I wish they'd killed me, too. They shouldn't have left me this way. I didn't listen to Mentor, and it's too late now."

So this was the Predator's plight, Malachi thought. How could a child come to terms with something like this?

"No one's going to kill you, Jeremy. You're going to get past all this. There are others like you, many thousands of them. Maybe they wanted to die, too, in the first days. You just have to trust me. My mother will help you. So will Mentor. He'll come and explain things and show you what to do."

Jeremy lay his head on Malachi's shoulder again, his face turned to the room. He had his arms loosely hung around Malachi's neck. "They need to come soon. Real soon."

Malachi shivered, thinking of the horses locked in their stalls and the look Jeremy had given them. He'd have to watch him. Maybe he shouldn't have brought him here. Maybe he should have searched out Mentor and begged him to take the boy. This was indeed a serious matter. To raise a child was one thing, but to raise one who was a natural born Predator had to be the hardest work in the world.

He took the boy up into his arms, standing with him,

and turned with him to look out the window. "Help me watch for my mom," he said. "I think she's coming."

Jeremy nodded his head. "Yeah. She's coming this way. I hear her thoughts. She's been to a hospital."

So now Jeremy could tap into them telepathically. That was new. He was growing not only in appetite, but in every way.

"Hospital?"

"Aunt Celia. She's thinking of Aunt Celia."

It was the cancer, Malachi suddenly knew. The cancer he'd detected in his great-aunt years ago. It must have come back.

"Oh, she's okay," Jeremy said, reading him now. "That's what you're mama's thinking. How glad she is Aunt Celia's going to make it."

Malachi walked to the front door and onto the porch. The car slowly maneuvered down the drive.

He didn't want to hear any more of his mother's thoughts until she was in the house where they could talk out loud.

The boy stayed quiet, probably having read his mind again. No one did that, not even his mother, unless he invited her. He wished Predators weren't so strong.

"Or so scary," Jeremy said, unable to resist finishing his friend's thoughts just once more.

"Stop it," Malachi said. "That's not funny." He put Jeremy on his feet and went down the steps to meet his parents. Thank God he'd have someone to help him out. He hadn't known just how frazzled he was from his days on the road until he saw his mother's happy smile and his father's beaming face.

* * *

Dell's heart leaped when she saw her son standing on the porch waiting. With all that was happening—Celia's surgery, rumors of an outside renegade force trying to take over, the complete loss of her blood supplies—she had been sick with worry about Malachi.

She raced up the path and hugged him hard. She thought her smile would break her face. "You've come home!"

"I've missed you, Mom." Malachi hugged her back and then let her go to hug his father. "How's Aunt Celia?"

"She had a radical mastectomy, but I think she's going to be all right now. At least as all right as you can be with a thing like that." The vampire hung back behind Malachi's legs. "Well, hello there. You're Jeremy, right?"

"We've got to talk about him," Malachi said, pulling him from his hiding place to face his parents. "He took your last meal from the refrigerator and he's still hungry."

Dell felt her smile dissipate and tried to get it back. Now what would she do? She was already feeling weakened from trying to dole out the blood to herself to make it last. "I'm afraid there's a problem. Upton joined with Balthazar and he's here now trying to make sure none of us get our deliveries. No one's been able to get through Upton's lines for two days."

"Balthazar's dead, isn't he?"

Dell knew that he was. She's talked with Mentor who assured her Malachi could come home. Ross had been sent to dispose of him. "Yes. Ross went to his caves and . . ."

"It was fire, Malachi said." It was the first thing the boy had said.

Dell looked at his feral little face and wondered if he really knew how terrifying death by fire could be for anyone, but especially for the vampire. She said, "Yes, that's right. Fire."

"I don't care about that guy anymore," Ryan said. "But something has to be done about this character Upton. It's all over the news about the fires set in Dallas. They think it was a group of arsonists, but your mother said it was Upton."

"He killed every Craven he could find," she said. "He knew they couldn't escape. It was an unbelievably wicked thing to do."

"Is Mentor able to stop him?" Malachi asked as they moved indoors.

She believed he could, but there was a small voice in the back of her mind that kept piping up and asking, *What if he doesn't?*

She shouldn't worry her family with her own doubts, she thought, so she said, "I'm sure he will."

Jeremy had surreptitiously slipped from Malachi's side and now stood very close to Ryan. He stood staring at Ryan's hand, his stare trained on the pulse he could see there, pulsing. He licked his lips uncontrollably. Dell moved toward Ryan and said, "You'd better see about the horses. They haven't been fed today."

"Okay. I think I'll take a ride, too. It's a beautiful day." He turned to Malachi. "I'm glad you're home, son. We missed you every day you were gone." His genuine words were accompanied with a crinkling around his eyes as he smiled.

Dell saw the boy's disappointment when Ryan left the room. She knew Jeremy's hunger, though her own was not yet nearly as strong. Over the years of marriage to a mortal she'd sometimes had to battle her own instinct to sink her fangs into her husband's throat and lap from his warm blood. She never would have killed him. She loved him more than anyone in the world. But she'd often been tempted to make a very small puncture and *taste* him. It was obvious the little Predator wanted more than a taste. If she and Malachi hadn't been right at his side, she expected the boy would have attacked.

"Malachi, go out and catch a chicken for your dinner. I'll fry it the way you like. First, catch one for Jeremy." Her small flock of yard hens had grown thanks to the unflagging efforts of a huge black rooster. Her son loved fried chicken that had been double-dipped in buttermilk and seasoned flour.

"A chicken's not going to be enough." Malachi gave her a serious look. "It's only an appetizer for Jeremy. I don't know what's happening, but in the last couple of days he's been that way."

Dell didn't know the boy's real need any more than she knew what was in his soul. She knew he'd come back a Predator, and a Predator was a more voracious feeder than the Natural or Craven, but how much more?

"Take two chickens, then." Malachi's face remained somber. "Okay, as many as he wants. I can always get more."

She watched as Malachi took Jeremy with him to the back door and outside where the chickens ran free every day. They roosted at night in a small enclosure with graduated shelves, but during the day the flock was free to roam, pecking at insects and clucking curiously over unearthed worms.

As she began to prepare the big pot of boiling water

she'd have to use for dipping the headless chicken into so she could pluck out its feathers, she watched her son and the little Predator beyond the window over the sink.

Malachi began to give the boy instructions on how to sneak up on a hen so he could catch it, but before he finished speaking, Jeremy was already on the prowl. Dell turned off the faucet and set aside the filled kettle. She had never hunted. The act mesmerized her.

Jeremy swooped over a hen scratching in the dirt and immediately pushed back its neck and sunk his fangs into the fowl's breast. It squawked and beat at his face with its spurs. Dell wanted to turn away, but couldn't. The boy's actions had also frozen Malachi in place. He stood by, his eyes wide in wonder, and, she thought, revulsion.

Dropping the hen quickly, its blood drained, the boy reached down where another hen had wandered near his pants leg, clucking and cackling crazily. He snatched it up and the deadly act began again. Unable to move from the window, Dell saw the boy go through eleven hens before he dropped the last one and turned with bloody lips to Malachi. She heard him say, "That's enough for now. You need more chickens."

Indeed she did. Her small flock had been halved in mere minutes. With one more feasting the boy would have finished off every bird on her property. This couldn't continue.

Shaking her head, she carried the kettle to the stove and turned on a burner. She wouldn't clean all of the hens. One was more than enough to satisfy her son. She'd have to take the others to the trash barrel and burn them to keep coyotes and other scavengers from coming into the yard in the night.

There was no way she could feed Jeremy. His appetite for blood far surpassed her own.

When Malachi came back into the house carrying one of the dead hens, he sent her a mental comment. *Jeremy's a real killer, as you can see for yourself.*

She could certainly see that. She'd have to keep close tabs on her husband and give the child Predator no opportunity to be alone with him. She'd have to go in search of wild animals on their two hundred acres and hand over her booty to Jeremy. What she really needed to do was find someone, another Predator, to take the boy. He was too dangerous to keep around for long.

That night she sat with him on the front porch. Inside, Ryan and Malachi slept in their beds. It was after midnight and the landscape lay beneath a bright moon.

"I'm bad," Jeremy said. "You don't have to tell me."

"No, you're just a Predator. Predators can't help their need for prey."

"I liked them. Your chickens," he said.

"I know. I used to like them, too." She meant when they were alive, pecking around her home and keeping her company as she went about her gardening.

"You drink blood. Why doesn't Malachi drink it?"

"He's part human. He's mortal."

"Oh. He smells like a vampire."

She knew what Jeremy meant. Malachi's scent wasn't as overwhelmed with human pheromones as it was impregnated with the scent of his vampire heritage. Vampires smelled to her like copper pennies—the hard, metallic odor that was so close to the scent of blood.

They sat a while quietly, and then Jeremy said he was going inside to sleep. She followed him mentally as he climbed onto the living room sofa where she'd fashioned him a bed.

While she waited for her mind to wind down and let her find rest, she caught herself licking her lips just as she'd seen Jeremy do it. She, too, was hungry and growing hungrier by the minute. She hadn't taken blood in twenty-four hours and something inside her screamed for sustenance. She thought of the hens and rejected the idea. They were her friends. She couldn't kill them.

She thought of the wildlife lurking just at the edge of the ring of blue-white light thrown by the yard light. She could sense living things there, hiding. She might find a rabbit if she would get up and leave the porch so quickly the wildlife never knew she was coming.

Still, she sat hungering, her mouth salivating, and struggled with the urge to move, move fast, and kill mercilessly. Until she absolutely had to, she wasn't going to give in. She just couldn't see herself in the same league as the boy

Predator. She was a Natural, devoted to leading a peaceful life alongside her human counterparts. She wasn't like Jeremy. She never wanted to be like him. She couldn't kill.

They had to get past Upton's people and bring her the blood soon.

They had to. Or she'd go get it herself.

She tried to concentrate on the sky rather than the darkness beyond the ring of yard light that illuminated her house and yard. Up there might be worlds like this, she thought, where men don't have to be vampires and take blood to live forever. Scientists had theorized man was a Type 0 civilization, the lowest in the hierarchy. Type 0s used the energy of dead animals and minerals to propel civilization. Type 1s used the power of nature itself. It was true this civilization was rapidly moving toward a Type 1, and it was predicted mankind would reach that higher world within a hundred years. If he didn't blow himself up first. That was the danger in moving from Type 0 to 1. As man harnessed the power to control nature—able to control hurricane, tornado, earthquake, and the deep hot heart of the volcano—he might also forget himself and set off a firestorm of antagonism between nations that would spell the end.

If it ever came to that and man's destiny was sunk, she figured ships would ferry passengers from Earth to a nearby planet made habitable by man's ingenuity. Would she and others like her go with them? She couldn't image they'd let themselves be left behind.

Or was it possible the vampire could one day guide man and keep him from destroying his own world? If that happened, the vampire would be thrust into the Type 1 civilization along with the mortal. *What a wonderful future,* Dell thought, realizing she wasn't suffering so much now from hunger pains.

Even a vampire couldn't harness the energy of nature, though they were able to bend it and use it for their own means. She thought the vampire might be the stepping stone, taking man from his inferior and dying Type 0 world into the new, powerful civilization of the Type 1. If one day man would study how the vampire bent natural laws governing the rest of the world, and discover how to enlarge that power to include taming the tornado and turning its great force into usable energy, the future wouldn't look so grim.

Whether this cooperation ever came about or not might depend entirely on vampires like herself who took the longer view. She had so much to look forward to.

Her mind was brought back to the here and now when her instincts alerted her to movement near her porch steps at ground level. A snake. It slithered past, oblivious to possible predators.

She could either rise and strike, taking the snake and drinking down the small amount of blood it contained, or she could have let it go on its way.

She sat unmoving. She let it go.

She was a superior being, fit to rise into a Type 1 civilization, that's all there was to it. A balanced world depended on control.

She licked her lips, her nostrils flared, and the snake crawled past the steps and into the long grass of the yard. That was when she heard the soft crying coming from inside the house. It was Jeremy, thrashing about on the sofa, weeping in his sleep from a nightmare.

She rose to go to him. She'd wake him so the nightmare would go away. She'd done this a hundred times for her son when he was young. She was surely competent to do it again, even if the boy she must minister to was a Predator.

She shook Jeremy by the shoulder. He jumped up suddenly, his eyes open and afraid as he threw his arms around her neck. His tears of blood dripped, wetting her throat.

"Shush," she said, cooing next to his ear. "Shush, it's just a dream, baby, that's all it is, a bad dream."

* * *

Alex drove up to Malachi's house and waited beside the car for his friend to come outside. He knew he'd heard him drive up.

Malachi waved as he came down the path to the gate.

"Hey, where have you been?" Alex asked. "I've been calling, and your mom said you were visiting relatives. Why didn't you let me know?"

Malachi seemed about to answer him when he turned at the sound of the front door slamming shut. A little boy came running down the steps. He called for Malachi.

Alex joined his friend at the gate. He said, "Who's the kid?"

Malachi caught the child by the shoulder to keep him from skidding into them. "This is Jeremy. My . . . uh . . . cousin. Jeremy, meet my friend Alex."

"Hi."

Alex held out his hand for shaking, but Jeremy didn't take it. He bounded past the two of them instead, heading for the horse shed.

"Jeremy, no!" Malachi was right behind him.

"Where's he going?" It seemed to Alex he kept asking questions and no one answered them.

Malachi caught up with the kid and swept him from the ground. He slung him over his shoulder. He turned back to Alex. "Wait here a minute. I've got to get Jeremy back in the house."

Alex stood around the horse stalls, petting Malachi's horse. When Malachi finally returned, he looked like someone with a very big problem. "What's with that kid?" Alex asked.

"He's just . . . uh . . . he's, like, hyperactive or something. We can't let him around the horses. He scares them."

"He kind of scares me, too." Alex laughed uneasily. "Now tell me, where have you been? Have you signed up for your first semester in Huntsville? I have to go down to Houston pretty soon and find a place to live." He meant for his first semester at Baylor College of Medicine. "I was thinking maybe we could make a day of it, me and you."

Malachi reached out and stroked his horse's head. "I don't think I can do that, Alex. There's some stuff going on around here. We have to try to help Jeremy. And there's some other things . . ."

"Well, hell, Mal, let's talk about it. Maybe that would help. I haven't seen you in months because I've been working so many hours. I've missed you, you big goof."

Malachi smiled now and Alex felt better.

"I can't really talk about it."

"Aw, you're always so secretive. You ought to let your fiends help out. Have you seen Danielle?"

"Not for a while."

Alex whistled. "You really are tied up, aren't you?"

"I'm afraid so. I might be able to tell you about it later. Right now . . . I can't . . . you know . . ."

Alex hung around for a while longer, but he couldn't get Malachi to open up. They parted with a handshake. Then Alex saw Jeremy come out onto the porch again and Malachi hurried back toward the house. "Thanks for coming by," he said, waving to Alex. "I'll call you, okay?"

Jeremy was off the porch and sidling around the side of the house, trying to get away from Malachi. Alex climbed into his car and as he drove away from the ranch, he saw his friend chasing the kid behind the house. *Whew,* he thought. *That kid needs a keeper.*

*   *   *

Bette Kinyo took the elaborately carved brass urn from the funeral director and held it tightly to her chest. In the car she placed it carefully in a box stuffed with newspaper on the front seat.

Alan.

With her again.

The police were stuck with an open criminal case, seeking an intruder she described for them. Not the monster who had really come. They wouldn't have believed that. They would have wanted to put her into therapy or lock her away. No, she described some scruffy imaginary man high on drugs. The police believed her, given her neighborhood, even when she wanted to scream the truth.

Now Alan was cremated, as he'd wished to be, and he rode beside her in the car in the beautiful urn she'd bought to contain his ashes. Some people drifted the ashes of their loved ones over a favorite piece of ground or into the sea, but she would keep all that was left of Alan with her always. His remains gave her some consolation. She felt his spirit close, hovering about, and superstitiously feared if she didn't have his ashes, he would disappear from her life forever.

Once Mentor had let her know where he lived in the city. They had been sitting on the stone bench in her garden late one night. He had told her more about his life in Dallas and how he lived it. He lived in a house, just like anyone else. Vampires hadn't ever lived in crypts and coffins. That was a fiction, he told her. Well, except for a couple of odd characters he had known, he admitted sheepishly. They believed the press on themselves and thought it quite romantic, so they adopted the lifestyle. For the most part, however, they all made their homes in human constructions, living quietly, seeking anonymity. They always had.

"Why do you want me to know where you live?" she'd asked.

"Because I trust you and if you ever need me and can't contact me, you'll know where I'll be."

Mentor loved her. One of the monsters loved her. The strange thing was, she accepted his love as natural. Destiny decided these things, she believed, and if she were to have a relationship, however one-sided, with a supernatural being, then it was preordained for her soul's growth.

Now she drove across the city toward that house. She had thought he'd be with her during the service for her husband, and when he hadn't arrived, she'd been disappointed. Some of her coworkers from the lab came and a few of Alan's family drove from different Texas locations to see him put to rest. But with Mentor missing, it was like a dark hole had opened up in the chapel to suck the life from the proceedings. She had come to rely on Mentor to alleviate some of her fears. When he wasn't there for the service, she gave in to her grief and saw life ahead as barren and empty.

The neighborhood she drove through now was an older one, though not as old or run-down as her own. The houses stood on larger plots, with plenty of room between them. Most of the houses were made of wood and many of them boasted covered porches and wide steps flanked by stucco pillars.

She found Mentor's house and pulled into the drive. *Mentor,* she thought. *I need help. I need so much help.*

The door opened, and there he stood looking at her sitting in the car. He didn't seem surprised. He probably had known she was on her way. She admired how the vampire could reach into another person's thoughts at great distances. Though she'd been born with some abilities of her own, they didn't compare to what Mentor and his kind could do.

She reached into the cardboard box and withdrew the urn. Her fingers were slow to warm the cold metal. She carefully let herself out of the car and crossed the lawn. On reaching Mentor she stood looking up at him, the urn again clutched to her chest. "I . . . I couldn't go home."

"I know. Come inside."

They sat next to one another in the darkened living room. His home was comfortable, though the furniture was older and rather worn. The place was spotless, not a speck of dust anywhere. A book lay on the coffee table. A novel by Steinbeck. She smiled to think Mentor read novels in his spare time. She wondered if he'd read all the authors of every age he'd lived through. If he had, she expected he was the best-read person in the world.

He offered her tea and she declined. "I'm sorry I wasn't at the service held for Alan," he said. "The vampire nations are in turmoil. I couldn't leave my duties."

"That's all right," she said, feeling it wasn't all right at all. She'd needed him.

Finally he asked, "How can I help, Bette?"

"All the joy has left my life," she said, feeling her statement was not too strong. It was the truth. Light had been extinguished all around her and nothing gave her any satisfaction—not her job, her home, nothing.

"It'll come back," Mentor said. "You're in a dark place, but there's a way out."

She had placed Alan's urn on the table. She stared at it as if she could will her husband to lift the lid and come out like a genie from a bottle.

"I believe you. I know it's true. But that isn't helping me now. I had to take time from work. I can't seem to get up in the morning. I drag around the house and don't even get dressed until most of the day has passed and by then it makes no sense to put on clothes." She felt a catch in her throat and had to swallow hard. "Do you know why I never married until late in life?"

"I wouldn't say your early thirties is so late."

"Maybe not for you. For someone like me, it was."

"Tell me why, then."

"You won't go into my mind and know the answer before I say it?" She looked at him.

"No, I won't."

"You don't know everything about me from the times you did go into my mind?" She referred to their first meetings when he and Ross feared she would tell the world what she knew about the shipments of blood from Dallas to outlets all over the Southwest.

"I know some things," he said tentatively. "Not everything."

"Well, the reason I didn't marry until I was thirty-two was because I thought I was better off alone. I'd convinced myself that was the way it should be. Except for Alan, I didn't date, didn't get involved. When he came to Dallas and stayed, I realized I had been fooling myself, protecting myself. Since I'd met him in college I'd wanted to be with him. I wanted to be his wife. But I'd put the thought so far out of my mind because we were going in different directions. He loved the healing profession. I loved research. His home then was in Houston, where he practiced. Mine was here. We met at medical conferences once or twice a year, renewing our affair and then parting again for months. It was killing me, but I denied my feelings."

"We all do that sometimes," he murmured.

She glanced at him. He meant his feelings for her. He'd denied them for as long as he could, and had only confessed them to her when he couldn't hold back anymore.

"I spent some of my best years alone because I didn't know how to get what I wanted," she continued. "I didn't know how to give up, how to sacrifice the career I'd made for myself here in Dallas. I built a small world in my home, created simple routines that kept my mind busy. I told myself I didn't need anyone in order to be fulfilled." She paused, the catch back in her throat. "I lied to myself."

"We all do that." Mentor sat still, not looking at her. She wondered what he was thinking. Maybe he thought she was whining about lost opportunity. And maybe she was. But it was thoroughly human and she couldn't help it.

"Now," she said, "I don't know how to go on. I waited so long to be part of a couple. It's been nearly twenty years since then, Mentor. I'm fifty-two. I thought we'd . . . Alan and I . . . would grow old together. But now I'm on my own again. And I've forgotten how to do it. I've forgotten how to live."

Mentor moved to put his arm around the top of her

shoulder. She leaned into him. It was amazing that she'd known this old vampire for two decades. They'd shared many secrets and come to know one another intimately. She'd been drawn to him from the first time he appeared in her kitchen to wipe the memories from her mind. She'd been on the trail of Ross' blood shipments that hadn't been tested by her lab. Alan came along and, investigating further, discovered the vampires, though she'd known from the beginning they were in some way supernatural.

She should have despised Mentor for meddling with her mind, but once she was past her fear of him, she understood the reasons for it. He was the Protector. He couldn't let her tell what she knew to the world. Their agreement of silence had bound them together for the rest of her life. He promised not to let Ross hurt her or Alan. In return, she promised never to speak of what she knew.

"You may have forgotten what it's like to be alone, Bette, but you underestimate your strength. I don't think I've known many like you," he said. "I believe you'll come out of this."

She closed her eyes. If he could believe in her, she might find a way to believe in herself again. "Can I stay here a while?"

"Yes. As long as you want."

"A few days? I can't seem to go back to the house yet."

"As long as you want," he repeated.

She settled against him and the weariness of the past days swept over her. It was as if she'd been given permission to let her mind drop into a dungeon where there was no emotions to tear at her spirit. She sought oblivion.

As she drowsed, she imagined the arm around her shoulder belonged to Alan and he was there caring for her. Loving her. Forever.

8

Ross stood next to Sereny in his home while she admired his art. He'd bought or stolen pieces that by all rights should have been donated to museums. It was a new sensation for him to share his fascination for his masterpieces with anyone. The women he brought here were for the most part uneducated and wouldn't know a Matisse from a Pollock. It would be all dots to them. He laughed to himself over his small joke.

His Predators weren't close to him, never expecting an invitation to his home or into his life. None of them even knew of his obsession. And Mentor, god. Mentor despised his collection. He was always uncomfortable when he visited the house. Ross knew what he thought of him. That he was pretentious. That he wasted the money he earned from Upton's former businesses.

Sereny was the first person who showed any appreciation at all, and her authentic awe for the vastness and quality of his collection pleased him enormously.

Over time he'd understood what the masterful paintings did for him. Unlike living beings, the world of mortals, whose passions were based on survival, art expressed true passion for him. Released from care about his survival, he had found artwork the only reason man should be allowed to continue. A few talented artists of every age captured the heart of what it was to struggle and overcome, or to fail and face the music. Whether their work was considered representational, paintings of life as most saw it, or allegorical, or cubist, or modern, the artist took paint and canvas and made of it windows into the eternal.

Though Ross sometimes scoffed at his own sentimentality, he recognized how his collection kept him from falling over the edge into baseness. He often teetered on the precipice where he might become the one true monster the world found most odious—that dark stain of destruction personified which walked without a soul.

Mentor would tell him that was not possible. It was his soul itself that had chosen the Predator life. And being Predator did not mean he was monstrous.

But Mentor had never traveled in his soul and didn't know how thin a line it walked between monster and human. He gave in to his appetites. He could feel no remorse. He didn't care how much suffering was inflicted on mortal men. They were like rats to him, multiplying without any care whatsoever about how they were overpopulating the very planet they called home.

Yet when he surveyed his art, actually fondling the frames and running his fingers across the beautifully applied layers of paint, he was closer to the man he had been before becoming Predator than at any other time. He remembered the taste of food and the abatement of thirst. He remembered his mother and his father, who had died as mortals, still loving him despite knowing what kind of creature he had become. He remembered the world had not been built by the vampire, but by the efforts of man, and all that he took for granted in his pleasure flowed from man, not vampire.

He forgave himself.

If it were not for his love of art, whether paintings, sculpture, murals in great chapels, or architecture that had stood for a thousand years, he knew he would be irredeemably lost.

What a great creature he might be one day if he could incorporate his passion into his daily actions. He would never be as compassionate as Mentor—who could? But he might be able to hang onto that portion of his human self that held him back from the dark fall and that would be more than enough.

As he thought these things and basked in the glow of Sereny's attention to his prize possessions, he was slow to note her mood had changed.

He said, "What's wrong?" She was as prickly as a cactus, the aura around her body having changed from soothing blue to sooty black.

She turned completely around, her back to the painting

they had been studying, and pointed to the rear of the
house. "Someone's coming."

He could have slapped himself for letting down his guard.
He knew Upton's plans included trying to get to him and
to Mentor. He'd let that slip from mind only for minutes
and if it hadn't been for Sereny, even now he wouldn't
know what was happening around him.

He tuned into the house as if it were a box lying in his
hand. He searched every room, every nook and cranny but
found no one. He then projected his intelligence to the land
surrounding his home. He picked up a faint transmission
of a Predator unknown to him.

"I heard two of them," Sereny said, moving through the
large open room to the hall that transversed the house and
led to the back patio.

"Two?" Ross followed on her heels, trying to pick up
the second Predator. He couldn't. "Two?"

She had stepped outside and stared toward the setting
sun in the distance. "Two who leaked their thoughts," she
said. "They're with hundreds. Upton will kill them for that
transgression."

"Upton's brought his entire army?" Ross was flabbergasted. He prided himself on how alert he was. He could
pick up another vampire within miles, yet he could only
detect one Predator while Sereny spoke of hundreds.
Upton and Balthazar had trained all of them in the art of
cloaking their minds, but it had been Sereny who found
them out.

"Yes." She turned to him and he saw flames in her eyes.
It was an illusion. Her thoughts made him see the future
coming for him. Flames. Death. Annihilation.

They didn't have to speak again. They didn't have time.
He took her hand and they both began to shimmer, their
matter changing to energy as it spun them away from
danger.

As her essence mingled with his own, Ross let go of his
identity, and together they formed a new energy that burst
into light and then vanished. They moved as one from the
ranch house and across the low, burnt-orange sky. He took
her to Mentor's within seconds, holding each and every
molecule of her close so he wouldn't lose her. She was an
incredible woman and a very powerful Predator. He needed

her. He hadn't known he would ever need anyone, but now, his being entangled with hers, the truth became clear to him.

When they reappeared in Mentor's house, they saw he sat on the sofa, his arm around Bette Kinyo. Mentor looked up and, reading Ross' face, he said, "They came for you."

Bette opened sleepy eyes. She flinched upon seeing the two Predators standing so close they could reach out and take her by the neck. A gasp escaped her, and she scooted closer into Mentor's embrace.

"They're not here to hurt you." Mentor removed his arm and stood.

"Can we talk around her?" Sereny asked, gesturing to Bette.

"Yes." Mentor came near. "She knows about us."

Sereny hesitated before saying, "All of them came. Every Predator Upton has."

Ross began to pace the room. "They'd cloaked themselves. All but two." He glanced at Sereny. No point in admitting to Mentor he hadn't been the one to detect them—that without the woman he'd be ash now. "We were lucky there were at least two with weak minds."

"I think it's time to call up our own army," Mentor said. "You have them ready, right? We can't have an all-out war. It'll attract mortals. We'll have to use subterfuge and hunt the enemy down one by one."

Ross agreed for once. He and Mentor often clashed over leadership and what actions should be taken, but this time he knew the old vampire was right. It was one thing to gather hundreds of Predators to attack him on an isolated piece of land, but if he and Mentor called up hundreds more there wasn't a place on Earth they could battle without someone knowing. Even if they went into the wastelands of the desert areas of West Texas, someone would see them, someone would know. Also, it wasn't Upton's style to fight a face-to-face battle. He would never agree to leave the city for a more secluded place.

Within minutes the house swarmed with their closest advocates. Dolan came, sheepish and guilty that he'd not saved the Cravens. Ross saw how he avoided Mentor's eyes. A few minutes later Dell arrived, the boy Predator with her, trembling at the experience of moving through space at such supernormal speed. "Malachi's coming," she announced. They all knew the *dhampir* couldn't astral travel the way they could. His noisy motorcycle could be heard a short time later as he drove into Mentor's driveway. He came through the door, breathless and flushed. There was excitement on his face, but no fear. Ross was impressed. He'd had little to do with the *dhampir,* but he'd heard of his mighty power in thwarting Balthazar's assassins. Dell had trained him well.

This small cadre had been on the same side for twenty years. They all felt they were Mentor's soldiers, except for Ross himself, who felt himself an equal. Nevertheless, he was thankful they'd all shown up. Together they could rouse the band of Predators Ross usually controlled alone. They must work together or risk Upton's sneak attacks on each of them individually.

"Should I leave?"

It was the woman Mentor had watched over for two decades. Ross suspected he loved her, but he didn't expect he'd ever let him know that. Loving a mortal, the way Dell did, caused problems for everyone. None of them approved of these alliances, though of course Mentor could do as he pleased. There was no one to oppose him.

"No," Mentor said. "It's safer here. It's too late anyway. Two of Upton's followers are outside the door."

At the same instant all of the vampires in the room knew it was so. They had cloaked their minds when called to Mentor's home. They hadn't wanted Upton to know all of them were together and easily attacked. But the two outside the door had come on their own, hoping to find Mentor alone. If they killed him, Upton would make them captains. Upton would give them power above all others.

Mentor read these intimate thoughts of the two Predators as he moved toward the door. "Come in if you dare," he called.

The lurkers outside slipped away into the twilight, muttering oaths. Mentor turned back to the assemblage. "They're gone, but not for long. They'll tell Upton we're all here. We have to leave soon. Let me tell you what we must do."

*   *   *

It was three days of hell on Earth. Unnoticed by the human population in the city, Predator stalked Predator. Bodies piled up, and Mentor had dozens working as burial parties, moving the dead away from the city into the surrounding countryside. Sometimes Mentor sensed Detective Teal at the crime scenes. Each time he went to him and walked him away, throwing confusion into his mind. The man was a regular pest. He showed up when least expected, standing over a body, making notes in a little notebook, or reaching for his cell phone at his hip. If Mentor had had the time, he could have done something permanent to Teal's mind to keep him out of the way, but as it was, he was lucky to reach him in time to stop him from interfering.

The war grew until each side rose with victory and fell again, usually within mere hours, Upton's Predators sometimes taking Mentor's troops unaware and narrowing their control. They left the dead where they fell, so that Mentor's people had to take their own dead companions to bury before too many humans saw the headless bodies. It was up to Mentor to go to the witnesses and steal their memories, hiding them beneath layers of more mundane memories in the depths of their minds. Still, strange news began to appear on the television and radio news. The newspaper ran articles about three bodies in the morgue with unidentifiable wounds. Humans speculated on wild dogs, perhaps rabid, invading the city. They began to lock their doors and empty the streets at night.

Mentor worked tirelessly, day and night. He, too, hunted the enemy and put them to death. It was a relentless battle. None of them stayed in one place long enough to be found. But to hunt Upton's Predators, they had to frequent every alley and abandoned building in the city. Every time Upton tried gathering his forces together, Mentor's Predators attacked, scattering them. They couldn't find them with mental telepathy, so it was a war of attrition. It was slow and dreadful, a deep-night hunt where Mentor put aside all his hard fought for compassion and allowed the predator in him full reign.

He hated to admit how alive it made him feel. He hadn't

killed that many of his own kind before. He had no idea
the hunt itself and the resultant death might make him
want to roar like a lion. The game of hide and seek raised
his tension so that he was a tightly wound wire. Yet it was
nothing compared to the feeling of power he enjoyed when
he actually confronted another Predator, one who had betrayed his nation to follow Upton. He felt no compunction
to talk them out of their negative path or save them from
themselves. All he wanted to do was kill in the most ghastly
and bloody manner he could manage.

After his first hunt where he'd killed three of the enemy,
he returned to his home to see about Bette. She looked on
his face and shuddered. His vampire nature was a fearsome
thing that caused her to quake and move away. He tried
to control it, tried to get back to himself when he came to
her, but his blood was too high. He'd taken blood with each
new kill and it gave him a feeling of majesty. Predators did
not have the same blood as a living being, but it was blood
just the same. Along with each vampire victim he drained
came that vampire's vitality until his whole body was suffused with strength and fire.

Usually a being who had abstained from murder and taking the blood of a victim, the war had given him a taste of
what it had been like when he'd first turned vampire. At
his very core, he was a killer. He might keep it under control for years, but he could never divest himself of the urge.
He *liked* killing Upton's followers. He enjoyed sending
them into the darkness from which there was no escape.

Bette could see that reflected on his face, and he wasn't
able to disguise it.

"What have you done?" she asked that first time.

"I'm trying to save people like you from a grim future."

"That's a high-minded goal, but that's not what I see. I
see a killer still high from taking life."

"What would you have us do?"

"I don't know." She wrung her hands in agitation. "I
wish . . ."

"Go ahead, wish me away. Wish me dead and all the
others like me. Maybe God will hear you and come out of
His silence. That's what *I* wish. For God to end this charade
I call my life after death." His bitterness was deep and
abiding, but not truly aimed at Bette. He sighed. "I'm sorry.

I can't make excuses for what I am anymore. What you see is the real Mentor."

"It's not the one I knew."

"Then you deluded yourself, didn't you? If I take blood without killing, I atone for all the murder I've had to do. But when I have to kill, I do love it. If I were a tiger you wouldn't judge me. If I were a lion fighting to the death with another lion, you wouldn't look on the victorious face of the conqueror and say he had done wrong."

"But you are not a tiger, Mentor. You are not a lion."

"No. I'm a vampire. And I'm fighting as much for you and mankind as I am for myself. Remember that."

The discussion left him feeling angry and depressed. He left the house to her and went out into the darkness to stalk another renegade. His wife had never admonished him for his nature. He had been more of a killer then than now. He had gone far and wide to take human victims so suspicion would never fall on him living as a man with a wife, but Beatrice knew when he came home suffused with blood. She knew what he had done. If she judged him, she kept it to herself.

He hadn't wanted Bette to see him this way, but he had known one day she might. Death wasn't as close to man in her modern world of medicine and doctors and heroic lifesaving measures. In his time with his wife, death was everywhere. Plagues, disease, floods, fires, and wars ravished the country as well as the city. Society experienced whole generations of cleansing where families and communities all died together. Life was shorter and more precarious. It was the rare man who lived to be forty and half the women died during their childbearing years.

Bette couldn't understand the death of her husband, and now she didn't try to understand the seriousness of his undertaking. Did she have no idea of how the world she knew would change if vampires like Upton ruled?

It was Mentor's ultimate imperative to stop him. If he could only find him, he would tear him into a million pieces. Every drop of blood he drank from Upton's followers fell on Upton's head. He was responsible for hundreds of deaths and all for what? Revenge, he could understand, but he knew Upton wanted much more than that. He always had.

9

Upton saw his force dwindling night after night. There were more Predators working for Mentor than they could combat. Though Upton had trained his troops to cloak themselves and to hide well, one by one they were found and destroyed. He pulled them together to present a united force, but each time he did, they were attacked so viciously, they had to flee to survive. He tried to tell himself they were simply careless, but he knew better. He hadn't really trained them long enough. They slipped and the cloak fell away, and then they were hunted down and killed.

After the fiasco when they'd gone en masse after Ross and missed him by mere seconds, Upton stood before his army like a general who has lost the pivotal battle. He looked out over the sea of faces and waited in furious silence. Whoever had screwed up was going to show nervousness, and when he did, Upton would move.

He stood there, glaring, waiting with impatience. Most of the Predators understood what he was doing, so they didn't dare protest. Someone had let down their leader. Someone had leaked his thoughts, and Ross had picked them up and fled.

It took most of an hour, hundreds of men standing in an open field before one man who never even blinked.

Suddenly Upton moved like a whirlwind, the flanks opening as he sped through them to the betrayer. There was a wild scream as Upton closed on the Predator, knocking him to the ground and holding him down with one foot while he swung a machete at his neck.

Even before the first Predator's voice was cut off, another made a grunting sound and began to flee across the fields for the forest. Upton raised his hands to his jittery troops and went for the fleeing vampire himself. He caught him just inside the shadowed line of trees, ripping off one of his arms before killing him. The gathered Predators in the open field could hear the screams that filled the air, scaring birds from trees to send them flapping across the sky.

None of his other followers would make this mistake again, Upton vowed. But he had lost Ross, and it was Ross who could command so many of the enemy.

It was a terrible blow to his strategy. If he could not separate Ross and Mentor, his plan might fail.

Invading the city again, they had done considerable damage to the Predators under Ross and Mentor, but not enough to overpower them. They tried, but couldn't take control of the city. Their numbers were no more than two hundred now and soon even those would be found and killed—or they would skulk away in the night, deserting. Upton ranted constantly in his mind and verged on mental collapse.

In the nights he had taken over an empty penthouse on the top of one of Dallas' downtown skyscrapers. He stood at the wall of windows overlooking the spreading lights that went on for miles. It reminded him of the splendor of the penthouse he'd owned in Houston and the one he was about to buy in Dallas before Mentor spirited him away to Thailand.

Thailand. The years and years in a cell listening to the chiming of the bells by monastery monks. Thailand, the native home of the body he now possessed.

If he could catch Mentor and, with the help of some of his men, overpower him, he would take him back to Thailand and put him into a grave there.

If he couldn't yet control this one American city, what if he did take a prisoner? Mentor. Ross. The woman called Bette. Someone important to wreak his revenge on. He hadn't come with a big enough army. He hadn't trained them right. They were made up of malcontents both he and Balthazar had gathered. More than half of them owed allegiance to Balthazar and hardly knew Upton.

He hadn't taken his time. First Ross and Mentor had killed his partner, Balthazar, and then there were too many of their clans to track and kill. The cat and mouse game was almost at an end. Before it ended, Upton must do something. He wouldn't be denied one small victory over Mentor.

Leaving the penthouse he went to the street and called together several of his minions. They met in the deeper darkness of a canopy over the entrance to a closed restaurant. "I want to capture someone," he told them. "If you help me succeed, you'll be my captains. We can't win, we've already had too many casualties, but we can take a captive and leave the country. Stay with me and we'll leave, but we'll come back one day, and we'll be stronger and smarter next time."

They vowed they would do whatever he commanded and, together, they began to seek out an opponent worth capturing.

*   *   *

Malachi was more tired than any of his comrades. He had tried to stay near his mother, but she had proved to be a significant commander, and was busily sending out groups to various parts of town where she thought the renegades might hide.

Tonight Malachi walked the streets with just one Predator named Clifton. They had run into one another in an alley where Clifton had just murdered one of Upton's people. They decided to go on together, the way Mentor suggested they hunt. "Go alone," he'd warned, "and you'll have more chance of being caught and killed."

Already he and Clifton had searched out three renegades, two of whom begged for mercy. Malachi stood back while Clifton dealt the deathblows, but he felt nothing. A renegade Predator was of no use to anyone, not even himself. He might pretend to be reformed, but he could never be trusted.

"Have you sent word for someone to pick up these bodies?" Malachi asked.

"They're on the way."

A lone car drove slowly toward them, then passed. Malachi and Clifton stopped, looking back. The car was going too slowly. It stopped at the head of the alley where the three dead Predators lay.

Clifton started back, but Malachi took his arm. "Wait, let me take care of this."

He saw a large man exit the car and head down the alley. He followed him. He tapped his mind and discovered this was a police detective and his name was . . . Teal? Tealiski?

He joined him at the three corpses and touched him on the shoulder. The detective jumped, having never heard his approach.

"This isn't you business," Malachi said.

"What? Step back, son. I'm with the police."

"I know." Malachi said. He couldn't do harm to this man. He sent out an urgent plea for Mentor.

The man was saying, "You know?"

"Your shoes," Malachi said, playing for time. He pointed to the big man's large black shoes. They were discount city shoes. Undercover officers who didn't accept bribes couldn't afford better.

Teal's lips showed a ghost of a smile. "My shoes," he mumbled. He reached for his cell phone.

Malachi took hold of his hand. "Don't do that."

Teal's eyes hardened. His voice deepened. "Are you the killer of these men? What's going on here?"

If Mentor didn't appear soon, Malachi would have to restrain the detective. He'd never done any sort of violence against a human. He didn't want to have to do it now.

There was a twinkling that caught Malachi's eye. He knew the mortal wouldn't have noticed it. He turned his head and said, "He won't listen to me, Mentor."

Teal twirled around and faced the old vampire. "Where'd you come from?"

"Hello, Mr. Teal. Let's go for a walk, shall we? We're becoming old friends."

Teal's eyes narrowed and then the skin around his eyes relaxed. "Oh, yeah," he said. "A walk. Sure."

Malachi watched them move away from the bodies and back to the street. He sighed. He didn't know what he would have done if Mentor hadn't come.

He rejoined Clifton and told him what had happened. They laughed about the policeman. He'd never know what hit him.

They wandered for hours, rarely speaking. They looked

deep into shadows. They threw out the nets of their natural telepathy, hunting for something out of the ordinary. They passed by humans, sending silent warnings to vacate the streets, they were in danger.

It was the hour when the city really slept the deepest. There were two more hours left before sunrise. The after-hour bars were closed and the traffic was almost nonexistent. Stoplights at intersections blinked monotonously, green, red, amber. Bugs gathered around lampposts, knocking themselves out to be near the light. No one walked the streets at three in the morning.

Malachi was musing about how much he and a Predator vampire were alike. He had always thought he was more like his father, more human than supernatural. But since assassins had been sent to kill him, he'd had to rely on anything but his human instincts. The more he used his inborn vampire abilities, the more he realized just how spectacular they were. The power was insidious and intoxicating. It made him feel omnipotent and indestructible. Which was a dangerous fantasy, of course, because even the most powerful vampire could be killed under the right circumstances. And he wasn't even a vampire.

As he argued with himself over the merits and faults of living the dichotomy that was his legacy, he paid little attention to his actual surroundings. He was relying on Clifton to be the lookout for any vampire presence. They were in the downtown area that seemed to draw some of the renegades after dark. Mentor thought it was because Upton was lying low there, drawn to the splendor of the lights and the tall buildings.

"He spent his life in the center of bustling cities," Mentor told them. "He's naturally drawn to the hub, the center, where he once lived like a king. It's why he wants this city first, why he picked it for his assault. You might think he's come out of revenge, come to punish me and Ross, but that's only half his motive. He used to run his massive conglomerate from here. With us out of the way, he could pick up the strings of his past life and start controlling the whole show again, taking over the corporation's board and installing a puppet chairman. He wants what he lost. He wants the money that fuels the power."

Charles Upton was a complicated individual, Malachi realized. There was more to him than a thirst for reprisal. He must have spent his years of imprisonment working out all the details. Mentor was right. Upton wanted the past back. He wanted to do it his way this time.

A swift warm wind kicked up, caressing Malachi's face. He smiled into it, pressing forward at Clifton's side. The first indication he was being hunted was when he saw Clifton slow and begin to swing his head back and forth like a hound, trying to pick up a scent.

Malachi suddenly knew that danger was close by. He took hold of Clifton's arm, halting him. They turned around, looking, but the streets and sidewalks were empty. "They're watching us," Clifton whispered.

"How long?"

"I just picked them up. There's . . . five of them."

Malachi wasn't afraid. He'd fought eight vampires at once in West Texas and he thought nothing could be worse than that. Besides, this time he had a weapon much more suited to the task. He hefted the machete from his belt loop and swung it at the end of his arm.

They began to move, backing up toward the granite wall of the nearest building when the attack started. Coming from above, miraculously descending from the air, the five renegades surrounded them before they reached the wall. Clifton leaped forward, slashing at the renegade nearest him, missing his mark. Malachi faced a renegade who stared angrily at him, an animal growl coming from his throat. As Malachi poised to strike, he saw the Predator's face change. It turned into a jungle cat with black fur and a wide mouth filled with razorlike fangs.

Malachi felt his heart go into deep freeze. The composite of man and jaguar was so startling it created a presence much more fearsome than that of Predator. It had to be Upton.

The transformation took Clifton's eyes off the others just for a second, and the whole group closed the circle in a flash.

Malachi hissed from between his teeth, swinging the machete above his head. Upton rushed him, coming under the machete and taking hold of the hand holding it. It happened so fast Malachi let out a surprised *Ah* sound and stumbled backward.

Tendons and muscles tore, and numbness took over his limb. He was forced to drop the weapon no matter how mighty a defense he put up. Now he was afraid. He had never been bested by a vampire. He realized suddenly that he had fought weaker creatures than Upton; Upton was not just a Predator, but one with the blood of Ross running in him, and the fire of revenge boiling in his soul. Had Malachi been less tired . . . or had he been with a group of strong Predators . . .

Now it was too late.

He felt Upton's Predators at his back, clawing at him. He saw a pair of vampires holding firmly onto Clifton, driving him to his knees.

Mom, Malachi thought desperately as his numb arm was being drawn hard behind his back. He struck at the Predator with the cat face over and over, but it was like swatting at an elephant. The blows bounced off the rock hard head of the cat, slipped on the fur, and fell away without having done any damage at all.

Now both his arms were bound behind him and the jaguar's snout came within inches of his face. "Malachi." He said the name as if it were a prayer. "Now I've got you," he said.

"You don't know me."

"A master always knows the weakest link," Upton said.

The feral eyes glowed, and a long pink raspy tongue slithered from the cat's lips to touch his cheek and slip up over one of his eyes. Malachi turned his head and saw Clifton's dead face staring up at him. They'd cut off his head and it had rolled near.

MOM! Oh, God, he thought. *Oh, God.*

"She's too far away. She won't get here in time. Come with me. We're going on a long journey, boy."

Malachi twisted and turned, trying to throw off his captors, but he couldn't. Not this time. These were tremendous creatures, much stronger than the ruffians sent after him under Balthazar's command. He knew now he had limitations. He'd been lulled into the belief he was indestructible. All his life he had escaped every harm, fought his way clear of every attack, and overcome every obstacle. Now this. He had come up against a creature unlike the others. He never thought Charles Upton would ever get near him. He wouldn't have imagined the vampire might want to capture him.

Upton took him by the back of his collar and hauled him off the ground. The two renegades at his back remained there, holding him, as they rose, too. The two Predators who had finished with Clifton hovered nearby.

"Say good-bye, Malachi. You won't be seeing your home again."

Mentor, Malachi cried. *Save me!*

* * *

Mentor hesitated, telepathically seeking the cause of the sudden disruption in the air. He had just come around a corner in the downtown district, the wind beginning to whip up the tails of his coat and abuse his long white hair. There had been no wind along the street from where he'd come. He had heard a telepathic cry for help from near this place.

He glanced all around, waiting for more instruction. Had that been Malachi?

It had been hours since he led the entranced Detective Teal to his car and back to the man's hotel. Since then he'd had been on the hunt and hadn't seen Malachi again that night.

As suddenly as it had come, the brisk wind died. The air was as still as a cold heart. There were no more telepathic cries calling for him.

He looked around in wonder. Then he looked up. A faint trail of darkness deeper than the background of space rose high and disappeared. It had been Predators. The renegades. Even now he could taste the distinct coppery scent they'd left behind on the sidewalk where he stood staring after them. He would have seen them in person had he come around the corner only a minute earlier. He didn't know who they were, but they must have known he was coming. That mystified him. None of the renegades ever knew of his approach. He was master of the cloak.

If they *didn't* know, then their taking to the sky held some other meaning that he couldn't yet figure. And had that been Malachi calling for him again?

Moving on, shaking his head, he crossed the city streets

and recrossed them, but did not find anyone. It was close to dawn. A street-sweeping machine came lumbering toward him and Mentor decided to call an end to the hunt. He would come out again when the sun set and fewer humans clogged the city.

He crossed a street and something stopped him before he reached the other side. He turned his head to look to his right. No traffic. Parked cars. And a block down a large blue trash bin, the kind garbage trucks backed up to and hooked onto to lift and empty.

Someone dead lay there.

Mentor hurried down the street to the bin and lifted the hard metal lid. Inside sprawled the body of a Predator, his head thrown carelessly at his feet. Mentor did not know him. In death it was impossible to contact the intelligence of a vampire, impossible to know his heart. He might have been one of Ross' clan or he could have been a renegade.

Mentor reached down into the putrid darkness of the bin and placed his hand on the dead Predator's chest. Maybe he could pick up traces of his living compatriots, friend or enemy. In that way he'd know if he should add this dead one to the list of their losses. As soon as his palm touched the vampire's bloody, sticky shirt, Mentor had a start. His hand blazed with a violent psychic imprint of the struggle the vampire had gone through, but, more importantly, his touch picked up a vivid picture of a *dhampir,* caught, but not killed.

Malachi.

Mentor withdrew, wiping his hand along his pants to clean it.

He turned into the stillness of the street and moved rapidly toward home. He could never follow the group who had absconded with the boy. They were no more than shadows speeding across the night sky. He must let Dell know. Upton might want to trade Malachi for something, though if he thought he could ransom him for control of the city he had to be more insane than anyone imagined. He couldn't win this battle through barter, not even with the *dhampir* as hostage.

Once home, Mentor sent out a call for Dell to come to him. He wouldn't let her know of the tragedy until he could speak to her face-to-face. His transmission was received, but Dell didn't reply. She might be in the midst of a battle, her concentration needed for the task of survival. She would come when she could get free, he knew.

Meanwhile, he would see about Bette. He'd left two skilled Predators to guard her and the little Predator boy, Jeremy, while he was gone. The guards stood outside the guest bedroom door, their arms crossed. They appeared to be asleep, but nodded as he passed and let himself into the room.

Bette was asleep. She'd kicked the sheet aside and lay on her side in the fetal position, knees to chest, chin down. She must be cold, he thought, and went to cover her. She woke with a jerk.

"I didn't mean to scare you," he said. He saw she'd placed the funeral urn on the bedside table. A lamp spilled a yellow lace of dim light around the urn.

She sat up, gathering the sheet over her lap. "Has it ended yet?"

"Not yet. But soon. There aren't enough of them left to do anything. We've been . . . thorough."

"Did you find the leader?"

"Charles? No, he's been careful so far." He thought of Malachi, who had not been careful, and worried about who had taken him. If it was Upton himself, they had a problem.

She ran her fingers through her hair, pushing it back from her face and his attention returned to her. "I can go home soon, can't I?" she asked.

"Only if you want to, Bette." He didn't want her to leave. Just being near her brought him an utter calm he could hardly find on his own. He recalled some reading he'd done recently about the six worlds of the Cabala, a Jewish mystical doctrine. There were many worlds, but six of them were named. Ayn was the world of Nothing. Atsiluth, the world of Origin, Briah, the Creation. Yetsirah, the Formation. Asiyah, the Physicality. And Qlipoth, the Debris. When alone, as he had been for more than a century, he was Ayn. Nothing. When around Bette, he was Asiyah, the Physicality. She brought the physical world to life for him. He lived in *Ka'an, Ka'eth*, the Here and Now. His hunger left him, his humanity rose inside his chest like a balloon of bright relief, and he was content to just be.

She was a grand gift in his life, but he did not know how

to tell her. He had loved her before she ever married, and he'd loved her all through the twenty years of that marriage. He'd kept his distance, only going to her garden to rest when he couldn't reach far off sanctuaries because of pressing duties at home. If she would ever consent to live with him, he would give her anything she wanted. Privacy when she needed it. Consolation when she was sad. Companionship when she required it. Though he knew she did not care for material things, he would shower her with anything she desired.

If only she would stay.

"I know what you want," Bette said. She'd been studying his face while he'd been lost in thought.

He felt as flustered as a young Victorian gentleman courting a proud lady and caught in the act of breaking protocol. She could not possibly know the depth of his longing.

"What do I want?" he asked.

"You want me to live with you."

"I . . . didn't . . . I . . . wouldn't . . ." Words escaped him. Surely she'd read his thoughts, either through his expression or . . . ? He didn't know how much she ever really knew. She possessed quite remarkable psychic talents for a mortal.

She took a dressing gown from the end of the bed and slipped it onto her arms. She stood and tied it at her tiny waist. "I can't make a decision like that right now." She stared at the urn before turning and going to the window. She pulled aside the drapes and looked out at the early silver dawn light in the sky.

Mentor's heart, had it been living, would have fluctuated in its rhythm. She hadn't said she wouldn't live with him. And she hadn't ruled it out. She seemed to be saying, in her way, that now was not the time to decide.

Only days before, she'd brought her husband's ashes to his house, and he would have never voiced his hopes to her so soon after her loss. She'd guessed his feelings or read his mind—regardless, she knew he wanted her to stay so much he dreamed of all the things he could do to make her happy again.

And she had not said no.

"Ka'an, Ka'eth," he said softly.

She turned from the window. "What does that mean?"

"The Here and Now. It's where I live only when you're around me. It's where I'd like to live all the time."

Her face softened and she came to him, taking his hands. "I'm sorry I judged you when you came back flushed with . . . with what you had to do these last few days," she said. "I had no right. It's not how I was taught—to judge harshly and without respect for whatever reality you're dealing with. If we should live in the Here and Now, as I also believe we should, then the past has no more power over us than a dust mote and the future is a dream we dream. In the Here and Now I have no opinion of what your nature tells you to do."

Oh, how he loved her, he truly loved her. He would, he realized with a slight shock, die for her if he had to. He hadn't loved a woman in so long it was as if he had never loved before at all.

He leaned over and kissed her forehead in a fatherly fashion though it was her lips he yearned most to kiss.

"I'm going to rest a while," he said. "I hope I didn't wake you too early."

He left her, the warmth of her hands still warming his own. He placed them against his cool cheeks and let them warm the flesh there. In his own bedroom he lay on top of the spread, closing his eyes, remembering every detail of the woman he'd just left, repeating in his head every word she'd uttered.

She couldn't make the decision to live with him now.

Her wound of loss was too large to permit it. That was the thing. He understood completely.

But perhaps one day she could decide. And the decision might be in his favor.

And he would not be Ayn, the Nothing, but Asiyah, the Physicality, in the *Ka'an, Ka'eth*.

10

Lewis Teal woke in a sweat. He had his suit on, his shoes, and he lay on top of the covers of the bed in his muggy hotel room. Again. Getting to be a nasty habit.

He sat up and rubbed at his thick brow. The room smelled like a wet sock.

Damn it all, what was the matter with him? Did he have a brain tumor? He kept going to sleep without remembering it and waking up in his clothes.

The last thing he remembered was . . .

He was . . .

Hadn't there been a blonde woman? Pretty, but with plumped-up lips that looked like they belonged more properly on a baboon?

He snapped his fingers. The reporter from Channel Nine. He had seen her . . .

Why had she come to mind? Where had he seen her? On TV, on the news? Well, of course she was on the news on television. But that's not where he saw her last. Was it?

Nah. This was crap. He had a brain tumor, he knew it. He had to get to a doctor right away. Maybe they could cut it out, or use a laser and zap it or . . . Oh, God. His memory was as full of holes as a tea strainer.

He climbed out of bed and went to the bathroom to wash his face. Cold water gave him a shock. He consulted his watch. Almost time to get up anyway. Where had the hours gone?

He had worked late. He found a body near the hotel. He went with it to the coroner's. He filed more paperwork. He came home, drank orange juice.

He stepped from the tiny bathroom and looked to the windowsill. Orange juice bottle. Yep. He had drunk the orange juice. Maybe he didn't have a tumor.

He just had to remember the rest of it.

Oh, no. No, no. Wait.

He was remembering the events from the night before. Today he'd gotten his spare suit from Mayfair Cleaners and it made him late for his shift. He spent the day fielding calls and trying to find out the identity of the body in the morgue. The one he had found lying partially beneath the holly tree at his own hotel.

He couldn't find out a thing about the guy. No ID on him, not even a wallet. No record of fingerprints. No missing person's report that matched him. And then the craziest thing happened. The coroner called and in a sheepish voice reported there were bodies missing from the morgue. He hadn't completed his autopsies.

"How many are missing?" Teal asked.

"Three."

"One of them is the body I found?"

"Yes. And two more with similar wounds in the neck area."

"Well, where did they go?" Teal wanted to know.

"I have no idea. They're just gone. This has never . . . it's nuts. This has never happened before."

The conversation made Teal hot-tempered. How could they have lost the bodies? Why would someone steal dead bodies? And how did they do it—did they walk right in and carry out the bodies over their shoulders? Wheel them out on gurneys to a waiting truck? Jesus.

Frustration caused Teal to snap at the receptionist, the secretary, and another detective. He told Travers, his own sergeant, to can it when Travers came over and told him the box of doughnuts on his desk was going to do wonders for his weight problem.

He left work early, his eyes feeling like lead sinkers. He needed to sleep. He had been up all night the night before. Doing . . . something.

He'd worked all day trying to track down the missing bodies from the city morgue, but no one had seen a thing. He couldn't find a witness, he couldn't find a motive, and the bodies hadn't been identified, so there was no one to question about them.

He came to the hotel, showered, went out for a double-patty jalapeno hamburger at the sports bar behind the hotel. He walked the streets a while, no longer tired. His feet hurt, his big thighs hurt, even his *teeth* hurt, so he returned and got into his car. He began to drive while his mind chewed on the problem of the murdered and missing bodies.

He thought he remembered driving somewhere downtown.

A picture of three dead bodies sprawled across one another in an alley flashed suddenly into his mind. It was like a faded postcard from 1923. Was his mind mixing this picture up with the missing bodies from the morgue?

He had to admit he was stymied. His memory was a mishmash of information that didn't connect. He was baked, fried, and boiled. He was a cabbage head.

He rubbed at his temples. He picked up the empty orange juice bottle and dropped it into the trash. He didn't let the cleaning staff into his room but twice a week. They'd pick up the place tomorrow.

He sat in the chair by the window and worriedly chewed at the inside of his cheek. If he could remember when the cleaning staff came, why couldn't he remember where he had driven earlier tonight in the car?

And what was it about three bodies in an alley? An alley was not a morgue. And he hadn't seen all three of the missing men from the morgue anyway. What was up with that? It was driving him crazy, this stuff about bodies.

He had to see a doctor, that's all there was to it.

As he gazed down to the city street, his eyes were slowly pulled to the clouds hovering over the skyline and he almost remembered something, but at the last second it escaped him. He decided he might make a visit today to the television station. He'd get the blonde reporter's phone number. He'd call and ask . . .

What? If she'd seen him two nights ago?

He dropped his large head into the palms of his hands and closed his eyes. Maybe he should take off his clothes and go back to bed until his alarm clock went off. He had a couple of hours yet before he needed to be up.

Maybe he'd remember then.

It was a scary thing to lose time, to lose memories. He had never been afraid of anything in his entire life. Not getting shot on the job. Not finding a woman to share his life with. Not his boss' opinion of him. Not anything.

But this scared him.

He rose, lumbered to the bed, and threw off his jacket. He emptied his pockets the way he always did before bed, placing his wallet, keys, ID badge, cell phone, notebook and pen, and his gun on the bedside table. He dropped his shoulder holster to the floor. He kicked off his shoes without untying the laces. He sat on the side of the bed, taking off his stained tie and sweaty shirt.

It came to him that he would probably never recall the lost hours. He figured he had lost time two nights in a row. And he'd never get them back.

He was sick. Or . . .

No, he was sick, all right.

He wouldn't call the blonde reporter with the fat lips. He wouldn't go to a doctor, wouldn't tell anybody about any of this. He'd keep his damn mouth shut.

That's what he'd do.

He took off his belt and slacks and calf-hugging, black socks, and fell back into the bed.

Had he turned that lamp on beside the bed earlier?

Oh, God. He couldn't remember.

*   *   *

It was as Mentor had surmised. Dell was caught in such a struggle that his call for her must go unanswered. She had slain three of the nest of renegades she and her Predators had discovered sleeping in the loft of an abandoned warehouse, but more came from the shadows to their rescue and it took all that Dell could do just to stay alive.

She'd been drinking the blood of the enemy, feasting after two days of starvation, and she was as bloodthirsty yet as any Predator under her command. She could not seem to get enough blood, could not restrain herself from draining the fallen vampires until even their skin shriveled and the moisture that made their musculature pliable stiffened in rigor mortis.

It was the second time in her life as vampire that she'd tasted the blood of another of her kind. Many years ago, before she married Ryan, when she was newly vampire, she had attacked Ross. Oddly, it had been in defense of Charles Upton. Ross had meant to drain him and she was too young and newly vampire at the time to understand she shouldn't interfere. She had attacked Ross. The small taste of his blood had made her crazy with hunger. If it hadn't been for Mentor stepping in, she would have thrown herself at him again to try for his jugular. Since then, for nearly twenty years, she had behaved as the Natural she'd chosen to be, living the lifestyle of a mortal. Whatever stray urge she felt to take blood from another being, vampire or human, was strictly denied, the very thought sent away.

Now that she'd fought Upton's Predators for days and killed her share, she needed the strength of her enemies. She'd needed their blood. She knew this was exactly what Upton wanted. He had hoped to force the Naturals to find prey. Those who didn't would soon die agonizing deaths, given his rule.

It was ironic to her that by fighting the enemy, she gave into him.

While fulfilling her ravenous need, supping hungrily at the neck of one of the three murdered victims in the loft, the shadowy ones attacked, catching her and the three veteran Predators with her by surprise. She turned, snarling, blood dripping from her exposed fangs, and with one arm knocked the vampire away. She jumped to her feet and saw what she'd have to overcome to get out of the warehouse alive. There were a dozen vampires silently spreading out across the dusty floor.

They would have to flee. They couldn't fight this many with any hope of victory. She glanced at her comrades and saw they knew they were outnumbered.

Before any of them could make a move to disappear, the renegades flew forward, feet never touching the floor. Their arms were outstretched, their fangs glittering in the moonlight that fell through the opaque high windows.

Dell let out a yell that spurred her into action. She rose up to the ceiling, hoping to draw off and splinter the group. Her ploy worked, four of the dozen rising with her to battle against the exposed plumbing and the concrete buttresses.

She spun, she swooped, she feinted in first one direction then another. She tore pipes from their moorings and used them as mallets. Below her the battle raged, Predator against Predator, wild cries of rage filling the cavernous loft.

Filled with foreboding, all she could do was hold off the slashing steel her enemies wielded. As she fought, fearing she might not survive many minutes longer, the ceiling-to-floor windows on one side of the loft imploded with a spray of jagged glass.

She hung from a pipe, about to wrench it loose, but now she turned her head at the rush of Predators coming through the open wall four stories up. She saw Ross and a woman and dozens more flying through to join the melee.

Now Upton's renegades were the ones outnumbered, and the tide had turned. Together, they fought with abandon, pinning the enemies to the floor, the ceiling, and the walls. They tore limbs off, pierced midsections with lengths of pipe, and once dominant, they swung knives, machetes, and even large jagged pieces of broken glass to deliver the deathblows.

Once it was over, Dell stood looking over the hideous scene of so many lying dead and dismembered. Though it should have sickened her, all she felt was the urge to go to her knees and lap at the gallons of blood that flowed from mortal wounds.

She trembled, resisting.

Sereny, the woman who now seemed to be Ross' shadow, showing up everywhere he did, came to her side and gently took the length of cast iron pipe from Dell's hand. "Something's happened to your son," she said.

Dell came slowly from the trance of fierce battle and vast longing to taste the blood.

"Malachi?" she asked dreamily. "What about Malachi?"

"Maybe you want to talk to Mentor."

Ross joined them and said, "Why did you say anything? You should have kept your mouth shut."

Sereny ignored his bad temper. Predators were frequently temperamental after a fight until the thrill of it had worn off a bit. "I was a mother," she said to Ross, though she knew that might not make anything clear to him. He had never been a parent before changing to vampire.

"Like that explains how you can't keep your mouth shut."

Sereny whirled on Ross and struck him a backhanded blow to the face. Blood rose to the skin and showed her handprint. "You will *not* speak to me like you do to the others. You will not disrespect my experience or second-guess my intentions."

Dell watched all this as from a distance. She was coming back to herself, but it took all her will. She felt lost in the flow of blood about her feet, drawn to it as if to a river of life.

"Tell me . . ." she said, haltingly. "Tell me about Malachi."

Ross, stunned by Sereny's anger, said nothing.

Sereny turned to her again and said, "We think he's been taken."

"Taken?"

"Captured. He's gone, Dell."

Now the words not only got through to her, but burned her ears like sizzling oil thrown against them. She physically flinched.

Before her knees buckled, Sereny caught her. The other woman spoke softly next to her ear, trying to soothe her. She couldn't make out what she was saying. Now her hearing was gone, the burning words still spinning around in her brain. Malachi captured. Malachi gone.

Gone.

*   *   *

Upton knew before he took the *dhampir* that the war was lost. He'd lost too many vampires; he'd been out-maneuvered.

Malachi was his ace. He might have lost the battle, but he had taken a prisoner whose disappearance would affect the opposition. If they thought to give chase, they'd think twice about it now.

The trip from Dallas across the face of the planet to Thailand didn't take long, but long enough for Upton to feel surprise at how it seemed he was going home. It *had* been his home in the monks' prison for many years. Though he'd schemed and worked daily toward escape, the place had taken on the look and feel of where he belonged. Not behind cell walls. But free to roam the country.

He expected part of his feeling had to do with the body of the Thai man he'd had to transmigrate into. Perhaps the cells of the body remembered, the way they remembered a phantom limb after the actual one was severed. His Thai flesh longed for the Thai landscape to wrap it again in jungle and mountain, in tropical heat and lush foliage.

Five Predators and the *dhampir* came down to earth into a sunny afternoon in Thailand. Mentor would never believe Upton might return to the place where he'd been incarcerated. He'd never search for him there.

"Where am I? Where have you taken me?"

Upton looked at the young man with narrowed eyes. He was jaguar and he thought unless he really had to show a human face for some reason, he would not bring it out again. If Thailand was his home, the jaguar was his face. "I won't tell you where you are. No one will ever tell you anything. But you'll be here for the rest of your life if I have my way."

He pushed the *dhampir* ahead of him through jungle thick with vine and entangled vegetation. Monkeys chittered, leaping from branch to branch overhead. The heat caused the forest debris to wriggle beneath their feet, alive with the boring of ant and beetle and worm. Brightly colored birds flitted in and out of leaf cover.

Ahead of them, they could see the majestic range of mountains covered with tropical forest. This had been the kingdom of Siam, ruled by a king who had built beautiful temples right out of the forest floor. The Blue Mountains of Australia had not been nearly this splendid or packed with such varied wildlife.

Upton did not know where he was headed, except he wanted to go deep into Thailand's interior away from any village or town. After some hours, with Malachi holding his peace and Upton's captains silently following at his back, Upton called for a halt. They'd come to a green terrace of land on the side of a mountain. It was a small natural area that had never been farmed. Around its perimeter the jungle encroached, rising high all around.

"Here," Upton said. "Dig me a hole. Make it eight feet deep by five feet in width and length. A square."

His captains went to work immediately, clawing at the ground with their hands, flinging sod and dirt behind them. Upton stood back watching, Malachi at his side.

"What are you going to do?"

The *dhampir* still sounded stout and strong, a rebel, but he'd lose that attitude soon enough. "We're going to put you in the hole," Upton said casually.

When Malachi didn't respond, he added, "It'll be your home for a good long time, the sky your roof. This is what Mentor gets in repayment for the years I spent in his monk's cell. Don't ever ask me for pity. None was ever extended to me."

It didn't take long before the square hole was finished. Upton told his men how to go into the jungle and find good strong wood for the crosshatched roof. Before it was dark they'd fashioned the enclosure he wanted, staking the sturdy roof to the ground with Malachi thrown inside.

Upton stood over him looking down at his face. The covering wouldn't provide any shelter from the elements. It was open enough that his prisoner could breathe and see his captors standing by. The Vietcong had made traps like this for American captives in Vietnam. Some of the men lived in them for months. Some died in them. Malachi would live in this one until he died.

"We'll give you food and water. We'll provide you with a bucket for wastes that we'll empty every seventh day. Beyond that you will be given nothing. Not conversation nor comfort of any kind. You may break through this thatched opening, but it'll do you no good. I'll have several of my people here all the time to watch you. Your first escape attempt will get you a beating. The second will be a torture you can't imagine. The third . . . Well, you won't survive a third attempt."

Malachi said, "They'll come for me, you know."

"No, they won't. Because they aren't going to know where you are." Malachi didn't know it, but he was going to be fed on a diet of native food, rice, and vegetables spiked with powerful man-made tranquilizers. Upton had thought of everything to keep his captive weak and hidden. The boy was purported to have the mental ability to reach others and to read them in return, just like the Predator

But he couldn't do much of anything if his mind was always clouded and unresponsive.

One good thing. He had to eat. He wasn't truly vampire, so he couldn't survive for too much time without sustenance. He lived on food the mortals used for survival. He'd never be given a morsel of bread or a cup of rice that wasn't first doctored. He'd live out his days so muddled he would be like a slobbering babe, unmindful of sensation. If Mentor or Ross or the mother of this creature ever did find him, they'd find someone mentally crippled to the point he wouldn't be worth dust to anyone.

Upton turned away from the dirt cell and went to his captains. They would stay to guard the prisoner until he gathered more Predators into a clan. He knew now how to go about it, who to search out, the type of vampire who could be swayed to join with him. It wouldn't take him nearly as long as before to get up another army, but this time he'd train them better. He'd take his time.

He had plenty of that. More and a world enough.

*   *   *

All through the night Dell sat in her home, calling to her lost son. Ryan had gone to bed, satisfied she was all right after her days of combat. He went away in despair, however, after she told him the news of their son's capture.

"We have to get him back," Ryan said, his years telling in the deepened wrinkles on his worried face. The news had first made him angry, then left him deflated and feeling helpless. He was only human. He merely loved. He could not fight the supernatural or save his son from its clutches.

Now Dell sat in the darkness in her favorite rocking chair, going over what had transpired and how she might find Malachi. Mentor related his story of coming upon the dead Predator and finding the trace of Malachi still lingering on his body. They all knew Upton had left the city. The few Predators he had left soon followed. Not one could be found anywhere.

Mentor didn't know where Upton might have taken Malachi. The Blue Mountains, where he'd first gotten the vampires together? Lanzarote, the Canary Island where Balthazar had brought together many more?

He could be anywhere in the world.

But why couldn't she reach him? She'd known his movements when he left home and traveled across Texas, trying to outrun the assassins. At any time in his life she'd been able to search him out and know how he was doing.

It seemed now he'd fallen into a black hole that had swallowed him whole. For the first hours after she learned of his kidnapping, she had heard faint echoes in her mind as if he were calling to her from another universe. She tried to link to him, but she couldn't latch onto the vibration. It was too weak, too intermittent, and then, finally, it was broken and there was nothing but silence. She had no connection with her son at all. It was as if he no longer lived.

She beat her hands on her knees in the darkness and swung her head back and forth in silent denial. He couldn't be dead. She prayed to God to take the thought away and not let her have it again.

He was . . . somewhere. He couldn't let her know where.

Even Mentor, who had much more power than she to find out Malachi's whereabouts, came up with nothing. He told her it was some kind of trick. Upton was malicious and he was brilliant, more so since escaping and being free for so long. He possessed most of Ross' great power, as Ross was his Maker, and combined it with his own massive intelligence, making him a formidable foe.

Mentor told her to keep trying. She'd find Malachi. Then he'd help her with the rescue. Meanwhile, he would keep trying to locate Upton. If they could find Upton, they would find her son.

If, if, if. But when? When?

She lay her head back in the rocker and closed her eyes, willing the vision of her son into the forefront of her mind. His tall lanky body that was so much like his dad's. His brown hair that showed more natural wave the older he grew. His dark eyes, so knowing and bright with understanding.

She would keep trying, of course, for as long as she lived if need be. She wouldn't let the son she loved be lost so easily. If she did not find him through telepathic means, she would hunt him down. She would have to leave her home and her husband and seek her son. She would begin interviewing vampires, traveling wherever it took her, until

she came upon someone somewhere who either knew
where Upton was or where her son was being held.

*   *   *

Sereny had taken the little Predator, Jeremy, off Dell's hands.
The woman had enough on her plate trying to find her own son.
Besides, the boy reminded Sereny of the son she'd left behind
when the change had come over her. During the nights when
they all made raids into the city, hunting Upton's vampires,
Jeremy had been left at Mentor's house in the care of guards
who also watched after the human woman there.

Jeremy took to Sereny right away, sensing she felt more
compassion for him than anyone else did. She had brought
him to Ross', where he ran after her through the house,
asking her to play games with him, watching her as she
performed the endless house chores that afforded her such
peace of mind. She learned all about his twin sister, Dottie,
and his grandfather, and the store they'd called Howard's
Rattlesnake Farm. Jeremy could spend hours talking about
rattlers and how much he liked them. He'd been fascinated
by his grandfather's milking them for venom.

Sereny settled into a sort of imitation life, one close to
normal, one like she'd lived as a mortal. A house to clean.
A man to care for. A child to raise. It was the last gift, the
child, that gave her the most joy. He was so bright and new
to the life. He needed her to teach him and stayed close
to her side, like a shadow. When she turned, he was there.
When she worked, he played nearby. When she slept at
night, he lay outside the bedroom door. They couldn't
make him stay in a room, he said. He had always slept in
a room with his sister. He didn't like it without her.

Ross came to Sereny only once during this time of do-
mestic bliss. She was afraid he might banish her. He wanted
her love every night, falling asleep locked between her legs,
but she wasn't sure that was enough to insure her perma-
nence. Ross had been a loner for a very long time. He
admitted he didn't know what love was or what loving a
woman was supposed to mean to him. Yet, he continued
to let her and the boy vampire stay, and the days raced past
as he got back to the business of supplying the Naturals and
few remaining Cravens with the blood they needed.

He came once to her and sent Jeremy outside, admonishing him not to enter the house until he called. He was never harsh with the boy, but he frowned on his impulsiveness and demanded his own commands be obeyed without hesitation. Jeremy complied, knowing in some way that this vampire was greater than Sereny, and Ross could break him to pieces on a whim of anger.

"Look," Ross said, seemingly in a hurry to get out what he wanted to say. "It's this way, Sereny . . ."

She watched him closely for any hint he was about to send her packing. She would go, if ordered, but she really wanted to stay. Ross was not the hard man the rest of the world thought him. He could be gentle in their lovemaking, stroking her for hours as if there was nothing better he could ever find to do. He had an abiding respect for artistic endeavor, speaking of great masters in reverent tones, as if they were his priests. Any vampire who could hold onto a love for the creations of men was not totally lost.

He was honest about his debauchery, and didn't for a moment think he should repent. If she didn't want to share him that way, that wasn't his problem.

He loved to kill. But then, so did she. If it were a sin, they were both going into hellfire together.

"It's this way, Sereny," he continued. "I like the way you keep the place."

She smiled. Balthazar had found it distracting and useless. But this was a large modern home, nothing like she'd ever lived in before. It had many rooms, gorgeous furnishings, exquisite items that must have cost fortunes. She wanted to care for them. She was very careful, moving slowly and humming throughout the day, caring lovingly for the house and the priceless objects in it.

"I even like seeing you with the boy," Ross said, still agitated. "That Jeremy's got what it takes, you know? He's a brat right now, but I think he'll mature well."

She knew firsthand that Jeremy did have what it would take to survive. She'd gone hunting with him in a small rural area far outside of Dallas, showing him how to read potential victims, how to take the ones who were already hoping to die, or who deserved to die. There were so many.

"Anyway," Ross said, "as long as you don't try to boss

me around, I won't boss you—and I'd like you to stay here. How's that?"

It was as close as he was going to get to saying she should be his partner, his mate. She kept smiling. "That's all right with me," she said. And then, without thinking, she stepped forward and kissed him until he put his arms around her back and drew her in close.

He pulled away. "You're a helluva woman, Sereny."

"And you're a helluva man."

That was the level they met on and which gave them both so much pleasure. Man to woman. She had always known sex was one way to get back to the mortal souls that otherwise languished inside their immortal bodies. She had taught him that and the lesson was taking hold. It pleased her unimaginably.

*   *   *

Mentor stood poised to hear the worst—Bette had decided to go home. His house was empty except for the two of them now. The Predator clan had gone back to their duties as sentries, lab workers, delivery men, and business entrepreneurs. The uprising had been put down and except for the missing *dhampir,* all was back as it should be.

Malachi's disappearance weighed on him. He spent much of every day and night telepathically trying to ferret out the boy's whereabouts without success. It was an enigma. A *dhampir* as talented as Malachi should have sent out a signal of distress. Unless he was dead. Like Dell, Mentor didn't want to believe that. Besides, what would the *dhampir's* death do for Upton? No, it was another trick, a sleight of hand, a magician's veil that he had to try to rip away.

"Well?" Mentor stood in the living room, the book he'd been reading in his hand at his side. Bette stood at the doorway. He didn't see the urn, but it might be waiting on the hall table for her exit.

"I'm coming back," she said.

His throat closed as if a fist had squeezed it.

"I have to go home to close it up. There are some things I want. My altar. A Buddha statue. My teapot," she said, as if just remembering it. "I think I'll keep the house. Keep paying the taxes, keep the lawn mowed, that sort of thing. For the garden." She smiled wistfully. "We both love the Japanese garden."

He set the book on the coffee table and came to her, taking her into his arms. She laid her head against him. "You're so right. I do love the garden," he said.

They held one another, and Mentor thought he'd never been so happy. "Let me go with you. I can help."

"No, stay here. I want to . . . say my good-byes alone. The house was my sanctuary, not just the garden, the way it is for you. But now after so many years of sharing it with Alan, I know I can't be there alone anymore. It wouldn't . . . it wouldn't be the same."

He let her go, watching from the window as she left, his gaze following until she disappeared from sight. He went to her room and found the funeral urn. He brought it carefully to the living room and set it on the mantel over the fireplace. It should be in a place of honor. The man within it had loved and cared for the woman he adored. In his death, he wouldn't be forgotten by either of them.

11

Malachi sat on the dirt at the bottom of the hole and stared into the twilight sky beyond the wooden latched opening. The first stars were coming out, tiny distant lights on a velvet display. It was as Upton had promised. He was fed. He was given water. He had a bucket sitting feet from him stinking of his own excrement and urine.

Nothing seemed to matter. The food was always tasteless to him and he only ate it because his stomach cramped if he didn't. When he thirsted, he drank from a canteen hung from a rope. When he must attend to his bodily functions he sat on the biting rim of the bucket and tried not to think about it.

After some days he realized the truth of his imprisonment. They were drugging him. Every time he ate a meal he felt woozy and disoriented and often fell over onto his side to sleep. He tried not to eat, but then he grew delirious anyway, and knew they were putting the drugs into his water. He could not go without either food or water unless he wanted to starve himself.

He tried and tried to think of a solution, but none came to him. If he did not eat or drink, he would die. Always, before he could get himself lucid enough to feel he could send out a call to his mother or Mentor, his captors would open the roof, climb into the hole with him, and beat him senseless with their fists and feet. He was too weak to fight back.

He caught himself daydreaming away the endless hours, piling little pebbles he found in the dirt into mounds before scattering them again. He found a pointed stick and scratched drawings and words into the earthen walls. He wrote his name. MALACHI. He wrote the word, GOD.

He wrote, HELP, INSANITY, and I'M NOT GOING TO DIE IN HERE. Meaningless. Meaningless.

When it rained, he sat in water that sometimes covered his legs, shivering and cold. They knew he would not get sick and he would not die. They were keeping him like a zoo pet, a mindless animal in a primitive cage.

When bordering on a lucid period just before his hunger forced him to partake of the tainted food, he sometimes felt a tear run down his cheek and he'd wipe it away with the back of his hand before any of the vampires saw. He was determined to endure it all. The drugs, the elements, the confinement. The silence.

One day his guards might make a mistake and turn their backs. One day they'd slip up and he'd notice and he'd get away. Upton had done it. Why couldn't he? Drugged or not, the food gave him strength and he needed that strength for the day opportunity presented itself. He convinced himself it would happen.

He just didn't know when.

He rocked on his buttocks with a rhythmic motion, his legs crossed, his hands gripping his knees. He watched the stars fill the sky. He saw the Milky Way spread across the expanse of space like diamond powder dusted across the heavens. Some time later, time being something he could no longer measure, the moon slid across the opening of his cage in the ground and he smiled up at it. It was a full moon, a Malachi moon. His moon, promising long life, promising freedom.

As long as he could see the moon ride the sky and he could smile, holding onto the hope of a night when he could walk free again, he would survive this hellhole.

Mom, he called weakly in his mind. *I'm here, Mom, can you hear me? I'm here in a jungle land, held captive.*

His rocking motion slowed and he ceased moving. He had fallen back against the dirt wall and his eyelids had gotten too heavy to keep open. Sleep slipped into his brain, paralyzing it. His hands fell from his knees and he slumped to the ground.

He drifted into the dreamworld that was becoming more real than his waking world. In his dreams there was no prison pit, no guards, no mad, lurking jaguar face lurid with curiosity.

In his dreams, Malachi wandered dreamscapes unlike the world he'd lived in. They were like the dreams of his childhood, without the silver wolf who stalked him then. The arid landscape was swept with moonshine. It was entirely devoid of life. Nothing moved, not even a breath of wind. Malachi wandered there thoughtless and lost. He walked for miles through every dream, the landscape unchanging, the moon above never setting.

On waking each morning he recalled nothing of the dreams except the vast emptiness of the land that left a residue of melancholy like a dry taste at the back of his tongue.

I will be free again, he told himself over and over. *I am not destined to die like a rat in a hole in the ground.*

Upton won't win this personal war. Mentor defeated him—and so will I.

To while away the hours when awake, but groggy with the drugs they fed him, he sometimes thought dreamily of Danielle. She'd promised to wait for him. He'd called her when he returned home with Jeremy, but he hadn't been able to meet with her before he was following his mother to Mentor's house, joining the battle.

Danielle had been so happy to hear from him. They talked of her college courses and her family. She'd delicately refrained from asking questions about where he'd been. She said she loved him. She missed him terribly, and she loved him.

Now he was missing from her life once more, this time without any explanation or good-bye. How long would it be before he heard her voice again? He couldn't hope she would wait for him if his imprisonment stretched from months into years.

But, God, it couldn't last for years. He wouldn't think of that again.

The roof rattled above his head, and he looked up to see one of the guards lifting it and dropping onto him.

Here they came again to beat him. They knew his thoughts, they monitored his dreams. They beat him near to death when they thought he made too much sense, even in his own mind.

"Stop it," he yelled, holding up his arms to protect himself. "Stop it, stop it!"

They never listened, they never relented. He tried to give as good as he got, but all his supernatural strength had fled him. The chemicals filling his bloodstream had stolen everything.

When he was conscious again, his mouth tasted of dirt and he found himself facedown in the pit. He sat up, dying of thirst, and lunged for the canteen. He drank deeply of the tainted water, gulping down the liquid until his belly expanded.

He sat back, his bones aching, and his bruises still evident. By tomorrow they would have faded and his body would be ready again to accept his captors' abuse. He even healed more slowly now.

He looked up at the night sky and saw it was nearing dawn. He'd been unconscious for hours. The moon, the yellow moon he called his own, was gone from sight. But not his hope. It was as vibrant and alive as the breath he drew and the slow beat of his *dhampir* heart.

He had hope for the future, knowing it awaited him. Hope that he'd see Danielle again, and his mother, and his father.

Hope he'd rise as a phoenix from the lowly pit.

They couldn't take that from him.

12

Dell woke with the sound of her son's voice echoing in her mind. He was calling to her. He was in a . . . jungle.

She threw back the covers and swung her legs to the floor. Ryan woke and sat up in bed. "What's wrong?"

"Malachi called to me. He's being held in some kind of jungle."

Ryan remained speechless.

Dell hurriedly dressed. She put on jeans and a matching blouse. She slipped on hiking boots.

"Where are you going?" her husband asked.

"To find him. I can't wait any longer. I know he's alive now. I have to find him."

Ryan came from bed and put his arms around her. "Don't cry," he said. He held her tighter. "You'll find him, I know you will."

She pulled away, wiping her eyes. "It might take me a while. It might take a long time. There are so many jungles . . ."

"I'll be here when you get back, waiting for both of you."

She kissed him and hugged him close. "I love you," she said. "I'll call you. I'll call every day I can. Tell Mentor I've gone. If I need him, I'll let him know."

Outside the house, Dell took a deep breath. She had waited for just this kind of message. She had never despaired and thought Malachi dead. Now she knew for certain he lived and she'd find him, no matter how long it took.

A jungle. Somewhere in the world. They held him prisoner.

It had been the faintest of messages, but she knew it was Malachi. It hadn't been a dream, a wish fulfillment. He lived in a jungle and something kept him from contacting her until now. He was weak, his powers lessened. But he was alive.

Where should she look first?

The most famous jungle that occurred to her was the Amazon. She would go there, then. She'd contact other vampires, looking for clues. As fast as she could move, it would not take her years the way it might a mortal. She hoped it might only take months, if that long.

She looked around the ranch once more, sighing at the thought of leaving her home, her husband. She had planted the roses and four o'clocks. She had watched the trees grow and mature. She gazed out at the herd of cattle in the fields where they rested quietly.

She'd be back and her son with her.

13

It had been a year. A long, desperate year of searching. Dell fought the fatigue of endless and fruitless days and nights. She had never again gotten a mental message from Malachi. She wouldn't give up, however. He wasn't dead, any more than he'd been dead before his plea reached her on that long ago night in her sleep.

She ran into vampires who gave her bad information, wrong information, and deceptive information. She followed down every possible avenue until it led to a dead end. She met renegades who threatened her, Predators who hadn't time to waste on her plight, Cravens who whined about their own lost or dead loved ones. She went to Naturals and pleaded with them to set up a worldwide network to share information.

She had trudged through the Amazon, Brazil, Chile, Peru, and most of Asia. She used to call home to Ryan every day, but her treks took her into the interior of wild lands where she couldn't call. She sent messages to Mentor, instead, who relayed to Ryan where she was so he wouldn't worry. She almost went home a few times, but every time she thought she had to go back and give up this hopeless mission, she thought of her son's sad, broken voice echoing in her mind. How could she give up on her son and leave him a prisoner? She straightened her shoulders and went on.

Mentor told her to go to Egypt, to Cairo, and to see Vohra. He was an ancient and he might be able to help her. She was in the city now, depressed by the steady sunlight and the dry climate. She was directed to a grand palace of a building where Vohra lived. She asked at the door to see him. She hadn't been invited. She didn't know if he would turn her away.

The servant returned to the door after announcing her

visit and allowed her inside. She was taken to a courtyard in the center of the building. She stepped outside and saw the great vampire sitting by a pool. He was dropping pellets into the water. He turned at her approach and she saw he was only a boy, a teen, younger than her own son.

"The body is deceptive," he said in English. "You look like a girl, yourself. Please sit."

She lowered herself to a cushion placed near the pond. She saw giant koi fish swimming in the dark depths. They swirled to the top and gulped the food before twisting and diving to the bottom.

"Your missing son is a *dhampir?*"

"Yes. He's been gone eighteen months."

"The one who has him has used the time well."

She wondered what he meant.

He spoke again, reading her mind. "He has an army again. But he isn't ready to use it."

"Where is he?" she asked.

"Thailand."

She almost leaped to her feet. She'd been through Thailand and there had been no one there who knew of Upton or his people so she had moved on.

"Did you know before now?" she asked.

He shook his head. He fed the fish, walking around the edge of the pool. It was encircled with brilliant tiles that reflected the sun.

"I did not know. It is only recently a visitor came who knew of the boy and the imprisonment. He was a former captain under your son's kidnapper. He defected and feared reprisal. He came to me to ask for sanctuary."

Dell thought she would explode with newfound happiness. Malachi would come home with her. She'd find and rescue him.

"This is the man who knows where he is," Vohra said, pointing to a shadowy figure coming into the courtyard. He walked into the sunlight.

Dell rose and greeted him. "You know where he is? Malachi? Is he well? Is he strongly guarded?"

The vampire put up his hand to stop her questions. "Please," he said. "Sit down and I'll tell you everything."

As the sun lowered and the courtyard grew cool and shady, Dell sat with the Predator and learned all that she could, every detail, leaving out nothing. Vohra had left them alone and not come back. When it was almost dark, servants came with lanterns, placing them all around the pond.

By full dark Dell possessed all the information she needed. This would not be another dead end, another lie. Malachi was not in good health, either physically or mentally. He was treated like a monkey. He was taunted, drugged, and mistreated daily. It was a wonder he had lasted this long, the Predator said. Her heart squeezed into a tight fist at that news. But he was alive. Alive.

The former captain told her he had once slipped her son extra food. He'd had a moment of weakness and felt pity for the youth. He'd been caught. Upton took him away and tortured him for days. When he let him go, he escaped and had come to Vohra for protection. There was no one who could save him from Upton except this ancient vampire in Cairo.

"You'll need help," the captain said to Dell. "The hills there are full of guards. They're brainwashed and loyal to the death. If they think Malachi is about to be rescued, they'll kill him before you get within a hundred yards."

Dell thanked the vampire and went to a servant asking about Vohra. She wanted to thank him. She was told the master had left the house and would not return tonight. He might not return for days. They would relay her message to him upon his return.

Dell left the building, feeling horrified at her son's torture and exhilarated at the thought she could free him.

She found a telephone and waited anxiously while she put in the overseas call. Ryan answered before the second ring.

"I've found him," she said simply. "Tell Mentor to come. Tell him to bring as many to help us as he can."

"Where is he?" Ryan asked.

"Thailand. The place where Mentor had Upton imprisoned."

"I thought you went there."

"I did, but he was too well-hidden."

"So you're sure he's there, you're sure it's Malachi?"

She assured her husband, hung up, and stood in the lobby of the hotel where she'd made the call. The world now was so bright and new. She noticed the colors in the carpets, the satiny paint on the walls, the chandeliers overhead shining so brilliantly, holding back the dark. She would always love Cairo. She would never forget Vohra.

And soon, she would get back her son. She would save him.

14

The dark, bulbous clouds covered the sun and another monsoon threatened. Malachi stared at the sky without blinking until his eyes burned and began to water.

From out of the sky, a chunk of bread fell, but he didn't want it. They couldn't hand him his food. They had to throw it into the pit, for the pig. He would not eat it.

He hadn't eaten in two days. They doubled the drugs in his water to compensate. It tasted like bitter oranges. He drank as little as possible.

"You should eat," the guard said. "You're only killing yourself slowly."

Malachi wouldn't answer. What did they care if the prisoner died of starvation? It was none of their affair. This was between him and his creator, whoever that was.

The rain began. It didn't start with a sprinkle or a shower. It came down in gunmetal sheets right from the start. Boom. Dark sky, black clouds, earsplitting thunder, and then boom—sheets of rain so heavy they might as well have been shovels of dirt filling the air. The rain slicked down Malachi's long, unruly hair. It sluiced over his body and began to fill the hole he stood in. The torn bit of bread floated, soaked up enough water to resemble pig fat, and sank.

Malachi sat down in the water. Maybe he could drink it. He hadn't tried that yet. If he drank it—untainted, undoctored water—he might get back his mind.

He reached out both hands to cup them in the muddy swirl at his feet. The guard drew back the thatched roof and threw rocks at him.

He couldn't drink. They wouldn't let him have anything but what they gave him.

He dropped his hands to his sides and the rock throwing

stopped. The roof dropped down. The guard laughed like a maniac.

Mom, Malachi thought weakly.

The roof lifted again and the guard leaned down and knocked him in the head with a club. The guard had heard that. He was a part of his prisoner's mind. He heard everything Malachi tried to think. That was his job.

Malachi fell against the muddy side of his watery grave. He felt an instant headache bloom and take over his whole physical being. All he could think about was the pain.

They dropped a pan into the hole. "Start dipping," the guard commanded. "Throw the water out before it gets too deep."

Malachi thought of disobeying, but only for a moment. It was no use. They always won. If he didn't do it, they'd beat him unconscious and, cursing him, haul out the water themselves.

He lazily dipped the pan and caught it full. He stood shakily and threw the water up and out. He did not know why he must do this. The rain kept coming down. Water streamed over the sides from the land. It was coming in faster than he could throw it out.

He dreaded the monsoon rains more than anything. Once it had filled his hole so fast they had to run to a village and get a pump. They had to suction out the water to keep him from drowning. They could have just taken him out of the hole during rains like this, but that was too easy. That might give him hope.

He must stay cold, hungry, thirsty, and miserable.

It was endless, mindless work to dip the pan. Fill it. Hold it steady. Lift it. Throw it over the top of the hole and hope the water did not slip back.

Dip the pan . . .

Fill it . . .

Hold it steady . . .

Lift it . . .

Throw it . . .

He knew now why he thought he might be insane.

"I'm a man, damnit!" he screamed up at the guards. Something had gotten into him, maybe a brain parasite that causes rebellion, because he rarely fought back anymore. It took too much energy.

He squashed the imaginary parasite and winced when

they said, "Shut up. You're not a man and you're not a vampire. You're nothing."

That is what they told him when he protested. He was nothing.

If he believed them, he would die. That is what they wanted, for him to die. It was boring duty to watch him in the hole. They took turns, but it was still an annoyance. They would be glad for him to die as it would set them all free.

He looked up at the rain, squinting.

He would not die.

He hoped they died from their boredom first.

He hoped someone would come and tear off their grinning faces and drape them on poles.

He hoped he could keep enough of his sanity to survive.

*   *   *

They were on their way. They had gathered at the foot of a mountain range in Thailand, a hundred Predators and Mentor and Dell. Dell knew where to go. They had their plan. Though it was raining, a cloudburst that poured buckets and soaked them to the skin, nothing would deter them.

Mentor touched Dell's arm. "It's almost over," he said. "Are you ready?"

She knew what he was really saying. Was she ready to discover her son after eighteen months of imprisonment and torture? Could she handle it?

"I'm ready," she said, but she felt sick. For the first time in years she felt dread.

They started out through the jungle, each of them moving soft and gentle as a praying mantis. They would have to surround the camp where Malachi was kept. They would have to surprise his captors. They all walked with their minds shuttered fast so as not to be detected.

They looked like a crazy pilgrimage of mystics, plodding up the mountainside in the drenching rain. A hundred and two vampires going to the rescue of one young *dhampir*.

*   *   *

The rain beat down in a homicidal rage. It stung Malachi's shoulders and arms and face. His shoulder-length, tangled hair kept getting in his eyes when he bent to scoop the water in the pan. He was the mechanical man, moving from habit, empty of mind and spirit. The guard, furious he was suffering in the elements because of his charge, taunted Malachi and threw rocks at him when he didn't move fast enough.

Malachi did not know how long he spent bending, scooping water, throwing it over the top of the pit. For all he knew this was the whole world and his entire existence in it. He could have been doing this since the day he was born. He'd done this sort of labor for years. His attention was narrowed to the water, the pan, and his cruel tormentor who screamed and pelted him with stones.

Thunder crashed, lightning zigzagged from sky to ground, striking the earth with a shudder. The rain was a berserk demon pounding the earth to submission.

At least two minutes passed before Malachi even noticed the voice had stopped babbling curses at him and the stones had ceased falling. He paused in the process of emptying the full pan of water, his arm held up above his head. His hand shook. Water sloshed out of the pan. Rain continued falling in hard, stinging droplets without letting up.

But everything had changed, everything. Malachi's dim mind struggled to distinguish what those changes were. He ticked them off slowly in his mind as he lowered his arm and swished the pan in the rising water around his knees.

One: The guard was gone. Or seemed to be.

Malachi couldn't see or hear him. He could see no one at all above his prison walls. It was the first time since he'd been brought here that he had been left alone.

Two: There was no evidence of the other vampires who he knew camped just on the rise above his pit. He always heard them and sensed them, even into the nights, and into his sleep. But now it was as silent as if a bomb had blown them all away and left him in his gravelike hole with only the steadfast drum-drum-drum of the rain.

He stood still, waiting. Surely the guard would peep over the side of the pit and leer at him and throw a stone, striking him in the eyes, dead center.

He blinked and grimaced in anticipation. That was it. That's what they were up to. Another trick to break his mind. Something to really drive him all the way over the edge, spilling his brains out his ears so he would start screaming and wouldn't be able to stop.

He waited, breathing through his mouth as the rain poured down his uplifted face.

Only the rain flowed. Only the splashing of the rain drummed around his legs.

Well, he thought, *this is new. I don't like new situations. It usually means they've thought of an even greater torment for me.*

Then he slumped into the mud and water, his bottom sinking down and down. His ragged shorts ballooned and then deflated. The cold water covered him above the waist. He let the pan go, and it floated away like the shadow of a silver moon.

He hung his head.

He couldn't take this any longer.

He couldn't take their cruelty and horrible tricks.

They expected him to crawl out and run away. That's what they wanted him to do. So they could spear him in the back or catch him in a net or trip him into a pit of sharpened bamboo. They meant to amuse themselves at his expense.

He was much too tired and dead to play their game.

He would simply sit and wait here for them to tire and return.

Mom. . . .

* * *

"Malachi?"

Yes, Mom. I'm here. Why won't you come get me? You don't know, you don't KNOW, how bad this is.

"Malachi!"

What? What do you want of me? I can't help it. I can't get up and climb out of this pit. They'll kill me if I do.

A hand reached over his shoulder and gripped the front of his sodden shirt. It was a small white hand. A girl's hand. It did not belong here. There were no girls or women in the camp. What was he thinking? He had hallucinated before. Once he'd even seen Danielle in the pit with him, stroking the side of his face, and crying. He had told her to go away. She made him want to die. She shouldn't see him this way. He loved her and he was about to die without her.

The grip from the small white hand tightened and pulled. The buttons on his shirt popped and plinked into the water. His shirt, the material old and rotten, was tearing apart.

He lifted his head to see who belonged to the hand. See what kind of torture they had in mind for him now.

He saw his mother.

He closed his eyes. *Dreaming. Just dreaming again.* Or maybe his guard had found a way to transform into the image of his mother. That had to be it. They would never let him go. They would run him out of his mind before they ever let him go. He couldn't even seek his own death because they wouldn't let him. They were too hideous to him, keeping him alive this way. If he had the energy, he would hate them.

His shirt ripped apart, allowing the rain to stream down his bare chest. Someone screamed his name.

He wished they wouldn't scream that way. It hurt his ears. But they were very good at screaming.

He opened his eyes. It was his mother. His young, pretty vampire mother. She of the small white hand. Crying blood tears that turned pink as they mingled with the rain. Pulling at him, trying to get him to his feet.

He smiled at her. It was a wonderful dream.

"Say my name again," he said. "Say it, Mama."

"Oh, Malachi."

He smiled.

"Malachi, please," she said, frantic to pull him from the watery pit.

He blinked, unsure, mistrustful. "Who are you?" he asked.

"Please, Malachi, stand up! Can you stand up? I'm your mother."

And he smiled dreamily as he rose from the muddy water and came, obediently, to his feet.

If she said his name just once more, he would climb from the pit.

"Son."

"Yes," he said, the smile stretching his lips and expanding his heart.

"Malachi." Her voice was pleading and sorrowful.

"Yes," he said and he climbed from hell into the world above.